THE RISKIEST MOVE IN BASEBALL AND IN LIFE.

STEALING HOME

BOOK TWO IN THE ST. MICHAELS DUET

HARLOW COLE

HOME RUN

BASEBALL ARENA

For A & R

For helping me believe,
and reminding me to wander.
Never forget your way home.

BRAYDEN

Ninety feet lie between the bases in every Major League park. When merged with home plate, they create a perfectly symmetrical diamond, transforming dirt and grass into a crown jewel. On game days, the distance is expertly measured within fractions of an inch. It's lined with stark white chalk, so the pathway stays clear.

For me, the distance home felt twice as far.

I'd been trying to reach it for years.

I kept pressing forward, one foot in front of the other, focused solely on preparing to slide into the plate beneath the tag. As best I could, I blocked out the noise of the crowd and the blinding artificial light. If I lost sight of my target, I held the panic at bay by looking up at the stars.

The real ones.

Not the men surrounding me with their names stamped on the backs of their jerseys.

The stars had long given me comfort. When I was fifteen, Mr. Foster took us for a night sail. We cruised out past the lights from town. Past the point where land darkened the safe edges of earth. Way out there, lost inside a deep black nothing, we lay on the deck and stared skyward. I listened, as he spoke about other men who, centuries before us, sailed out into the ocean and lost their way home.

The stars became their guide.

Trusting in their power, those sailors wove magical tales of celestial beings. They followed their path, even when they couldn't clearly see their destination. In the darkness, those tiny points of light brought them safely back to port.

Back where they belonged.

I am a ghost ship now. Abandoned at sea.

Left to pray the stars will lead me home.

ASHLEY

The nickname Brayden gave me, when I was still a little girl, played on my name. Ash. Soot. The little burning embers.

What's left behind.

I could still trace life back to all the special moments when a spark lit inside me. My mind stored those memories as torn snapshots. I tried not to pull them out very often. They remained tucked between pages I never turned. The faces those images captured were young and naïve, unscorched by the pain of loss and loneliness.

That's the problem with flying high without fear attached; you never see the collision coming before the crash and burn.

After he left, I awoke to my own destruction, reflected in the rearview mirror by the sting of hindsight.

I could still wear a smile. It just formed beneath cracked lines, invisible to the naked eye. They weren't put there by age; they'd been cemented by life experience.

First love is unconstrained. It doesn't fear the rush of heartbreak or know what it's like to watch a fire flame out.

Once you witness that tragedy, in slow motion, paralyzed to do anything to stop it, you lose that untethered feeling. Your happiness knows its own bounds. You live cautiously, aware that, at any moment, life could deal a different set of cards with another losing hand.

The only thing good about surviving the free fall? Once you hit rock bottom, there's nowhere to go but up.

I loved.

I lost.

Then, I lost some more.

Surely, the new hand I now held had to scrape bottom. How could there possibly be any more room to fall?

I am the ashes left behind to smolder and wonder if I'll ever get another spark.

STEALING HOME

"Stealing home is one of the most sensational plays in baseball . . . It is a play that requires a lot of quick thinking . . . The chap who has slow-moving feet and a slower-moving brain had better never try to . . ."

—*Billy Evans*
Baseball Hall of Fame, Class of 1973
Youngest Major League umpire

"You'll know when the time is right."

Her voice didn't waver. I envied her sense of certainty.

"How will I know? How can you be so sure?"

Doubt clouded everything for me—from the edge in my voice to the far corners of my brain. It always had. I'd never been able to escape it. But there she was, telling me someday I'd find clarity. Telling me my fear would eventually turn to resolve.

I clung to her words and to the belief that as she lay there, lingering so close to being joined with some higher power, she had a direct line to divine premonition.

I had a plan. Scratched out on a sheet of lined paper.

I just didn't have a motherfucking clue how to make it all work.

"You will." Her hand grasped mine too loosely.

I already missed its familiar strength. I yearned to feel its warmth stroking over my back again.

"I promise, you will."

"I wish I had your faith." I exhaled a shaky breath, determined to hold it together in front of her. I'd come to give strength, not to suck the last shreds out of her.

"Listen to what I told you. You have to start at the beginning before you'll ever know how the story ends."

"I'll try."

Her eyes squeezed shut. Pain creased the edges of cheekbones that had grown too hollow, too fast. My heart stuttered. I hated every single part of this. This damn room. The smell alone made those invisible hands put a vise grip around my chest. I fought them back, forcing my mind to break their hold.

I wouldn't let them win today.

We both fell silent, listening to a nurse push a cart down the hall outside her door. An errant wheel squeaked with every turn. It quickly faded away.

Like everything else in this place.

"They'll be coming soon," she whispered. "It's almost time to say goodbye."

"I don't want to leave you. I wish there were more I could do. I wish I could make this all different."

"I know. But this was in the plan, too. This is part of it. We don't get to decide. It's okay. I'm at peace with it." She lifted my hand and pressed her cheek against it. Her skin felt like wrinkled paper. "Thank you for coming. You have no idea what it means to me to see you with my own eyes. I have my happy ending now."

I nodded my head. I couldn't speak. I didn't want to relive this scene again. The back of my throat filled up with too much sadness. It thickened past anything I could hope to swallow down. Ripe pain. I should've been an expert at dealing with it by now. I should've been skilled at playing out my role in this endless nightmare.

Bubbles formed in my lungs, holding back the screams I desperately wanted to shout at the dark. I'd been waiting far too long for a dawn that would never come.

"Go out and find *your* happy ending. Don't give up until you get it."

"I love you. I should have said that before now."

"I love you, too. I always have. You are loved. Let yourself feel it."

"I'll try. I promise."

"I need you to make me one more promise. It's a favor. Something I hope you'll do for me."

"I'd do absolutely anything. What do you need?"

"For my part, I know nothing with any certainty, but the sight of the stars makes me dream"
—*Vincent van Gogh*

HOME RUN

BASEBALL ARENA

CHAPTER 1
BUSTED DOWN & BROKEN

ASHLEY

"Why don't we stop at Lucky's and get some lunch? I'm starving."

Okay, so I lied.

The pit in the bottom of my stomach didn't yearn for cheese fries and a mushroom burger with special sauce. It begged me to inhale half the bottle of antacids I had hidden under my seat.

I would never admit that to him though.

For Nathan, I adopted this whole fake persona. When he entered a room, plasta-girl emerged. She wore a painted-on smile and spoke one octave higher than normal.

My brother didn't deserve my turmoil.

"Don't be funny," he replied plainly. "It's annoying."

I stole glances at his profile as I reluctantly turned the truck toward home. His dirty-blond hair hung limp, pulled into a greasy ponytail that made my skin itch. Joey needed to cut it.

I stopped short of suggesting that.

More fertile battlegrounds awaited our next war.

"I was thinking we should schedule an appointment with Darcy next week. I don't think it's a good idea to keep skipping sessions with her. You were making good progress, and Dr. Zeleski just said—"

"Stop, Ash. Just stop." He turned to glare at me. His jaw clenched as he immediately pressed the heel of both palms to his forehead.

Anger spawned migraines. All those weird electrical connections that still misfired inside him. I should've waited to bring it up. Or I should've just scheduled the damn therapy appointment and dragged his ass there.

He'd never go back willingly.

"I know what you're trying to do. Knock it the fuck off. You and I both know we cannot afford to—"

"Nathan, let me be the one to worry about that. You don't need to think about all that stuff. I've got it covered."

"I'm so not in the mood for your bullshit and lies today." He groaned again and shut his eyes, resting his head against the passenger window.

The side of a closed fist thumped against his left knee. He did that a lot. Any excuse to beat himself up a little more.

His legs were almost misshapen now. Weak and spindly where once there had been great strength. I tried to avoid looking directly at them.

"You have enough things to worry about," he muttered.

"Nothing is more important than—"

"I know about the deadline."

My mouth snapped shut to his declaration.

"I saw the notice in the mail last week. Stop worrying about me. There are other things that need and *want* your attention. Other things that are even more broken than me right now," he added below his breath. "Focus on saving the business and try to stay the fuck out of mine for a change. I'm fine the way I am."

Fine. My least favorite four-letter word.

Nothing about it applied to our situation.

I wanted to yell and scream. To vent some of the frustration boiling beneath my plastic veneer. But what the hell would I say?

You don't look fine.

You're not even trying.

You'll never get better like this.

He dug in his sweatshirt pocket for his earbuds and phone, plugging himself in to cut off our conversation.

Those stupid freaking letters. The bank kept sending them. As if I'd suddenly forgotten the jumble of angry numbers printed inside.

They could've saved themselves the postage.

I hated that he'd seen them.

Hated that my brother knew I had failed him once again.

I pulled the truck as far up to the garage as possible, shortening his path. This part still bugged him. The strangled dignity of having to wait for my help. I moved as fast as I could, dragging open the tailgate to extract the heavy chair, rolling it up next to the passenger side.

"I got it. I got it," he mumbled irritably as I wedged my body between the chair and the door, giving him something to grab on to. The bulky muscles in his shoulders strained, compensating for the weakness he suffered everywhere else. He lowered himself down to his rolling prison.

I started to push. Forgetting myself.

"Stop," he said, snapping at me, as his hands turned the spokes, sharply pulling back. "I'm good. I don't need you to mother me."

He always knew just the words to cut me.

By the time I'd shut the side door, he was already halfway up the wooden ramp to the converted garage apartment. I knew better than to ask if he wanted help getting inside.

"I have to go over to the marina for a little bit. How about I bring some pizza home for dinner?"

"Whatever."

In the place of optimism, I'd settle for apathy.

Thank God for small victories.

I made it a mile and a half.

That's when the thunder rolled in as pregnant clouds started their daily dance across the bay. I used to love watching a storm blow over the water. Back in the lazy days when I could sit and enjoy their dark power. My mind used to soak up their energy.

Now, I mentally calculated lost revenue.

The rumbling earth and violent strokes of light served as one more reminder of just how little I could control. Adulthood sucked the joy from so many things.

I turned on the radio to give my pity party a soundtrack and to drown out the scrape of the windshield wipers. Angry Adele accompanied my mood. I dived right in, singing full steam, as my hand smacked against the cracked blue steering wheel like a drum.

The old girl couldn't take the beating. As I hit the high note in the chorus, the whole truck lurched once and then suddenly lost power.

"No. Not today," I groaned. "Come on."

I pumped the gas pedal a half-dozen times, trying to will the thing back to life, as I coasted to the gravel shoulder on the side of the road.

"Seriously?" I looked up and pounded my open palm against the roof. "Why can't you cut me just a little bit of slack? Do guardian angels take holidays? You're supposed to be watching out for me."

I slumped forward, resting my forearms and brow against the oversized steering wheel, locked inside disbelief of the shittiest luck possible. I'd become one of those blow-up punching dolls with the sand in the bottom. The kind fists keep pummeling 'cause the stupid thing never has the sense to stay down.

Begrudgingly, I popped the hood release and hopped down out of the cab. I had no clue how to diagnose the problem, but broken-down suckers on the roadside always pretend to look at the engine.

I played along.

Stepping up onto the rusted front bumper, I stared at the pile of dirty metal while daydreaming about tossing a match inside and walking away. At least bending over under the hood shielded part of me from the rain.

The sound of tires crunching through the gravel behind the truck brought a sigh of sweet relief. I looked back up at the heavens and felt bad for not trusting my angel to send help. Jumping down from my perch on the bumper, I brushed my hands down the front of my khaki shorts as I rounded the front of the cab to call out to my hero.

Cruel disbelief blossomed in the back of my throat.

"You've got to be shitting me. This is not happening."

He's still in town?

It had been almost a week. A week of trying to make myself believe our run-in at Foxy's was just another bad dream. Six freaking days of convincing myself life couldn't possibly be that cruel.

I'd avoided the town gossip machine buzzing furiously about his sudden return. But no one else would drive that car. It looked like money on wheels. The black paint and sleek lines made my truck's chipped blue exterior and scratched marina logo look even more pathetic.

Some folks in St. Michaels had seen a Maserati.

Nobody in town *drove* one.

Certainly not one with New York plates.

I lifted my face to the rain, letting it wash away my urge to cry, as the driver's side door popped open, and my worst day of the week took a turn for my worst day *ever*.

"Really?" I grumbled, shooting a snarky eyeroll toward the angry sky. "This is who you sent?"

He was dressed casually in a pair of shiny black athletic shorts and a plain gray sweatshirt, slightly frayed across the bottom hem by time and fondness. The hood bunched up around his neck, framing the sharp jawline that sported thick, dark scruff.

Brayden Ross turned gym-rat attire into the costume of a sex god.

He suffered from that strange anomaly that saddled people with fame and fortune. As a little girl, I'd seen it in his father and his father's friends. They seemed crisper around the edges or something. Like brand-new bills freshly spit from the ATM instead of crumpled dollars that spent life stuffed in back pockets and sweaty bras.

He didn't walk toward me; he prowled. Slow and steady with this sexy gait that deserved its own theme music.

The rain didn't even try to touch him.

This second sighting didn't level the same sucker punch. More like a queasy dysphoria. A bad case of déjà vu that punctured skin and vein. Half of me wanted to run, throw my arms around his waist, and hold on for dear life. The other half wanted to put my hands around his neck and squeeze hard.

I remained stuck in place, combing a hand through my own dripping hair. My light-pink T-shirt was soaked down to the skin, letting the outline of my white lace bra peep through. As he closed the distance between us, I futilely pulled the material away from my chest, trying to appear half as trashy and plain as I suddenly felt.

"Ash?" he called out. "You need a hand?"

He didn't bother to wait for an answer. He walked around me and stuck his head under the hood, pretending the same way I had. He tinkered long enough for me to get an eyeful of his ass. I stood and ogled it like a stupid mute, squelching down memories of digging my nails into him while I screamed out his name.

"You've got a broken belt. It looks like it's snapped clear through. But you've got some kind of liquid spilling out, too. This is pretty fucked."

Okay, so maybe he did know what he was looking at.

"You heading into town? Let me give you a lift."

"No. No, I'm fine. Thanks for stopping, but I'm all good."

Thunder crashed overhead. Punctuating my ridiculous statement.

Fine. That damn word again. Nothing about this was fine. Not the constant rain. Not this old, pissed off truck. And certainly not the way standing beside him still made me feel.

"Ashley." He didn't say anything else. Just my name. In that way that always made me feel childish.

I sighed, weighing the options between bad and worse.

"I have to grab a box out of the back. I was taking it to the marina. I don't think it's even gonna fit in that thing." I motioned to his four-wheeled mortgage payment.

He was already back around me, pulling down the lift gate and extracting the heavy box I'd labored to get in there alone. I considered his injury too late. He'd already hefted the package onto his hip with his good arm and was carrying it to his trunk.

The car smelled like his aftershave and buttery leather. They both assaulted me as I slid into the soft luxury of the passenger seat.

"Nice car," I said purely to have something to say as he settled in on the driver's side.

He pulled his door shut, sealing us into unnatural quiet.

Being this close to him, tightly confined by metal and glass, was a very bad idea.

"It's just a car," he said nonchalantly as he pressed the button to fire the engine.

It purred in Italian, refuting his irreverence.

"So, you're still here? I thought . . ."

I'd become the master of all things obvious. I pinched the bridge of my nose as he turned to look at me. Blue eyes burned. They soaked me in and held me captive. My nipples turned into rocks, painfully stretching against wet lace. I crossed my arms to hide them.

He misunderstood my discomfort.

"Fuck. You're soaking wet." The huskiness and deep rumble of his voice jolted me.

"Christ," I murmured. Hearing him say those words felt like the worst kind of foreplay. They stirred more memories and sent involuntary sparks to the part of me that hadn't felt tingles in a very long time.

"You must be freezing. Here." His large frame struggled against the confines of the claustrophobic interior as he shrugged out of his hoodie. He pulled it free, leaving his hair standing up on end so he looked even more like my Brayden than he had before.

"No, really, I'm fine."

"Wrap this around you at least."

He didn't wait for me to accept or take no for an answer. The material, coated in his body heat and musky scent, pressed around my shoulders and neck. We stared at one another. Long enough for that familiar burn to reignite between my legs.

How the hell did he still do that?

He hadn't touched me, but I felt him all over my skin.

"Yeah, I'm still here." He finally broke the silence with an answer to my earlier question. He motioned to the back seat where a bag from the hardware store lay haphazardly. "Have some repairs to make around the house."

I nodded my head and bit my bottom lip, staving off the need to ask exactly how long that would take.

I needed him gone. Like yesterday.

He pulled away from the curb. The volume of the music magically increased along with his speed. Satellite radio spun from a nebulous-one-hit-wonder to a new song by Rihanna. My hand instinctively reached out to the dash, searching for a way to shut it off. My fingertips hovered, hopelessly desperate. The music died as he touched a button on the steering wheel.

"Fucking Rihanna," he muttered.

My gaze shot to his profile. He was smirking. That stupid half-mouth thing.

We'd fucked to Rihanna. A lot.

When he first downloaded the album, I made fun of him. Then, he drove into me to the pace of the downbeat, and I understood the appeal. He used to murmur that same phrase in my ear as I came.

Her voice had been our sexual anthem.

Now, it brought too much pain. I refused to listen to a single chord of her latest record.

"Brayden."

He turned to look at me. The desolation on my face chased away his sexy grin.

"Don't," I whispered. "Just. Don't."

BRAYDEN

I fought back my innate need to touch her.

It hurt. Being so close. Chaining up all the things I wanted to say. The things I'd waited too long to tell her. For years, I'd lived in a glass prison, hundreds of miles away. I finally had Ashley back beside me, but I still stood behind bars.

"I can get that." She said it like she really believed it.

As I popped the trunk lid, her little arms reached out toward the heavy box.

"Seriously?" I chuckled a little. "Get out of the way, baby girl."

She inhaled sharply. I hadn't meant to use the endearment. It just slid out of me. She was being ridiculous. Stuffing too many books in her bike basket all over again. The box weighed half of her.

Even soaking wet.

She'd left my sweatshirt in the car, treating me to the final round of a free wet T-shirt contest. White lace. Fucking white lace. I wanted to rip through it with my teeth to get down to the prize I knew waited beneath.

I pulled the box out with my good arm and cocked it against my hip. I swiveled around to ask her where she wanted it just in time to see some jackass with a man bun and too many teeth bounding up to us from one of the docks.

"Sorry I'm late," Ashley called out to him. "Damn truck broke down again. And, of course, you know me, dead cell."

"No worries." He greeted her with a private smile.

I hated him immediately.

"Here, let me take that for you." He held his arms out toward me.

I started to stammer that I certainly didn't need any help, but the dude was already taking the box from my grasp. Never would've happened if I still had two working arms.

"Are these the parts for the pontoon engine?" He smiled at her again.

This must be the guy working for her. I had a copy of his background check on Grams's old rolltop desk. It failed to mention he looked like a hipster straight out of the Abercrombie & Fitch catalog. He put the box down at his feet and slung one arm around Ashley's shoulders.

I twitched involuntarily.

"Oh, hell, where are my manners? How you doin'? I'm Logan."

I took his hand in a shake two or three notches past firm. "Brayden Ross."

I never introduced myself that way. Ever. I never gave my last name. It sounded presumptuous. Like, *You should know who I am.*

I didn't usually have to introduce myself at all.

People act weird when they recognize a face. They blush and hunch their shoulders forward. Sometimes it's only slight, but, after you've witnessed it a couple thousand times, you can spot it on instinct.

On a rare occasion, like this, when my face didn't give me away, I'd only use my first name. Then, I would bask in the glow of being plain old me for a fraction of time. But, the caveman inside me, wanted this guy to know both my names.

Much to my chagrin, he didn't seem impressed.

"Thanks for helping Ash with the lift, man. She's always forgetting to charge that cell phone. I reminded her last night, but she has too much on her plate. She forgets the little things." He smiled down at her, pulling against her shoulder more.

It made my stomach burn. The way he was so familiar. He'd said *last night* like it must've been pillow talk he happened to ramble about after they shut off the light and were drifting off to sleep. Together.

Bad shit started going down in my head. I'd been back in town less than a week, and already, I could feel sixteen-year-old Brayden ready to creep back in and bust heads.

I cracked the knuckles on both my thumbs.

I hadn't done that in years.

"Worst of the storm is already blowing north," he said, holding his palm out to grab hold of the misty drops that lingered in the air. "I'm gonna get started on these." He extracted himself from my girl and hefted the box back up off the ground.

"Nice meeting you, Brandon," he called back over his shoulder.

Brandon? Seriously?

I rubbed the pad of my thumb against my bottom lip to keep my inner thoughts from spilling out.

"Listen, I'll run over and get the guys at Mr. Uxley's shop to go tow your truck. I'm sure they can get it fixed fast."

"No." She held up a hand like a Stop sign. "No. I don't need you to—"

"It's no problem. I can just swing by and . . ."

The pinched look on her face made the words die in my throat. It looked like a strange combination of fear and embarrassment. I wanted to suck back in whatever part of my offer put those feelings there.

"I'll get Joey to call Conner. He'll come and fix the truck. He's good with cars. He does it all the time. I can't . . ." she stammered, and her voice grew quieter. "I can't afford the tow. Or the shop. So, just don't, Brayden."

"Ash, don't worry about the money. I'll get them to fix it. It's on me."

"No. I don't want anything from you." Her bottom teeth tugged against the little pucker of her top lip. "Thanks for the lift, okay? Good luck with your house repairs."

She was dismissing me.

I took a deep breath and tried to channel inner patience I didn't have.

Sometimes, you had to walk a batter. Purely because the timing called for it, you would force yourself to throw balls instead of strikes. You'd coast weak shit to the outside when you knew damn well you could send heat down the pipe.

This wasn't the time for my fastball.

Stick to the motherfucking plan, asshole.

I squeezed my eyes shut against the silent reminder.

"If you change your mind . . ." I said, letting my words trail off with less than a subtle suggestion.

Change your mind, damn it.

Look at me, and tell me you don't feel it.

"About letting me help with the car, I mean."

"I won't." Her voice didn't waver. "Look, let's not make this weird. Well, weirder than it already is. If I don't see you before you leave . . . good luck, Brayden. With the house and with your rehab."

She turned and walked toward the office without looking back. The masochist in me couldn't stop the reflex. I stood there and gawked at the sway of her hips, daydreaming about watching them swivel on top of me.

I gazed back down at the dock where hipster boy appeared hard at work.

I knew their deal. He was a partner of sorts. A professional sunbird. His kind floated up and down the eastern seaboard, looking for temporary shelter and a way to score charter jobs. He owned his own boat. A fifty-two-foot Viking Convertible. He got to run it out of the marina in exchange for free room and board in the apartment above the maintenance shed. She got a cut of his daily excursion fees.

When I read the dossier on him, it sounded like a win-win. On paper, it still was. But now, face-to-face, I had to question what else that guy had scored with this deal.

It'd damn well better not include any part of her.

This plan needed to work.

Fast.

CHAPTER 2
ROTTED PIECES

ASHLEY

"I think you've finally sniffed too much hair dye."

My left leg swung back and forth, tapping on the metal bar used to raise and lower the chair. Joey's broom swept across pink linoleum, clearing away remnants of the day's last client. Riley, the new shampoo girl, smiled from her perch behind the reception desk.

Joey rested both hands atop the wooden handle as she stopped her work to stare at me and sigh. "He came to see me," she said, her voice as soft as her sudden change of heart.

"What? When?" I asked, my brow creased.

So not what I'd expected her to say.

"He came into the shop. I cut his hair yesterday." She paused for a moment, considering her words. "His hair really is pretty damn fantastic. He bought a deep conditioner. I mean, people think that shit just happens, but the boy truly does respect the hell out of what God gave him."

"Seriously? The guy boosts weekly product sales, and you go all googly-eyed? Who are you, and where did you chain up my best friend?"

"Oh, he brought her coffee, too. He brought us all coffee actually," Riley said enthusiastically, standing up and rounding the counter to join in on the shitshow going down before me. "He went to The Grind and asked Kacey if she knew our favorite drinks. Came in with a whole load of coffees and muffins. Those lemon poppy seed ones. I'm never gonna lose this baby weight, but they are so worth every single calorie." She placed a palm against an imaginary bulge.

Riley was a sweet girl. She'd been a star dancer, working toward a scholarship at Juilliard, until she got knocked up her senior year of high school. Her mother watched little Chloe while Riley worked her tail off, scrubbing heads and answering phones at the salon.

She'd become Joey's latest pet project.

I almost felt bad for the girl.

"Riles, don't help, sweetie," Joey said, bending down with the dustpan to finish her job and escape the scalding look on my face.

"The dude brings you a cinnamon chai latte and some empty carbs, and suddenly, you're BFFs?"

She huffed out a breath and stood back up to thoughtfully look at me.

Pensive Joey scared the crap out of me.

"I'm just saying, you should consider the idea."

"What good could possibly come from it? Please don't use the word *closure*."

The therapist my mother forced me to see right after the accident had used that word a lot. It was a sweet notion really. Learning to tie things up and put a shiny bow on them sounded like great, big, beautiful make-believe.

"There are some things you just can't talk out. Nothing we say to each other would change the fact that my brother lives out each day in a wheelchair and we're the ones who put him there."

She tucked a strand of fiery-red hair behind her ear. "He said some things, Ash. I just think . . . he's different. I think maybe you should hear him out. Give him a chance."

"You know I can't do that. I can't, Joey. I don't have a choice."

She knew.

Better than anyone else.

Joey was the one who held me while I cried. She was the one who force-fed me until I gained back some of the weight stripped away by grief and a broken heart. She drove me to those therapist appointments, sat in the waiting room, and held my hand as we walked back silently to the car. Every time life shredded me, Joey had been by my side, ready to sweep up the fallout.

"You know what I was like before, Joe. I can't go through all that again."

"I know, babe. But he's carrying some pretty heavy baggage, too. I think he felt like you sent him away. He didn't think you wanted him to come home and—"

"Oh, please. I sent him to get help. I didn't change my number or move to an undisclosed location. He's the one who forgot all about us. He moved on, Joey. Very quickly, if you recall."

"I'm not sure he's moved on at all actually."

"Please." I rolled my eyes at her. "He moved right into a big, fancy life, just like his father planned out. The rest of us can't move on. We're stuck, living the nightmare he just woke up from and conveniently forgot. That's all we are to him. An uncomfortable memory. A past he chose to never revisit. Nothing, Joey. I've got nothing. He never sent a card or a note. Never picked up the phone. He doesn't even know about . . ." My voice trailed off.

It still hurt to say the words out loud.

It made the loneliness real.

"He's just back here now 'cause he got hurt. The Jack Ross master plan finally hit a speed bump. That's all we are to him."

"I think you're wrong. I think you might be part of the reason Brayden is here."

"Oh, sure. Bet banging all those movie stars and supermodels got too tiring, and he decided to go back and look up an old flame. I mean, look at me." I gestured down to my baggy sweats and the white T-shirt bunched up at my waist, secured with a stretched-out hair tie. "I'm totally Brayden Ross material."

"You sell yourself short. You always have. You've never stopped seeing yourself as that skinny girl with pigtails, but you haven't been her for a long time."

She was wrong. I saw myself clearly. I didn't have time for glamour or the money for high fashion. Brayden Ross hung out with women who never wore the same thousand-dollar outfit twice. They woke up, prepped for a blow job, a blowout, and a French mani-pedi. I woke up, wondering how to cover the mortgage and pay for groceries. Life had cracked me into busted up pieces that I held together with Scotch tape and sheer will.

"He's back out of guilt. You're right about that. But it has nothing to do with me. Getting hurt forced him to stop and look beyond the sixty feet between him and home plate. He didn't want Jack to sell the house and toss all of Grams's old things. He'll be gone in a week, and we won't ever hear from him again."

Tying up loose ends.

That was his only purpose.

He'd pack all of Grams's stuff up in neat cardboard boxes and tuck them away in a storage room. Stacked somewhere on top all his boxed up memories of me.

"I'm not saying you have to forgive him. I just think you should sit down and talk." Her voice had that soft edge again.

They must've handed that out at his fan club induction.

"It's not like spending time with him would be a hardship. I mean, sweet Jesus, he's smokin' hot," Riley added. "I thought I was gonna pass out when he walked in. He's even better-looking in person. All those muscles and those sultry eyes. I almost had an orgasm while I washed his hair." She fanned her hand in front of her face. "Maybe you shouldn't talk to him. But you should *definitely* fuck him before he up and leaves."

"Riles, you're helping again." Joey smirked along with her admonishment. "We need to find you a man soon, sweetie. We have rules about spontaneous orgasms around the customers." She directed her gaze back at me. "I honestly think Brayden might be the only one who can help dig you out of the mess you're in. And, good grief, we all know he owes you."

"No one could ever repay what we've lost. And, besides, he's not the only one with an unpaid tab," I murmured the last part under my breath.

"Talking is still free, you know." Her perfectly sculpted brow pointed straight up.

"How are you, of all people, suddenly sitting front row in the Brayden Ross bandwagon?"

"I know. It's weird." She shuddered and fluttered one hand in the air. "Trust me, it's totally skeeving me out, too."

"When did you even start using his real name?" I shook my head in disbelief and started picking at my thumbnail. "I'll never take anything from him, Joey. My father wouldn't take Jack's blood money four years ago, and I won't take any of it now. I might fail at saving everything else, but I won't hock the last of my family's pride."

Fire spread through my lungs. Everything inside me wanted the pain to stop. The lack of air, the stitch in my side, and the damn pebble rolling beneath my left instep, all worked to remind me why I hated this so much.

I didn't run because I liked it.

Running fucking sucks.

But gasping for my next breath gave me a respite from every other worry. I liked the last stride across the finish line. I just bitched inside my head every other step along the way.

Picking different routes kept me from obsessing about how far I had left to go. I'd never allowed myself to wander near the old path by the water, but with angry P!nk shouting in my ears, my feet just took me in that direction.

The breeze coming off the water dampened some of my misery and distracted me as I approached the old building.

Twenty feet away, I heard a noise that didn't belong. A staccato thumping so loud, it punctured through the bass of my music. I slowed until I came to a stop, staring toward the memorial I'd planned to ignore.

As I pulled the earbuds free, the thumping stopped, replaced instead by a string of muttered curses.

I couldn't stop myself.

The old barn door sat wide open.

Brayden stood three rungs up the ladder, holding a nail between his lips the same way he used to hold a cigarette. A hammer hung loosely in his left hand. His jeans sat low enough, I could see the top waistband of black briefs. A wadded up white T-shirt spilled out of his back pocket, leaving the overly defined muscles spread across his chest on full display. They glistened with a sheen of sweat. His new haircut hid beneath a baseball cap, turned backward on his head. It wasn't crisp navy blue anymore.

This one, I recognized.

Worn and red and perfect.

"Motherfucking stupid thing," he grumbled out of the corner of his mouth, letting the nail wobble back and forth, as he studied the board above his head. "This is never gonna work like this."

"What the hell are you doing here?" The words popped out of my mouth before I could apply a filter. The question Joey had planted in my head. The one I'd been trying to torture myself into forgetting.

He turned, clearly startled. Blue eyes swept down the length of me. The black sports bra and bright purple running shorts, which had seemed like a good choice to match the humid air, suddenly felt indecent. Using both hands, I tugged my ponytail tighter, pretending that small improvement would transform me into looking more Lululemon model than standard hot mess.

The action just made my boobs bunch together and unintentionally poke toward him. His attention paused there a fraction too long before his eyes met mine again. He stepped down off the ladder and pulled the nail from his mouth. A half-naked Brayden Ross wasn't the kind of torture I needed. Muscles I didn't intend to work on suddenly woke up and flexed.

I struggled to keep my own gaze above his neck.

"What the hell are you doing?" I repeated, motioning around us.

I avoided looking into his eyes by staring instead at the tattoo I'd seen peeking out from his shirtsleeve at the bar. He took two steps forward.

I inhaled a deep breath, turning my head to put more space between my eyes and his body. Soaking in our surroundings didn't make anything better. I hadn't been inside in years. Not since the last time we'd stolen away from the world and come here to get our fill of one another.

Forgotten laughter echoed off the walls around us. I could hear his voice whispering dirty things in my ear until I cried out his name. I could see the way his eyes always darkened when he told me he loved me.

Staying away from here had been a very smart decision.

I surveyed the room, cataloging things that didn't belong. A pile of new lumber, some kind of plastic sheeting, a can of paint, and a box of nails.

"I told you I was fixing some things."

He held out the hammer in demonstration and followed my gaze around the room. A patch of light shone down from the window up in the loft, creating a sundial against the weathered boards near my feet.

"I'm surprised it's still standing. This place should've rotted into the water long ago."

"Nah. This place will last a couple more lifetimes. Strong foundation. Just needs a little TLC." He smirked and took one more long stride in my direction, tucking the end of the hammer in his other back pocket and the nail behind his ear. "You run by here a lot?"

"No. Never. I never come here."

His eyes darted to my lips, half-hooded with something I knew all too well.

One corner of his mouth turned up as he mumbled under his breath, "That's not how I remember it."

Everything in my lower half stirred against my will. It was too much—being this close to him, surrounded by ghosts, weathered happiness and guilt.

"Well, I'm glad you're here now," he added.

The arrogance in his voice grated on me.

"Don't."

"Don't what?"

"You know what."

One brow quirked up along with a cocky half-smile.

"Stop that, too." I waved a finger at him. "Don't play games with me, Brayden."

His eyes met mine again, more serious, but the playful smirk remained. He slowly ran a hand down his chest and over his abs, pretending to wipe away the sweat. Knowing full well my eyes would trail down along with his fingers.

Driven by reflex, I ogled my way to the button on his jeans, past the small patch of thicker hair and sinfully carved hip bones. My eyes snapped back up to his sly look.

"I'm fixing things that should've never been left to fall into disrepair. Things should never have gone unattended this long." His eyes grew darker as he stressed each word. He paused and then held out both arms, gesturing around to the rotting wood. "I mean, look at this place. Someone has to fix it. Can't be left like this."

"Leaving shouldn't be a problem for you. You're good at it."

The playful expression died on his face. Resentment, and its close friend bitterness, quickly took up residence.

"Now, who's playing games? There's a difference between leaving and being exiled."

I groaned angrily. "I knew nothing good could come from us trying to talk to one another."

I couldn't handle another word. Flight won out over the fighting words I was ready to hurl at him. I turned on my heel and started back for the door.

His hand grasped my arm before I could escape.

"Soot."

My eyes squeezed shut.

One word. Searing pain.

"Will you just answer one question?"

I rounded slowly back toward him. His grip on my arm slackened but didn't fall away.

"Have you spent all these years hating me?"

"*Hate* is a strong word. I don't hate you," I replied, clenching my jaw. I watched as his shoulders sagged by a fraction. Bubbling fury made me want to soak up that relief and toss it right back in his face. "I feel nothing for you at all."

He stared at me intently, forcing my poker face under a spotlight. His blank assessment provided no response. Our chests both rose and fell in counterbalance. Too many beats passed before he gave a brief nod and let his hand gently fall away.

He bowed his head.

"I'm sorry. About your mom. So sorry." Sad eyes looked back up into mine. "If I could've been here . . ."

"Joey told you, huh? I heard you two are besties now."

He didn't respond, just bit down on his lower lip.

"Thanks," I finally said, swallowing down my own emotion. "It was fast. Once they found the tumor, we only had six months." My voice faltered. "She asked for you. Toward the end. I didn't know how to find you."

My mother's ghost sat on my shoulder, a murmuring angel fussing at me for using her to inflict pain. But instinct forced me to lash out. I used those words to turn the knife just a little bit, to break off and share a piece of the heartache I'd been served up in spades. I wanted to see his perfection marred. Wanted to leave him with some scars to match my own.

He was right. I sent him away. But, for too long, my foolish heart clung to some naïve hope that he would eventually turn back around and fight for us.

He never did.

He walked away and started a brand-new life. He gave up on me, the exact way his mother had so easily given up on him.

He'd repeated more than just the sins of his father. He'd turned me into a carbon copy of his former self. Broken by drugs, spilled fidelity, and the sadness of being too easy to leave. The same resentment I'd witnessed in his eyes all those years now resided in my own.

I didn't hate him. I couldn't.

I'd spent the time since he left too numb to hate.

But seeing him broke through that haze. Too many feelings were bubbling up now. Those prickles that burn a sleeping limb were breaking out all over my body. The sooner he left, the sooner I could return to an anesthetic existence.

"How long do you think this is gonna take you?" I impatiently motioned to the pile of new wood. "Is this even good for your arm? How are you gonna nail all those down with your left hand?"

"I can do it. I just have to take it real slow. Chip away at it a little at a time." Something about the hoarse tone of his voice made me question whether he was talking about a hammer and nails.

"I thought you said you'd only be here for—"

"Yeah. So, that might have been a small white lie." He held up his thumb and index finger, pinching them close together.

"Brayden," I replied, admonishing with only his name.

"I can't do my rehab in the city. There are too many eyes watching. Too many opinions. My father and my coaches all telling me what to do. I needed a way to lay low for a while." He held his arms out. "This was always my favorite hideout. I can't think of any better place."

"You can't be serious. I told you, my brother can't—"

"I'll be careful," he interrupted. "I'll avoid Nathan if you don't think he should see me. But I'm not leaving here anytime soon."

I exhaled sharply, giving too much away. He closed in on me again, reaching out to brush the pad of his thumb across my bottom lip. I shuddered against the sudden tenderness.

"You feel nothing at all, huh?"

I turned my cheek away from him and his cockiness, but his index finger quickly curled under my chin, forcing my eyes back toward his.

"Ash, I could fix other things, too. Let me help—"

"No. We've managed without you just fine for all these years. We don't need any help from you now. Do whatever it is you came here to do, Brayden. Get it over with. Then go back home to your big city life. Just make sure you stay the hell away from Nathan." I huffed out a loud breath, punctuating my angry words.

He studied me without flinching, in that old, all-knowing way that punctured too deep.

It stole secrets I couldn't afford to give him.

"I promise to stay away from your brother, but I won't promise to steer clear of you. We both know I couldn't if I tried." His hold loosened. The side of his finger whispered over my cheek. "You were never good at lying to me. And I was never good at keeping my hands off you for very long."

CHAPTER 3
CONFESSIONAL

BRAYDEN

The strong hand that clamped down on my shoulder startled me.

I'd been flying low. I'd slipped in the back door at Foxy's and found a spot at a high top toward the side of the bar. It was more crowded than last time, so I'd pulled my hat down low enough I could watch without being seen.

I'd long mastered handling the hard approach—fans who come up at unexpected times with big voices and small demands.

Things had exploded near the end of my second month in the majors. I threw a no-hitter against the Sox, helping to clinch the American League East. After that, the press stopped labeling me a genetically gifted flash in the pan.

And I devised a faster signature.

These days, I couldn't go many places in New York where someone didn't stop me to sign something, to smile at their camera phone, or occasionally, to offer armchair coaching advice about what the organization kept doing all wrong.

I expected it there.

Knew how to prepare for it.

Here? I had no freaking clue what to expect. I'd half-feared I would come back the town pariah. The jerk who gutted his girl and broke his best friend and was never heard from again.

But, while there weren't any red carpets or banners on Talbot Street, no one had spit in my face yet either. Maybe time really could shorten memories. Or maybe I'd just reached the point of celebrity where an automatic free pass licked away the skid marks left by fucked-up choices and bad behavior.

Over the last week, I'd garnered some curious stares and soft smiles as I walked through town. The girl behind the counter at the coffee shop found the courage to ask for a selfie. The old guys at Lucky's Diner still weren't pleased with my curveball. And Marty at the hardware store wanted to know why the hell Eddinger had traded away Coniski—a move I'd never understood myself.

I enjoyed each of those conversations. I stopped and took time with all of them, dropping the need to stay on message and contain my words into publicist-vetted sound bites. In this town, I could trust again. Could talk openly. Without worrying someone would turn around and sell me out in the press by the following day. Plus, talking baseball filled in some of the emptiness of missing the game.

But, other than those fairly benign interactions, everyone else had stayed in orbit around me. No one had gone for a hard approach.

Until now.

The hand on my shoulder squeezed again. I mentally prepared myself to be on—to be Brayden Ross the ball player instead of Brayden Ross the human being.

"Well, look what the tide dragged in. I heard a rumor The Great One was back in town."

I smirked, relieved by the familiar voice, as I rounded on a face I hadn't seen in far too long.

"Fuck. Hey, man." Slipping off the stool, I greeted Dillan with a one-armed man hug and a slap on the back. I held my hand out to the empty seat opposite me. "God, you are a sight for sore eyes. Been way too long."

The last time I saw him I was apologizing for half-smashing in his nose.

I studied him as he scraped the stool out from beneath the table and settled into it. It was sort of like looking at a weird time-lapse photo. He had his hair cut military short, and his biceps looked pretty fucking badass, but otherwise, same old Dillan.

"Well, whose fucking fault is that? You've been busy up there, lighting the world on fire, and busting up your arm real good." He smiled and good-naturedly tipped his chin toward my elbow. "You healing up?"

I cleared my throat.

"Rehab is going great. Should be able to start throwing some by the end of summer."

The canned response sounded just as hollow now as it had the hundred times I'd repeated it to reporters before I fled the city.

"Must feel weird as hell not to have a ball permanently attached to your hand," Dillan replied.

"Yeah. Never been away from the game this long. It's making me a little stir-crazy. You still play at all?"

"Hung up my cleats for a clipboard. Just took over coaching the junior varsity team at the high school. You oughta come out to one of our summer practices sometime. Those kids'll shit themselves if they get to meet you."

I smirked softly. The thought of that old field softened some of the tension in my shoulders. "I'd love to. That would be fun."

He turned and motioned to a cute blonde behind the bar. She smiled at him and started filling a pint glass.

"So, nice outfit. That thing loaded?" I asked, nodding to the gun holstered on his hip. "I always thought you'd end up in a uniform, but truth be told, I thought you'd turn into a priest, not the town deputy."

He chuckled and patted the shiny gold star pinned to his starched black shirt. The words *St. Michaels Deputy Sheriff* were etched just above his last name.

"Decided freshman year I liked the law but had no intention of following Bobby to law school." He shrugged his shoulders. "Got my associates degree in criminal justice and came back here. Sheriff Kincaid retires next year. Needed an heir apparent. Figured there were far shittier places in the world to hang your hat. 'Sides, the most action we ever see is busting up high school parties and drunk sunbirds wandering around town. It's a fairly cake gig."

I nodded my head and smiled at the waitress as she brought his beer and offered us menus. I used the distraction to make a sweep of the room, checking to see if Ashley had come back inside. Her tables were all out back tonight, probably a ploy to stay far away from me.

I finally caught sight of her talking to the hostess in the corner of the room. I turned back to see Dillan staring at me with an all-knowing look.

Dude should've been wearing a collar.

He could sniff out sins from a mile away.

"She's been through a lot. Too much," he added defensively as he set his glass down and toyed with the corner of the cardboard coaster lying beneath it.

My brow furrowed. I stared down at my bottle, running my thumbnail under the bottom edge of the label. "Yeah. I know about her mom. I've kept tabs on them every now and then." I managed to keep my tone light.

I sought her out again and couldn't help but enjoy the view as she hefted a heavy tray, carrying it toward the back door. Her jean shorts were pulled tight across her ass. They rose up a little too high, showing off the creamy flesh at the backs of her thighs where I used to press my fingertips. I visibly exhaled and then turned back to see Dillan looking at the very same thing.

Well, fuck me.

Not exactly white-collar material after all.

We exchanged a discerning glance and let the conversation die away.

After we ordered food and more beers, we started running through a where-are-they-now laundry list of people I hadn't bothered to care about in years. I kept watch for her on instinct—an old habit that slid right back on like a game-worn glove. She kept skirting around our table, maintaining a wide enough berth so she could pretend not to see me.

Dillan and I weren't the only ones who noticed her. A dozen eyes followed her around the room. She'd already squelched down the dreams of two fuckwit sunbirds seated at the end of the bar.

They were lucky they still had their hands attached.

She came in the back door right before Dillan got up to hit the head. Weaving his way toward the restrooms, he made an unexpected stop beside the bar. He approached her from behind, but she quickly spun around with a bright smile. Her arms flung out to greet him with an exuberant hug.

The kind I didn't deserve but would've begged for.

He only returned it with one arm, but he pulled her in tight and held on a fraction longer than casual.

"What the hell is this?" I murmured out loud.

I couldn't read lips, but I hated the way she bounced on her toes and talked to him with happy eyes. The thing stabbing me in the heart smelled a whole lot like fear.

Five minutes later, he was back at the table, double-fisting new beers for us. He started to mention something about the game of the week playing out on one of the TVs.

Chavez was throwing like shit again. The Sox were already six games ahead. Fucking chumps. If they won the pennant, while I sat on the disabled list, I'd never hear the end of it.

I waded through our banter, waiting painfully long for a third out so they'd cut away to a commercial, and I could slide into a new topic of conversation.

"You and Ashley certainly are chummy." The last word came out with more bite than I'd intended.

He eyed me in response. Studying me with an assessing gaze.

Half-cop. Half-heavenly father.

"She's a sweet girl," he finally said plainly.

I stared at him with one raised brow.

"What's that look for?"

"Just wondering if there's something I should know about between you two."

His nostrils flared slightly. He swallowed a hard swig of beer and set his glass back down with a weighted thud. "I helped her with a project this week. Rebuilt some old dock benches. She was thanking me for offering to finish painting them this weekend."

He sighed and blew out a long breath. "Why the fuck am I

telling you this? God, you've fallen right back into the old pattern, haven't you? Sitting here, stalking her. Watching like you own her. At the ready to tear up anyone looking her direction."

I sat up taller in my chair as his voice grew angry. Angrier than I'd ever heard him before.

"What gives you that right?"

I didn't respond. I started counting in my head. From ten, going backward. Forcing my chest to rise and fall. Anger Management 101 involved a lot of low-level math and deep breathing.

"Why are you here, Brayden?" he asked, insistent.

"I came for a beer," I said, raising my bottle up and down. "And to catch up with an old friend."

A frustrated hand rubbed down the side of his face. "I don't mean, why are you in this bar? I mean, why are you back in town? Why now? What are your intentions with her?" His eyes narrowed.

That badge did fit him better than a white collar.

"How 'bout you tell me yours first?" I'd made it all the way to four, but my tone still had an angry edge.

"Jesus," he muttered before sucking in the sides of his cheeks and heaving out a breath.

He stared back up at the TV long enough that I wasn't sure he intended to answer.

"Not that you deserve to know 'cause you don't," Dillan added emphatically as his eyes cut back to mine, "Ash and I are just friends. I can't lie and say I haven't thought about it a hundred times. Because she walks around town, looking like *that*"—he motioned in her direction—"and she's one of the best people I know. She's never left her brother's side."

I swallowed hard.

"But, no, there's nothing going on. You dropped off the face of the earth, but going after her still felt like a major violation of bro code." He sighed. His face softened. "I'm her friend, Brayden. And, trust me, she's needed all the friends she could get the last couple of years. You have no idea."

His words held a bitter tone. They wiped away the nausea in my stomach, yet simultaneously left me feeling like the world's biggest asshole.

He was wrong, of course. I had every idea.

Every fucking idea in the world.

He set his beer down, so he could point a finger at me. "Don't hurt her. She's been through enough. She doesn't need you coming down here, twisting her inside out, and then running back home to the big time."

"Dillan, the big time hasn't changed who I am. I'm still the same guy you grew up with. And I still think of *this* as my home."

I chewed on my bottom lip to stave off the emotion that admission uncorked. My therapist would've marked that down as a giant step and sent me a bill with an extra zero.

"And I think you know me well enough to understand that I would cut off my own nut sac before I ever hurt her again."

I gazed around the room, trying to decide if I wanted to show some of my hand. If I was ready to admit to more. Only three other people knew my whole plan. And that was only because I needed their help to pull it off.

What-the-fuck-ever.

A cop and a priest both love a good confession.

"You want to know my real intentions? Fine. If anyone asks, I'll say I'm here to escape the heat of the city. Needed to find a quiet hole-in-the-wall to get through my rehab without everyone breathing down my neck."

I licked my lips and stared him in the eyes with the same intensity I used against a batter standing at the plate.

"But just between old friends? I'm not here by coincidence or because I decided I was overdue for a trip down memory lane. I'm here to fix the things I broke." I briefly focused my gaze toward Ashley before turning back to face him. "And God help anyone who stands in my way."

"Yeah? Well, one of the things you broke can't stand on his own two feet anymore. But you sure as hell better be prepared for him to get in your way."

BRAYDEN

"So, what? Is carpentry your fallback plan if the whole baseball superstar thing doesn't pan back out?"

My brush paused mid-stroke as I swallowed down her sass. I dipped it back into the can, loading it down with more paint while pretending to ignore how close she'd just come to the mark. I started to casually smile up at her, but my chest seized as I was greeted with an eyeful of mile-long legs.

Ashley stood above me, granting a whole new angle with which to fall in love. She had on those crazy, skintight bootie-short things girls always wear to the gym and a tank top that exposed enough plump cleavage to make me salivate.

God bless the inventor of spandex athletic wear.

The outfit highlighted just how much she'd changed since I'd been gone. Curves in sinful places. Less girl. More woman. As if my dick needed any more reason to stand at attention and salute her.

I went back to work to hide my involuntary reaction.

"At the risk of repeating myself, what the hell are you doing here?"

She cocked an angry hip to the side, planting her hand against it. I tried not to smirk at how adorable it made her look. Or the way it made her left boob push up a little higher, gifting my eyes another quarter inch of lickable skin.

"Most people call it painting." My response came out cool and easy. Pretty much the exact opposite of everything happening below my waist.

"I get that, genius. Why are you doing it? Dillan built these for me. He's coming to help me paint them this weekend."

I knew that. He'd already told me. That's why I was beating him to the punch. Saint Dillan, and his fucking one-armed hugs, could stay far away on Saturday. The job would already be done.

Outwardly, I ignored her. Partially, because I didn't want to explain myself. And partially, because I knew my silence would drive her nuts. I continued my work with long, even strokes, adding in a low, quiet whistle just to really get under her skin.

If I couldn't have her hugs, I'd take her ire.

Anything beat the hell out of nothing at all.

"Brayden."

"What's that old cliché? Why put off till tomorrow what you could get done—"

"I don't want your help," she said, with snapping impatience. "How many times do I need to say that? No one invited you here. No one asked you to do this. You're trespassing."

I reloaded the brush once again and moved around to give the other side my attention. She stood and watched, hands on both hips now. She huffed out a few noisy breaths to make sure I knew she was good and pissed.

"You're not gonna just go away, are you?" she finally asked. "You can't just leave well enough alone?"

Without responding, I finished up the first coat and leaned back to survey my handiwork with pride. "Not bad, huh? Think I'd better do a coat of polyurethane when it dries."

I stood up, unfolding my frame until I towered over her. Her teeth were clenched so tight, it looked painful. I wanted to run my fingers down the side of her jaw to ease the tension. Or offer her other services I knew damn well would leave her totally relaxed.

In place of the dirty thoughts, I couldn't share, I settled on continuing to taunt her.

My index finger tapped lightly on the end of her nose. She didn't have on a stitch of makeup. A light dusting of summer freckles danced across sun-kissed cheeks.

"No time to chat, Soot. Got eight more to go." I motioned to the other work ahead of me.

She groaned and stomped off toward the office, hips angrily swaying and hair flouncing behind her in the breeze.

I couldn't contain my grin.

"Mission accomplished."

Working with my left hand made everything feel backward. The whole job took twice as long as it should have. By mid-afternoon, my back was baked by a cloudless sky, and my throat resembled fine-grit sandpaper.

It was time to give in and see the warden.

My knuckles rapped lightly on the door left open to the office. She sat behind the desk, looking the part of a sexy headmistress. Her dark hair was piled up on her head in a messy bun held in place by a pencil she'd shoved through it. A few rebellious tendrils framed her face. Papers lay scattered all around her as her short red fingernails angrily hunted and pecked their way across the keyboard.

A small grunt accompanied my entrance. Her eyes briefly shot in my direction. I motioned toward the water cooler in the corner.

She just poked the keys harder.

I filled a cup, greedily sucking it down while I studied the photographs lining the wall. They'd all been taken during happier times.

My eyes lingered on one of Mrs. F. She stood at the helm of *Net Profit*, hair blowing in the sea breeze, with full-fledged laughter spread across her face. My hand clutched against my chest, pushing against the familiar pang of grief.

Not a single photo showed the three of us. I felt certain there'd been many at one point. The reminders must've all been purged. I fought back that old, customary feeling of rejection.

Earning a punishment fair and square didn't make living through it any easier.

Clipped up next to the photographs was a sheet of scratch paper with a hand-sketched map. Squares and circles mixed with arrows and words. The top was labeled *Master Plan.*

"What's this?" I asked, tipping my head sideways to read the scrawled print.

Her pecking stopped briefly. "My mother's last scheme. Her pipe dream for revamping the whole place."

My eyes squinted as I studied it closer. "Does that say pool?"

"Yes."

"Wow. What are these things? These rectangles?"

"Guest quarters. She wanted to build a little inn, so people could book a slip and decide to come and stay in a real bed. There's on-site storage and a convenience area, too. Small groceries, laundry, business center. The works."

"Your mom was a visionary."

She let out a tired sigh. "That's the way everything is going now. People don't just want a beat-up old dock and a place to pump out and refuel. They want the whole resort experience. They opened that same basic scheme in Kent Island almost two years ago. Sucked away all our business. Right about the time we found out she was sick."

I turned back to the cooler for a refill. I had to choke down the idea that Mrs. F had to forfeit her dreams, too. Some things, I was too late to save.

I adjusted my hat back and forth on my head, getting myself back in check.

Her keyboard pecking resumed for a minute before she paused and called out to me, "I'm surprised that hat still fits on your head."

She meant it as a dig, but her continuing to send any words in my general direction felt as good as locking up a game in October.

I turned back to see her hands hovering over the keyboard, eyes trained on my faded St. M cap. I'd hunted it up like long-lost treasure within minutes of first entering Grams's house. I'd left it behind all those years ago, plucked from my suitcase and abandoned on a shelf. Part of me had known I wouldn't be able to handle the reminder. The other part had secretly hoped, if I left a little sliver of my old self, I would have a reason to come back and retrieve it.

The thing still fit like a glove.

"Some things, you never outgrow."

She'd apparently never outgrown her ability to show major fucking attitude with a simple eye roll. She blew out a breath and tugged at the pencil, letting her hair cascade down her back. Frustrated fingers combed through it as she returned to staring at the paper in front of her.

"How bad is it?" I asked, growing serious. I took a few steps forward to snoop.

"How bad is what?" she asked, not bothering to look up.

"I thought we weren't playing games. I have eyes, Ash. Half your slips are empty. And the dockside benches aren't the only things needing replacement or repair. Just how much business have you lost?"

"Things are . . . difficult right now."

Difficult. Interesting word. It didn't come close to describing the dire reality I already knew she wouldn't divulge to me.

"My dad is taking a trip. He went down south to find some winter work and—"

"I heard."

Her brow raised in question.

"Joey told me." One more tally in my string of lies. I was getting used to the sour taste of my own half-truths.

"He's down there, working—"

"Is that what we're calling it?"

Her face fell a little. "He just needed some time. Losing my mom so suddenly, on top of everything with Nathan . . . she was his other half. You know how they were. He's broken without her. He had to get away for a while before we could sit down and form a new long-term plan. He's coming back soon. I think," she muttered the last part under her breath.

"I get it. He's trying to numb the pain." I crushed the paper cup in my palm and tossed a sinker into the trash can five feet away. "Been in those shoes. Never works out well."

She blinked. Her face softened with pain I immediately felt guilty for putting there.

"When he gets back, he'll have a way to fix all this," she said defensively.

So, her faith wasn't completely broken.

She believed in white knights.

How would she feel about one dressed in sheep's clothes?

I was pretty shit at this slow and patient thing. I wanted to dive right in. Wanted to walk around the desk and pull her into my arms and plow my hands into all that hair and make her remember those happier times.

Instead, I closed the distance between us and perched on the edge of the desk, fingering a stack of envelopes that all looked like bad news.

"Ash, change your mind. Let me help you." I held up a bill with a red stamp that clearly said *Final Notice*. "I can make this all go away. All of it. I can take all of this off your plate."

Her eyes turned cold. Her posture straightened as her back grew rigid in response to my words. "Don't you dare come in here and try to throw your money at me. My father didn't want it then, and I'm not taking it now. Nothing in the world could make me that desperate, Brayden." Her tone grew angrier with every word. "Look, I don't know why you've suddenly appeared here like the Ghost of Christmas Past, but let's get one thing straight. I don't need or want your pity, *or* your charity."

"So, you're just gonna let some stupid sense of pride—" I hadn't meant to raise my voice, but my frustration leaked through. I took a breath. "Lots of businesses take on investors when they're in trouble. I could be a silent partner if you won't accept it as a gift."

"A gift or a bribe? What is this? Some kind of twelve-step program where you come to buy your way out of guilt? Is that why you're really here? Some kinda hometown tour to earn absolution?" Green eyes cut into me. "Besides, my pride has nothing to do with it. *He* would never forgive me. If he even knew you were sitting here, talking to me, right now . . ." She shook her head. Fingertips grazed across her worried forehead.

Her words gouged deep into wounded places I'd learned to keep covered. She wouldn't take my help because she didn't want to hurt her brother.

Her brother, who rightfully hated my guts.

Her brother, who I fucking stole everything from with my own selfish weakness.

Dillan thought Nathan would be the one standing in my way, but clearly, he was wrong. I had to get through Ashley's anger before I would even have a chance to get to her brother.

I dealt in things that moved ninety-plus miles per hour. Slow-moving targets fucked with my head. But chipping away at her resentment couldn't happen fast.

I wanted to tell her the whole truth. I should have. She'd given me an opening. But I knew her pride wouldn't handle it well, and my uphill climb already felt steep enough.

Her cell phone interrupted the inner battle waging a war inside me. She cringed as she glanced at the name on the screen and then quickly answered the call.

"Hey. Different day, same story?" She paused and listened. "Crap. Yes. Yes, I know." She sighed in frustration. "Okay. Can you hold tight for a few minutes? Logan took off with a group all day, and I have some kids out sailing. They should be coming back in soon. I can't leave until . . . yeah. Thanks, Emory. Thanks for taking care of him. I'll be there as soon as I can."

She threw the cell back onto the desktop and blew out a shaky breath.

"What's wrong?"

"Nothing."

"Did you know, when you're sad, the corners of your mouth turn down a little? It flattens out your top lip."

Her mouth instinctively puckered, fighting off my observation.

That's it, baby girl. Nobody knows you like I do.

"Nathan is over at the Wharf Rat. I need to go get him." She blew out a quick, frustrated breath.

I couldn't help the instinct to check my watch. Yep. A smidge early for happy hour. The people who hung out at the Rat during the day had one objective. Drunk oblivion.

"Is that place still a grungy shithole? He hang out there a lot?"

Her top lip flattened again.

"More than he should. He bums a ride there with some degenerate who has a permanent seat at the bar. Emory runs the place. She keeps my number handy." A palm ran down one side of her face as she got up and walked to look out the window. "Dillan went and got him last time. I don't want to bug him again."

A group of rough and tumble kids went out in Sunfish boats thirty minutes ago. I'd watched her help them secure life vests and push out into the water. I walked closer, standing behind her, fighting the need to press my chest against her back and wrap my arms around her.

"Go. I'll wait for the kids to come back in."

Her shoulders rose with added tension.

"It will be fine. Go take care of your brother. I'll stay here till you get back or till Logan comes in."

She turned and stared up at me, hesitation on her face. I swallowed against the burning need to touch her.

"I don't want your—"

"Jesus, Ash. All I'm gonna do is sit here and wait for some kids, and then help them drag their boats up outta the water. You can't even accept that?"

Resignation settled slowly across her features. "Okay. Okay, you're right." She dug her purse out from under the desk and was halfway to the door before she turned back around. "Thanks, Brayden," she added softly.

I'd spent my whole life fighting for big victories. I'd never realized the small variety could feel so sweet. I nodded in response. It felt more appropriate than the fist-pumping going down in my head.

After she left, I used my phone to snap a photo of Mrs. F's master plan. Then, I helped myself to the desk chair. The power bill sat on top of the closest pile. Two months overdue. I started sifting through the papers in front of me. More letters. More cancellation notices. A clusterfuck of red ink.

She was drowning.

With no one around to throw her a damn life preserver.

I could wipe this all away without blinking. Stroke one check and make all these papers and all her worries disappear. She was sitting on a mountain of debt I could work off by throwing six innings. I wouldn't even have to last till the stretch.

She would never willingly take it. I'd already known that coming in.

She'd work two jobs. Face twelve-hour days. And barely tread water. She'd already cashed in all her own dreams. Her pride was the only thing she had left.

My lies would take that away.

Right before they slayed her white knight and exploded in my face.

That very first summer we met, I bought her a new bike basket. It was way bigger than the cheap, white plastic daisy thing she had barely clinging to her handlebars. I picked one with a fancy lid, fashioned to keep her many things from spilling out. I didn't present it to her. I just cut the old one off and strapped the new one down tight. I thought when she saw it, she would get that glowy little smile that always lit me up inside.

She did not.

She showed up the following day with a bag full of quarters and a mouthful of sass, telling me where to stick my benevolence.

That memory haunted me now as I leaned back in the desk chair and closed my eyes. "I have to find a better way to do this."

I sighed and pinched the bridge of my nose, leaning forward again to regain my focus. A screen saver floated across the darkened computer monitor. Random images spewed up from the hard drive.

I almost fell off my seat.

There, in the top corner, was a black-and-white photo from those happiest of times. I could still remember the day Mrs. F took it. It was from a Labor Day party where we claimed childish liberties with cans of whipped cream. We squirted it directly in our mouths and then shot it straight at each other. Three smiling faces. Heads covered in sugary foam. Arms slung around one another's shoulders.

I sat, dumbstruck. Tears wedged in my eyes.

They hadn't purged *all* the reminders.

The faces in that photo stared back at me with proof of the fairy tale.

Once upon a time, we were a family.

I had the summer to fix my busted up arm *and* my busted up past. I stared at those smiles and knew exactly which I would pick to save if I could only choose one.

I wanted to take away all of Ashley's troubles and give back her dreams. But slow and steady required baby steps before giant leaps. I couldn't just tear off the old basket and expect the happy smile.

That image reminded me of where I had to start. The first thing I had to give her back, was the same thing that photo gifted me.

A little bit of hope.

I heard the kids before I saw them. Whooping and hollering as they made fun of the last guy struggling to steer his boat back to shore. The first two dudes didn't need me. They had youth and testosterone on their sides. They tucked their boats up onto the little sandy beach, sails neatly secured.

Funny, I hadn't been on one of those things in half a dozen years, but I could still hear Mr. F telling me and Nathan to make sure we'd properly tied down the lines.

"Ashley had to go run an errand. You guys know where to put your vests and stuff?"

"Yeah, man, we're cool."

"Hey, Evan!" the second one shouted out to the third kid, still struggling twenty feet off the shore. "Hope you get in sometime today. Last one to Lucky's is buying."

They took off up the grass toward the vest bins stationed beside the dock house.

I took pity on the last kid. Slipping off my shoes, I waded out to my knees and helped pull him in the last ten feet. Together, we dragged the boat up onto the sand.

"Nice day for a sail, huh?" I asked, making conversation.

Sun and exhaustion ripened across his face. He had a scrappiness about him—shaggy midnight-black hair and puppy-dog limbs he hadn't quite grown into yet. Something about his demeanor reminded me a whole hell of a lot of a kid I used to stare down in the mirror every day.

"Motherfucking boat is the stupidest piece of crap I've ever seen. Those jerk-offs just get how it works. I spent most of the time trying to figure out how to turn around. This is only the third time Miss Foster's let us go out past the inlet without her. I didn't want to *F* it up."

He shook his head and started securing the sail all wrong. I took the line from his hands.

"Here, watch. Like this. Loop this through and pull. Then, loop it through again." I untied it and handed it back to him, silently watching as he repeated the steps the right way. "Yeah, man. That's it. You got it."

He allowed a small smile.

"Turning sucks at first. You've gotta get used to the idea of doing all the shit backward. How did your friends learn so fast?"

"They're not newbs. Lived here their whole lives. I just moved here last fall. Those A-holes I hang with have been sailing with their pops since they were little. I ain't got a pop. It's just me and my mom. And I've only been sailing for a month. I need more practice, but Miss F says I gotta stick with her or my buddies. I can't go out alone on account I might capsize and drown myself. But I can't concentrate with those buttholes yelling and taunting me. I need to stick with lacrosse. I can kick their asses at that."

I smirked as he shrugged out of his life vest, revealing a concave chest ribbed with the new muscles of a kid trying to force his way through puberty.

"Did Miss Foster take off or something?"

"She had to go do something for her brother."

He nodded and pursed his lips as we started walking back up to the dock. "I help her sometimes. Usually, haul all the stuff up to the storage shed at the end of the day. She's kinda little to do all that shit herself, ya know?"

"That's nice of you. I bet she appreciates the help."

"Yeah, man. It's the least I can do. She doesn't charge me for the rental. She knows I can't afford that shit. My mama's a nurse over at the hospital. Already pulling extra shifts to make our life work. Know what I mean? Miss Foster, she's real cool."

"She's one of the best people I know," I replied, stealing Dillan's words as I palmed the bill of my hat and tried to keep my tone light.

"You guys friends? I've never seen you around before."

"Old friends. Used to be friends," I stammered as I squinted and shrugged my shoulders. "Used to be more than friends, actually. I've, uh, been gone a while. Had to go on a long trip."

My explanation made no fucking sense, but the kid bobbed his head up and down.

"I feel ya. So, you're, like . . . tryin' to be *old friends* with her again." He grinned and tipped his chin.

I cocked my head and chuckled. He couldn't be more than fourteen.

I was already hell on wheels at his age.

"I'm thinking maybe, if I do some stuff to help her out, she'll let me hang around, too," I answered simply.

He nodded and looked back down to the beach where the tubes and kayaks were stacked. "Well, man, let's quit talkin' about it and do the work."

I didn't accomplish half as much as he did. It was sort of embarrassing. Fucking left arm. But the conversation kept me highly entertained, and the job went quickly. Some dude came in with a Hatteras Sportfish. I taught Evan how to tie a hitch knot as we helped secure the boat to a slip. Had to pat myself on the back for remembering that shit, too.

When we were all done, I bought us Cokes from the vending machine. We sat on the edge of the dock, downing them in thirsty man gulps.

"We make a good team, kid," I said, holding my can out to bump his.

"Yeah? Thanks."

"My name's Brayden by the way. We were never formally introduced."

He sputtered a mouthful of soda. "Dude, I know who you are. I can't sail worth shit, but I'm not slow or anything."

It was my turn to smile.

"You're sort of a badass, you know? And kinda a legend around here. I didn't wanna say nothin' on account my mama told me we aren't supposed to gawk at you or bug you too bad. Folks are sorta hoping you'll stick around. Think they probably got the idea you might draw more of a crowd. City slickers will wanna catch a glimpse of you. Might bring more business to town or something. God knows, this place could use it." He gestured around us.

"Things have been pretty sad around here. Miss Foster . . . she's been hurting pretty bad, I think. She don't know I see it, but sometimes, I stop and say goodbye before I leave and catch her cryin' at her desk. I don't gawk at that shit neither. People oughta be able to cry over their troubles without an audience."

I mulled over his words as I watched the boats on the horizon.

Out sailing toward happiness.

That's what Ash used to say.

Chasing after dreams that never docked here anymore.

I glanced around at all the empty slips. The place was haunted by old memories. Three kids laughing and jumping off the end of the dock. The ghost of a mother I'd always secretly wished could be my own.

Four years ago, my fuckup cast the first stone. It made a ripple, that built into a wave and, eventually, knocked everything off-kilter. Before it, the Fosters had enjoyed a perfect little life.

The accident marked the start of their ruin.

Now, every single rotted board heaved up toward me. The worn umbrellas tipped their fingers, pointing in my direction. I'd helped break this place apart. I needed to work faster to put it back together.

Slow and steady was for bastards with patience. Everyone knew that wasn't me. Wasn't my style.

Evan's words rattled around in my head.

Draw more of a crowd.

"Evan, you might not be the best sailor in the world yet, but you are a motherfucking genius."

"I am?"

"You do social media stuff?"

"Like Snapchat and Insta? Yeah, I got that shit. Twitter, too. Don't spend as much time on it as my girl, but I got a respectable follow list. Why?"

"How do you feel about selfies?"

"I mean . . . I don't usually take 'em with other dudes, but seeing as you're not regular people . . . I think I could make an exception. My mom thinks you're hot as shit, so she'd probably be impressed, too." His head bobbed up and down. "Yeah, man. I'm down with it if you wanna snap with my ugly mug. No filters though. That shit's straight up for girls."

I pulled out my phone and took one of us. Heads pushed together, smiling like fools who'd known each other a lot longer than an hour.

"What's your Instagram?" I asked.

"BigLaxMan22."

"Seriously? Big Man? Dude, we need to work on that." I lightly punched him in the shoulder and then sent him the photo. "Do me a favor. Post that picture to your accounts. Tag me in them, okay? And check in our location. Post something about us hanging out here."

"Okay, I can do that." He shrugged with teenage nonchalance.

"What are you doing Thursday afternoon? Wanna meet me here and go sailing? Promise, I won't bust your ass like your friends if you screw up."

"Seriously? You yanking my chain, man?"

"Totally serious. Most of my friends here have either moved away, work all day, or . . . really hate my guts. I need some new friends to get in trouble with. I bet you and I will get into all kinds of trouble out there together." I pointed out to the water.

"Holy crap. Yeah, I'm up for that. That would be lit."

I held my fist out for him to bump.

"Is it cool if I go to Lucky's and kinda rub all this shit in my buddies' faces?"

I chuckled. "Go give them some hell. I've got some more work to do."

His brows furrowed. "I can stay and help if you need another hand." He glanced back around to see what tasks lay undone.

"Nope. You go dish up some revenge on your boys. I gotta go do some research." I cracked my knuckles and added, "Money can't buy everything, kid. Trust me on that. But I think you just reminded me of a way to score a little happiness and hope."

"Progress always involves risk.
You can't steal second base and keep your foot on
first."
—*Frederick B. Wilcox*

CHAPTER 5
SAVAGES

BRAYDEN

"You've become a regular fixture around here, haven't you?"

Logan stopped beside me on the way to his truck. The acid in his tone needed a good reminding that I'd been around here a hell of a lot longer than him.

I slammed my car door and tucked the bag of food against my hip, rounding to face him. The dipshit had traded in the man bun for a ponytail and Billabong visor. A fucking bright yellow visor. Lord. I tried not to roll my eyes.

Ashley damn well better not have hooked up with this loser.

"Just enjoying being out on the water," I replied with a slight edge of my own. "Going out sailing with a friend again."

"Yeah, sure you are. So are the other half-dozen guys who cruise in and outta here every day, trying to get in her pants. Word from the wise, buddy, I don't get the feeling she wants you around. Maybe it's time to catch a clue. Go back and find another supermodel's heart to crush."

Interesting.

So, he clearly knows my name isn't Brandon after all.

This dude was pissing in the wrong pool. The inside of my palms itched. You could never totally take the fight out of the boy. I turned my head and spat on the ground. A familiar warm-up before lighting up a bastard. I got real close, so he'd understand my special English.

"You know, I pay a lot of people a fuck-ton of money to give me advice. Not looking for the unsolicited variety from you."

As I walked away from him, I bumped his shoulder. Just a little, for the fun of it.

Maybe he was right about one thing. I had met a lot of supermodels. But, their emaciated stomachs and fake tits never made me half as hard as I was now, walking toward the office, and watching Ashley's body as she made her way up from the dock.

I stopped to appreciate the natural sway of it, tucked inside a navy-and-white-striped bikini top and tight little board shorts. I stood at the counter outside the dock house, sporting a bag of food and a boner, as I waited for her to close the remaining distance.

"I swung by Lucky's for lunch." I held up the familiar red-and-white bag. "Bacon and avocado club was the special today. Couldn't stop myself. I know it's your favorite. Swindled two dill pickles, too. And there might be a bag of M&M's in the bottom. Peanut, of course. Although have you tried the pretzel ones they have now? They're a fucking travesty."

"Brayden." She stopped just short of me.

I saw her glance quickly down to the bag and then at my chest. I'd left my shirt in the car. On purpose. No sense in it getting wet while I was out in the water.

I smirked.

"Why the heck has every teenager in town been loitering around here half the day?" she asked, annoyed.

I took a few steps forward to get a better look at the crowd formed down on the man-made beach. Twenty-five teenagers. Hanging out in kayaks, laying in tubes, and trying to knock one another off paddleboards. She must've had to empty out the whole shed.

Evan was already in the water. His Sunfish and mine stood at the ready, fifteen feet out. He was macking all over the cute redhead he'd told me a lot about. He'd asked me for advice about her. I'd tried to give him a PG version of why I was the very last person qualified to talk about how to handle women.

"Evan and I invited a few more friends today. Kid did really well last couple of times we've been out. We thought it was time for him to show off a little bit. That chick he's with is his new girl. She's cute, huh? He's a great kid."

She didn't say anything. Just stood there, blankly staring at me.

"How many rentals you have today?" I asked, feigning innocence.

She pursed her lips and rolled her eyes. "We're sold out."

"Huh." I cocked a cheeky grin. "Go figure. That's great. You sure you don't wanna play hooky and come out with us?"

"Some of us have work to do."

I held up the bag of food and smiled knowingly. No chance she'd pass it up.

She finally huffed and grabbed it from my hands.

"See ya later, baby girl."

She stomped toward the office, but I caught her peeking in the top of the bag as she went.

I'd lay odds she ate the M&M's first.

By late afternoon, half of St. Michaels High was assembled on the beach. They sat in camp chairs and took turns out in the water. The vending machines had long been emptied. Someone had a radio playing bad pop music. A few boats came in and tied up to the open dock, drawn in by the crowd.

I sat back, lingering on one of my newly painted benches, enjoying the flip side of people-watching.

Evan finally broke away from the pack to check on me. "Hey, man, you tired of smiling in selfies?"

I held my fist out for him to bump as he sat beside me.

"Nah. It's all good. The dude who asked me if I'd sign his forehead before the picture was sorta colorful."

"That's my friend Aaron. We all think he was dropped a lot as a baby."

I chuckled and watched as his eyes sought out his girl in the crowd.

"You remind me a lot of my teenage self, kid."

"Yeah? How's that? My striking good looks?"

I smirked and nodded in his chick's direction. "You always know where she's at. You seriously dig this girl, huh?"

He shrugged his shoulders and tried to fight off a shit-eating grin.

I bumped his arm. "Be good to her. Hold doors open. Tell her hair looks pretty. Take her flowers . . . don't be a fuckup." I didn't add, *Like me.*

He turned to look over his shoulder toward the dock house. "How are things with you and Miss Foster? Any thawing of the ice?"

"I'm trying to learn a life skill they call patience."

"Yeah?" He snickered. "How you doin' with that?"

The kid had gotten to know me too well already.

"Off the record?"

He nodded.

"It totally fucking sucks."

His eyes lifted, along with his smile, but then narrowed just as suddenly. "Looks like that douchebag is back to bug her. He's like a bad habit that won't shake off."

I swiveled around to follow his gaze. Ashley was standing up at the counter, talking to a group of half-baked sunbirds who'd just climbed off their daddy's yacht. I recognized two of them. They'd been at Foxy's that night I met Dillan. The two from the end of the bar with leering eyes and wandering hands they were lucky they'd been allowed to keep.

"Those guys regulars?" I asked, playing it cooler than I felt.

"Unfortunately. The one in the pink polo likes to get a rise out of her."

As Evan spoke, the dude he mentioned finally turned to the side. A face I knew all too well. Finally seen in the flesh.

"Think there's some kinda history there," Evan continued, oblivious to my sudden change in mood. "The last time he dropped by here while I was helping her out, she asked me to stay until he left. Said he wouldn't bug her if I was around. 'Safety in numbers,' is what she called it."

I stood up and rounded toward them. I watched as the pink-shirt-wearing prick leaned over the counter and said something that made Ashley push him in the chest. He grabbed her wrist, only dropping it after she snapped something back at him.

"As if I needed another reason, asshole," I murmured to myself. "I'll be back, kid," I called to Evan, already on the move.

By the time I reached the dock house, Ashley had retreated inside the office. The crew of sunbirds stood around with contraband bottles of beer and an elitist air of entitlement. I lingered on the fringes, pretending to sift through the bin of life vests as I sized them up.

They looked like a Ralph Lauren outlet on Easter Sunday. White Docksiders, madras plaid shorts, and pastel polos with starched up collars. One had Ray-Bans tucked on top of his head, and the other had a pale yellow sweater tied around his neck. They reeked of bad weed and department-store cologne.

Fucking tools.

"You're laying it on pretty thick with this one, Preston. I thought for sure you'd be switching it up to that little waitress over at the inn this summer."

"Nah. Her tits are like goose bumps. So not my thing. This one . . . I don't know. She's a pain in the ass, but swear to God, this chick did some kinda voodoo shit to my dick last year."

"I don't know, man. Looks like she's ready to break your balls now, not suck 'em."

"Yeah, Xander's right. I think you burned that bridge hard. No way she's gonna spread that sweet cunt for you again this summer."

"I rode that bridge hard, motherfucker." They all chuckled and high-fived. "Come on, boys, remember where we come from. Girls like that don't turn guys like us down. I got two Benny Franklins that say I bang her again by Fourth of July."

"I'll feel you on that wager. But we want some proof, asshole. Video, or it didn't happen. And no dropping a forget-me in her drink, or the bet's off."

My back teeth ground together.

Patience was a dumb fucking life skill.

Mine had about all dried up.

"Nah, dude. None of that shit. That chick is a wildcat in the sack.

Gotta tame that bitch full throttle." Pink Polo held his fists out and thrust his hips back and forth like a total D-bag. "This is a win-win for me. I get to dip back into that pot of honey, *and* I get to take Xander's money."

Clause 18-A.07 of my contract. I knew it well.

No fighting.

Micky had hounded my ass about it my whole first year in the League. Told me guys would be trying to goad me. Dickweeds in bars and nightclubs would all make a play for me to throw the first punch. He'd seen it before with young up-and-comers who'd gotten hotheaded and had to write big fucking checks.

Those days were behind me. I'd been a choirboy, never even tempted toward violence. But, right at that moment, the only thing that could improve Pink Polo's face was a handprint of my fist.

"You all talking about Ashley Foster?" I called out.

Their chatter stopped as they turned to look at me. All three of them sized me up. In that pretentious, are you good enough for us to talk to, way used by pompous rich boys.

"Yeah. You know her, man?" the yellow sweater wearing pussy finally asked. He lifted his chin in acknowledgment. "My buddy here is her ex."

"I know her pretty well. We grew up together."

"Well, you probably don't know her as well as Prestie here. Dude knows all about things that chick can do with her tongue . . ."

". . . apparently . . . good . . ."

". . . if you know . . . ever had a chick do . . ."

The blood rushing in my ears blocked out half their words. They kept laughing and pounding each other on the back.

I closed my eyes for a moment and channeled all the things Doc Wolfe would say. Her nasally voice would ask me to inventory my emotions. She'd tell me not to use anger as a mask for disappointment and sadness. Remind me to practice assertive expression, to demonstrate my hurt through nonviolent means.

Blah. Blah. Blah.

I'm not the one who needs to hurt here, doc.

I could smell the stale air freshener saturating her office in fake vanilla. I could feel the soft velour of her couch, my fingertips brushing back and forth, while she ping-ponged between her textbook knowledge and my real-life brain.

I knew how to handle this properly.

I'd employed her techniques a hundred times.

Stay calm.

Pink Polo laughed at something else his buddy said. The static in my head grew louder, drowning out the doctor and my last shred of good sense.

His teeth were too straight. And blinding white. His parents must've spent a fortune at the orthodontist.

Sure would be a shame if they all got knocked out.

Micky had told me to count on a hundred K for every punch. He'd said that was the going rate. There were two more of them still lounging on the deck of the yacht. And these three dimwits.

Five altogether.

I was staring at half a million dollars in the face.

My head flipped to another channel as it conjured images of grainy black-and-whites. Two smiles. My broken heart. Lonely nights mad at the world, madder at myself. Stuffed between two thighs I didn't really want. Hating what I couldn't have.

What this asshole had taken.

What I fucking let him have and can't get back now.

This pastel-wearing, white-toothed joker became the mascot for all that pain.

"Fuck it. I've been waiting for this for too long."

I lunged forward, grabbing on to Pink by the collar. "If you're smarter than you look, you and your fuck-nugget buddies here will turn back around, row out of here in your daddy's little boat, and never look back again."

Doc Wolfe had gone to med school for twelve years to learn her craft. I'd only need fifteen seconds to practice my God-given right hook.

"Whoa, dude. What the fuck?" his friend asked, bemused.

Pink Polo turned his head and spat on the ground near my shoe. "Wrong answer, asswipe."

I tightened my hold just as Ashley rushed out of the office and Evan came tearing up the hill with a few of his buddies in tow, like they were grown enough to play backup.

"I don't know who the hell you think you are. But you lay one hand on me, and you have no idea the wrath my father—"

"I'm the guy who makes sure dickweeds like you don't touch her."

"Too late, man, 'cause I know every inch of that pussy."

He tipped his chin up toward Ashley. His arrogant grin badly needed a matching set of my knuckles. My fist flexed by my side, crying out for a taste of the action.

Ash knew I was about to strike. Guess she'd seen me in this position enough times in her life.

Rounding the counter fast, she grabbed on to my biceps with both hands. "Dallas," fell from her lips. That one simple word stirred a thousand memories.

I froze, caught beneath the weight of it.

Her hands and pleading eyes pulled against my own, slowly forcing my hold to release.

Pink Dickweed took a step back, stupidly worrying over the wrinkles in his shirt. He should've still been worried about getting out of this alive.

Ashley stepped in close, leaving only a breath between us. My vision filled with her. The rest of them faded into the background.

"Dallas," she calmly said again, staring back at me with intense green eyes I knew better than my own. She carefully stressed the word with one brow pointing upward for emphasis.

She wasn't using my real name.

Wouldn't say it out loud, confirming my identity.

"Don't do this."

"Give me one good reason I shouldn't rearrange this guy's face right now, baby girl. One reason. If you heard the shit he just said about you . . ."

She tilted her head to the side, gesturing quietly toward the larger group of teenagers now filtering up from the beach, at the ready to catch a glimpse of the action.

She stood up on tiptoes, mouth and breath brushing against my ear. "Every single one of those kids is armed with a camera phone. All of them will be happy to brag they witnessed you punch this jackass out. Not the attention you want, or the kind this place needs."

As she spoke, her fingers trailed down my arm, lightly brushing across my scarred elbow. Owl-wide eyes bored into mine, silently adding, *He's not worth your arm.*

Of course, she had no way of knowing. I'd learned *some* lessons from my father without repeating his mistakes. The morning after the Yankees called me up to the bigs, I'd insured my right arm. Rearranging Dickweed's smile would be worth half a million in lawsuits, but it sure as fuck wasn't worth forfeiting my career, even for a sixty-five-million-dollar claim.

I gave her a curt nod, letting reason sink back in. Taking the prints she'd left on my skin as a consolation prize for letting this jackass walk.

"Preston"—she swiveled back around and glared at him—"get the hell out of here. I don't want your business. I don't want *anything* from you."

"Oh, shit," his friend muttered, awkwardly staring at me. "Are you . . ." His eyes narrowed.

He needed thirty more seconds to place my face. I slid my cap down lower, hiding the eyes that always gave me away.

My top lip curled in a snarl. "You heard the woman. Get the fuck off her property."

The other friend pulled on Preston's arm, forcing him to walk backward. "Let's blow, man. Had enough of this dump anyway."

Ten feet away, the quiet one punched Pink Polo in the arm. "Dude, do you know who I think that was?"

I leaned against the doorjamb, staring at her from across the room.

"Thank you, Soot."

It didn't escape me that she no longer bristled at the sound of her special name.

"For what?"

She kept her back to me as she stood motionless, staring out the window. The late afternoon sun cascaded through the glass. It circled her dark hair with angelic light, making me feel even more like the devil.

"For protecting me back there. Not using my name. Stopping me from doing something stupid. I'm not a dumb teenager anymore. It's been a long time since I used my fists to make a point."

"I did it to protect the business. Not great advertising to have a fight break out with half this town's youth on the lot. Although, trust me, I would've enjoyed seeing Preston's face getting deconstructed."

I pushed off against the doorframe, giving in to my need to get closer. "They're all still here, aren't they? Circling like always."

"Who?" she asked, bemused.

She turned to face me. That soft pink upper lip teased me, flaring out, tugging on my dick from across the room. I closed the distance between us, crowding her back on purpose. Her chest visibly swelled, responding to the instant pull that formed every time we got this close.

"The vultures," I finally answered. "They're here, just like they always were." My hand roughly cupped her cheek. Fingertips pressed into her hairline. "Wanting what's mine."

The pad of my thumb rubbed harshly across her bottom lip. Back and forth. Erasing anyone else who'd pressed up against it.

"I'm not yours." The denial came out as a whisper, a silly little breathless lie.

"Yes, you are," I said forcefully. "You always will be. And I think I'm fucking done with playing nice about it."

I didn't give her a choice.

Or bother stopping to evaluate where this fit into my master plan.

My lips just forced their way onto hers, rebranding the skin that used to hold my mark. It was harsher than I'd intended, but jealousy burned a toxic path right through me. I had to wipe away the last inch of that guy's words with the taste of her mouth.

Prickly sparks shot up my spine. My cock went from slightly pissed off to diamond hard. Dude didn't want to hear my head whine any more about patience. He'd waited four long fucking years for this, and she tasted too much like sweet memories and promise to turn back now.

My hand tangled up into her hair, turning her so I had a better angle to suck on her bottom lip.

I should stop myself.

I knew that.

But greed wouldn't let me.

Neither would her low, needy whimper. It gave me the perfect opening.

My tongue plunged into her mouth, igniting every possessive nerve in my body at once. Both my hands slid down her hips till I cupped her round ass and pulled her flush against me. She melted into me, the fight and resistance evaporating behind shared lust and primal need.

"I hate that he's touched you. Fucking hate it, baby girl." I barely pulled back to murmur my angry words against her lips. "Fucking hated every second you were with him."

One of her hands threaded into the hair at the back of my neck, tugging me hard back toward her. I forced my tongue back inside her mouth, thrusting it in and out. Circling slow. Withdrawing just enough so she'd feel it good when I drove back deeper, demonstrating what I really wanted to do to exorcise Pink Polo's memory.

She gave as good as she got. I don't know how I ever thought we would have some trophy hello kiss. A sailor coming home to dip his girl over his arm. We never worked that way. We never kissed syrupy sweet on the front porch. Not from our very first time in the hall outside her room.

Kissing Ashley always felt like everything but the final act. Pulling closer, grabbing harder. Brutal, hungry lips. Biting. Hot, heavy breathing. Grinding. Praying for pauses to catch hold of a single breath.

Her lips were always a full-fledged addiction all their own. With absolutely no tolerance, I should have prepared myself to get totally fucking stoned from the first hit.

She moaned against the continued onslaught. Her nipples pebbled against my chest, coaxing me to dig my fingertips harder into her ass. I nestled her fully against my tortured cock. That poor bastard had activated his homing beacon and was motherfucking desperate to feel any part of her rubbing up against him. He wasn't gonna feel ashamed for trying to frantically dry-hump her.

"God. So. Fucking. Good."

My teeth plucked against that pouty top lip. As I was about to lift one of her legs up against my hip, to give my cock a better angle, her two little fists loosened their death grip on my shirt. They reared back instead to pound against my chest.

Drawing away, I looked down at her with hooded eyes. I watched in disbelief as her face morphed from sheer need to undoctored anger.

Her mask of pride snapped fully back into place.

It looked funny next to her shiny, swollen lips.

Her index finger jabbed into my chest. "You can't . . . we can't . . . don't do that again." She dragged the back of one hand across her mouth, like she naively believed it could wipe us away. "You can't just come in here all Neanderthal, act like you have some kinda territory, and manhandle me. You're no better than Preston."

"Manhandling? Is that what you want to call what just happened here?"

She nodded, but I didn't miss the way her breath still caught in her chest.

I smirked.

"Fine. Tell you what. I'll wait for you to come to me, if that's how you want to play it. I'll wait for you to beg even, if you want. But know this. I'm done playing nice, Ashley. You never liked it nice anyway. I think the time's finally come for me to start reminding you."

CHAPTER 6
STRINGS ATTACHED

ASHLEY

"Why are you in such a pissy mood?"

I stirred a spoon through my watered-down crab soup, one of the only half-edible creations in the crappy cafeteria where we'd eaten too many meals. The place smelled like antiseptic and burned shoe leather—the perennial special on their weekday menu.

"Just wish they'd come and give us the results," I replied. "We could use some good news."

Nathan leaned back in his wheelchair and looked away from me. "Yeah, well, don't hold your breath."

We were waiting for the results of one more MRI. One more confirmation of what they all kept telling us. On paper, the surgery last year still looked like a complete success. The experimental procedure we'd decided couldn't possibly make things worse, should have made them better. There should have been groundbreaking progress. The doctors all thought the nerves were healing enough that he could regain feeling. Move. Stand. Maybe even learn to walk again.

Only he wasn't.

Couldn't or wouldn't?

I'd squashed down that annoying doubt for so many months. They had to be missing something.

Why would he choose to stay in that chair if he didn't have to?

My phone rang while I studied his sullen profile.

"What's up?"

"Hey. It's me," Logan replied. "I know you're busy, but we kinda have a weird situation here. I think you'd better stop by on your way home. I'm not sure how you want to handle this."

"Handle what? What's going on?" My voice had enough concern, my brother turned with furrowed brows.

"We got a new tenant this afternoon. I know you said I could fill out seasonal contracts, but this guy sounds like he's looking for something more long-term, and his request is . . . well, this whole situation seems a little unusual."

"Uh, okay. I'll be there as soon as I can." I disconnected the call and stared down at my phone.

"What's that all about?"

"I don't know. Logan wants me to come by. I'll take you home first and then—"

"No, it's fine. Let's get out of here. Doc will call us." He rolled his chair back from the table. "I'd rather get bad news over the phone anyway."

I discarded our trash and followed after him, trying to recall images of him as that optimistic, easygoing boy I used to know.

"What the hell is that?" Nathan asked as he hoisted himself down into his chair.

My mouth couldn't produce an answer. It was hanging open too wide. He pushed his way toward the ramp near the back of the dock house. Logan stood, waiting there, with an older gentleman in an old-school captain's hat. As we got closer, I shielded my forehead with one hand, so I could fully soak in the magnificence of the sleekest luxury yacht I'd ever seen.

"Holy shit. That thing has to be at least a hundred feet," Nathan said.

"She's a hundred twenty. Pure beauty," the older gentleman corrected, holding out his hand in greeting.

I shook it and tried to soak in his words.

"Name's Jake Resnick. Brought her up from West Palm Beach. Was told to deliver her to ya and sign for you to keep her. Gonna take up four or five whole slips I'm afraid, but luckily, looks like you folks have some room to spare right now. I have a check to cover the security deposit and to prepay the first three months' rent."

"Paperwork all looks legit, Ash. You just have to sign."

"How did this . . . who . . . did my father send you?" I took the papers from Logan's hand, searching for details that would fill in the gaps.

The owner's name was listed as a trust.

A name I didn't recognize.

Five slips times three months. My mind turned over the numbers. I might've had a lifelong hatred of algebra, but even I knew that added up to a crap-ton of money. Not to mention, the free advertising. This thing would cause a stir. Everyone sailing by would see her. Want to gawk at her. Park next to her.

My finger trailed down over the fine print. I set it down on the counter and picked up a pen to sign at the bottom.

"This might be the best gift my guardian angel has ever . . ."

The exuberance died in my throat. Words caught as I noticed the name buried halfway down the page.

"Have you captained this yacht before?" I asked, trying to cover the budding anger I didn't want my brother to hear.

"No, ma'am." His fingers smoothed over the gold braided strips on the cuff of his jacket. "Purchased a few weeks ago from what I understand. Detailed and retrofitted for the new owner. Renamed, of course. I don't know much more than that. They just hired me on to bring her up here safely. This is my retirement gig. Used to sail much bigger boats for the Navy."

I didn't mean to be rude, but I'd started walking away before he even finished his explanation. I needed to see it for myself.

"Ash? Everything okay?" Logan called out from behind me.

My strides grew longer, my pace more impatient, as I neared the end of the dock. As I drew closer, my perspective changed. The thing grew taller, lurching up right out of the water. It completely overpowered me with its hulking size.

The sleek lines of the design were capped off by glistening silver rails and polished teak decking that glowed like honey in the midday sun. I reached the stern and peered down at what I already knew I'd find.

Toward Happiness.

St. Michaels, Maryland.

"Goddamn it, Brayden."

I didn't bother to knock.

Never have before. Why start now?

Voices filtered in from the back patio. I stomped my way toward them; the paper half-wadded in my fist. He was deep in conversation with a guest—the tall, athletic guy I'd seen him with at Foxy's that first night. They were seated at the table, inspecting a mass of papers spread out before them.

"I'm telling you, with these latest results, I know this will work. I just need you to get him . . ." The guy's words tapered off as he looked up at me.

Brayden turned suddenly with wide eyes and a raised brow. "Ash?"

"What part of no don't you understand?"

They both blinked.

I rested my hand against my hip and prepared to dive. "I know it's not a word you hear from many women, but do I look like I want to be your charity case? I told you I wasn't going to take your goddamn handouts."

His friend gathered the papers into a stack and scraped his chair back to stand. "Uh, I'll just give you guys a minute."

He shyly smiled at me. His kind eyes seemed oddly juxtaposed to his hulked-out body and armful of tattoo ink. On closer inspection, he looked more WWE wrestler, or renegade superhero, than he did a ball player.

He walked off in the direction of the guesthouse.

Brayden pushed his chair back and stood, sliding his cap around backward to unveil those wicked eyes. His board shorts and wifebeater tank highlighted the tan earned from all his sailing. A cocky grin lit his face as he pushed against a lock of hair that had fallen across his forehead.

"I guess she arrived, huh? You didn't have to bring me the contract personally. Is she a beauty? I promised Evan he'd get to smash the champagne bottle, but you and I could christen her in a different way." His voice rumbled, deep and sexy to match his lewd suggestion and the accompanying fuck-me eyes.

"I'm so done with you." I pinched the bridge of my nose between my fingers. "You've got to stop all of this. You've got to go back to New York and leave the past where it belongs."

"Can't do that. Not till I get what I came for."

"What the hell *did* you come here for, Brayden? That's what I keep asking. What I can't figure out. Do you think this is fun? You came here to fix your arm and just decided it would be sporting to mess with the rest of us while you're at it? What kind of a sick bastard are you?"

He rubbed his hand across the scruff on his jaw as he stepped toward me. "I came because it's time."

"Time for what? For you to wave your money around like a magic wand? That's not gonna work. News flash, you live inside a fairy tale. You don't even know reality anymore. Come wear my shoes for a day. I'll serve you a double helping of the real world. There's no magic that can change the past. It needs to stay buried. Where it belongs."

"I disagree."

"Yeah? Well, that just makes you sound like a lunatic."

I closed my eyes and tried to channel my need to launch myself over and smash him right in the nose.

"You said you didn't want a handout. I'm not giving you one." He shrugged with sarcastic innocence. All the muscles at the top of his shoulders bunched up near his neck. "Just needed a place to park my boat. Simple as that."

I snickered at his pathetic attempt. "How the hell am I going to explain this to my brother? He's going to ask who that behemoth belongs to. He's going to find out you're here."

"Ash, by now, I'm sure your brother already knows I'm in town. You need to let me see him. I can help him, too. More than you know.

At least let me try." His Adam's apple bobbed as his voice grew thick. "I came back here because it's time to heal more than just my arm."

I hadn't even noticed him swallow up the distance between us, crowding me like always. I needed to wind myself up in yellow caution tape, so the motherfucker would back up off me.

He did it on purpose. He knew it left me off-balance.

"You feel it, don't you?" he asked softly. His index finger trailed down the side of my arm.

On the drive over, I'd promised myself I wouldn't let him touch me.

"Feel what? Annoyance that you still don't get the concept of personal space?"

"The pull between us. That thing that happens as soon as we're in a room together. The burn."

"Most people call that indigestion. There are home remedies for it. You should try one."

He chuckled low in his chest, amused instead of put off.

I turned my back on him to stare across the lawn toward the water's edge. The blue expanse stretched out beyond us with too many miles of better-forgotten possibilities.

"You can still feel my hands, can't you?"

Hot breath lingered near my ear. I could smell his aftershave, almost feel the prickle of his two-day beard.

"Molded to your hips. Digging into that sweet spot right where your thighs meet your ass. Did you let yourself dream about it the other night after I kissed you?"

The side of his jaw lightly grazed the skin on my right shoulder. Not close enough for contact, just close enough to tease.

"Did you close your eyes and imagine my middle finger coaxing you open while my tongue pressed flat against your clit? Did you touch yourself, thinking—"

"Stop," I ground out the command on one long exhale as I clenched my hands into fists.

"I dreamt about that noise you make in the back of your throat right before you come. It's what I hear every time I squeeze my cock in my hand."

"Brayden." Turning abruptly, I pushed with both hands against the hard wall of his chest. "You have to stop this." My voice grew more demanding. Unfortunately, so did my desperate need. My body was reacting too violently, recalling too much about the dirty things he'd whispered.

He grabbed ahold of my wrists, refusing to let me go. "I don't think you want me to stop."

Warm lips barely brushed across my temple. My breath came out in short, panting bursts. He slowly released me, letting my hands fall back to my sides.

"Close your eyes, and feel me, baby girl. Let yourself remember how good we are together. Think about all the things my hands love to do to you."

Fingertips grazed across the flimsy strap of my tank top.

"Don't." I meant it to sound like a direct order, not a sad plea for mercy. I glared up at him, fighting tears that wanted to form. "Why are you doing this to me?"

"Because I want you. And you want me. Give in to it. It's that simple."

His words threatened to break me open.

Giving in to simple notions could only lead to more extravagant pain. For me. And for Nathan. How would my brother ever face the person who'd ended his future before it ever began? Simple choices no longer existed as a luxury for me. I couldn't let Brayden spin me up into his make-believe.

"You really think anything between us could ever be simple?"

"Yes," he answered without hesitation.

"Then, you're a fool. Nothing was ever that way for us. We didn't start out simple. And you made certain we didn't end that way."

His eyes narrowed as my biting words hit their easy target. He eased back away from me, face somber. I took greedy gulps of air, trying to calm my body and clear my mind, as he strode slowly back toward the table.

"You've turned down my offer to help you financially. And you've turned down my offer to take care of you physically," he added with hardened impatience. He fingered a piece of paper left sitting on the table. "I hope that doesn't mean you'll be the fool and turn down my request for a favor."

He turned back to face me, holding out a crisp white page folded into thirds. My name was scrolled on the outside in black ink.

"I was going to bring this by later, but since you're here now . . ."

"What is this?" I asked, tentatively taking hold of the letter.

"A job offer."

"I don't need another job, Brayden. I have one too many as it is," I said, unfolding the paper.

Another contract. More fine print. I shook my head involuntarily. There was a comma and zeroes.

I glanced back up at him. "What . . . what is this?" My voice faltered.

"That magazine has been after me for months. They want to do a piece on my rehab. Pick me apart a little. Figure out if I'm washed-up or not. Micky wants me to do it. And my publicist. They're both hot to keep my face out there. Put a spin on this shitshow. Make-believe we know for certain I'll be back at the top of my game." He absentmindedly rubbed his elbow, doubt and worry clouding his face. "I told them I'd do it on one condition. I get to pick the photographer and the cover shot. They agreed." He slowly licked his bottom lip. "And I picked you."

I looked back down at the page.

"Twenty grand is a lot of money, Ash. They want some test shots to start. That's all you have to commit to for now. If they like what they see, which they will, you'll get an all-expenses-paid trip to New York to host a full-blown shoot in their studio. Carte blanche. Anything you want."

Like the man standing before me, tears filled my eyes with no regard for my wishes. I turned my back to him again, shielding my reaction.

"Oh, and Joey told me you sold all your equipment. I'd obviously resupply you with new stuff. All you have to do is say yes. Like I said, it's simple."

My finger rubbed across the figure on the paper.

So much money.

The cashier's check was already burning in my back pocket. I'd come here, ready to tear it up in his face. To tell him he had two days to find another place to park his ostentatious new toy. But that check and this contract might buy me more time. More time until my father rode in on a white horse, ready to come back home and save us.

I pictured old words scratched inside a notebook. Dreams that had died and shriveled up. He'd caught one in a trap. Had it there for the taking, taped right down to his silver freaking platter.

Joey had rules about accepting gifts with strings.

These strings came attached to a strange fluttering in my belly. Something I hadn't experienced in quite some time. Excitement. That pull toward something more. I'd learned to squelch that feeling down. I didn't deserve more than I already had. The blame didn't all rest at Brayden's feet, so he couldn't take on all the punishment.

"I can't."

The words left my mouth before my brain caught up to them. I turned to face him and held the paper out, passing back my dream. Blinking rapidly, I shut off the hint of emotion I'd temporarily let through.

"I'm not right for this. They need a professional photographer. I'm a small-town girl who once had a hobby."

"Ashley . . ." He started forward again, his cockiness suddenly edged with alarm.

"No." I held up a hand as if my palm possessed superhero powers that could propel him back. "I told you, I can't take your charity, and that's all this is."

I walked past him, dropping the letter back onto the table.

I paused with my hand on the door. "Nothing. I won't change my mind about any of it, Brayden. Your job offer. Your hands. Or letting you see my brother. Nothing will ever be simple for me again."

CHAPTER 7
SPILLED DIGNITY

ASHLEY

A mother with a screaming child sat in the waiting area. Full-out, red-faced wailing. The kid had dropped his sippy cup, spilling the last of his apple juice all over the floor. His world had ended. That upturned bit of happiness had fostered an epic meltdown. Little fists beat against the floor, tugged against his mother's leg, and then thrust wildly toward the sky, as if to say, *Why, God? Why me?*

I understood him completely.

Two decades spread between us, but at that moment, I had more in common with him than anyone else in the room.

"Ashley, you don't know how badly I wish I could help. Back in the old days, they let branch managers have a say in these things. We knew our customers and could bend the rules to help them. These days, it all comes down from corporate. To them, you're just a number on a page. There's just not enough there for them to give you better terms right now."

The kid wailed again. A real ear-piercer. I turned to look over my shoulder to where he now lies on the floor beside his mother's feet. Obviously embarrassed, she kept trying to sop up the mess while offering him something else.

A better deal.

Different terms.

I wanted to scoot out of my chair, lie down beside him, and thrust my hands up at God to ask the very same question.

Why me?

"I don't foresee them moving further with an eviction as long as you continue to make the good-faith payments. And you still have some time to exercise the redemption if you come up with the rest of the balance. Are you owed any more from your mother's life insurance? Maybe your dad will find a way . . ." The bank manager's voice trailed off, tamped down by dying hope and pity.

My father hadn't called in four and a half weeks—the longest he'd ever gone without contact. Things weren't getting better. He was still lost at sea, impaled by his own misery.

"I'm not sure about the life insurance. I've never found the paperwork. My parents' files aren't exactly well organized. They come in as direct deposits into my folks' savings. He just randomly forwards them to the business account. I don't know how all that works."

That was a lie. I did know how it worked.

I'd just given up on asking for more details.

The last time I'd mentioned it, my father started crying. I wouldn't do it again. Wouldn't ask a grief-stricken man about his dead wife's price tag.

My father didn't cry easy. He used his whole body. This gutted sound from deep in his chest, unfiltered by the unknown miles between us, or the liquor I felt certain coated his breath. Alcohol laced through most of our conversations. Sometimes to the point he didn't make sense.

When I'd asked about the policy, he'd broken down and then mumbled a slurred string of, *I'm sorrys,* before hanging up the phone.

I wouldn't live through that again.

My father had checked out. And I had no reassurance he was any closer to checking back in. I just believed in my heart that he eventually would.

I needed to find a way to hold on, a way to keep everything afloat until he found his way home. I would. I had to. Taking care of this was my penance for ruining my brother's life.

I could feel the guilty paper lying in my back pocket. It seared right through the denim, leaving a heated scar.

Choices.

So few and far between.

I wanted to stand on my own two feet and boot Brayden's ass back into the harbor. To tell him where he could shove his money and his happiness.

He wouldn't even know if I cashed the damn thing. He probably had no clue how much money sat fat and lazy in his checking account. The withdrawal wouldn't even register against his easy fortune.

He'd be happy I took it though. I could see the little half-smirk. I knew the way he craved victory. In all things. He needed it. I didn't want to give him this one. Small victories were the only kind I had a shot with these days.

"I have some money I can pay today. I was hoping maybe making another payment would buy me some more time."

I slipped it from my pocket, unfolding the pressed creases against the desktop. Pyxis International Trust. At least I didn't have to stare at his signature while I handed over my dignity.

Banks don't deal in the currency of pride. Lenders want their money, or they want to take your land. They don't care if that includes the business your mother created from the backs of half-torn envelopes.

After we lost her, we'd planted vines of bougainvillea next to the office door, along with a little plaque that had a picture of her and words of memorial. Technically, the bank owned those now, too. They could tear it all down, scuttle the whole place, and have it rezoned for luxury townhomes or condos. My only prayer was to buy it out of hock before they did.

"Wow. This is great," Mr. Garrett said, reaching his hand out toward the paper. His eyes grew wide when he saw the amount. "This will help, Ashley. How wonderful."

Our fingers were almost touching—his keen to accept the money, mine still suffering the forfeit.

The kid finally stopped crying. My gaze collided briefly with his mother's as I turned to find out what settled him.

She'd picked him up. He sat, safely tucked against her chest, his puffy, wet cheek nestled into the side of her neck while he greedily sucked his thumb. Happiness restored. He was soothed by the protection only his mother could provide. I smiled sadly. Their connection brought me one more reminder of loss.

My fingers slipped from the paper.

"I'll call up to the division VP myself, make sure he sees the updated balance." He ran his hand down the gray beard that covered his double chin. "Another payment like this, and I might be able to talk them into renegotiating those terms."

Mr. Garrett had run this bank for the last fifty years. He'd probably dealt with lots of sob stories, seen lots of people lose it all. I was determined not to cry all over him. I balled up my fists to hold it in.

"Let me print a new statement that will show you exactly where you're at after this payment." As he stood, he pushed his glasses higher on his nose. The overhead lights glistened against his bald head as he cracked a genuinely pleased smile. "You just keep up the hard work, young lady. Eventually, luck has to fall on your side."

I held back my snicker.

Luck. A frivolous idea held by those with the luxury of time. I wished like hell I could sit around and wait for it.

I had to make this happen on my own.

With good old-fashioned pain and sweat.

CHAPTER 8
TRACTOR BEAM

ASHLEY

The space wasn't perfect.

The dark walls and tall ceilings soaked up all my light.

I'd obsessed about that all afternoon, second-guessing the placement of homemade soft boxes I quickly DIY'ed from coat hangers and old white T-shirts. It took me over an hour to set up the long, white backdrop I borrowed from a local wedding photographer. I'd done some moonlighting for him, back before I pawned all my camera equipment online. Using the yoga studio had been Joey's latest brainchild. I wanted neutral ground. Somewhere quarantined from shared history. This place couldn't possibly trigger memories or flames. It used to be a scummy, old tackle shop. A few years ago, a local woman named Toni, bought, gutted, and revamped it into a place where folks could get in touch with mind and body.

Those were the two things *I* now had to keep separated. My mind needed to stay far, far away from Brayden's half-naked physique.

When I'd finally caved in, telling him I would agree to the test shoot, I'd known full and well what it meant. I had already surfed the magazine's covers back dozens of years.

The models were always shirtless. Ripped abs and oiled arms. Steely gazes and blistering smiles. Hollywood celebs, star athletes, and rock stars, looking like the millions they got paid. The cover shots hocked those perfect bodies. To dudes who passed newsstands, sporting a couple bucks, and the hope that deadlifting glossy pages would turn a beer belly into a six-pack.

I really needed to not fuck this up.

Keep it professional, clinical.

Get in, and get out.

I inwardly groaned as my mind immediately scattered to a different kind of in and out.

"You sure there's nothing else I can get you before I leave?" Toni asked, poking her head into the room as she prepared to call it a night.

"No, I'm great. Everything is all set. Joey should be here anytime now. She's coming to give me a set of extra hands. So, I should be all good." I didn't add, *She's coming here to supervise 'cause, after last time, no way in hell I'll be alone with him again.* "I promise, I'll lock up and drop the keys off to you as soon as we're done. Thanks again for letting us use the place."

"Glad to help, babe. You know how happy we all are to see you doing this. This is your calling." Her smile was half-bittersweet. "Wish I could stay and watch, but the last time I got home after bath time, Rodger had washed Addie's hair with Head and Shoulders instead of Johnson and Johnson. We were lucky all her hair didn't fall out." She pointed a finger at me. "But you better let me see all the shots you take. You know a man with a strong core does special things to me."

I wandered out to the main reception area to watch Toni leave and double-check the street for any signs of Joey. She'd promised an early arrival and a pep talk.

"Please don't be thirty minutes late for once in your life," I murmured, turning the sign in the window to Closed. I sighed and retreated to the studio to recheck everything one more time.

Ten minutes of paranoid fluttering and pacing passed by before the little bell on the front door rang out. Footsteps tracked me down the hall.

"Well, it's about time. I was getting worried you weren't gonna get here until after he . . ." My head turned toward the door.

"Joey isn't coming."

"You're early."

We spoke at the same time and then stood there, silent and frozen, staring at one another through the diffused light. He looked way too damn good. Black jeans molded to his thighs, and other parts I wasn't supposed to be noticing. A tight white V-neck highlighted muscles covered in a deep golden tan.

"What do you mean, Joey isn't coming? How do you know?"

"Check your texts. She sent us both a message."

I broke his gaze and poked in my bag to locate my phone. A long string of blue bubbles greeted me. Joey never sent just one.

Don't kill me.

Can't come.

Martha Dingle tried one of those store kits again. Her hair is avocado green. Have to stay and fix it, or I'll hear it from Kathy.

You kids don't need me anyway.

Assden, you've had your picture taken a million times. Just smile and act pretty. Don't piss her off. Use that pomade I gave you. Wet your hair first.

Ash, you've got this. Stop picking at your nails and cursing me under your breath.

A string of colorful emojis with praying hands and hearts followed her words. I indeed cursed every one of them.

Kathy was Conner's mother. She hated Joey with a brutal passion. Thought she wasn't Catholic enough for her son. She wanted him to reunite with an old high school girlfriend who had a blue-blooded pedigree and a diploma from Notre Dame. She didn't want her precious chicken heir dating a small-town hairdresser with a penchant for leather skirts, colorful hair, and kinky sex in the barn. Getting caught in the hayloft hadn't been one of my bestie's grandest plans.

Joey just kept beating her head against a wall, convinced she could still win Kathy over by working miracles with her friends' bad perms and dye jobs. Martha was a repeat offender from Kathy's inner circle.

"Did you put her up to this?" I asked, scowling at him.

Brayden's hand flew to his chest in a gesture of claimed innocence. "I promise you, I didn't ask that old lady to dye her hair green."

I blew out a breath and eyed the duffel he had hefted over one shoulder. "Did you bring the stuff I asked about?"

His hand patted the bag. "It's all here. Just tell me where you want me. I'm all yours."

It sounded benign at first. Then, he slowly licked his bottom lip while eyeing me from the tips of my toes all the way up to my hairline. He lingered too long in taboo places.

I'd worn a navy-blue maxi dress on purpose. The empire waist gathered beneath my breasts and hung all the way to the floor. I figured, if he couldn't see most of my body, maybe he'd keep his hands to himself. But, now, under his assessment, the thin cotton felt too clingy against my hips and belly.

I attempted to ignore him, pulling my tripod out farther and pretending to check settings on the back screen.

The thing was an orgasm with a motor drive.

When the UPS man asked me to sign for it, I'd acted surprised, but I should've known Brayden would go overboard. It was the Cadillac of Canons. When a second box arrived, full of lenses and filters, I'd almost wept. They were things I'd been eyeing in magazines and catalogs for years. Things I'd dog-eared but never thought I'd own.

Not that I could keep them.

When we were done here, I'd give them all back. Every single piece. Keeping them wouldn't be right. I wouldn't allow myself such nice things.

I'd done nothing to earn them.

But my inner masochist wasn't going to ruin the fun of using the hell out of them for the next hour. I was ready to shut out the world and let my senses take over. Ready for the fast heartbeat and the rush that came as soon as my face pressed against the black metal.

"I made a call sheet. This details the shots I plan to take and the wardrobe changes. There's a changing room at the end of the hallway.

Joey was going to help style you, but . . ."

He studied the piece of paper I handed him, smirking at my businesslike tone. "I think I can handle it." Eyes twinkled as they sought my own. "Be right back."

I thought I was prepared. I honestly did. I'd erected a wall and preplanned every detail. But I forgot one simple weakness. My ultimate downfall.

Sweet mother of God.

Brayden Ross in baseball pants was a fucking work of art.

He returned in the tight, form-fitting white pants that clung to his hips and cupped his assets. They showcased every single inch of him. Inches I wanted to run my eyes over, back and forth, until I soaked in every naughty detail.

Put a man in baseball pants or ballet tights, and every woman on the planet is gonna look one place first. It's human nature. Nothing to be ashamed of.

At least, that's what I told myself.

A blush blossomed across my chest before I could stop it. The strapless maxi dress was a dumb idea. I should've worn a damn turtleneck. And tinted eyewear.

"Uh, so I just need to take a few shots to check the light. Can you . . ." I motioned to the space in front of the backdrop.

Of course, it was all wrong. I had to move everything. Too many shadows hid one side of his face. Split light wasn't what I had in mind. He stood, watching me, rubbing the pad of his thumb across his bottom lip in a way that made me want to replace it with my tongue.

As soon as I returned to my tripod, he did something that blew me away even more. He faced the camera and morphed into someone I'd never met. Sultry eyes, stiff posture, chin raised just the right amount, head perfectly level.

I didn't have to move him an inch.

He just dialed in.

Of course. He'd done this a million times. He'd done shoots like this for big names. Shoes, cologne, sports drinks, athletic apparel.

He'd been well-trained by professional photographers equipped with teams of the best people.

Watching him through the lens suddenly made me feel very, very small.

"What's the matter?"

My head popped up as he broke out of character.

"Did you want something different? Just tell me what you're looking for."

"No. No, you're fine."

"But you're not. Something's off. You're not . . . you." He stepped out of position, walking forward to escape the haze of lights.

"What does that mean?"

"You're not smiling. Or doing that little breathy-gasp thing. Ashley, you've photographed me enough times in my life, I know when there's something you don't like."

He was closer now. I tried to look past him, but one bent knuckle pressed against my chin, forcing me to look up.

"I'll do whatever you want, okay? You're in charge. Just tell me what you want. I promise, I'll make myself into whatever you need."

His finger slipped away, but the heat of his skin was replaced by the heated words that slid through me like melted chocolate. Warming parts that needed to shut the hell up.

"Just be you," I replied softly. "Not the superstar. Not the guy they think they know. Smile. Be loose. Feel comfortable in your own skin. Cocky, but sweet. Be . . . be my Brayden." I didn't mean for that last part to translate from my brain to my mouth. It just slipped out. Fueled by something smoldering between us. I could feel it. Building like smoke around the corners of the room. Pressing in on me.

I knew he could feel it, too.

His eyes already had me naked and facedown on a mattress.

Lord have mercy, if I could've captured them on film, those magazine editors would just use the test shot on the cover. Women would buy extra copies to keep under their beds.

"I can do that," he replied in a husky voice.

We made it through five or six different positions. Back turned, profile, side view with arms flexed. Intense, no-bullshit gaze. The half-smirk, full smile, and full-fledged laughter.

We both knew what was coming. The anticipation grew. Something was passing between us. We fed off the energy crossing through my lens. The temperature in the room kept rising, heated by the bright lights and our own scorching wattage.

"Okay, I think we're ready to move on," I said, lifting my face away from the camera and tilting side to side to crack my neck.

"So, uh, this is a little awkward, but can I have a minute before the next set?"

My brow furrowed. "Of course. Are you okay?"

He nodded and went to his bag for a bottle of water. I started flipping back through my shots, watching a dozen versions of him zoom past on the camera's small screen.

His sudden movement had me almost pushing over the tripod, knocking everything over under the force of my shock. He'd dropped down to the floor, positioned perfectly on his left arm, right arm tucked behind his back. He was pressing up and down, doing single arm push-ups that made the muscles in his shoulders and back scrunch up. They strained against the microfiber shirt that formed a second skin. Tattoo ink stretched angrily around the top of his biceps.

I didn't speak. I couldn't. Every muscle in my lower half spasmed. Muscles in places long neglected. I watched like a voyeur, wondering why calisthenics porn wasn't already a thing.

He did a couple sets and then rolled over in one swift motion before doing hammer crunches at lightning speed. I bit my lip and didn't even pretend to look away.

He smiled sheepishly when he finally stood up. His cheeks warmed a touch by exertion and embarrassment.

"Don't make fun of me, okay? I'm not trying to be an asshole. I've neglected a few too many workouts since the surgery, and I've got about ten pounds of soft right now." He rubbed a palm across bulletproof pecs. "If I'm gonna take this shirt off, I gotta jack up what I have left."

He put his hand behind his head and started slowly pulling the neck of his shirt, exposing his abdomen a sliver at a time. Ripples against rib cage. The crazy cleft at the top of his hips. A dusting of hair that teased down toward his belt.

I'd seen him on display plenty at the marina. But the unveiling striptease, when my nerve endings were already unraveled, left blood pooling in my own cheeks.

"I think you look fine."

Fine? Seriously?

Fuck that word. It never applied to anything. Certainly not to what stood in front of me.

He didn't look fine. He looked like a freaking god. My own vagina clenched in anger at my understatement.

He smirked again.

"First shoot I ever went to, the stylist spent thirty minutes reaming me in front of the crew 'cause I showed up without doing a pre-workout. I didn't realize it was a thing." Shoulders shrugged. "Promise, before the real shoot, I'll workout beforehand, and I'll have kicked my habit for the coffee-shop cinnamon rolls." He sucked in a breath, hollowing out his cheeks. "That's gonna be harder than I want to admit."

He repositioned himself in front of the lights as I tried to collect my fine motor skills and keep all remaining saliva inside my mouth.

Luckily, capturing his beauty didn't take much work. The camera loved every delicious inch of him. The shutter growled like an animal in heat.

I took some with him fingering a ball and thrusting it out toward me before I zoomed in on fuzzy laces with him looming sharp in the background. Then, I switched up to his jersey barely hanging over his shoulders, unbuttoned down the front, exposed underneath.

Every shot got sexier.

A fine sheen of sweat built up on his skin, pooling between ridges of hard muscle. Perspiration cascaded down my spine, teasing the top edge of a thong that was already soaked in more ways than one.

Every angle I snapped felt like foreplay. He stood fifteen feet away, but I felt him all over me. He stared into the camera like he already had the tip inside and was ready to bury himself deep.

"Can you . . . I want to try something," I murmured. "Can you take off your belt?" I asked, keeping my face hidden behind the camera.

He didn't question me. His gaze never left my lens as he slowly undid the black buckle and started tugging it free. It took seconds that felt like a goddamn century. He tossed it to the side, out of the frame.

"What kind of . . . do you have on . . ." I couldn't say it. I knew he was wearing a cup. Knew he'd come with a complete uniform. I could see the telltale bulge. "Does the waistband have a brand? Are you allowed to show . . ."

I swallowed.

Am I asking him to do this?

BRAYDEN

My hand was already stationed on my zipper.

Fuck yeah. Let's do this.

"You want me to unzip?"

I adjusted myself to the side a fraction of an inch.

Women have no idea what it's like to get a hard-on inside a jockstrap. It hurts like a motherfucker. Unzipping would free the poor bastard up a little bit. Dude was ready to drill right through the plastic to get to her. Ashley's body was his favorite drug, and he'd given up fighting his addiction.

That dress she had on . . . damn. Women thought they had to show skin to be sexy. She'd wrapped hers up in long, flowing cotton. It stretched across her tits and clung to her hips and the top of her ass. When she walked, it swirled around her legs. My palms burned from the need to rub my hands across the material and watch it bunch up in my fists. She might as well have tied a little bow around herself and hung a sign around her neck, begging me to dream about every hidden inch.

The inches I kept thinking about the whole time I stared into the camera.

I could feel her eyes on me, studying my body through the glass lens. The whole room filled with an electric charge that left the hair on the back of my neck standing straight up. When she had me turn around and look over my shoulder, I was afraid she'd be able to tell.

Unzipping for her? Yeah, not a problem.

My zipper lowered an inch at a time. The only sound in the room was her breath and the metal casing coming apart. I lifted my hands and let the front flaps of my pants fall slightly open, exposing the top of the bulge that cried out for sweet mercy. I let my hand slide down, roughly cupping my crotch to adjust myself further.

She couldn't quite camouflage the sharp gasp my action inspired.

I'd never been aroused during a shoot before. Last year, I'd posed for a cologne ad with three buck-naked models half-climbing my body. Bare breasts pressing against my back and my side. Sets of hands clinging to my thighs. One of the stylists there had offered to tape down my dick in case I got wood.

Didn't fucking happen.

I'd felt nothing.

That shoot had taken forever though. The photographer got a bug up his ass and kept saying the chakras on the set were all wrong.

I didn't know what the hell he kept yammering about at the time, but now, I got it. My chakras were alive, well, and quickly falling victim to the tractor beam pulling me across the room.

She thought she was hiding, coy and protected, behind her black metal tripod. She forgot how well I knew her body. Didn't realize that, after all those years of watching over her, I knew exactly how to read every expression. Her face and skin always betrayed her attempts to hide emotion.

She was sure as shit turned on, too.

"How do you feel about showing your scar?"

My brow wrinkled in question. I turned my arm to stare down at the five-inch red mark that curved around the inside of my elbow.

"Uh, that's fine, I guess." I shrugged. "It's pretty ugly."

"I don't think so. It's no different than the tattoo really. It's a part of you now. Tells who you are."

My fingers rubbed across inked skin.

If you only knew.

"I just think . . . I mean . . . you're all hulked out and perfect. But what if you show just a little bit of the real you? Everyone reading this article has things about themselves they don't want the world to see," she added softly. "Why not show them you have scars, too? Sort of Superman with human skin."

My arm instinctively went up, palm flattened against the back of my head so that my bicep swelled and my scar lay on full, trusted display.

I'd been covering it up as much as I could. Not necessarily because I didn't want the world to see the ugliness, but because I didn't want to. I had to live with it for the rest of my life. It would either become the trophy of my greatest victory or the parting gift from my greatest defeat.

But I didn't mind showing it to her. I'd never had to hide any of my scars from her. She knew every single one of them.

The ones I had inside and out.

As her motor drive whirled, I knew she didn't get the significance. I didn't let my guard down easily with anybody else. I could always tell her stuff—since those days huddled in the library or cuddled up on the futon in the boathouse. She saw a side of me no one else ever got the chance to see.

Her Brayden.

A version of myself I'd missed, almost as much as I'd missed her.

"God, that's amazing. Don't move. Totally blank expression. You're not happy. You're not sad. You're just determined. You're not gonna let this scar mean anything. It's not gonna stop you. Lex Luthor had better not think you've gotten soft 'cause you're coming back, and you're gonna knock the shit out of him."

My nostrils flared at her words.

Photographers all did it. They fed you lines of bullshit. Forced you to snort their compliments till they got inside your head and got what they wanted to see. I was used to it. Usually, I ignored it. Prayed they'd press the shutter button and shut their mouths.

This time was different.

Her words struck at those things I was worried about in deep, dark places. Things I'd only shared with my inner demons.

Would I be as good again? Could I get back to where I'd been? Was this scar a memento to mark the end of my career? What would I be without baseball?

No Soot *and* no baseball.

How would I do life without them both?

Pressure built behind my eyes. I sucked in against my cheeks to hold it at bay. The shutter whirled faster. She exhaled between parted lips, completely lost in the world behind the glass.

When her head finally popped up, I was still standing there with my fists full of feelings my shrink would love.

"I think we're all done. You did great."

She came around the tripod, dress swishing around ankles and bare feet. She snapped off one of the bright lights, eliminating one heat source while turning up another. The room was bathed in the muted glow of one small lamp and the lust that still pressed in between us.

I was drawn to her. Couldn't stop myself. I never could. I had to be as close to her as possible.

Always.

Her back was to me. Her neck exposed as her hair cascaded to the side. I drew the side of my index finger over the curve of her shoulder.

"You were incredible," I said, my voice thick and raspy like I'd just fucked her hard and enjoyed a cigarette.

I'd said I wouldn't kiss her again without permission. I never promised I wouldn't touch her.

She inhaled sharply and turned slowly toward me, pulling herself away from my finger but bringing the rest of her closer to my naked chest.

"You feel it, don't you?"

"Brayden, don't."

"But you want me to. You do."

Our eyes locked. Something I saw in hers bolstered my confidence. Ashley wanted to give in. Her body just needed to supersede her mind. She was teetering on the edge; I needed to give her one big push.

"What you really want is for me to pull the front of this dress down and press my chest against those cotton-candy nipples. You want me to slide all this material up the backs of your thighs and wrap my hands around your ass till I can feel how wet you are against that thong."

Her lips flattened, pressed together, and quickly parted again, desperate for air.

Give in to it, baby girl.

"You wore the thong for me 'cause you know it makes me insane when I can see that little strap. When I know I could slide it to the side and press my fingers up into your cunt. Snap that strap against your ass while you're riding me."

She spun back around, her back to me again. The diversion couldn't hide the way her chest heaved now, filling up with need in place of oxygen.

We both want this . . .

My hands ghosted over her hips. No real pressure, just enough so she could feel me. "You know it's gonna happen, baby girl. How long are we gonna play this game? How long are we gonna keep pretending we don't both want it? Let yourself remember. Remember how good we are together. How tight you fit around me. How good it feels to explode around my cock."

"I can't . . ." Her voice wavered.

"I promised I'd wait for you to come to me."

"It's not gonna happen, Brayden. You're gonna have to wait a very long time."

"I've already waited too long." My hands slid away as I took a step back.

She shivered, unconsciously chilled, as the extra space soaked up the combustion between us.

"You just gotta come to me, Soot. I'm right here, but you gotta take that last step."

"It's hard to beat a person who never gives up."
—*Babe Ruth*
Baseball Hall of Fame,
Inaugural Class, 1936

CHAPTER 9
BREAKING POINT

ASHLEY

I rang the doorbell. For the first time . . . ever.

I stared at the brass door knocker, counting my breaths and the number of reasons this was a monumentally bad idea.

The front porch light flipped on as the door swung open.

"Ash? Are you okay?"

Brayden's whole face measured my disheveled appearance—worried eyes, wrinkled brow, pursed lips.

A yellow cotton nightgown, edged in frayed white lace, skimmed halfway down my thighs. I'd hastily pulled an old raincoat over top it. The belt hung uneven and forgotten by my sides. My hair still felt damp from the cold shower I'd taken hours ago. It lay parted into two thick braids that rested against my shoulders.

Nothing about me looked sexy.

I was less Victoria's Secret, more Salvation Army.

Maybe I'd come that way on purpose. I stood before him, wrapped in the rags and hope. Hope that his Clark Kent laser vision would see I was too fragile for this misbegotten idea and toss me back out into the night.

As grand plans went, this one rated epically dumb.

I'd lain in bed for hours. Staring at the ceiling. Feeling the old memory of him against the sheet beside me. Allowing the mere thought of his hands to coax me near climax. In a moment of violent weakness, I'd thrown on the coat and padded barefoot to my car.

A ghost drove me here.

A ghost of a girl I used to be.

For just a little while, I had to let her take the wheel.

I stepped forward, over the threshold, violating his personal space for a change. His breathing quickened as his eyes inventoried the rest of my body, checking for injury or pain.

My skin and bones remained fully intact.

My mind had just gone completely insane.

"This isn't gonna be nice. I don't want nice. I don't want soft and sweet or slow and easy. I need to get this over with." My palms pressed flat against his chest, gliding across the ridges of hard muscles I had captured on film and seared into my brain.

"Get what over with? What are you talking about?" Confused hands latched on to my wrists, seizing them before they could reach all the way up to his shoulders.

"I need to fuck you out of my system. Once and for all. I can't stand the tension anymore. I can't stand thinking about it one more second. We're gonna do this. Right here, right now. I want you to fuck me hard and fast and dirty—down so deep it chases all this away. Then, you're gonna leave me the hell alone. Pretend like I don't exist. Go back to living your other life. Quit taking up so much space in mine."

His hands loosened, palms pressed flat on top of my hands, melding them back against his hardened nipples. Hooded eyes stared into mine. His lips hung open, speechless.

"This isn't me saying yes to any of your bullshit. Get that straight in your head right now. This is just about taking something from you. I'm taking this. You don't get anything back from me in return."

I pulled one hand free from its cage to poke three times at his hard chest. He took it without flinching, freely inheriting a little taste of my pain.

"I don't owe you anything. Not a damn thing. Do you understand me?"

"We can play this however you want, baby girl."

He kept staring at me with those intense blue eyes that always pierced too deep. I forced myself not to cower or to let them suck me entirely under his control.

I shrugged awkwardly out of my coat, letting it fall to the floor. He didn't wait for me to say anything else. His hands tread roughly down the length of my body, over the sides of my breasts, over my waist, and down past my hips to the top of my thighs. Pushing my flimsy nightgown up, he palmed my ass, lifting me like a feather to smash against him. I wound my legs around his hips as he turned, forcing me back against the wall beside the door.

The hard bulge smashed against me left no doubt that he wanted this just as bad, but he halted suddenly. His eyes were affixed to my mouth as perfect white teeth worried his bottom lip.

"Ask me, Soot. I told you I wouldn't do it again till you asked me."

"Kiss me, Brayden. Right now."

"Thank Christ."

He ground his mouth down on mine. Nothing like the teasing kiss in the office. This was possessive and angry. Tongue and teeth and hot breath. As our mouths tangled, his fingers dug into my ass. He thrust involuntarily against me.

I could feel all of him.

Devouring me. Claiming me. Forcing broken pieces together. Those same jagged shards I'd held in bloodied hands, never able to fit back into place on my own.

It was more than I asked for.

More than I wanted.

The only thing separating us was the lace of my panties and the silky material of his athletic shorts. I scraped my nails across the back of his neck, trying to leave him permanently marked, the way he'd left me too many years ago.

He groaned and slid his mouth across my cheek, trailing wet and hot down onto my shoulder. He bit into the soft skin and then drew his tongue across my collarbone, dragging the scruff of his chin over that damn spot that always threw a switch inside me.

Fucker always knew right where to find it.

He kept swiveling his hips against me. Rocking back and forth against my clit, already too sensitive from all his suggestive words and our photographic foreplay.

"I need you inside me. Right now, Brayden. I want you to pound into me. I want it to hurt."

Make it hurt.

Make it hurt, so I don't feel anything else.

My rambling plea spurred him on. He eased his head back. In the space of a single breath, he tugged the little tie at the top of my nightgown, tearing it open so my naked breasts fell out, heavy and sensitive against the chilled air. My nipples pebbled, begging for his touch. One finger slid down over an upturned peak.

Gentle. Too gentle.

"Holy hell," he groaned painfully. "This is the shade of pink I dream about every time I jack myself. Fuck, baby girl, I've missed these tits."

His head bent. Warm breath danced across aching flesh. My fingers threaded through his hair, angrily demanding more. I called out his name again right before his mouth finally claimed me.

He sucked greedily, pulling my nipple so hard between his teeth, I thought I'd explode from that simple touch. My hands grabbed ahold of his waistband, urgent and needy.

"Now, Brayden."

"Not yet," he murmured. His lips returned to softly brush over my mouth, breathing his next words into me. "Not like this."

In one quick motion, he bent down and slid an arm under the backs of my knees. He lifted me and turned to carry me up the stairs.

He didn't stop at his old bedroom door. He continued down the hall and into one of the spare rooms that had some of his clothes scattered about. The lamp on the nightstand cast a glow of dark honey. The duvet sat rumpled. I must've interrupted the paperback book that lay unfolded on top.

I snickered at the title.

Of course.

"I'm tenth on the waitlist for that at the library. Is it any good?" I asked as he gently set me down next to the bed. The backs of my legs met the smooth cotton sheet.

"It's amazing. You can have my copy." He smiled with one half of his mouth and reached out to carelessly fling the book off the side of the bed. "Ash, I'll give you anything you want," he added huskily.

My fingers dropped to the lacy hem at the bottom of my nightgown, gradually drawing it up my thighs. Demanding hands moved to stop me.

"Let me," he whispered gently, staring into my eyes.

Instead of lifting it over my head, he used one finger to coax the right strap off my shoulder. It slid down my arm, leaving goose bumps in its wake. The side of his finger followed its path, tracing lightly across the pebbled skin, warming it again. He repeated the motion on the other side until the whole garment cascaded down my body and pooled at my feet.

Something was changing in the room. The air felt too thick. My neediness too raw and exposed. He kept slowing down when I wanted to speed up. I needed to get this over with.

My hands grappled again for his waistband.

"Wait." His quiet demand stilled my assault.

In slow motion, he sank to his knees in front of me. His arms wrapped gingerly around my hips, and fingertips dug into the top of my ass. A rough, stubbled cheek pressed against the sensitive skin of my belly. He was . . . hugging me. Fucking hugging me, like he needed it to breathe.

I stood, frozen. A knight with no armor. Fighting off his gravity.

"One thousand four hundred sixty-eight days." His words fluttered across my skin.

"What?"

"It's been one thousand four hundred sixty-eight days since I held you like this. Since I made love to you."

My brows drew up in confusion. Brayden's face tilted up to meet mine.

"How . . . how do you know?" I asked, stammering.

"I've counted them all."

I needed to run. Far, far away. From his words and from the tears forming in his eyes. His fingers pressed into the sides of my hips, locking me in place, preventing my escape.

"No," I said irritably, pressing against his shoulders, trying to force his emotion away from me. "No, Brayden. Don't. You can't do this. I told you how this has to be. Don't make this into something it's not. My terms. Or nothing at all. You said this could be simple."

I pushed against him harder. Insisting. Begging. Praying he would let me go. I chanted ugly things at him. Ranting again about how this had to be. My anger flowed up like carbonated bubbles held too long beneath hard glass.

He knelt there and took it, his chest rising and falling rapidly, as he soaked in more of my pain. Absorbing all of it until, finally, a growl ripped from his throat. He stood at once, lifted me straight off my feet, and tossed me back onto the bed.

Yes.

Yes, that's more like it.

That's what I'd wanted. I had come here to tie things up, rough and dirty, with a nice, neat bow. Closure. They'd all been telling me to find it for years.

For one thousand four hundred sixty-eight days, apparently.

Well, this was my way of getting that. I'd fuck him right out of my system and then walk away from him the way he'd walked away from me.

"You sure you want it hard and fast? 'Cause I can do that, baby girl. You think this is what you want?"

Strong hands ripped my panties down the middle, tearing them away from my legs, as I struggled to exhale. He pushed his shorts down and tore the shirt over his head in one motion. He stood before me, magnificently naked and totally over-equipped for what I needed.

He harshly fisted himself as I shamelessly watched, studying the rigid head of his cock and the thick veins that swelled up around the side. I felt jealous of that strong hand pumping back and forth. He kept it moving over his skin as he walked to the dresser. He used his free hand to rifle through the top drawer.

"What are you doing?" I pushed up onto my elbows.

"I assume your idea of a hard, fast fuck still includes protection."

"I'm on the pill."

Both his hands stilled. Anger drained out of the wide eyes that shot back to mine.

"Stress messed up my cycle. I got sick of it," I explained.

"You're sure you . . ." He stopped short of asking if I trusted him. Smart move, considering we both already knew the answer.

He strode back to the bed, sat on the edge, and cupped my cheek. "I swear, baby girl, I've never . . . other than that one time in your car, I've never *not* used protection. I'm clean. I would never put you in any danger like that."

My eyes narrowed. I batted his hand away. "Don't twist this into me giving you something special. That's not what this is about. I'm taking this. For me. This isn't about you. I need this over and done with and you out of my life. As fast as possible."

His gaze sharpened, nostrils flared. Anyone else in my position would have been scared.

He leaned toward me, placing his hands on the mattress next to my hips. His face hovered inches from mine with eyes still rimmed by liquid emotion. "If that's how you want to play this, *fine*. You want to fuck me out of your system? Super. 'Cause I'm more than ready to fuck you so hard you forget every guy who's followed after me. I'm gonna make you come till you only remember my name. Till you only want me."

He pulled back and fisted himself again, pulling ferociously. I moved up farther onto the bed, spreading my legs wider. My hand slid down over my stomach, and then my middle finger drew circles over my clit.

"Fucking hell," he said, groaning as he climbed onto the bed. "You know what that does to me."

His weight pressed down on me. His forearms rested on either side of my head, caging me in. The tip of his cock lined up with my entrance, pushing just against the outside.

"I'm gonna fuck your pussy till you finally remember, Soot. I was your first, and I damn well plan on being your last."

I wound my legs around his hips, digging my heels into his ass to shut him up.

"Shit. I knew you'd do that, too," he hissed into my ear, his cheek pressing against mine.

With one swift motion, he plunged into me, so vicious and deep that my back arched up off the mattress. His head reared back as his mouth spewed a string of dirty expletives.

So fucking good indeed.

Our mouths sealed together as his hips started circling bitterly against me. My lungs begged for air.

Dear Lord, I'd forgotten how thick and perfect he was, how he filled places no one else had ever come close to finding. I moaned as he hit my favorite spot in three quick thrusts. He took me right to the edge too fast, pumping into me until skin slapped together. Bruising fingertips dug into my hips, forcing my body back and forth as he slammed forward.

"Oh God. Dallas." I said it once. One lousy time, I cried out *that* name. A stupid reflex, I couldn't hold in.

His mouth responded, softly meeting mine in a kiss that no longer matched the hostility of his strokes. It was sweet. Gentle and giving and calm. My tongue lashed out, trying to amp it back into something different. I didn't want sweet. I wanted simple and dirty. Biting teeth and hard pressure.

He wouldn't let me get my way.

His cock kept fucking me, but his mouth started making love.

I banged against his chest, beating him back away from me, begging for sanity and space. I immediately wished I hadn't. His thrusts slowed. His hips began circling in a quiet, steady rhythm. They were still maddeningly deep but no longer gifted the hard, raunchy thrusts he'd treated me to before.

I knew what he was doing. Trying to suck me in. Trying to add emotions to something I couldn't let be more than purely physical. He pulled on strings I'd only ever allowed him to hold.

"Stop."

"I can't help it," he whispered, his voice laden with an emotion I wouldn't allow myself to name.

My heels dug angrily into the backs of his thighs.

"Stop, Brayden. This isn't right."

I balled my hand into a fist and punched against his chest, just above his heart. He levered himself onto one hand and used the other to grab on to my wrist, pressing it over my head to stop my assault. He stared down into my eyes.

"This is abso-fucking-lutely right. Everything about it. Don't you feel that? The way we fit." He pulled back, withdrawing till he was almost gone. Then, just as slowly, he plunged back into me, full hilt. We both panted in unison. "Did you honestly think we could do this and not feel it? Not feel one another all the way down through our fucking souls?"

I squeezed my eyes shut and tried to block out his words.

"Look at me."

I shook my head.

"Look at me, Soot."

My traitorous eyes fluttered open. His hands grasped my cheeks. Smooth lips brushed across mine. He withdrew and then drove brutally deep again. I gasped involuntarily at the contrast, the emotional battle of body and will.

"*This*. Is. Home, Soot." He punctuated every word between thrusts. "We're finally home," he repeated, softer this time as he rotated his hips.

That did it. Something inside me snapped. A strobe light flashed over happier times. Our first night under the Christmas lights in the boathouse. Our last time—a rushed little quickie in the back of his Jeep before he'd had to get to practice. Never knowing that those hastened moments would become some I'd try so hard to forget.

His hand cupped my breast. The sensation shot through me, triggering too much. In my mind, I could hear our laughter, feel his hands cupping my breasts under my white bikini as I stood at the kitchen counter making sandwiches.

I'd suppressed that image for so long, never letting it out of the carefully sealed box. I couldn't let real life damage the snapshot of the very last day I remembered being happy.

Turning away from his hold on my face, I pressed my cheek against the sheet, trying to hide the feelings that were coming now whether I fought them or not. Tears spilled over the bridge of my nose and across my other eyelid to pool on the crisp white cotton. Lips immediately skimmed over my shoulder. I turned to face him, opening my eyes to see his sad smile and tears of his own cascading, unashamed, down both his cheeks.

"Please . . . please, I can't . . ." I was cracking. Hurtling toward all the pain I'd locked up deep, deep down. It would all bubble up if I let it. It would swallow me whole again.

I couldn't let it all tumble down off the shelf all at once.

"Shh . . ." He kissed my eyelids and then trailed his lips across my wet cheekbones. "Don't cry. You know I hate it when you cry. It breaks things inside me, and I don't want to be broken anymore. I want to feel whole again, baby girl. We've both been living half a life for too long. Let me do this. Let me give you this. Give it back to me. Give me back the piece of myself I left behind."

My hips met his in answer, tentatively pressing up to meet him halfway.

"That's it," he coaxed, thrusting a little harder with deeper, smoother circles that curled against that very best spot.

His hand slid down between us. Callused fingertips pressed into my clit, forcing me to cry out his name.

"That's it," he repeated. "Let go of all of it. Just feel me. Feel us. Crawl over the edge with me. I want to pump myself into you so bad, baby girl. I've never . . . I want to feel you pulse around me, and then I wanna watch my come slide back out of you. I wanna mark you in a way I never have before."

A series of deep, unhurried thrusts shoved me down against the mattress and had me gripping on to the sheet with both fists.

God, I'd spent years assuring myself I'd romanticized Brayden's sexual prowess.

Maybe he wasn't that good?

Maybe the others were just skill-less duds?

Yeah, I'd been lying.

"So close. So . . . it's so good."

"Always was. The best. We're the best together, Ash. 'Cause this is where we both belong."

He sped up the pace again, so deep tingles and sparks and blue stars lit behind my eyelids. I couldn't fight it. Couldn't fight his words or their meaning or my own tears. Couldn't fight the things inside me that soaked up all the emotion he was pouring into me.

We drove together, clinging to one another like we had to hold on. It kept building. Higher and higher until everything suddenly tensed and snapped. Over and over, I pulsed against him as he grew impossibly harder.

"Fuck yeah. Jesus, Ashley. It's so good. God. It's never . . ." His breath skittered out. He couldn't finish his words. They stuck in his throat as sensation took over.

He followed right after me, convulsing in hot, wet streams of spilled seed that would stay with me long after he withdrew. I already knew the memory of this night would last even longer.

Long enough to haunt me.

When I'd told him he could go bareback, I'd just wanted to hurry him up. I hadn't thought that far ahead to the new connection it would form.

Another first.

He'd taken them all.

He pulled back, sliding out of me with a wet pop. Strong arms encased me. Gentle kisses traced across my hairline. He finally propped himself up to look down at me. His index finger drew a line from the top of my breast and down over my belly button until it slid through my folds. He traced it back and forth through the wetness leaking out of me. His eyes traveled down the same path, staring in awe.

"Holy shit. Look at that."

I couldn't fight the urge to follow his gaze.

I should have resisted. Seeing his finger against me in the most intimate place, drawing through proof of our reunion, was the most erotic thing I'd ever witnessed.

And the most destructive.

My shoulders shook as they caved in against emotions I'd promised to never let back in.

BRAYDEN

I held on to her, smoothing my hands over her tangled braids. I kissed her forehead and murmured her name, trying to gently coax her toward a different kind of release.

It felt so good. Having her in my arms, feeling like I was protecting her from something.

Something I wouldn't admit was myself.

She stayed quiet; her back spooned against me. I thought it was to put some distance between us. Physically. Emotionally. But she let me wrap my arms back around her, let me curve my cheek into the crook of her neck.

We lay there in silence for a long while, lulled by a temporary truce and the sound of our breath intermingled with the crickets and cicadas chirping outside the window.

I'd been in turmoil for so long. I felt peaceful now. Almost drugged. Riding a high I had not let myself experience in a very long time.

Soft fingertips trailed up my arm. They stopped to dance across black ink, tracing the edge of flames and barbed wire that wrapped around the image of a compass at the very top of my bicep. Ashley shifted a little, looking down at it. I propped myself up on my other arm, so she could see more.

"How long have you had it?"

"Almost four years. Got it done at an all-night tattoo parlor just outside of Toledo. It was one of my very first road trips in the minors. Our bus broke down, and we got stuck there for the night. The guy who did it had one glass eye and a tremor, but I showed him a picture of what I wanted, and he got it just right."

The tip of her finger whispered across the scrolling letters stretched inside it. "What does it say?" she asked tentatively.

"It's French," I replied. "*Le pardon est gagné.*"

"What does it mean?"

"Forgiveness is earned."

ASHLEY

The nightmare woke me. The same one. My mother's voice screaming. Calling for me. My brother's voice shouting. Nurses' faces. Scenes blending together. My brother hurt. My mother ill. Men in dark suits, laughing. The marina parking lot full of bulldozers.

It startled me awake at least once a week. I'd gotten pretty good at rolling over and falling back into an exhausted, fitful sleep, but tonight, I couldn't do my normal toss and turn.

The warmth of Brayden's chest soaked into my back.

I eased out of bed an inch at a time, careful not to rouse him. I padded my way down the hall, pausing at his old bedroom door. The hinges still squeaked as it opened.

My hand covered the shock that forced my mouth wide. I don't know what I'd been expecting. I guess part of me feared a time capsule. Homework on the bed. Rumpled sheets and broken glass. Trophies and old team photos. Shelves of shared paperbacks and a nightstand full of lies.

The smell of cheating.

But, the room held none of it. Not a single shred of youthful memories or broken promises.

It didn't hold a single thing.

All the furniture was gone. The walls stripped bare and repainted. No longer blue, they were now a harsh, stark white. The carpet had been torn up, exposing plywood. Old nails lay strewn across the floor.

Everything was gone.

He'd wiped it all away. The bad. And the good.

I didn't know how to feel. About the room and about all the stuff he'd said. Everything jumbled in my mind like heavy bricks layering to form my own tomb.

I crept down the stairs, intent on washing down some of my turmoil. I sat at Grams's old kitchen table, staring around the room with an odd sense of déjà vu and a juice glass full of tepid tap water.

The sound of a phone vibrating broke through my introspection. It buzzed against the counter next to the fridge. In my little world, a chiming phone at two a.m. still spelled emergency. Reflex forced me out of the chair.

The bright screen provided the only light source in the room. It glowed against the darkness, bringing to life the lock-screen photo of Brayden and a smiling woman.

She was beautiful. Not supermodel gorgeous, but very pretty. Sharp features, nice eyes, and great hair. The soft, not-from-a-bottle blond lay piled on top of her head.

Their arms were around one another's shoulders. He wore a uniform, a bright navy shirt that brought out the insane blue of his eyes. She had on a form-fitting T-shirt tucked into skinny jeans. His number stretched across her breasts. She looked happy.

I must've smiled like that once.

The screen darkened and then immediately lit again. Another vibration, accompanied by more words.

Just got back to ur place and found my package waiting. U r the best. Luv u so much, B. Missing u bad. City is no fun without u. C u soon, bb. Xoxo.

The tears in his eyes, the soft touches, the whispered words and promises—the mirage I'd let myself have for a while—blew away with one breath of truth. He wasn't here to reclaim me.

Injured birds sputter home, heal, and then fly away again.

He already had someone to go back to.

Does he say the same things to her in the dark?

I am so stupid.

The glass of water I still held slid from my hand. It didn't shatter. It rolled across the floor, spilling into a puddle along with the contents of my heart.

I wouldn't shatter either.

I was already broken.

I stepped over the water, staggered to the front hall to gather my old coat, and soundlessly walked out the door.

BRAYDEN

I woke to the first pink streams of daylight and the smell of her hair. It filled me with short-lived relief. My hand stretched across the sheet, searching for warmth I wouldn't find. My eyes opened to emptiness.

My empty bed and my empty heart.

She left me. Again.

Loneliness backfilled all the dark fucking holes inside me.

BRAYDEN

I found her.

Standing at the counter outside the office with her back to me. Cup of coffee in one hand, a clipboard loaded down with papers in the other. I'd given her a head start, waiting until the sun had fully come up. Long enough to get my shit together and long enough for her to think about what she'd done wrong.

Last night, she didn't want nice.

She was about to learn how not nice I could be.

She must've heard the door shut. Her head turned slightly. She didn't need to turn around; she already knew it was me. The room immediately with *us*. With that thing that happened every time we shared space. The extra electrical charge that scorched my brain and shot straight to my dick.

My dick that was still chafed from waking up alone.

My dick that made her come three times and still held the scent of her pussy.

We got it back last night. Our connection. The fucking thing that had lived and breathed between us since the day she walked in that library and stole my chair. Miles and years and broken heartbeats hadn't killed it. I sure as hell wasn't going to let her run away from it now.

I didn't need hope. I had proof. In spades.

What I didn't have anymore was patience.

Patience is an excuse anyway, dreamt up by losers to explain why they didn't win. That wasn't me. I wouldn't accept defeat. We'd busted up slow and steady real good last night. I wasn't going to go back there.

She stayed still as I approached her from behind. I stopped just short of pressing myself against her.

"You left," I snapped.

She set her things down and let her arms drop to her sides, bracing herself. "I told you, last night was not the start of something. I was very clear."

I ghosted one fingertip from the top of her hand all the way up her arm until I reached her neck. Her head tilted instinctively into my touch.

"I told you how this had to be, Brayden."

Her words said one thing.

Her body said another.

I placed my hand flat against her belly at the same time I pressed my chest against her back, squeezing her to me in violent possession.

"Come home." I wasn't asking. My tone made that pretty damn clear.

Her shoulders sagged beneath the weight of her world and my simple demand.

"We can't do this."

She needed to remember last night. How it felt, being connected to me again. Yes, we'd both left some pain hanging in the air. Yes, we'd torn some stuff wide open. We still had work to do. I got that. But I wasn't gonna let her walk away from this. If she kept on running, I would chase her.

Anywhere.

I ground my pelvis forward against her denial. Fuck. I was already hard as a rock. I wanted her to feel that. What she did to me.

"Too late. We already have. And we are again. Right here, right now. For as long as needed until you remember."

Message received apparently because her breathing changed. A couple short, little pants that matched the timing of my hips. Her neck tilted again. I pressed the side of my chin against that sweet spot that made her crazy. Rubbing the scruff of my jaw back and forth. Rough against silky smooth.

She whimpered.

Bingo.

Her hips moved, an almost unperceivable amount, but just enough for me to register she was pressing herself back against me, letting my cock settle in between the cheeks of her ass. I used my free hand to slide up the back of her thigh, tracing fingertips under her tiny athletic shorts, over the seam of her panties.

"Why did you leave me?" I asked the same old question. The one burned forever in the mind of a boy who had been left by his mother and by the only girl he'd ever loved.

They all leave you.

You're not good enough.

Be better. You have to be better.

The siren voices sang to me their lullaby of bullshit. They mixed with Dr. Wolfe's nasally accent, reminding me the only path around them was to bleed out the anger and hurt.

I growled deep in my throat, forcing the voices to quiet. Sticking them back in a cage where they couldn't harm us. I'd let my fucked-up insecurities cost us both too much already.

I could do this. I had to. We both needed it.

I'd waited years to be strong enough. To be ready.

You couldn't go around the voices. The good doctor's textbooks had that part all wrong. If you tried to outrun them, they followed. Anytime, anywhere. Singing their broken serenade to level you at most inconvenient times.

I knew better now. I'd played their tune for as long as I could remember. The path around them wouldn't work. The only sure way to wipe out the hurt was to walk right through it. To sound a battle cry and run headlong forward.

That's what I came here to do.

I just had to find a way to drag her along with me.

After last night, winning over her body still felt like the best, fail-safe method, to get her on my side.

"I—" she started to speak, but her breath caught as I slid the edge of her panties up to the crack of her ass, exposing creamy skin that needed to be taught a lesson.

I grabbed her there. Rough and harsh and mean—the way I'd felt waking up in that empty bed.

"I never intended to stay," she answered.

I squeezed harder, exorcising the pain her words caused. She gasped in pleasure.

Good girl.

"I wanted to wake up and make love to you. Sweet and slow. I wanted to taste you while you were still half-dreaming and have you wake up and understand it was real."

"Brayden, I told you—"

"No. I don't want to hear any more denials right now. I thought you got it last night. I'm not letting you just walk away. I'm not letting you ignore this . . . us. You and me. You wanted to get fucked last night. And I wasn't totally prepared for that. But, now . . . now you've pissed me off. And a good fucking is just what you need."

I swatted her exposed backside, pinking soft flesh. She gripped the side of the counter and heaved out a breath. I grabbed on to her shoulders and spun her around to finally look at me. Her bottom teeth dug into her pouty top lip. The cheeks on her face were blossoming, too. I pressed my fingers into the skin beneath her ear, preventing her from looking away.

"Tell me you don't want it. Tell me you don't want me to rip these shorts off you and take you here right now."

She didn't speak, but her eyes darkened as her arms slowly threaded around my neck. That was the only answer I needed. It snapped clear through the last of my resolve.

My palms cupped her ass, pulling her up against me until she wrapped her legs around my waist. I carried her through the office door, pausing only to slam it shut with my foot. The frosted glass rattled. I marched her backward toward the old wooden desk, perching her just on the edge of it. A sweeping arm cleared the space.

I pulled her hands from my neck, slowly letting them fall away until she was forced to reach back and prop herself up on her elbows.

My hands skimmed up her inner thighs and under her shorts until I could trace the damp band of elastic blocking me from my ultimate goal in life. I snapped it against her. Just a little sting to make sure she was with me. Then, I yanked the lace underwear down her legs, forcing the flimsy shorts to follow along.

I inhaled, filling up my lungs, letting my chest expand and contract. Without ceremony, I slid my shorts down, letting them fall to the floor so that I could palm my greedy cock. Three harsh pulls brought zero fucking relief.

She leaned up on the desk more. I froze as her slender fingers reached out and replaced my own. They wrapped around me. Short red fingernails gripped me just right. She ran her hand up and down, testing me.

Torturing me.

Jesus Christ, I need this to happen right the fuck now.

I stared at her movement, crippled by that primal contact. Needing to give it back to her.

"I want you to watch this time, baby girl. I want you to watch my dick sink into you. Watch our connection while I fuck you. Think about why it feels so right. Don't fight me. You want this. Let yourself have it."

My hand replaced hers again. I leaned over her, pressing her back down to her elbows. I teased her entrance with the tip of my dick, sliding back and forth to make her wonder when I'd give in and do it.

"Brayden, this is crazy." She exhaled loudly as I pressed the head inside. "Logan will be here soon."

"Great. Let's be real damn loud then. I want him to hear you screaming my name. One more asshole who needs to take a hint."

"Is that what this is about?" she asked defensively, leaning up more. "You making sure no one else can have me?"

"This is about taking back what's mine. I told you last night. I've never given up on you, Soot. Someday, you're gonna finally see that. Right now, I want you to stop thinking altogether. Shut off your brain, and just feel me."

I thrust into her without preamble. She didn't need it. She was wet as hell. I slid right in to the hilt, pushing her back against the desk a little. Her eyes were staring directly into mine. I shook my head.

"No, baby. I want you to see this." I looked down to where we joined.

Slippery skin slid back and forth. Her gaze dropped hesitantly. Her eyes widened as she finally looked.

"See that? You see how we fit together? Perfect. We're perfect, Soot. You and me."

Her chest was rising and falling faster. I traced a finger around the folds just above where we met. Pushing in and out of her brutally slow while I teased her clit.

Her head fell back as she groaned.

"Let it feel good, baby girl. Let me have you."

Her head snapped back up, her gaze intense. That was my cue. I harshly thrust into her, cutting off whatever evil thought she was about to let flood her mind. Her eyes dropped back down to watch me plow into her, pushing relentlessly against the spot I knew would drive her insane.

It drove me pretty crazy as well.

"This is sliding home in the very best way." I punctuated the last three words as they passed through gritted teeth.

"Fuck, Brayden." It came out a breathy whisper as she wound her legs back around me, digging her heels into my ass, as the last of her resistance gave way. "Harder."

"Jesus," I managed. I leaned over her, pressing my forehead against hers. "You sure?"

She nodded to me.

"Hold on to the edge."

For once, she did as she'd been told. Her hands grabbed ahold of the end of the desk. My hips got wild. She was gripping me from the inside out. Taking everything.

My cock and my heart.

I squeezed my eyes shut, trying to keep my shit together this time. She was making that mewling noise in the back of her throat that always made my balls burn.

"God, I've missed that sound."

It spurred me on. Harder. Faster. Till the desk started sliding back and forth, squeaking as the legs scraped against the old wood floor. As she began to pulse around me, the only voices filling my head were her string of soft chants.

"Don't stop. Don't stop." My new favorite words spilled from her mouth.

"Yes, yes, yes, yes . . ."

I'd wondered if the second time would feel different—less starving man, more average Joe. Last night, my senses had become hyperaware. When you're desperate and drowning, you count every breath. But the light of day didn't dull a thing. That feeling of frenzy cemented what I'd always known.

I'd never get enough of her.

I watched her ride out her release and then quickly followed, filling her up, with a reminder I wanted to slide down her legs for the rest of the day and a feeling I wanted her to need for the rest of her life.

My forehead stayed pressed to hers as we both came down from the high, panting against mingled breath. I brushed my mouth across hers, a soft contrast to the raw energy we'd just shared.

I slowly pulled out, just so I could see the sticky wetness trail behind me. Tracing a fingertip down the top of her inner thigh, I tried to fight off my worst caveman smile. She leaned up again, looking down at my hand. She blushed. All over her body.

Jesus, I loved that shit.

"Brayden, we need to think about—"

"No. Hush. We don't need to think right now. Stop with all the goddamn overthinking."

"This is just sex."

My brows shot up.

"Great sex," she added, rolling her eyes with a little smirk before she sobered again. "But that's all it is."

She pushed up off the desk, reaching down to retrieve her shorts.

"How long are you gonna go on telling yourself that?" I asked, watching her shimmy back into them.

She turned her back to me before she spoke, "For as long as it takes. Until you walk away again."

"Ashley—"

"That's all it can be, Brayden. We crippled our chance to ever be anything more."

CHAPTER 11
HAND OUT

ASHLEY

Happy hour hadn't officially started.

The hard-core clientele had another hour to slog their way through the weekend traffic crossing over the Bay Bridge. A few early birds were already stationed at the best tables near the deck rail. They nursed beers and sunburn beneath the cloak of bright red umbrellas with flaps that swayed gently in the breeze.

Trent, the lead singer of the house cover band, came over to chat while his buddies finished setting up their gear on the far corner of the deck. I dodged the hints he dropped about scoring the headliner slot for the marina's Labor Day party. I didn't have the heart to tell him that annual rite of passage into fall had no chance this year.

I knew people would be disappointed.

My mother had turned it into a well-loved tradition.

Last year, I'd lost my sanity and a couple grand, trying to pull it off.

I tried drowning my dejection with the mundane tasks of restocking liquor and wrapping napkins around silverware. The sound of a stool sliding back broke through my stupor. I did a double take when I saw Brayden's houseguest sitting casually near the end of the bar.

Mirrored aviators covered his eyes, but he didn't have a hat this time. His dark brown hair was cut neat and super short. A plain white polo and khaki shorts looked formal and crisp, fitted perfectly to a set of muscles no woman could ignore. His attire was oddly juxtaposed to the vibrant tattoos that fondled the inside of his forearm and crawled up under his sleeve.

I couldn't help the curiosity that bloomed inside me.

Who the hell is this guy?

I used a damp dishrag to wipe down the bar on my way over to him. That excuse let me approach slowly, sizing him up as I drew near. He had that same grin as before—friendly and welcoming, more little boy than man.

This guy was a study of contrasts I would've loved to photograph. Black-and-white film with just the ink on his skin lightly shaded into color. I itched for the challenge of capturing the hard strength of those muscles and the beguiling warmth of that smile.

I placed a little cardboard coaster in front of him and tried to return his grin. "Uh, hi. I know we haven't really . . . I mean, I'm Ashley."

He pulled off his glasses and set them on the bar.

His eyes matched his smile. They curved up at the edges and made you feel at home.

"Matt Sullivan. It's nice to finally meet you, Ashley. Officially."

He cleared his throat of the same awkwardness I was suffering. I shook his outstretched hand.

"Um, yeah. You, too. What can I get you?"

I poured the draft beer he'd requested, returning to set it down in front of him.

"So, you in town long? You work for the Yankees?"

"Me?" He chuckled low and deep. "No. Well, I used to work for a different kind of Yankees." He lifted his shirtsleeve to show a tattoo of a globe with an anchor and an eagle. Scrolling script encircled it.

"You're a Marine?"

"Ex-Marine now. Retired. I'm a physical therapist."

"Oh." My eyes widened with surprise I couldn't hide.

My brother had worked with dozens of PTs. None of them had looked like Matt Sullivan.

"I'm here for the summer. Stealing a little downtime and making sure the Yankees don't lose their shining star."

I returned an appropriate smile. Reminders about who Brayden had become still somehow felt like a punch in the gut.

"So, which do you like better? Being a soldier or soldiering through rehabbing athletes? I imagine you deal with some big egos, huh?"

"I don't know yet actually. Brayden is my first. We met a year and a half ago at a charity event for wounded vets. I was there with a guy from my old unit. Dude who was pretty busted up. Huge Yankees fan." He held his arms out wide and smiled. "Brayden was the rookie sensation everyone was talking about. He heard about my friend somehow. Visited him a bunch of times while he was rehabbing. Helped my buddy get his head straight, if you know what I mean."

I nodded. Half the battle of recovery happened between your ears. I knew that all too well.

Nathan always let his head get in the way.

"Anyway, I'd just gotten out of the service. And, by that, I mean, I was sitting on my butt, missing being a Marine." He paused and then added, "Once he found out my background, Brayden wanted to pick my brain about some stuff. We struck up a mutually beneficial friendship. He's the one who talked me into becoming an independent contractor, starting up my own practice. He forced me to pursue my passion."

"What's that?"

"Helping soldiers get back on their feet. I work with guys at Walter Reed."

"So, how did you end up here?"

"Brayden drives a hard bargain when he wants something really bad. He's sort of relentless."

"Yeah, I know something about being on the other end of that." I rolled my eyes.

He chuckled again. "He claims I was the first person he called the day after they scheduled his surgery. Said he needed someone to fix him. Had in mind he wanted to get out of town to do it. Asked me to come here for the summer." He rubbed the pad of his thumb across his bottom lip. "The check he wrote was mighty tempting. Then, he said he'd double down what he was paying me as seed money to start my own foundation. Couldn't say no to that. That money is gonna help a lot of people."

I nodded my head as I tried digesting a story so far from what I'd been expecting. I'd thought the guy was another meathead tied to Brayden's new world, not a gentle giant with a penchant for helping people.

"Is he gonna be all right? Can you fix him?"

"Brayden?"

I nodded.

"Healing the body is far easier than healing the mind." He sipped his beer and carefully set the glass back down, mulling over something he obviously wanted to add. "His arm I can work on fixing."

For just a moment, dark brown eyes seared into mine. Eyes well trained in the art of intimidation.

"His head? I don't know. You tell me."

When Matt Sullivan stopped smiling, the sun died. The sticky-sweet boy fell behind an eclipse of a serious man—the old-fashioned kind who walked with swagger, knew how to handle a gun, and always looked out for his friends.

My instinct didn't want him as an enemy.

But I didn't know how to respond.

Luckily, the boyish grin returned as quickly as it'd fled, and he didn't seem to expect an answer. "Don't take this the wrong way, but it's kinda weird to finally meet you in person. He's told me a lot about you and your family. You're sort of a legend in my mind already."

"Me?" My brows creased as I shook my head, further blowing off his assessment. "I'm a nobody, I assure you."

He toyed with the edge of his coaster. "I'm saying too much. Probably even violating some kind of patient confidentiality bullshit." He ran his hand across the small cleft in his chin. "Brayden's arm will be fine—if he follows instructions, which he has so far. This is my first Tommy John procedure, too, so we're both learning as we go along. But I'm very happy with his progress."

"Do you work with a lot of arm injuries?"

"No." His eyes locked on mine. "My specialty is SCI."

My eyes widened as that statement spread through me. "You . . . you mean, you . . . you work with spinal cord injuries?"

He studied my reaction. A tiny bit past the point of weird. "I usually work with guys who come home from the Middle East with busted up backs and missing limbs or legs that don't want to work anymore. We have too many of them, ya know? On the outside, those guys look like the rest of us mortals. But on the inside? On the inside, those guys are made of tougher stuff than the everyday Joe."

"God, that sounds incredibly hard . . ."

Watching Nathan struggle leveled me most days. How would anyone live, surrounded by the suffering of so many?

"Nah," he replied quickly, "I'm not the one doing the hard work. By the time they get to me, they've already been through hell. I'm the lucky one who gets to stand on the sideline while they learn new ways to climb out."

He made it sound so easy. So . . . possible.

Tears welled in my eyes. My mind fought off that thing again—that feeling I'd had while reading that magazine contract. It crawled up my back and sat on my shoulder, whispering in my ear like a morning bird full of excitement and . . . *hope*.

The only four letter word I hated more than *fine*.

I'd been taught one lesson while watching my mother battle hand-to-hand with death. Hope suffered many a fool. It deluded its victims with fabricated promise. It built up a pretty facade and then cruelly uncovered a fragile illusion. Hope lived as a paper-thin false front.

Easily crushed.

For us, hope had looked like alternative medicines, clinical trials, experimental treatments. A chance at life.

Reality?

Reality was three to six months. Morphine drips and feeding tubes.

I'd learned the hard way to hold hope with two iron fists, always pushed back to at least an arm's length.

Standing that far away from this guy suddenly didn't feel far enough.

Matt Sullivan spoke with a slow confidence and moved with a self-awareness that translated into pure power. Something about him invited trust. He was a natural protector. A giver. The kind of guy you couldn't help but like. A guy you instinctively wanted to be near because his very presence promised safety.

I needed to get far, far away from him.

To regroup and catch my breath.

To make sense of him—this smiling poster boy of possibility.

"Ashley, I know you're in a rough spot. But just be careful with him, okay? I don't think you understand how hard he's struggled to get back to this place."

Brayden and struggle seemed like an oxymoron. He lived a gilded life. Perfect and shiny. He probably ate hope for breakfast, mixed into a protein shake.

"Brayden? How hard he's struggled to get back to St. Michaels?" My eyes narrowed, and pride reared forward. "Is that a joke? His toughest choice was to fly here in a private jet or drive down in a two-hundred-thousand-dollar sports car. The whole town is googly-eyed over his triumphant return. They're ready to rename streets after him."

"I don't mean he had to fight to come back to this town. He had to fight to come back home to you." He paused, taking two breaths to let his statement ping-pong through my skull. "You know, it sucks when our own mistakes cost us things we want. I see it all the time. Big, strapping soldiers who were fine one minute. Out walking a post. Strong. Invincible. Saving the world. Everything going as planned. Then, boom. One step. One split-second decision." He snapped his fingers in the air. "IED takes away everything they knew."

"That's horrible," I whispered, bowing my head.

"It is. It's pretty fucking awful. But the only thing worse than taking that step and hurting yourself is taking that step and watching the fallout hurt someone else. Those are the guys who don't recover.

The ones who step on bombs and blow themselves up—those aren't the guys I worry about the most. Most of those guys work their asses off to form a new life. They still have that sense of fight in them. It's the guy who steps on the bomb that takes out his buddy walking next to him that I fear for the most. Those are the ones who don't want to live. They mentally check out, won't rebuild." He paused and then added softly, "They don't think they deserve to."

I gazed out across the deck, watching white sails on the horizon instead of the whites in his eyes.

"What about the guy who stepped on the bomb and walked away, unscathed? The one who found that new life and forgot the people he left behind to finish the battle?"

"No one walks away, unscathed. Guilt is a nasty motherfucker that eats you from the inside out."

I snickered. "Yeah, I know something about that, too."

Tears filled my eyes. I looked back down at my feet, fighting them off. Fighting off his words, too, because I didn't want them to seep inside me. Didn't want to consider their meaning.

I'd spent too many years thinking of Brayden as the bad guy. My accomplice in ruining my brother's life. I'd spent too much time thinking of him as the one who got to move on while the rest of us were stuck.

Bitterness became my best friend when my first love left town and never looked back.

"Don't mistake him not being here for walking away. I know it doesn't compare, but he lost something, too."

"He didn't lose anything. He's living the life we dreamed—" I stopped myself short. "He's living the life he, and his father, always dreamed of."

"He lost the thing that's the most important to him. His family. A man and woman he loved like they were his own parents. The only brother he ever had. And the girl who he would've died to protect." He paused, waiting until I looked up at his face. "The girl he'd still die to protect."

I blinked. Unable to form words now.

He downed the remaining swig of beer and pushed his stool back to stand up. He pulled his wallet from his back pocket.

"No," I said, holding up a hand, "this one's on me." My voice cracked.

He tipped his chin. "I'll owe you one." He turned halfway before pivoting back around. "You know, in basic training, they teach us a lot about dealing with battlefield injuries. When you're hurt, sometimes it's best to dress your own wounds and clean yourself up, before you reach a hand back and help the guy who fell beside you."

I bowed my head and bit my bottom lip, praying I could hold it all in. That I could stop myself from the epic breakdown that was coming now whether I liked it or not.

"Please don't hate me for saying too much. Honestly, I'm a good guy. I specialize in giving people second chances."

He smiled the same as before, back to the little boy who didn't play with such heavy things. The one he must've locked somewhere inside him, protected from the trauma and sadness he'd witnessed.

I tried to force the edges of my mouth into a smile as I met his gaze.

He opened his wallet, fished out a crisp white business card, and held it out over the bar. "If there's anything I can ever do for you, anything at all, all you have to do is ask."

"That's very nice of you," I said slowly, taking it from his hand.

"Once a Marine, always a Marine. Helping people is what we do." He leveled me with one more knowing stare. "And, if you know anyone else who could use my help, you just let me know. I owe you one now, remember?"

"I was driving past on my way home, saw the lights on down here . . ." My voice trailed off.

The wind tugged a swirl of hair across his forehead. I knew the exact length of time it would take to annoy him. I counted backward, waiting for three fingers from his left hand to swipe it back out of the way.

I didn't want to see Brayden differently. Too much of him

mirrored the boy I'd spent years trying to forget.

Joey's voice taunted me. "*He's different.*"

But, I stood there at the end of the dock, with lead feet and fresh eyes, trying to reconcile a merged version of that boy I'd known and the man Matt Sullivan had described.

"The kid and I went for a sunset sail earlier. He's starting to look like he knows what he's doing. Turns out, I might not suck at teaching." He smirked and leaned over the yacht rail. "It was too nice a night to just go straight home. Want to come aboard? Check her out firsthand?" He'd already started moving, walking toward the gangway with an outstretched palm.

A helping hand.

At the ready.

Free for the taking.

I stared at it with wide eyes. Did I trust it? Did I take ahold of it and just let my pride and my anger go? Could I learn to accept any of the things he'd offered?

Tangled emotions and those cement feet held me in place. I was stuck again, hiding out from dealing with heavy decisions I didn't want to make. I'd spent so many months—so many years really—with no choices at all, with little control over the path I had to take.

Now, there were suddenly too many.

His fingers curled slightly, like his body sensed my hesitation and knew to silently coax me forward. His hand held there, steady against the dark night, just waiting for me to clasp ahold of it.

Would the strings attached, take me in and shelter me, or suck me into the undertow and leave me drowning all over again?

I'd been asking the same question ever since he arrived.

Why are you here?

Maybe I finally had an answer.

"Ash?"

"Did you bring him here for Nathan?" The words rushed out as I stepped closer to him, beginning to walk up the metal plank with determined fists clenched by my sides. I hadn't even provided a name, but Brayden's eyes softened with acknowledgment as they studied me. His hand hovered in the air, still offered freely, but also prepared to grab hold without permission if I fell.

Protection—even when I hadn't asked or wanted it.

"Yes."

We took three steps toward one another with the slow motion of a magnetic pull.

My lips parted in surprise. "That's why you want to see him. You want to talk Nathan into working with Matt."

"I've already had a work crew gut Ginger's boathouse. I'm turning it into a new space. Part of my deal with Matt. The boathouse and the guesthouse are both going to be remodeled. He's gonna use them as a retreat for patients who need a place to hit reset. I'm just the guinea pig. I'm gonna use it till my arm is back to full strength."

His fingers curled again, instinctively reacting to me moving closer still.

"I intend for your brother to be his first real patient."

My hand reached out without further thought. Fingers interlaced with his, doubling my strength, as Brayden pulled me all the way toward him. His arm wrapped around my shoulders as he guided me the last steps onto the massive deck.

A bird cried overhead.

That same morning song rang in my ears.

A lullaby about paper wings.

"Welcome aboard."

BRAYDEN

She came back the next night.

And some of the nights that followed.

I started planning my day around the sinking sun. Every evening, she made a final sweep, checking to ensure every boat was tucked in and tied down and that overnighters had what they needed. I made sure not to miss it. I would stand at the rail of *Toward Happiness*, trying to look casual, holding a can of PBR that washed down with the taste of adolescence and old friendships.

I finally coaxed her aboard a second time with some lame excuse cast on the end of a hook. After that, we settled into a pattern.

We had dinner one night. Bad Chinese out of cardboard cartons. The noodles stuck to our chins and the ends of flimsy wooden chopsticks. She accepted a chilled glass of chenin blanc after a day that wore heavy across her face and shoulders. I desperately wanted to ask, to bear some of the load, but I didn't push.

I needed to learn her all over again.

The new her.

She kept coming to me. Meeting me halfway. I had to keep playing things just right. Had to call upon the skills in my arsenal.

People generally thought of my arm as my greatest weapon— the reason for my success. But that was a crock of shit, supplied by amateurs who'd never stood alone on a mound of dirt. My success hinged upon one thing—my ability to study opponents, to crawl inside their heads, learn their greatest weakness, and then use it against them.

I studied batters. Every single one. Their stride to the plate. Their spit trajectory. The way they tapped the bat against the bottom of their shoe.

I saw my catcher's fingers splayed between his thighs, flexing impatiently, waiting for my nod. His sign came from the encyclopedia he kept tucked inside his head. Catch knew if the batter swung flat or could take a curve for a ride. He knew if a guy craved heat or always took the first ball. In the back of my mind, I knew the same things.

We watched the same tape.

So did the coaches who would stand on the periphery, tugging on ears and swiping hands across aged bellies. They all thought they knew better.

But the secret between throwing a ball or a strike lay behind the one thing none of them could ever see. The one thing I always had.

A batter's eyes.

Eyes tattletale. They give up the covert story, the whole library of human emotion. From sixty feet out, I could predict batting averages based solely on cockiness or fear. Then, I used that knowledge to craft my approach.

I had to do the same thing with Ashley now.

My favorite green eyes were still filled with the same defiance and pride as the independent little cuss who'd once made me stand on the side of the road and watch her struggle to change a flat. That same girl, who'd ridden away from me with too many books in her basket, still didn't want to accept my help.

She didn't want to need it.

I understood why. It was a bitch of a thing to need the help of someone whose missteps had wrecked your life. I'd worn those same shoes when I woke up that first morning *after*.

Day one on my countdown.

After the accident, that first morning home from the hospital, I woke up to find my father sitting at the kitchen table. He was disheveled from a lack of sleep and aged by worry. A blank legal pad sat in front of him along with two business cards and an orange sticky note covered in girlie handwriting I knew too well.

"What are you doing?" I asked.

"Wondering where the hell we go from here," he answered.

I was still working off that page. That lined paper we sat and filled with a new plan. My father's bottom line inevitably ended with the same dream—getting me to that anointed mound of dirt with a pin-striped jersey on my back. His mistakes had warped my whole life, but I agreed to accept his help and keep following his dreams.

I just never told him about the things I added later.

Things I copied from a different sheet of lined paper.

My own penciled-out dreams were still far from realized, but now, every time Ashley climbed aboard, I knew I was finally getting closer to happiness.

The fucking boat was aptly named.

I'd come this far. Gotten this close. I could feel her skin, smell her hair, taste her on my lips again. But Ashley's eyes told me not to push. They held me back with a force she didn't know she had. By sheer size, I could easily overpower her. But there she stood, still pint-size, still holding my nuts and my heart in a vise.

This girl could crush me. She had before.

Whether she knew it or not.

Those first few weeks after the accident, my father wouldn't leave me alone with my shoelaces. That was when the need for a magic pill had burned so deep beneath my skin, I finally knew I had a problem. I pined for her. Grieved for her. Begged for her.

Wanted to die without her.

Since I was little, people who watched me play always said I had superhuman strength. But adapting to a life without Ashley taught me just how much I'd always leaned.

Blowing out my arm, losing the only other thing that mattered, was the final piece falling into place. A stark reminder that I couldn't do life without them both. The weakness of injury finally prodded me toward the strength I always needed.

Her.

She thought she didn't want my help. I knew I had to have hers. Her mother's strength lived deep inside her. I wondered if she even knew she had it.

When she came aboard each night, I didn't make her talk. It felt like progress, just coexisting in the same space.

Most nights, she left with a suddenness that broke me. One minute, everything felt perfect, and the next, she was bolting for the dock and mumbling goodbyes behind eyes riddled with guilt.

I moved around her in orbit. In my mind, I kept my arms held out wide, caging her from bolting like a newborn colt with faculties not yet in sync. I stayed loose. Didn't pressure, or push, or force myself on her again.

I sensed her need for extra time, and so long as she kept coming back, I didn't mind giving in to it for a while.

Slow and steady wasn't half bad when you weren't going it all alone.

"This thing probably has five staterooms and fifteen couches. Why are we lying on the deck?"

I adjusted the pillow behind my neck. I'd scattered a half-dozen of them, plucked from the nearby loungers, to make a soft bed on top of the glossy teak floor.

"This is the best spot to see them." I lifted my hand, drawing my index finger across the dark sky.

"What are you doing?"

"Tracing Hercules."

"The constellation? Is he what you used to look at through that fancy telescope Grams gave you?"

"Yeah. He's one of my favorites."

"Where is he?"

My palm wrapped around the back of her smaller hand, loosely extending her arm beneath my own. Overlapping fingertips pointed into the night. She let me guide her, etching a path across the stars, connecting the dots to form a man.

"Why do you like him?"

"We have a lot in common," I replied softly.

"Overly muscle-bound? Wielding a big bat?" She giggled.

I wanted to bottle the sound.

"Chauvinist much?" she added.

"He's not what people think," I answered quietly.

My fingers slid down her arm, leaving a lazy path of goose bumps. I turned my head on the pillow, drawing her hand down to my chest, as I stared into her eyes.

"He was a bastard. Zeus screwed around on his wife with a mortal chick. Made him. Hercules wasn't even his real name. He was cursed, went a little nuts, did some real bad shit. Was sent away for years. Had to complete twelve tasks to atone for his sins. People think of him as a hero now, his name is synonymous with strength. But he had sort of a shady underlayer. A genesis and past mistakes he wanted to leave behind him."

She curled onto her side, inching closer to me on the makeshift bed of pillows. Letting me lean as she soaked in my words.

"I missed this in New York."

"Missed what?" she whispered back.

My fingertips stroked the back of her hand, forcing her palm to loosen. I pressed it flat against the thumping inside my chest. Our eyes collided as unspoken words passed between us. A gentleness settled over me that felt like old times. Back before everything. Before the really good times. Before the really bad ones, too.

Back when things had been simple.

I swallowed against the ache in my throat and the sting in my eyes. Being with her like this turned me into a fucking basket case. If she walked away from me again, these were the moments I knew would haunt me.

"The stars," I finally answered. "You can't see them very well in the city. Too many tall buildings, too many lights soaking up the dark. I always knew I missed seeing them, but I'd forgotten just how bright they were here. The memory was half as beautiful as the real thing."

My eyes never left hers.

I made sure they told my tale, openly revealing I wasn't talking about the damn night sky.

"Brayden," she said my name like a whisper, barely cloaked by need.

She felt it, too. All of it. That same frustration. I wanted to give in to it. I wanted to devour every inch of her. With my eyes first and then with my hands. I could feel my lids droop under the heaviness of lust. My dick begged for denied attention.

She inched closer to me again.

Millimeters sprouted into measured giants.

"I missed you, Soot. So much."

Her hand startled, pulling away from my chest. I clutched on to it, unable and unwilling to let her go.

"Don't. Don't run. I'm trying real damn hard not to scare you away."

Her shoulders relaxed, and her hand fell limp beneath my own. "If I run, you'll just chase me down, won't you? You'll use that freaky tractor-beam thing to suck me right back in."

Half of my mouth twisted into a smirk. "You finally get that, huh?"

She nodded in response.

I bent toward her, resting my forehead against hers. "Don't make me run after you tonight. Stay. Just a little longer. Let me hold you. When was the last time you let yourself lean on anyone? For just a little while, let's stare up at these damn stars and forget about everything before this night."

"Like this is our first date?" Her breath fanned across my cheek, lips so close to my own. "Like we just met?"

"Fuck yeah." My lips rested against the edge of her hairline, brushing lightly back and forth, as my arms circled her. I drew her into my chest and held my breath, waiting to see how she would respond to tenderness.

Slowly, an arm gently encircled my waist.

I tried to hide my sigh of relief.

"I'm Ashley," she said softly. "But most people are lazy and just call me Ash."

Her words echoed in my head. She'd spoken them with the voice of a grown woman, but they conjured images of the girl with freckles and pigtails, boldly sitting in my seat as she made the same introduction.

"It's nice to meet you," she added.

"I'm Brayden," I replied, playing along.

Her smile tickled my neck. "I know. Everyone knows who you are. You're a big superstar. I've seen your picture in all the magazines. With fancy models and movie actresses."

"Nope. You're wrong. People say I look like him, but I'm no one special. Just a guy. I saw you walking along the dock earlier and had to know who you were. You're the most beautiful thing I've ever seen."

Her little fist lightly punched me in the side. "You always lay it on this thick on the first date?"

"Nah. But I've never wanted to have a second date this badly."

She nestled in closer, her hand fisting the back of my shirt. We lay there in amiable silence, listening to night sounds and each other's breath. Dampness against my skin and the uneven rise and fall of her back beneath my hands alerted me to the sudden change.

"Ash?" I pulled back, smoothing her hair away from wet cheeks. "I'm pretty sure Joey has hard and fast rules about crying on a first date," I added quietly.

A sad little smile made the tears well up and spill faster down her skin. I swept them with the pads of my thumbs.

"I just . . ." She huffed out a breath and pulled farther back from me. "It's just so much. All at once. I feel . . . so overwhelmed." The back of her hand swiped angrily at her cheek. "God, I'm just being stupid. I haven't let myself . . . I don't usually cry like this anymore."

"Maybe that's the problem. Let me be the shoulder for a while."

"I have to stand on my own, Brayden. Life's made that abundantly clear too many times."

"You've been doing this alone for too long. Leaning doesn't mean you're weak. It means you're strong enough to ask for help."

Her brows furrowed as she looked at me, sarcastically bemused.

"Where'd you learn all that fancy crap?"

I laughed and used the lightness of the moment to pull her back to me. "Rehab. Followed by hours upon hours of therapy."

My laugh rumbled in my chest. A shaky breath and sigh combined as she settled back against me.

She let me hold her. She let herself cry. Let that release valve open just enough to share some of the bottled up pain.

I stared up at Hercules and tried cutting that bastard a deal. I begged him to send me some strength for the feats I still had left to conquer.

I would do whatever it took. I'd hurdle anything and everything that stood between me and a million more nights like this.

ASHLEY

The only way to survive grief is to block things out.

That's the gift given by time. You don't ever forget; you just shove the memories that hurt the most into back corners and onto the top shelves of your mind. You learn to cram them in, using your back and all remaining strength to shut them inside. Then, you spend each day praying they don't tumble out when something random accidentally cracks the closet door back open.

I hadn't forgotten how good it felt to lay, protected, in Brayden's arms. I'd just squelched down the memory of the way those big arms could wrap all the way around me, the way my tears could easily fall and dry, absorbed by his skin and the rough cotton of his shirt.

I cried for those losses.

And for all the nights like this one that we never had.

Eventually, my eyes ran dry. The tiny hiccups in my chest subsided, and I let one more recollection out of the dark cupboard. It wouldn't be allowed to stay for long, but maybe, for a while, I could let myself remember what it felt like to love him. To rely on him.

My fingers found the hem of his shirt. They lightly scraped beneath it, against chiseled skin and the tiny patch of coarse hair. His breathing changed. A deep inhale, followed by a chest that expanded and then held unnaturally still.

After the rough sex on my desk, he'd backed way off. The crude suggestions, the open wickedness, and teasing caresses had given way to something softer and gentler. Part of me despised it. Not just because I hated to admit I liked that side of him, but also because I knew him too well. Knew why he was doing it.

He wanted to lure me in. Again.

I still didn't want to give in to him, but maybe I could give in to myself for a little while. I'd learned to pack away my feelings once. I could do it again when I had to.

"What are the rules about hooking up on the first date?" My fingers climbed up farther beneath his shirt, spreading across warm, tight skin.

He sucked in a breath between clenched teeth. "There are exceptions to every rule."

I skimmed up over hard pecs. Across a galloping heart.

"Are you seeing anyone else?" I played along, role-playing my way through the question I didn't want to ask. I hadn't forgotten the girl on his phone at two in the morning. I'd just tucked her image in a box, double-sealed with packing tape, shoved high up behind winter boots and mismatched mittens.

I'd fought off the urge to Google him. To find out for myself how her face linked to his name. I'd seen the pain of those investigations too many times. I could still picture him, a younger Brayden, tethered to his father by a search engine query and a gossip rag post. I could imagine him, seated at a computer, seeing his mother's face for the very first time.

I wouldn't fall into the same trap myself. Not knowing was the best possible answer. But, even playing out this role, I hated thinking of myself as the other woman.

I'd walked in on that once, too.

I didn't ever want to be her.

He scoffed at my notion. "Of course not."

I couldn't tell between truth and playing along. It didn't matter. Most likely, she was one of many. The Prince of Gotham probably had a vast array of hearts in his collection. She probably sat in his display case with all his other shiny toys.

His hands splayed across my back, dropped down over my waist, and then squeezed my ass through the thin cotton of my dress. They heated my skin and expertly forced me toward making my next move in the game.

The flip side of weakness is strength. Where you find one, you can always dig deep to find the other.

Giving in didn't have to make me fragile. I could take solace for just a little bit and then stand strong enough to let it float away. I wouldn't become a puppet if I kept holding all the strings.

My foot tangled with his and then toed up the inside of his calf until my inner thigh hitched across his hip. His fingers dug into me harder.

"Make love to me, Brayden." The words came out so softly, they almost got lost in the breeze blowing across our nest of pillows.

"Goddamn, I thought you'd never ask."

He rolled on top of me in one swift motion, like he'd been standing at the ready for those words his whole life. His elbows bent at the sides of my head, caging me in. Our eyes searched one another, opponents suddenly placed on the home team.

My head turned to the right. I gently leaned over to place my lips against the jagged red scar on his inner arm, kissing away the hurt. He drew in a deep breath. As soon as my head turned back, his lips crashed down onto mine, and his lower half pressed down against me.

My hands found the back of his neck, nails digging into flesh. His hands responded in kind against my hips, drawing my dress up around my thighs. His lips trailed wet kisses down the side of my neck, over my collarbone, and to the top of my breasts that peaked over the hem of the scoop neck. It was held in place by a string that laced up the front and tied in a bow. He pressed up onto an elbow again, staring down at me with glistening lips and hooded eyes. A hand tugged on the end of the string, unraveling me in more ways than one. He plucked at the laces, slowly loosening them, revealing cleavage as he went.

"I've missed this, too. God, how I've missed this."

"My boobs?" My laugh stalled as his index finger traced a straight line between my breasts.

"No. Little sundresses that skim across your thighs and barely hold in these tits. Pale cotton against sun-kissed freckles. Fucking teases the hell out of me. My dick burns to get to what's underneath. All those stupid women out there, wearing skintight dresses that hide nothing. So dumb. You. Right here. Right now. This is the sexiest thing in the world to me."

He pulled my dress all the way open, letting it gape down the front to expose the white lace of my demi cup bra. My hands instinctively reached to cover myself. The mention of all those fancy women out there, the ones who'd shared morphed names and magazine covers, left me feeling simple and plain. The Hollywood actress probably wore brand names Joey would drool over. Surely, the European lingerie model did.

"I don't think all your women wear bras from Target."

Harsh eyes scolded me. His hands pushed mine away.

"Do you know how many nights I've closed my eyes and prayed I'd fall into a dream about these tits? Prayed my mind would let me relive sucking on your nipples till you arched up off the mattress and begged for my dick? I don't care what the fuck they're wrapped up in so long as it comes off easily."

He demonstrated by gruffly tearing at the cups, pressing the lacy fabric down underneath my flesh so that it plumped up, standing at attention, ready for him to make good on what he'd described.

It didn't take long.

"That's it. Just like that," he said, teasing, as his fingertips traced down the arch in my spine.

"Brayden, I need . . ."

"I know, baby girl. I know exactly what you need. You've just gotta learn to trust that again."

He pulled himself up, kneeling between my legs in one swift motion that left the cool night air dancing across heated skin.

"What—"

My protest was interrupted by forceful hands that jerked my dress down my body. I sat up to meet him halfway, reaching back to unclip my bra, desperate to have my skin against his as quickly as possible. All my doubts and fears were gagged and stuffed away in that closet, back behind the happy memories of moments like this that I'd temporarily exposed under the moonlight.

As soon as my upper half was bare, I fumbled for the hem of his shirt, tugging at it with disdain, until he used one hand to lift it off with a simple pull from the back of the neck. Copper muscles ribboned under my hands. He shivered as my fingernails grazed down, across his sides to the V of muscles that bunched above his hip bones. I cupped him through his shorts.

"Now, Ash. I gotta get inside you right now. I'm gonna take it so fucking slow tonight, but I need you around my cock as fast as humanly possible."

His words spurred our hands. They tangled together, coaxing his belt open, and then teamed up to push his clothes down over his hips. As they fell to the ground, he stood, pulling me up with him. My arms wound around his shoulders, already well versed in his next move.

Expected hands lifted my ass, forcing my legs to wrap around him, pressing us together in places that drew groans from both of us. He walked us backward toward a plush banquet seat that stretched across the stern. He sat with me straddling him, his cock pressing impatiently against my belly.

I turned to glance over my shoulder, checking for eyes lurking through the night. The marina was sadly quiet these days, but the deck rail didn't give total privacy from the few who might wander by. Some overnighters would stroll into town for dinner and drinks and then come back to crash in their staterooms. And Logan lived in the little apartment above the maintenance shed.

"No one can see us," Brayden murmured against my lips.

I pulled back and looked up, drawing his mouth onto the pulse of my neck. The stars overhead met my gaze.

"You forgot about your buddy Hercules."

"That dude's a perv. Told you he and I had a lot in common." His lips smiled against mine. "Let's give him a show."

He hoisted me up like a feather, positioned me just right, and then pulled against my hips so I easily slid back down, impaled on his cock.

His chest heaved as fingertips dug into the fleshy skin at the top of my ass. "Swear to fucking God, that takes my breath away every single time. There is no place on earth like the inside of your pussy." He leaned back on his forearms and tore his gaze from my bouncing breasts to look up at the sky. "Be jealous, motherfucker."

BRAYDEN

"Stay with me tonight. We can sleep right here. The commute to work in the morning will be amazing."

"I can't."

"Ash, please."

My fingers trailed down the inside of her thigh, still slick from both of us. I'd lost track of the number of times I made her come. I'd been a man on a mission. I had an insatiable need to banish her memories of anyone else who had come between then and now. I could only do that by giving her some new ones.

Ones she couldn't walk away from so easily.

Tonight felt different than the times before. Those had been about stealing what we needed. Filling a burning desire that had to be quenched. But tonight had been more about giving than taking.

She'd pressed her hips forward, meeting my every thrust. Our fingers stayed clasped over her head as we drove toward that first release, our eyes locked on one another.

Open.

Vulnerable. That was the difference.

I could fucking feel it in every breath we'd shared. That barrier Ashley always left between us came down for a little while. Her anger and reluctance had been stuffed down. She'd stayed out of want instead of need.

Tonight, with every breathy gasp, every plea for deeper strokes, every muttered curse, we'd chipped away at one more brick in that wall.

I didn't want to let that feeling go. I didn't want her to walk away and force me to fight to get back to this place all over again tomorrow.

There was still an air of bittersweet between us. That scent that lingers when no one knows if it's the last time.

Before tonight, the last time we'd made love and had time to linger in each other's arms, was at the boathouse, a dozen nights before the one that sealed our fate. I was still sweaty from practice. She said she didn't care . . .

"You'd better hush up and fuck me right now. I've been waiting for you all afternoon. I was about to give up and resort to my own hand." She stripped off her clothes and held out her arms.

A sassy little witch with perfect nipples. Her fingers trailed down her belly to tease me.

"Now, Brayden. Right here. Up against the wall. Hurry."

"I don't want to hurry. My whole damn life is in a hurry right now. You're the one thing I'm gonna do real damn slow."

I ate her out till she was on the cusp of pulling out all my hair. She'd thrashed around like a banshee every time I stopped. Eventually, I'd given her a release. Then I'd spent the rest of the night teasing her till her pussy screamed around my cock.

Over the years, I'd replayed that night in my mind a million times. I could remember the exact outfit she'd left rumpled on the floor. I could remember the smell of coconut on her skin, the lime-green nail polish on her toes and the twisted braid in her hair. Every detail had crystallized.

I didn't want this night to end, because, in the back of my mind, I fucking feared this would turn out like that.

A night I held on to in the dark.

All alone.

My fingers traced through her folds, soaked from our love.

She swatted at my hand. "Swear to God, there's no way I can possibly go again. We've already broken the world record."

"We have a lot of time to catch up on." I pushed past her hand again, zeroing in on her clit. Slow, soft circles.

"Brayden, I have to go. I should've been home hours ago."

"One more."

"I can't."

"I don't know that word. I don't do *can't*. And, now, you know you've thrown down a challenge I have to accept. If I make you come again, you have to agree to something."

"Lord. What do I have to agree to?"

"That second date."

My lips trailed across the length of her neck and down over breasts, flushed deep pink from over attention and the scruff on my jaw. She arched up as I scraped my chin across the skin of her belly, descending past her oversensitive clit. I sank to my knees on the side of the banquet seat, looking up at her with a shit-eating grin.

"Brayden." She said it like a protest, but her thighs clasped around my head as soon as I buried my face between them, flattening my tongue against her. The quick flicks back and forth brought her nails scratching into my scalp.

That shit drove me insane.

"You know better than to challenge me with this, baby. You know I can always make you come this way."

I thrust two fingers inside her, curling them forward till she arched up again. Her cunt squeezed me.

It wasn't even a challenge.

"Second date, Ash. A real one. Dinner at the Inn. A ridiculously expensive bottle of wine. A slow walk in the moonlight by the water, and you and me falling asleep in my bed. Naked and spent. After we've broken tonight's record."

"Brayden, I . . . this can't go on. I can't . . ."

"There's that word again."

My fingers curled again as my tongue worked to drive that word right out of her.

CHAPTER 13
FORBIDDEN

ASHLEY

"You're home awfully late."

My palm pressed to my chest, barely containing my shocked gasp. "God, you scared the shit out of me, Nathan. Why are you sitting in the dark like a creeper?"

I flipped on the lamp beside the couch.

He didn't respond. A half-dozen empty Coors Light cans littered the table beside him. Another sat open in his hand, providing all the answer I needed to what he'd been doing all night long. He was sporting dirty sweatpants, a ratty T-shirt, and a three-day-old beard.

He hadn't left the house since last Tuesday.

"Where've you been?" he asked. He had that tone. The accusatory one that convicted without trial.

"I was at Foxy's. Susie called in sick. I went to fill in for her."

I hated lying. But the words fell from my lips with almost no effort. An old habit. Little white lies spread like warmed butter, so easy and tempting.

"Pretty dressed up for work."

My hand smoothed down the front of the cotton sundress I knew held wrinkles across the back. I wondered if my eyes were still starstruck or if my cheeks were still beard-stung and flushed.

"It was last minute. I didn't want to pull a shift in my grungy stuff from the marina. I walked over to Joey's and borrowed this from her."

"I called your phone. Three times."

"It died. I forgot to charge it last night."

Another lie. My phone was at the bottom of my purse somewhere. I'd been otherwise engaged and never heard it ring.

I was a bad sister. A horrible person. What if he'd fallen out of his chair? What if he'd had a migraine and he couldn't find the medicine? I always answered when he called me at work.

One night with Brayden, and I was already shirking responsibility, acting like someone I didn't have the luxury of being anymore. A carefree young girl who had time for love and stargazing. I'd spent my whole night caught in an old fairy tale.

He raised the can to his lips, sipping as he stared over the lid at me. I turned away and started back toward the kitchen, trying to escape the need to continue my deceit.

"I know he's here."

My hand gripped the white molding of the doorframe.

"Did you think I was too stupid to figure it out?" His tone snapped like a whip. "My legs don't work, but my ears function just fine. Whole damn town is in an uproar. The hero has finally returned home."

I half-turned, keeping my traitorous eyes focused on the chipped oak planks lining the floor. I could still feel Brayden's hands all over me. His scent surely lingered on my skin.

"You weren't gonna tell me, huh? You've seen him, haven't you? Were you with him tonight?"

"What? No." My voice faltered. "I told you, I was at work."

"Mm-hmm."

"What's that supposed to mean?"

"It means, I know you've seen him."

I swallowed and finally met his gaze. "I've run into him. He sought me out. Not the other way around."

"What does that jackass possibly have to say to you?"

I licked my lips and prepared to dive. This was what I'd been hoping to avoid. This dose of guilt. It weighed on my shoulders, as heavy still as that very first night in the hospital. "He's said a lot, Nathan. He knows about the mess we're in. He wants to help."

"Oh God. That's fucking comical." He threw his head back and snickered. The can lifted to his lips as he swallowed down my news. "We wouldn't be in this mess if it weren't for him. I would've gone off to college. Might have been playing minor league ball now. Dad wouldn't be drunk and hiding out who knows where. And Mom would still be alive."

"Jesus, Nathan. Brayden didn't give Mom cancer."

"He's what started the chain of bad luck. He upended every plan this family had. And at what cost? His life didn't change. He ran off and left a wake of destruction. I hold him responsible. For all of it."

"And me, too, right? Say it, Nathan. Just say it. You hold me responsible, too."

He shook his head and drained the rest of his beer before crushing the empty can in his fist.

"That new yacht at the marina is his." There was no way I could uncover just how far I'd fallen back into Brayden's web, but coming clean about taking some of his money checked one lie off the list.

"Fuck. Of course it is," he replied sarcastically.

"He's trying to help. He's . . . made other offers . . . things that would help dig us out from underneath—"

"Oh, I'm sure he wants to help. I'm sure he wants to ride back in here and save the day. Throw around his money, sign some autographs, and maybe fuck you a time or two, for old time's sake, before he sails back off into the spotlight with a clear conscience."

I stared back down at my feet. There was no use in trying to add any more fuel to the fire. I knew this would be my brother's reaction. Knew him finding out would send him into a downward spiral.

I'd left the marina riding too high.

I had to pay the price for that now.

"Has he?"

"Has he what?" I asked.

"Already made his play for you. He has, hasn't he? Don't lie to me."

"I'm not stupid. I see Brayden for what he is."

"As if." He snickered. "You never did. Whatever. Go ahead and let him have his way. Act like a filthy slut and spread your legs for him again. He'll use you and then break your heart all over again. We both know it."

"Shut up, Nathan. Just . . . shut up, okay? I'm not letting anyone do anything to me."

My thoughts didn't match my words. He was making me feel foolish and feeding into the insecurities that I'd just started to squelch down in my mind.

"You'd just better damn well be smart enough to realize you and this town are small potatoes to him now. He doesn't give a damn about you. He has way bigger and better things to go back to. Sweet, small-town girls like you have no business tangling with people like him. You two aren't cut from the same cloth anymore. And don't start thinking that he's some superhero who can fix all our problems. That's a line of shit. Probably like the lines of crap he pumps into his body."

He meant it as a dig toward Brayden, but in the back of my mind, I was still listening to Coral Lynn tell me I'd never be enough. I was still seeing her standing beside the bed, half-naked, hurling, *I told you so*, at me from across the room.

His words opened the door and let those memories tumble down on top of my head. I couldn't stuff them back inside all at once.

"He's here because he needs a backup plan, Ashley Jane. That's all this is. Got himself hurt and finally stepped out of the spotlight long enough to realize he has nothing else in his life. No one there to give two shits about him. He's not looking for redemption. He needs a crutch. That's all you'll ever be to him, Ash. Someplace safe to fall."

I sucked in a breath, watching my earlier happiness slip away in tattered shreds.

"He's different, Nathan," I said quietly. "Maybe you should talk to him. He wants to see you. I told him no, but maybe I was wrong. Maybe it would be good for you."

"I want him gone."

"Nathan—"

"No. Stay away from him."

"He brought someone I think you need to talk—"

His hand violently smacked down onto the table beside him, silencing me. "I don't want him, or anyone he knows, anywhere near our family. Do you understand me? I think you owe me that much, don't you?"

He'd never mentioned it that way before. Not once. My culpability in the whole disaster. He'd never directly placed the blame at my feet. Not that he needed to. I already felt it lying there like shackles.

"You asked something of me once. And I did it for you. Without question. Well, now, it's my turn. Stay away from him. I can't carry you now. I won't be around to pick you up off the ground when he breaks you again. We're done with him. All of us. Make sure he knows that. He needs to turn right back around and get the fuck out of this town. That's what I want. Him. Gone. The whole damn town knows *he* owes me that much."

"Ten more."

"You trying to kill me, man?"

"Haven't you heard? If it doesn't nearly kill you, it won't make you stronger. Ten more. Quit being such a pussy."

I'd shouted for Brayden all through the house but acquired nothing for my trouble. His car sat in the driveway. A cup of coffee remained on the counter, still lukewarm to the touch. He had to be home.

After the house proved fruitless, I'd wandered down the path, too numb to think about the last time I'd taken those same steps. My bare just feet kept moving, one in front of the other.

I hadn't been near Ginger's boathouse in years. The outside looked the same, aside from the fresh pot of white impatiens next to the front door that I'd let myself inside.

Like Brayden's old bedroom, nothing remained the same. Gone were the bodies and the pumping bass. The couches and chairs, the lamps and drywall. Everything was gone. The entire space had been cleared out, gutted right down to the studs. One massive room remained, renewed, with windows that looked out over calm, crystal water.

It was breathtaking and disorienting at the same time.

So was the man, half-naked from the waist up, down on a mat doing one-armed push-ups. His back glistened with sweat, muscles coiled around every square inch of him, jacked up from exertion.

"That's it. Three more. You've got this." Matt jotted notes down on a clipboard and then added, "This is even better than yesterday. You're stronger than you think."

I watched, mesmerized, fighting against the gravity that naturally pulled my body toward Brayden's. I searched for any mark I might have left on him the night before, any sign I'd managed to leave behind showing he was mine again, for a little while.

Now, I had to give him back. To his new life.

To all the other women with their skintight dresses and French-made lingerie. To the girl on his phone at two in the morning.

The last time I'd done this, I'd meant every word, but hope always lingered somewhere in the back of my childish mind. Hope that, somehow, someday, he'd return, and things would work out.

That's the wretched thing about hope. Even when you pledge not to subscribe to it, it crawls in through the seams, back into a fragile heart it can crush all over again.

This time had to be for real.

This time had to be for good.

"You have to go." My words fell out on his final repetition.

He stalled halfway up. Matt swung around to stare at me, clearly surprised he hadn't heard me come in. He probably wasn't a guy people got a jump on very often. He assessed my disheveled appearance, finally staring down at my bare feet.

I hadn't even combed my hair. I never managed sleep. My pillowcase hadn't absorbed my tears as well as Brayden's shirt. I was still clad in pajama shorts and a braless tank top. I'd crawled out of bed, desperate to get this over and done.

Before I had another minute to regret it.

Brayden lifted himself off the floor with ease, but he grunted and stretched his right arm across his chest to alleviate obvious discomfort.

"You have to go. Today," I repeated.

"Go where, baby girl?" He smiled as he accepted a towel Matt thrust out toward him.

"This is a nice surprise." Brayden looked at Matt as he wiped the sweat from his face. "This part of the training? You knew I wouldn't wimp out if I had an audience."

"Brayden." My voice cracked.

A look of alarm replaced his smile as he finally picked up on my tone. Both men stared at me, suddenly on alert.

"What's wrong?"

"You have to leave St. Michael's. As soon as possible. You can't stay here."

Matt looked back and forth between us. "Uh, I'm gonna go fix up some breakfast. Keep stretching it out." He tapped the clipboard against the side of Brayden's shoulder and smiled at me with a sad nod as he took his leave.

I bowed my head and stared at my feet until the front door latched shut. "He knows you're here."

Silence filled the space between us, bubbling up with the same discomfort as my words. He walked to a bench on the side of the room and guzzled down half a bottle of water.

With his back to me, he finally spoke, "That's good. It's time for us to sit down and talk, face-to-face."

"He doesn't want you here, Brayden. He wants you to leave. Immediately. He forbid me to see you anymore."

"Jesus Christ. He forbid you?" He quickly rounded on me, anger spreading where that smile had been. "You have to let me see him."

"No."

"Ashley, I'm not walking away. I can't. I won't do it again. Don't even think about asking me to."

"I'm not asking, Brayden. I'm telling you. You can't stay here. And we can't see each other anymore."

"Bullshit. You're not a child. He can't make your decisions for you. Tell me that's what *you* want. No lies, Ashley. No bullshit. Tell me *you* want me to go, and I'll consider leaving."

I squeezed my eyes shut as I turned my back on him. I couldn't face any more white lies today.

"The sex was great. Last night was fun. But you're delusional if you think it was anything more. It's over now. I've had my fill. You should go back to the city. Get on with your life. Let me get on with mine."

The water bottle was hurled against the far wall, hitting with a pop. He strode to me, gripping my arms, spinning me around like a top. He shook me hard as his thumbs pressed into both my biceps, marking me.

"You're fucking lying. I don't think you've ever lied to me. Why are you starting now?"

My tears welled up as I finally looked at him. It was a bad move. The desolation in his eyes nearly struck me to my knees. His hands cupped my cheeks, fingertips digging into my hairline. I thought for a moment he was going to kiss me, but his brows creased again with anger.

"How long does he get to control you? How many dreams do you have to give up to pay penance for *my* sin? You *have* choices, Ashley. You deserve to have a life. There's a huge world out there, waiting for you, but you're letting him keep you here like a prisoner. Why are you letting him do this?"

I couldn't answer. I was too raw. If I spoke the words, my heart would just crack further apart. Hot tears spilled down my cheeks.

"You've always said you would do anything I asked. You'd give me anything I needed. I need this, Brayden. I need you to go now and never look back."

His forehead pressed into mine. "Don't do this," he whispered. Thumbs brushed across my wet cheeks.

"I have to," I replied softly. My words renewed my resolve.

I lightly pressed my hands against his chest. He let me push him away.

"What do you want me to do, Brayden? He's my brother."

"I asked you once, why I'm so easy to leave. Why I'm so easy to send away." He stepped farther back, shaking his head. "You think I walked off and never looked back. But you're so wrong. I don't know how you never felt my eyes on your skin. Don't do this. Don't try to force me out of your life again."

Fresh tears silently spilled over. I knew what was going on inside him. Somewhere, beneath his layers of muscle and cocky self-assurance, there would always live the cracked little boy who'd been tossed aside by his own mother.

"I have no choice."

For the second time in my life, I turned and walked away.

CHAPTER 14
ANGELS & TAILLIGHTS

ASHLEY

The grass was freshly cut. Manicured and perfect.

As if the people lying there cared what it looked like. Like they'd complain if everything didn't appear just right.

I shucked off my shoes and sat down next to her, toying with the fresh flowers peeking out of the vase. They were the only symbol I had of my father. I didn't want to be the asshole who wondered how much he spent having them delivered each week.

My mother would've loved them.

I came a lot. To talk to her. To beg for advice. To ask her for a leg up with the powers that be. She'd told me to do it. In her final hours, she'd told me to come here and visit whenever I needed a good haunting.

Those were her exact words.

She'd smiled and laughed when she said them through obvious pain. She'd made it a joke, but the message was clear. She would always be listening.

"I miss you."

I traced the letters engraved in the marble below her name.

Beloved.

Simple. Plain. True. Chosen by my father on the day he'd clung to the sides of a wooden church pulpit and tried to find an adequate phrase to describe what my mother meant to him.

He'd called her *his one*. His one friend. His one lover. His one partner in crime. His beloved.

"How do you say goodbye to the person who was all those things to you?"

The agony on his face gave the unspoken answer.

For a second time in my life, I faced the same misery.

"He can't stay, Mama. I know he can't stay. I thought I was strong enough this time. But I'm just so, so . . . tired."

I whispered the words as cracked pieces shattered. The tears I'd held back while I stood in front of Brayden fell hard now, cascading down my cheeks into my waiting palms. I curled onto my side, lying in the soft grass, as close to her as I could get, pretending her fingertips swept back and forth across my forehead.

I stayed beside her until my eyes ran dry and the sun grew bright, sweeping away the softness of morning. I was late. Logan was probably done with setting up for the day and plotting ways to kill me. Things were no doubt falling apart. But how the hell was I going to put anything back together today?

I didn't hear footsteps. But a shadow fell across my shoulders, blocking the harshness of the sun.

"Joey told me you might be here. She said you come here when you're upset." His voice speared through me, making everything worse.

Brayden stood over me, hair slicked back and crusted with dried sweat. He wore the same gym shorts, paired with a crisp white T-shirt. It matched the bouquet of fresh tulips and bright purple hyacinth blossoms he held in his hand. Bending down, he carefully arranged them in the marble vase, adding them to the ones already there. He stared down at her headstone and scrubbed the back of his hand against his cheek.

Seeing her name did that. Her name with an end date too close to her beginning. The short dash in between had cheated us all.

His head bowed. He brushed his other cheek.

"I loved that you chose the yellow dress. There was so much black. And all those tearstained faces. Your dress was like one single ray of sunshine."

"She asked me to wear it," I said quietly.

His words kept skimming past my simple answer. The connection took me a minute longer, like the prongs of a plug wrestling with the slots of a light socket.

My eyes stretched wide as they sought his own. "How did you know?"

I glanced back down at my mother's name etched into the smooth white stone.

She had asked me to wear that dress. She'd handpicked all our outfits. My brother and father donned bright blue ties, the exact color of a cloudless sky. I wore a bright yellow dress, the color of sunflowers. That's what she wanted on her coffin. No bloody roses. Wildflowers—the kind you could find and gather while running in a field.

Throughout the service, I'd held a single sunflower. A tear-mangled tissue stayed balled up in my hand, wrapped around the fuzzy stem.

"You were here." The words fell from my lips as an acknowledgment instead of a question.

His eyes darted up to meet mine, a small nod confirmed the statement. "I snuck into the back of the church after the service had already begun. I stayed in my car during the burial, so no one would see me."

I looked back down at my feet, trying to conjure up visions of that day, wondering how I'd never sensed he was near.

"She would have wanted you there. She kept asking for you near the end."

"I know. I got to see her."

My brows furrowed.

"The night before she died, I stayed with her. I had to come. I had things I needed to say to her before . . ." His voice cracked as his body shook, overcome. He clutched on to the front of his shirt and inhaled deeply through his nose and mouth. "She sent me a note. Through Micky. She mailed it to his office. It was just two words with Memorial Hospital as the return address."

He visibly swallowed. His fist slowly loosened against the white cotton of his shirt. He had sad eyes that made me want to wrap my arms around him and crawl back into that bubble we'd re-created last night.

My father and brother were both so closed off.

I never had anyone to share my grief.

"What did it say?"

"Red twenty."

"What does that mean?" I asked, bemused.

"It was a play name we always used on our all-star team. The first summer we had to memorize them, she kept a list pinned to the refrigerator. It was the call sign Coach used when he wanted us to steal home."

My eyes filled up again. "She was telling you to come."

"I was on the next flight. I had to see her. Had to thank her."

"Thank her?"

"She saved my life. In more ways than one." He glanced off into the distance again with a bittersweet smirk that held more secrets. "When I woke up that first morning—the first morning home after the accident—I stood at the bathroom sink and thought about swallowing a whole bottle of pills. I didn't know how to exist." He paused, giving me time to take the breath I needed.

I'd worried about him in those first days. Worried about where he was, whom he was with. Wondered if his father used the information I passed along. Not knowing where he was felt so foreign in the beginning. For so long, he filled so much noisy space in my life, and suddenly, there was just . . . nothing.

That's how I learned loneliness doesn't have a sound.

After the note on my car windshield, he just evaporated. I struggled against the void.

When he reemerged, just in time for the draft, the void only grew deeper. His name was splashed across the Internet and highlighted on *SportsCenter* as it played in all-day waiting rooms. That's when my emptiness had morphed into full-fledged rage.

When I'd known he'd just gone on and forgotten us.

"I didn't think of myself as suicidal. I didn't want to die. I just didn't want to be alive either." He licked his lips before he continued, "She sent me a note then, too. Right before I left town that afternoon. She had the sheriff drive it over. I was pretty sure he was coming to arrest me. Figured the tests they'd run at the hospital showed I was high as a kite when the accident happened."

"My mother sent you a note that day?" My voice gave away my added surprise. She'd been sitting in Nathan's hospital room around the clock, beside herself with the awesome depth of a mother's grief.

He nodded his head. "That one only had two words as well." His head lifted. "*Forgive yourself.*"

I stared down at her name again. The marble shone in the sun, perfectly complemented by the blooming white and purple flowers.

Another memory tumbled out of the closet.

"Brayden?" I plucked one up from the vase. Twirled it in my fingers before settling it back into a better place. "Why did you bring these exact flowers today? How did you know?"

Another puzzle piece fell into place. A bouquet my mother asked me to move to the table beside her bed that final morning. Bright purple blossoms surrounded by pure white.

"They're the prettiest ones in the room. Move them closer, would you? I want them closer to me now," she'd said. The pain in her eyes had softened when she looked at them. "Don't know where he found tulips this time of year."

"They're from you, aren't they? You have them delivered every week. They aren't from my father."

My eyes darted to his face. He held my gaze with confirmation.

"She liked boys who brought flowers."

Something inside me crumbled around his words. Pieces that needed to cave snapped as I stepped forward.

Being close to him suddenly felt like a new connection to her. He knew things about her I didn't know. New things.

When you lose someone, you lose all the newness. Retold old stories soften with age. The connection to them slips each time they're reheard.

Every word he spoke, now felt like an untouched gift.

"The white ones are a symbol of love, the purple ones a symbol of forgiveness," he added.

I sniffled and finally got the courage to ask, "What did she say to you that night?"

His fingertips brushed across my hairline. "She told me, most things happen for a reason, if you look hard enough. But you can always choose to make a reason for the things that don't come with one ready-made. Even for the shitty stuff. Even babies born to mamas who didn't plan on them. Car accidents and heart attacks. All of it."

I smiled sadly.

"If life doesn't give you a silver lining, that doesn't mean you can't stitch your own," I muttered softly. "We went out sailing one of the last days she was still feeling pretty good. It was a gorgeous, clear day, and she begged to be out on the water. That's what she said to me as we were coming back to shore."

I brushed back my tears. "What else did she say to you?"

He paused to clear the emotion stuck in his throat. "She told me she'd always loved me like I was her own son. And she made me promise to wait for the time to be right."

"The time to be right for what?"

"To put our family back together."

Swallowing deeply, I turned my back on him to collect myself. I gazed out across the expanse of deep green, past the tall oak tree that shaded a statue of Mary, past the rows of neatly ordered headstones to the expanse of deep blue water that lingered across the horizon.

A single white sail hovered in the distance, blowing out toward the edge of the world.

Out toward happiness.

A place I could see, but never touch.

BRAYDEN

I stared at the rigid shoulders in front of me, splayed out before a backdrop as close to heaven as I could picture. As final resting places went, this was a good one.

I just refused to let anything else I loved come here to die today.

I'd admired Mrs. F's certainty and told her of my doubts that I'd ever find it myself. But, as I stared at her name beside those purple flowers, I knew for sure.

It was time to start laying my cards on the table.

"She told me to start back at the beginning without taking any shortcuts. So, that's what I did. And she told me I'd know when the time was right to come back. Told me I could go back to my old ways and fight like hell if I had to. I had no idea what she meant about timing. I'd been killing myself, wondering how I'd know."

I cleared my throat, fortifying my nerve. "I watched you, Ash. I never stopped watching you. I couldn't. That's my freaky addiction that no amount of rehab could ever cure."

She rounded on me again, brows furrowed with confusion. Soft cheeks were marred by tracks of new tears. It hurt me not to sweep them away.

I could hear the good doctor's voice in my ear. Telling me to make myself vulnerable. "Vulnerable fucking sucks," I'd once told her. She'd assured me it was the only way to let people in, to form the connections I craved.

Time to let out my crazy.

"I think your mother busted my arm." I chuckled at how stupid that sounded out loud.

Stupid. But true.

"Most guys with this injury lose it over time. They play through pain for a while. Mine wasn't like that. The day I blew it out, I felt it snap. I knew the second it went. It hadn't been sore. I'd been throwing full power, and then, suddenly, it was just gone. I was all over the fucking place. It was like someone turned a dial from ten to zero." Instinctively, I flexed my right elbow, needing to prove to myself that broken things could be fixed. "I knew before they told me. I lay in bed for the first couple of days, feeling sorry for myself. 'Cause it was just gone. Everything I'd worked for. Everything I had left." I snapped my fingers. "I thought, *Well, this is pure shit*. And then it hit me. It was. Total shit."

My eyes searched hers, imploring her to hear me, to feel my next words.

"That's when I knew. Just like your mother said I would. I knew there was a reason. I knew it was time. I was supposed to come home. To beg for forgiveness and try to move forward. Together. Like she wanted."

She turned her back on me again. Her shoulders visibly shook. I couldn't take that shit any longer. My hands wouldn't keep to themselves. My feet closed the distance, so fingertips could lightly brush up and down over the soft skin on the sides of her arms.

"I don't know how to forgive you when I can't even forgive myself."

"What?" My fingers stalled against her skin, squeezing a little.

"You don't hold all the blame for my brother being in that chair, Brayden. Some of that burden is mine."

My fingertips pressed into her skin, leaving a mark. "How the hell do you figure that? I'm the one who got whacked out of his mind and got in his car. I'm the one who plowed into Nathan, head-on."

"But I'm the one who sent him."

I froze.

Everything stopped. The breeze, the birds flying overhead, and my own heartbeat.

"What?"

She turned in my arms, looking up at me with fresh grief that counterbalanced my confusion.

"Nathan was coming to check on you. As a favor for me. I asked him to go."

"Ashley—"

"He was home when I got there that night. He carried me in the house. Calmed me down. He got a text from Bobby about you going nuts. I was worried that you'd injure yourself or someone else and hurt your hands in the process. I didn't want . . ." Her face twisted with the irony. "I didn't want you to lose me and baseball in one night. If you broke your hands or hurt yourself, I knew it would screw up the draft. I didn't want you to throw it all away. I needed to make sure you were okay. I had to save you one more time."

Tears pebbled in her eyes.

"He did it as a favor. We'd made up that night. We'd talked. He didn't want to leave me so upset, but I begged him to go. Everyone's always assumed he was out, driving Cindi home. But you were coming to me, and Nathan was going to you. I'm the reason the accident happened. I put him right in your path."

"Jesus fucking Christ." I pulled at the ends of my hair and blew out a loud breath.

The spring after I'd turned fifteen, my team had gone to the district championship. On the ride to the field, we'd all bragged about needing more shelf space for the trophy. We had that game all sewn up. We'd over prepared for the other team's quick bats and lightning-fast feet. They would have to call the slaughter rule by the bottom of the fourth. But, as we'd taken the field for the anthem, a six-foot giant sauntered out of our opponent's dugout. They'd drafted a ringer—a kid who topped his Wheaties with screws and nails and looked well poised to spit them back out at us.

The sinking feeling I had while staring at that kid, was the same one I had now, trying to stomach Ashley's new wild card.

My hands shook her, more roughly than I intended, but the panic welling up inside me felt desperate to make her suck the words back in.

It had taken me years to learn how to forgive the people around me.

Hard, gut-wrenching work.

Unlocking your own cell door and claiming freedom didn't come easy. I'd come here to teach her the same lesson. To show her that staying angry with me would only keep her locked behind bars.

I thought I could teach her what I knew. Could hold her little hand and lead her down that path. But there was one lesson I'd failed at miserably. One thing that remained an invisible ball and chain I'd made peace with dragging around.

Forgiving others? No problem.

I could teach that to anyone.

Forgiving yourself? Yeah, not so much.

I'd never forgiven myself. Never absolved my own actions.

I would never forget forcing Bobby to retell every small detail of the things my memory couldn't form the next day. I'd wanted to hear it all. The desolation on Ashley's face when she'd walked in that room. The smell, the words, the anger that had spread like wildfire. The way she'd hit Coral Lynn.

The shattered glass. A woman screaming. The blood. So much blood.

The images of my bedroom where I broke my best girl. The roadside where I broke my best friend. Scenes my mind had blocked to protect me. They'd warped and blended together over time, coming back to me in bits and pieces of nightmares that threaded together over years spent alone in the darkness.

Forgiving yourself was the hardest part.

I couldn't teach her what I didn't know how to do myself.

The wall of tightness spread across my chest. "Is that what you've been carrying around? Is that why you're here, half-killing yourself, trying to keep everything afloat? Why you've forfeited all your dreams and chained yourself to this town?"

"Yes."

"Holy shit."

I started mentally counting backward. Warding off the tentacles before they could surround me.

Ten, nine, eight . . .

In. Out. Breathe.

Seven, six, five . . .

My hand fisted against my abdomen, feeling each breath, reassuring myself I could get this under control.

"None of this mess was your fault. Do you hear me? None of it. You've gotta get that shit straight in your head right now." My finger waved at her. "I did this. Me." I poked myself in the chest. "Blame me. Fucking hate me if you need to. But you let go of this silly notion of hating yourself. Let me earn your forgiveness. Let me fight for it.

It's gonna be hard enough a task on its own. Don't add more layers, Soot."

"I can't help it. Every time I look at my brother, the guilt eats me alive. Being near you again makes it even more excruciating. You're the worst kind of torture, Brayden. You're old happiness and fresh pain."

I couldn't hide the tears that spilled over onto my cheeks.

Yep. Vulnerable still sucks.

Hers trailed even faster than my own.

I couldn't take it anymore. My arms engulfed her, pressing the side of her cheek against my chest. Her back shook from the bottled-up emotion.

"I know, baby girl. God, I know."

As I smoothed a hand over her hair, the tightness in my chest vanished. Having her pressed against me chased the demon away. I was still stuck in hell, but I could breathe easy again. I always could with her near me. That shit still worked. My lips pressed against the top of her head, willing my touch to somehow become a salve for her pain, too.

"People think my life is a fantasy." My voice came out muted against her hair. "But I'm not living a dream. I'm living a nightmare. Every good thing that comes my way is a reminder of what I stole from the people I love. I feel like the worst kind of thief. The kind who got away with it and was left to rot in a cell made of shame. I don't want that for you, Soot. Above all else, I don't want you to live that way, too."

She pulled back to look up at me with watery eyes. The pads of my thumbs scraped roughly across her cheeks.

"My mother told us both, everything happens for a reason, but what could possibly be the reason for all this grief? All this sadness?"

"I don't know the reason for all the shit we've been through. It's pretty hard to believe things were supposed to get this fucked-up. But I feel certain of one thing—we won't find the answer alone."

I watched Ashley's taillights slip away from me, forcing myself not to pull out behind and follow her home. We were stranded somewhere between good and right. I'd made a deathbed promise to her mother; she'd promised Nathan she'd run me out of town.

Either way, we would break an oath and piss someone off.

She needed time to work things out with her brother. She'd used the one word that made any dude's balls shrivel on impact.

Space.

She wanted a few days to think. I sure as fuck wasn't gonna give her that long but tailing her bumper might've given that away too soon.

I leaned back against the headrest, letting the chill of the air conditioner settle over me along with my resolve. Everything was starting to unravel now. I had to be ready to lay down my whole hand, to go all in at any moment.

I fished my phone from my pocket, firing off a text.

Change of plans. Moving things up. Come as soon as possible. Bring her with you. It's time.

Her response was immediate.

Squeeeeee!

She followed it up with a string of *X*s and *O*s and a dozen goofball emojis. God help me, I really had missed her.

I smirked as I dialed another number from memory.

"S'up, boss?"

Steel drums played in the background.

"Afraid it's about time for me to cut your vacation short."

"Damn. I was just starting to like this assignment."

"I'm sure you were." I chuckled. "Need you to start tying up loose ends."

"I comin' to you? Or we meetin' in the city?"

"I'm staying here for now."

"Got it. Might take a little time to dry things up here."

I sighed. "I was gonna send the plane. But maybe the slow boat is a better option."

"Now, you're just spoilin' me. Guy could get used to this lifestyle. You wouldn't believe the honeys down here. If I were ten years younger"—he whistled suggestively—"I'd be scoring left and right."

"You'd better make my delivery and get your ass home to Theresa. She's gonna have your nuts in a vise."

It was his turn to laugh. "Hey now, I'm bringing her home one of those fancy shot glasses with the name of the hotel."

"She's sure to know you were thinking of her the whole time."

"I'm joking, big man. I ain't that stupid." His voice sobered. "How you want me to play this one out, boss? Clue him in? Or strong-arm him?"

"I'll let you decide. Do what you gotta do." I quickly reconsidered. "Don't make a scene, Vincent."

"Ey-yo. You know me." His Jersey leaked out. "I can blend when I gotta."

Vincent was a six-foot-six school bus with a shaved head, Gold's Gym arms, and a penchant for facial piercings. He didn't blend in with any crowd.

"Seriously, boss, I got this. I'll keep you posted."

He'd also always had my back.

I ended the call and put the car in gear. Pieces were going to fall into place quickly now.

I stared out across the field of angels and prayed for the two who had raised me to watch over us.

The only way for this to work was to go through *him*.

It was time to break another promise.

"The difference between the impossible and the possible
lies in a person's determination."
—*Tommy Lasorda*
Baseball Hall of Fame, Manager, Class of 1997

HOME RUN

BASEBALL ARENA

CHAPTER 15
PLAN B

BRAYDEN

"Was wondering when you'd get the balls to show your face here."

The sound of my former best friend's voice stunned me more than it should have. I thought I had it etched into my memory like glass. I would replay it sometimes. I'd hear our voices calling out plays, make-believing we were in the bottom of the ninth, game seven, all tied up with bases loaded.

We always took turns pretending to hit the homer.

I'd see his face sometimes, too. The tears in his eyes as he charged me on the mound the first time we won a district title. His smile the first night he scored with Cindi. His rosy cheeks the first time we got drunk in the old shed behind Bobby's house. The green tinge, that mirrored my own, as we hurled in the bushes afterward.

I tried to focus on those kinds of memories.

Not the ones full of ugly words that had come later.

When you part with someone on bad terms, you're forced to play those mind games. You walk through all the things you should've said, creating whole dialogue that never happened.

That kind of make-believe was the only thing that had settled my stomach some nights. In my head, I'd already had this conversation a million times.

"Figured you were just gonna keep fucking my sister behind my back again."

Nathan rolled his chair forward, out of the shadows. I held on to the porch rail, stuck halfway up the steps.

I thought I'd prepared myself for seeing him face-to-face in the wheelchair. I'd psyched myself up for the firsthand gut punch of just how much I'd cost him. But I couldn't fight off the wave of nausea and doubt.

Part of me wanted to turn and run and never stop. The part of me that knew I didn't deserve to be here. The part of me that used to sit in seedy hotel rooms in minor league towns and contemplate an easy way out. Me and a whole bottle of pills and a sob story about what could've been. I'd finally get what I should've had coming that night.

The night I threw away everyone I loved.

It should be me in that chair.

I swallowed the familiar taste of guilt and let myself look past the metal spokes of his prison.

The damn chair wasn't even the most unsettling thing about him. He looked like hell. Not even a shell of his former self. He'd always been pristine, perfectly coifed, and pressed to the point we called him GQ.

My version of Nathan didn't do sloppy.

His disheveled appearance shouldn't have come as a shock. I'd seen photographs. But the lens had filtered the harsh reality.

He looked like an old war vet who'd gone off clean-cut and preppy but came home wearing long hair, a scraggly beard, and a chip on his shoulder.

His hair lay greased back without the need for product, pulled into a nappy ponytail with strays tucked behind his ears. His clothes hung from his frame, looking bed-worn and stained. Muscles still stretched tight across his shoulders and veins crawled up the forearms that rested against the sides of his wheelchair. But, even with baggy sweats covering his legs, I could see they were a fraction of their former self. He'd aged faster than the days passed. His features were hardened by trouble and sadness.

I'd come over here, all piss and vinegar, ready to demand he cut his sister some fucking slack. Looking at him now felt like a swift punch in the junk.

I stood silent, forgetting the first line of my script. Nathan's angry gaze left me raw and mutely ashamed.

"Of course, I heard the buzz about the prodigal son returning. And, of course, I knew you wouldn't be able to keep your dick out of her."

I inhaled through my nose. Willing myself to stay cool. Fighting back game-day nerves.

You've gotta do this. Sack up.

"I've wanted to come see you. Wanted to come and . . ." I trailed off, unsure of how to introduce those two words that sat between us with the weight and stench of a caged zoo animal. "Ashley wouldn't let me. She made me promise to stay away from you."

"Well, at least she hasn't lost all her common sense."

I bowed my head. Picking a fight with a dude in a wheelchair suddenly felt like a lame-ass idea. Picking a fight with a dude you'd put in the wheelchair felt even worse.

"What could you possibly have to say to me?"

When I didn't reply, he used his hands to turn the chair, angrily stroking the spokes to move away from me. He glided toward the ramp that led off the side of the porch.

"Go home, Brayden," he said, calling back. "And, by home, I mean, New York. You aren't welcome here."

In my mind, his words shape-shifted into the ugly chant I'd told myself over and over as a child.

You aren't wanted.

You aren't wanted.

You aren't wanted.

Half of me yearned to lash out. The other half needed to turn tail and bust ass all the way to the county line.

I knew coming here, coming back to this place and this town, meant I'd crossed over the point of no return. It cemented the fact I'd become a full-fledged asshole, dreaming of entitlements I didn't deserve.

His dismissal made me second-guess myself again. But, as his wheels reached the top of the ramp, I kicked myself into motion.

I took the final two steps up, squelching the voices of doubt still shouting in my head.

"Why don't you return Cindi's calls?"

He stopped suddenly, wrists pressed against metal spokes to block his retreat. "What the fuck do you know about that?" he asked, his back still to me. His head tilted slightly to the side, revealing a clenched jaw.

"I know."

He spun the chair back around. "You don't know shit, pretty boy."

"I know she tries to contact you once a month. I know she leaves messages. I know you've returned every single letter. She gets tears in her eyes when she talks about it."

His chest rose and fell rapidly as his nostrils flared. He glanced out at something in the yard, suddenly unable to face me. "You've seen her?" His voice softened by a fraction.

"Yeah. I went to see her a couple years ago. To tell her how sorry I was. To tell her how fucking badly I wished I could take back that night. How I would pretty much do anything if I could." I prayed he got the message loud and clear. "She's in nursing school at NYU now. We keep in touch."

An open palm ran down his face, pausing to scratch back and forth across the scruffy hair on his chin. "How is she?" he asked quietly.

"Why don't you pick up the phone and find out?"

His eyes narrowed with renewed bitterness. "Why the hell would I do that? So, I can hear all about her peachy-keen life? So, I can hear how she loves school and has some dipshit boyfriend who can still fuck her like normal and who plans to give her the life she deserves?" He snickered. "No, thanks, asshole."

He started to turn away from me again.

I gripped the railing and called out to him in desperation, "Nathan, I know what it's like to lose the love of your life."

"Oh, that's rich." He held his hands out to the sides. "Go ahead and cry me your sob story. I lost everything because of you, so excuse the fuck out of me if I don't feel like letting you waltz back in here to take whatever you please. My little sister included."

"I can't give you back what you've lost. I can't give you back how these years were supposed to be. I would give up anything if I could. I'd hang up my glove. I'd forfeit everything I own. But I won't give up on your sister. Stop giving her ultimatums. At least give me the chance to earn *her* forgiveness."

He scowled as he rolled his chair back toward me. I knew that look. If he could've thrown a punch, it would've been a knockout.

"I know why you're here. You think I don't know?" He licked his lips and gave me a slow, condescending nod. "You've forgotten how well I know you. You've had *just* enough time, haven't you? Just enough time to sit on your ass and wonder if it's ever gonna come back." He tipped his chin toward my arm. "I know how that feels."

He turned and spat on the ground with the precision only a ballplayer knew.

That guy was still in there somewhere.

I just had to scratch and claw my way to dig him out.

"First couple of months, I would wake up every morning, wondering if I'd ever walk again. The wonder is the worst part, isn't it? Then, I started with the nightmares. The ones where shit just doesn't work. Did you have those, Brayden? All those people, the bright lights, you standing up on that pile of dirt. Did you wake up sweating? Trying to move your arm? Screaming in desperation 'cause, even in your sleep, it won't move the way you want it to?" He paused and then added, "That's how I wake up every night."

I swallowed deep, concentrating on trying to breathe. My eyes shut briefly, needing a respite from that brutal stare.

And the brutal truth behind his words.

"I know *exactly* why you're here. My sister is either still too naïve or too stupid to see it for herself. You need a plan B, don't you? What happens if those nightmares become a reality? What happens when the golden arm never works again? Where are you gonna go? What are you gonna fall back on? Got no real family." He slid his jaw back and forth as that sucker punch landed. "So, you just decided to fucking come back and try to steal mine again."

"Jesus," I whispered, shrinking back from him as my hand covered my mouth. "You really think a lot of me, don't you?"

"I think you put me in this fucking chair. And didn't have to pay any price for it. You rolled right on with your life. And you should've just kept on rolling. No one needed you to look back. There's no place for you or your backup plans here. If your arm is fucked, it's 'cause God finally got around to dishing you out some of the Karma you deserve."

"Nathan, I'm so . . . so—"

"Christ, don't say that crap to me. You think I care? You think I care how *sorry* you are now? Now that you need something? The rest of us have needed a lot these last couple of years. Thanks for fucking asking."

He shook his head and turned his chair back around, rolling away from me.

He stopped again, just at the top of the ramp.

"If my sister decides to be a repeat victim, more power to her," he called back to me. "If she decides to spread her legs for you and get her fucking heart smashed again, that's on her. I'm clearly not gonna be the one to catch her when she falls this time."

CHAPTER 16
CAT & MOUSE

ASHLEY

"I can't believe he's doing this."

"This dude has it seriously bad for you."

"Why the hell is he here?"

"Is that Brayden Ross?"

Joey and Riley turned to look at Toni.

Joey smacked her lips. "Yep. In the flesh."

"Damn. He's even better-looking—" Toni cleared her throat. "I mean, he's even taller in person."

All four of our heads cocked to the side as Brayden did a deep lunge, stretching his quad and opposite hamstring. We all ducked and tried to act nonchalant when he twisted his torso around toward us.

Well, three of us did.

Riley openly gawked.

"Have you ever given any thought to filming a sex tape?" she asked, mesmerized. "You don't have to put it online. You could just share it with a select group of us."

A few of the other women coming through the door did a double take and quickly joined Riley in openly appreciating the view. When he twisted in the opposite direction, his shirt rode up, uncovering a chunk of rippled abs. There were a few hushed gasps in the crowd. Half the Lululemon in the room was already damp from something other than sweat.

"He's seriously gonna take my class?" Toni asked in a hushed whisper.

"This is his idea of space," I muttered, shaking my head. "How did he even know about this class?"

Joey turned away and started rolling out her mat.

"Oh, you're so busted." I poked her in the boniest part of her ass.

"What?" she said, all bluster and fake innocence. "Maybe he saw the class schedule when you brought him here for the photo shoot."

"Yeah? Pigs don't fly, Joey."

She hid a sheepish grin as she ran a hand down her newly dyed jet-black bob.

Toni walked to the front of the room and clapped her hands together, bringing everyone milling about to attention.

"Okay, ladies"—she made a show of turning to smile at Brayden—"and gentleman . . ."

He pressed his hands together in a perfect namaste.

"Let's get started."

Riley punched me in the shoulder. She had the smile of a bona fide fangirl now. She'd been glowing ever since he walked in and warmly greeted her by name.

Halfway through the class, she kicked me in the leg, forcing my head up, as she pointed to Brayden's ass thrust up into the air in downward dog. She balanced on one hand and made a squeezing motion with the other. I rolled my eyes and kicked her back, feigning like I wasn't interested. But, truthfully, the sweat trailing down my back had nothing to do with my body movements and everything to do with the burn between my legs.

Space, Ashley. You're giving yourself space.

Riley and Toni weren't the only ones affected. The whole class fell under his spell. Even the blue hairs who usually stayed on the fringes of the room and barely bent over. Gail, the eighty-year-old bat who ran the town garden club, almost killed herself while trying a full sun salutation. She smiled and fluttered her lashes when Brayden helped her up off the floor.

When he held on to an expertly balanced tree pose, Tamra

Evanston, a newly divorced mother of three, not so quietly announced, "If I hadn't sworn off men after Ricky, I would climb the hell out of that."

The entire group around her nodded their heads in agreement while they openly objectified Brayden's flexed ass.

By the time fifty minutes passed, they'd all given up on trying to outdo one another and begun full-fledged swooning. As soon as class wrapped, they descended on Brayden like schoolgirl groupies, giggling and making small talk with more barely concealed innuendos. I busied myself, helping Toni wipe down the mats.

Most of the room cleared by the time I walked to the little cubbies near the window to retrieve my bag.

"Your ass, all twisted up in these little shorts, is one of the hottest things I've ever seen. That was like working out with porn live-streaming in the mirror behind me." He stood close enough to whisper the naughty words in my ear. So close, I could feel the heat of his sweaty chest against my back.

I hadn't chosen the bootie shorts and strappy sports bra for his benefit. Usually, I was among friends—women friends—and it didn't matter if we let it all hang out.

Having him stand so close felt more unnerving than usual. That tree-climbing idea was still too fresh in my mind.

"I got an earful from my brother a couple of nights ago," I replied coldly.

"Yeah. Sorry I didn't give you a heads-up. I knew you'd never allow it, and I couldn't wait any longer. It had to happen. You have to trust me on that. He's not exactly forbidding you to see me anymore, is he?"

"I think the phrase, *Go ahead and royally fuck up your whole life*, was used a few times." I sighed, trying to forget the hurt I knew lingered behind my brother's angry words. "You have to give me some time to work through things with Nathan. Did you say anything to him about Matt?"

"Not yet. That's next." His mouth still hovered near my ear.

Goose bumps covered my arms. Being near him was like a plated chocolate cupcake on the first day of a diet.

After you tell yourself you can't have something anymore, you want it twice as bad.

"You were supposed to be giving me some room to think."

A large hand splayed across my belly, inches above where my body really wanted it. His chest pressed fully against me as he thrust proof of just how turned on he'd become into the crack of my ass.

"Can't help it. How am I supposed to stay away from you when my dick is hard as a rock?"

"Brayden," I answered in an angry whisper, turning my head to the side to gauge who was in the room, playing witness to his stealthy advance.

If Connie Cularko, the president of the elementary PTA and the town's resident loudmouth, saw Brayden's hands on me this way, she'd have her network buzzing by lunch.

"Sorry, baby girl. Now, you've gotta stand here a minute till I get myself under control. Unless you want everyone to see the state I'm in. Just keep still and give me some cover while you think about how badly I wanna peel these things down your legs and bend you around my cock. I haven't been inside your pussy in eleven days. That's way too much space."

His other hand pulled against my hip, grinding me back harder against him.

"Doing that isn't gonna help your situation," I said, hissing at him, as I turned my head enough to look over my shoulder.

"The only thing that's gonna help my situation is me throwing you over my shoulder, carrying you out to my car, and driving as fast as possible down Route 33 till I find a deserted spot where I can lay you out on my hood and fuck the daylights out of you."

My lips puckered as I fought against the O my mouth wanted to form. His eyes mirrored my response, dipping down to stare at my lips. He smirked like the devil.

"Don't do that."

"Do what?"

"Give me the fuck-me eyes and that cocky, lopsided grin. It's not fair."

The side of his mouth crooked up a little higher. "Did I ever say I intended to play fair?"

He threw the gauntlet, just hard enough, I decided the time had come to play him by his own rules.

Game on, mister.

"You're right." I twisted around, putting a little breathing room between us as I threaded my hand up and tugged a little on the hair at the back of his neck. Then, I trailed my fingers down over his collarbone, so I could feel up his pecs. My palm flattened out against him, fully groping without shame. "But I think I'd rather you spread me out on the hot metal and went down on me first. My clit misses your wicked tongue. And that might be safer for your paint job."

His mouth dropped open, stunned.

My hand fell to my side as I took one more quick step back, far enough to glance down at the impressive bulge in his shorts. "I've gotta get to work. Too bad for you. You know I always return the favor, and as I recall, you always thought I gave great road head."

I moved around him faster than he could grab me, slinging my bag over my shoulder as I walked to the door. He muttered a string of expletives and took the Lord's name in vain.

"Good luck with your little issue, Dallas. Hope you get it figured out."

I paused as I finished my challenge. Connie and her crew of gossip whores still lingered in the hallway, just outside the door. They were salivating like they'd just watched the best reality TV show ever recorded.

I put my head down and plowed through their knowing smiles.

BRAYDEN

Ashley didn't *really* want space.

But I figured giving her some might help her figure that out.

I kept a low profile, avoided the marina, didn't venture into town. Kept hoping a couple of days might actually make her miss me. I focused on pushing myself a little, doubling up on my workouts.

A calendar hung on the wall with a big red X marking the spot. The date beneath it simultaneously felt way too close and far. The skin on the tips of my fingers had grown annoyingly soft. I missed the feel of the ball. Missed rubbing it across the seam running up my thigh. Missed the scratch of the laces in the center of my palm.

I wanted all that back.

But the thought of that first throw, that very first one, made chunks rise in the back of my throat. Nathan was wrong about a lot of things, but about the night sweats and terrors, he was right on the mark.

When you make a living playing a game, a big ego becomes a part of the uniform. You slip it on every day as you drive to the park.

When I stood on that mound and stared down an opponent, I had to believe I would wreck him. In my mind, every time I wound up, I could already hear the ball pop into my catcher's glove. I could already see an orphaned bat, fanning nothing but air.

People think an athlete's ego comes from success. But it's the other way around. Success is fueled by the ego, by the inability to believe you'll be anything but great. Every professional ballplayer has two sources of protection. The piece of plastic cupping his balls and the massive ego cutting off the nerves from his brain.

I couldn't get the latter to snap back into place. The only thing more screwed than my elbow was the space between my ears. I couldn't stop myself from wondering how long it would take to tell if I'd be back to the old me or back to being totally fucked.

Taking care of things with Ashley served as a perfect distraction. Giving *her* space, gave *me* too much room to think.

It didn't help that Micky kept calling to rattle my chain.

"You're killin' me here, kid. All this free time you've got, I could've retired on these endorsement royalties. I'm turning stuff down left and right. That hometown pussy must be pretty damn sweet to keep you away from the bright lights and all this easy money."

"Mick. Man, cut the crap. You have no idea."

"Fuck, kiddo, of course I do. Went through the same damn thing with your old man. I've seen this shit a thousand times; I'm old enough to be your great-grandpa. But let's not mess with business, eh? Dip into the honeypot, and then get your ass back to work. *Capisce?*" He paused and then added, "How ugly is this girl? Can't ya bring her with you? I'll add to our list of prerequisites, space on the carpet for arm candy."

"Mick?"

"Yeah, kid?"

"You're an asshole."

"Tell me something I don't know. You think I got us all this rich by being nice?"

I hung up on him and almost didn't answer when he called again the following day.

Well, truthfully, I didn't answer. Then, he sent me a shouty text.

GOT NEWS ABOUT YOUR SWEET CHEEKS. ANSWER YOUR FUCKING PHONE.

"Your girl's in."

"What?"

"The hoity-toity snowflakes running that magazine love her. They want a full shoot. They're booking space. Need to know your short list of possible dates. Looks like you have to come back home after all."

"I am home, Mick. *This* is home."

"Whatever, kid. Quit giving me heartburn. You can't hide down there in la-la land forever. Time to get to work. Get your chickadee on a plane. Buy her a hot dress. I'm tryin' to line this up with the Loweman brothers' big opening. Your ugly mug needs to be there. People in this town got short memories. You don't remind 'em who the fuck you are, they'll start throwing their dead presidents somewhere else."

"Get it lined up. Call me back with the details."

"Josie! Josie!" There was a commotion in the background as he called out for his long-time assistant without covering the phone. "Get on the horn to those pansy-assed magazine people. Tell them to get their shit together, stat. The boy wonder's coming back to

Gotham." He chuckled in my ear. "You just made that old hag's day, kid. We'll be in touch."

I hung up and dialed back the need to rush right over and convince Ashley this was good news. I didn't want to pile too much on her all at once. Hitting her with meeting Jess would be overload enough.

On a good day, Jessica made Joey look normal.

We'd entered the part of my master plan where things got sorta fuzzy around the edges, where I had to start making things up as we went along.

I'd invite Ash to dinner. Let them get to know one another.

Then, I'd spring the idea of a trip to New York.

ASHLEY

Brayden had been avoiding me all week. Like a tease, he was playing an old-fashioned game of cat and mouse. I refused to fall into the trap.

He'd texted me the dinner invite.

I'd only agreed to go because he said Matt would be there. They wanted to talk about how to coax my brother into treatment. Matt could lay out new options and delve into the idea of alternative therapies.

It was a business dinner. Plain and simple.

I hated to admit, I sort of wanted the company. Joey had spent the week gallivanting at the beach with Conner, Logan had taken a crew out for a three-day cruise, and my brother still flat-out refused to speak to me.

Early in the week, Nathan had called and canceled a doctor's appointment purely to avoid the car ride with me. His only form of communication had come via the printed articles and pictures he kept leaving on the kitchen counter. He must've thought the old gossip clips about Brayden and other women would silently drive home his point.

My brother had wicked skills with twisted knives.

I'd tried to toss them in the trash without looking.

For Brayden's not-a-date dinner, I dressed the opposite of all the flashy women in those pictures. I wore white capris and a prim yellow top. Conservative. Classy.

We'd sit across the table, eat all our vegetables, and act like adults.

It was one of those rare East Coast summer evenings without shirt-wringing humidity, so I walked over along the path past the old boathouse. The fresh paint was an exact match to the original, but it made the whole place look brand-new.

Walking by it didn't hurt as much anymore.

For the first time in years, the main house seemed alive. It glowed from one window to the next. Bubbly pop music streamed out of the kitchen door. I paused on the threshold to dream up the million ways I was going to poke fun at him for having it on.

I threw the door open with a little more force than normal, imagining I would catch him in the act of shaking his ass to the mechanical beat.

Confusion and alarm broke over me like a wave.

My instinct to dive lay as frozen as my mouth, which hung wide open.

She stood near the stove, stirring something in a big pot. Her hips swayed back and forth as her head bobbed to the beat of the music. When the chorus began, she started singing along in a high-pitched voice that threatened to break glass. Her slender arms stretched into the air, and she jumped up and down like she'd just melted into the crowd at a packed club.

Blood pumped in my ears as the scene before me morphed with another night when I'd opened a door in this house to the shock of my life.

I must've gasped. Or knocked into something, because she turned suddenly, her face registering the same surprise.

She was beautiful in that maddening, no-makeup sort of way. Her coloring was the complete opposite of me. She had soft blond hair that hung in a long ponytail down her back, ice-blue eyes that barely looked real, and porcelain skin unblemished by a single freckle.

She wore a weird little headband covered in plastic daisies and a white mesh half-shirt that barely covered her tiny string bikini. It showcased a body blessed by perfect DNA or a calorie-free diet of organic tree bark and grass.

She was breathtaking, one of those girls other women smiled at sweetly but instantly hated on sight.

I recognized her, of course. We'd met before. One night in this very kitchen at two a.m.

I'd stuffed away the image of her face, rebuffing the notion that I could be the other woman, and refusing to ponder the question I now heard myself ask.

"Who are you?"

"Oh, shit," she muttered. In startled haste, she put her hand against the side of the pot, scorching that perfect skin. "Fuck me!" she cried out, crossing to the kitchen sink to run it under the faucet.

Fight and flight battled with one another.

I don't want to know.

I really don't want to know.

Panicked, I turned on my heel and started back through the door. I was halfway back down the side path when I heard her shouting, "Brayden! Fuck a duck. Brayden! Where are you? She's early. She's here. Do something!"

I didn't turn around. I quickened my pace, even as I heard the *thwack* of the screen door slamming shut and footsteps closing in fast behind me. I'd just decided to break into a run when arms wrapped around my waist.

It took me a second to realize my feet were no longer on the ground. We were still moving forward, but in one swift motion, I was in the air and thrown over his shoulder.

"Put me down." I kicked back and forth, swimming in his hold.

"No."

"Put me down, goddamn it."

"No. Not until you listen to me."

He swatted my ass when I didn't stop kicking. It stung. Pretty bad.

"That hurt, asshole."

"It got your attention. Keep kicking me, and I'll do it again."

I quieted down. He carried me toward the back patio.

Standing in front of a lounger, he asked, "If I put you down, are you gonna stay put and stay quiet, so I can explain some shit to you?"

"Depends. If I run, are you gonna chase me?"

"Damn straight. I can run a sub five forty. Wanna test me?"

I grumbled some incoherent stuff and then finally said, "Put me down."

He unceremoniously dumped me onto the lounge chair and then squatted down in front of me in a catcher's stance.

"There's some stuff I haven't totally filled you in on. Stuff I didn't think you needed to know till now."

"If you remember, I asked if you had a girlfriend, asshole."

"I've had one real girlfriend in my life. She's a sassy-mouthed little wench who kicks really hard."

"Well, maybe I should've clarified. I meant, fuck buddies, too. We both know you've got a lifelong list of them."

He snorted and licked his lips, impossibly fighting that stupid little smile. "Jess isn't a fuck buddy, Ash."

The side of his fist lightly tapped the top of my knee. He paused, looking up at me until I returned his gaze.

"She's my little sister."

CHAPTER 17
DOMINOES

ASHLEY

Brayden's eyes stared back at me.

Looking into them felt completely surreal.

Framed by blond curls, they were filled with the compassion of a woman who'd lived through hard times and the wisdom of one who'd come out on the other side.

Watching her walk through the kitchen door had registered as twice the shock. She was nearly the mirror image of her daughter.

She had a bombshell figure, glossy hair, and porcelain skin. Her light features made those clear blue eyes stand out even more. Brayden had once described them to me as the eyes of a whore, the piece she'd left behind with him. Staring back at them now felt so strangely familiar.

Her mouth quirked up into a timid half-smile that struck me hard with another strange sense of déjà vu.

I'd seen that smile my whole life.

She'd shared more than just her eyes.

"Brayden's told us so much about you. We feel like we already know you." Her sweet, homespun accent had the cuddle-up feeling of soup and biscuits on Sunday.

I wanted to sit a spell, rock beside her, and just listen to the way her mouth made words sound so different. It reminded me a whole lot of the way my Brayden used to turn on a little Texas when he wanted to get his way.

"You have to forgive Jess for being so exuberant. She's been dyin' to meet you."

Jessica had attacked us as soon as we walked back through the door, apologizing a million times for surprising me. She'd tightly hugged me, like a teddy bear misplaced and then rediscovered. After Brayden pried her off me, she'd jumped up and down and clapped her hands.

"I can't believe she's finally here!" she'd said while throwing her arms around him in the same teddy bear hold.

He'd laughed and whispered something in her ear that made her stand down. After kissing him on the cheek, she'd given me a half-wave, and taken off up the back stairs.

Now, I gazed out across the pool toward the guesthouse where Brayden had wandered after his second introduction stole my breath.

He'd wanted to give me this time alone.

With his mother.

"I'm so sorry about your mom. I lost my father to cancer three years ago. I know how terrible it is to watch someone you love go through that hell."

I nodded my head, unsure of what to say.

"I wish I'd had the chance to meet her. I owe her a great deal."

"My mother?" I asked, my voice laced with wonder, my hand pressing to my chest.

She gazed out across the lawn to the sloping hill that reached down toward the water's edge. "She helped raise Brayden. The stories he tells of her . . . he loved her deeply. She sounds like an amazing woman. Movin' y'all here like she did. Startin' a business. She must've been very brave."

"She was, I guess. I never thought of it that way. She was incredibly brave in the end." I swallowed.

"Bravery is a quality I greatly admire. I didn't have a lot of it as a young girl." Her voice filled with regret. "I'm not proud of who I was back then, back when I was just a little younger than you are now."

Her hand smoothed down over her long blond hair as she considered her words. "I grew up in a tiny town in Texas that few folks ever leave. I was desperate to get out. I was suffocatin' there. I wanted to go to college so badly. But my daddy was a cattle rancher, and my mama taught preschool. We didn't have the money."

She sighed softly. "You have to understand, in Texas, football players are royalty from the time they're little kids, barely big enough to wear shoulder pads. So, when a friend told me she could get us behind security at a Cowboys game, it sounded like the perfect chance to rope myself a prince. We hitchhiked our way there and back."

She paused and looked out toward the water for a few more minutes, letting me digest an angle of the story I'd never even considered. I'd spent so many years feeling angry with the very idea of her that I never considered the reasons for her actions.

"I was young and stupid, and Jackson Ross was high on life when I met him. That's a bad combination. I convinced myself he'd come for me with a glass slipper in hand, ready to whisk me off. In the fairy tales, the prince is never totally in love with someone else." She smiled sadly.

"When I found out I was pregnant, I didn't know what to do. My folks sent me to live with an aunt in Mississippi until Brayden was born, so no one in town would know. I was so lonely and scared." Her voice quivered, weighted down by the kind of pain that time never dulls. She patted her fingertips across the corner of one eye.

"I felt bad when his girlfriend answered the door. I didn't mean to ruin his life. But there was nothing I could do to take it back. I had nothing to give my baby, but his daddy was a king. His face was all over the TV every Sunday. A spitting image of my little boy. I thought I was doing the right thing."

Her watery eyes forced me to reach out my hand. To somehow share her pain. My fingers loosely grasped her own. She squeezed them tight before letting them go and smiling a little brighter.

"From the outside looking in, I went on without my son. But there wasn't a day when I didn't think of him and wonder what could've been."

I tried to picture her as a younger version. I'd spent so many years with conjured images of the locker-room whore with teased hair and a short, tight skirt. But this woman had a gentleness about her. She had a calm voice and soft creases near the corners of her eyes. She wore a long cotton skirt and a flowery peasant top that gathered all the way up to her collarbone. A small gold cross hung around her neck.

Nothing about her fit my childhood assumptions.

"Ashley, I owe your mother for more than the years she helped raise Brayden. I owe her for giving me back my son."

My head jerked back to look at her, curious.

"Brayden coming to find me was her idea."

Realization slowly washed across my face. "She told him to start back at the beginning. She wanted him to find you."

She nodded.

"If your mother hadn't been ill, if she hadn't sent for him and instructed him to heal his past—from the very beginning without shortcuts—I wouldn't be here. My family wouldn't be complete."

"Everything happens for a reason. Even the shitty stuff," I murmured, looking up at the sky. I hoped my mother's haunting abilities stretched this far, that she knew this wish came true. "If you can't find one, make your own silver lining."

She'd made one. As my mother lost her battle to watch her kids grow, she passed that chance to a woman who'd lost her son.

"Yes. Goodness, when I was your age, I would've thought that was a real sack of horseshit." She chuckled.

Even her curses sounded sweet.

"But years and hindsight have a way of proving it ain't. And the funny thing is, as I've gotten to know my son, I've come to realize I wasn't just a domino that led toward his mistakes. I was also a domino that led him toward things he loves. If I hadn't left my baby in the arms of a man who didn't love me, he never would have ended up here, in this sweet town. He never would've gone to that library and found his silver lining—he never would have met you. So, yeah, I don't believe it's just malarkey. 'Cause, darlin', when I see the look in my son's eyes, every time he says your name, all I see is reason."

I sat quietly, picking at the hem of my capris, trying to digest everything she'd told me. Her words had lifted the veil on the stickiness of life. Situations that seemed so simple as a child had turned out to be a whole lot more complex.

Storybooks teach us to see heroes and villains.

Real life doesn't cut people so plainly.

She rubbed her hands up and down her arms, chasing away the cool dampness of the summer night air. I sat beside her, numbly still, chasing away the monstrous image of her I'd held on to for so long. She was imperfect and flawed. She had regrets.

Damn if I couldn't relate to that.

"I'm sorry I grew up hating you." I'd meant to apply a filter before the words tumbled out, but my mouth had moved ahead of my brain.

She nodded slowly as her hands stilled.

"I just always wanted him to be okay. But he wasn't okay without you. You were a missing piece in his life." My words caused her to bow her head, nodding sadly.

"I don't mean that to sound cruel," I added quickly. "I just . . . I'm still trying to wrap my head around all of this. And I think you should know, he always missed you."

I prayed she'd see my words as a gift, not as ugliness.

She patted my knee. A simple gesture that rekindled so many memories of my mother. For the first time since she'd passed, I let myself think back on a memory of her and feel comfort instead of grief.

"I don't deserve the forgiveness Brayden's given me. I know that. But he gave it to me anyway. He initially gave it just to free himself. Finding me was a stepping-stone he thought he had to cross. Something he had to do to get back to the family he'd loved and lost."

She exhaled a shaky breath and wiped the back of one hand against her cheek. I pressed my lips together to hold off my own growing emotion.

She continued, "When Brayden told me your story, what happened that horrible night . . . I can't explain what it did to me.

He's told me you feel partly responsible. And I know he feels wholly to blame. But there were dozens of dominoes that toppled over and led to that accident. A perfect storm of unfortunate decisions that started with my own. They all combined and led to your brother waking up in that hospital bed. We all share a piece of that burden. In so many ways, what happened in that locker room between me and Jack Ross kicked off one helluva chain reaction."

"It's hard for me not to play the what-ifs."

"Lord, I know, honey. I'm a champion at that myself."

We smiled softly at one another.

"When Brayden first found me, I asked a million what-ifs. What if I'd had all those years with him? What if I'd kept him to raise him myself? But I've learned to make peace with it. Instead of looking back, I've learned to focus on the future. On what can be." Her voice cracked with emotion.

Instinct made me reach out to her again. I loosely grasped hold of her hand. She exhaled and gripped tighter on to mine, shaking it with something that felt like relief.

"I begged Brayden to let me come here as soon as he thought you were ready. Thanks to your mother, Brayden found me. But, now, you've become his missing piece."

She turned her head and smiled at me, so much like her son that I had to blink back tears.

"Ashley, I came here to return the favor."

BRAYDEN

"You're doing the right thing here, Brayden. You just have to stay the course."

"I'm not so sure Ashley's gonna see it that way," I replied.

"You're keeping your promises. What more can you do?"

"I could set things to right and walk away. Let her have what she deserves."

"What she deserves or what she wants?"

"Both."

"Be the man she deserves. You're already the one she wants." My mother smiled and patted my hand before I could refute her claim. "Trust me on that. Woman's intuition."

"Thank you for coming all this way."

"Brayden, there is nowhere else I'd rather be. Thank you for letting me see your home." She lifted a hand to my cheek. "It's everything I prayed it would be."

I nodded, pretending like hearing her talk about our past didn't still make me a basket case.

"You think she'll ever really forgive me?" I asked quietly.

"You know that better than me, don't you? Don't know anyone else who's ever done as much big forgivin' as you. Most folks would've never believed you and I could be standing here together."

I tipped my chin as I stared down at my feet, avoiding more of that damn vulnerability.

"My papa used to always say, 'You can't catch a fish if you don't cast your hook in the stream.'" She squeezed my shoulder. "That's Texas for, *You just gotta keep tryin'*."

I nodded.

"If you don't want her to give up on you, you can't give up on her."

"I never gave up on her," I replied quickly.

"When the time comes, you tell her the whole story and make sure she sees that."

ASHLEY

Jess hadn't stopped talking.

She'd told me stories about her former roommate, her classes at Columbia, and the day she'd found out she had a big brother.

She had this magnificent freeness about her, an innate ability to overshare. She interspersed light and dark, happy and sad, with total disregard for prejudice over which she preferred to tell.

I'd misjudged her on first sight. She wasn't the girl everyone wanted to hate; she was the girl everyone wanted to be near—the life of any party.

She and Joey were gonna be thick as thieves.

She'd driven over to the marina with Brayden and Evan, but as soon as she saw the dock full of shirtless sunbirds, she'd decided to forgo the sailing lesson and hang out with me instead.

"This is the best view in town. Will you look at that one? Jesus, that's some good DNA. Please tell me he's a regular."

I smirked as she leaned over the counter to get a better angle. Her white plastic sunglasses slid down the bridge of her nose.

"I think I need to come stay here for the rest of the summer. Bray needs his personal assistant with him full-time. And he needs to take this rehab thing real slow. He's gotta convince his general manager to let him stay here into the fall."

I tried not to let it bother me. The mention of a deadline and Brayden's other life. The one he had to go back to. Eventually, the crystal slipper would fall off again. And I'd be left like the sweet little field mouse.

She must've sensed my disquiet. She levered herself up to sit on the counter, facing me instead of the man-whore view.

"You know he's scared, right?"

"Scared? Who?"

"My brother."

I was really trying to get used to hearing her call him that.

"What does he possibly have to be scared about? Seems like he's got everything figured out."

"That's an act," she said matter-of-factly as she pursed her lips. "He's terrified he's never gonna play again. Or, he'll play but not be any good. He'll be that dude everyone says was great once upon a time."

She spoke of sad things, but her legs swung back and forth, loose and free of her own worry. I wondered what it was like to live like that.

"He'd kill me for saying this, but he's also terrified of things not working out here. You have no idea the lengths he's gone to, to try and make things right."

"What do you mean?"

"He's just—"

"Miss F!" Evan called out to me, interrupting her answer.

"Oh, shit. What's wrong with him?" Jess asked, scooting down off the counter, as she plucked the glasses off her face.

Brayden was limping a little, stumbling up onto the path, while Evan tried to climb under his shoulder and pretend to carry some of his weight. As they clambered up toward us, I could hear the muttered curses falling from Brayden's mouth in one long compound string.

"What happened?" I called back, already rounding the desk.

"I hope you know how to handle this shit—I mean, stuff. Dude is suffering," Evan replied.

"I'm suffering from being an idiot," Brayden said, looking down at me. "You still got meat tenderizer and baking soda stocked up here?"

"Oh God. How bad is it?"

He turned around, unveiling his back to us. Ugly red welts stained his skin. They curved down along his shoulder blades and all the way to the side of his rib cage.

Jessica's hand flew up to cover her mouth. "What the fuck is that?"

"Jellyfish," Brayden and I answered in unison.

"Biggest motherfuckers I've ever seen," he added. "Things had six heads and mile-long arms. Fell in the water, trying to turn near the point. Stupid freaking rudder just got stuck."

"You were leaning way too far, man," Evan said, piping up the real answer as he tried unsuccessfully to squelch a knowing smile.

"Well, look who's the expert now, hotshot. Don't you have somewhere to be, kid?" Brayden reached out and lightly punched him on the shoulder.

"I can't leave you all busted up like this. We should drive over and see my mom. She'll know what to do."

"Nah. I grew up covered in these damn things. Ash is gonna doctor me up with some crap that's gonna sting real bad, and I'll live to see another day. We ain't ever going out near that damn buoy again though; I can tell you that." He smirked and then grimaced in pain again. "Don't keep your girl waiting. Get out of here. Jess, can you drive him home for me? Left my keys under the mat."

He turned back to Evan. "Go brag about how you had to pluck my ass outta the water. Make it sound real good. Like superheroes against giant man-eating squid. Make 'em think we saved the town or something, m'kay? We've got a reputation to uphold here, buddy." He pointed a finger at Evan and chuckled. "Don't go telling them I fell over."

Evan laughed and smiled at me before he followed Jess toward the parking lot.

"I have some in the office. Come on, let's get you fixed up. That has to hurt pretty bad."

He followed me inside, shutting the office door behind him. I dug through the first aid drawer to find the Adolph's canister.

When I turned back around, he was standing right behind me, arms folded behind his head so that both his shoulder muscles and welts were on full display. I licked my lips and tried to ignore the sexual charge already building between us.

"Try to stay still."

I started with his back, moistening his skin with a cold, wet towel. Then, I spread on a thick paste I'd mixed by hand. He groaned a couple of times as I turned him, so I could reach the most tender part near his ribs. My fingertips trailed down his sides, grazing the redness as softly as I could.

When I hovered near the edge of his waistband, he reached down and pulled the tie on his board shorts, loosening them enough to slide down onto his hip bones. I followed along the length of the deepest welt. He sucked in a deep breath as he watched my fingers moving against his skin.

"Does that hurt?" I asked just above a whisper.

Our eyes met briefly before he dropped his gaze down to my mouth. His tongue darted across his bottom lip.

"It doesn't hurt half as bad as being this close without touching you." Bent knuckles brushed down the side of my cheek. "You about done with this needing-space thing?" He stepped closer to me, wedging his leg between my own. The pad of his thumb skimmed across my bottom lip. "'Cause, right now, I think you need reminding of just how good it is when there's no space between us at all."

My lips parted as he pressed his thigh flush against me, granting me rough friction where I needed it.

"Brayden." I said his name to broadcast a warning, but my voice came out too husky. It sounded more like, *Please fuck me hard now*, than, *Back up off me*.

He didn't need further invitation.

His lips pressed against mine in a slow, drugging kiss. Little pecks became nibbles with just enough pressure to make me want to beg for more. His leg pressed harder against me, forcing me to squeeze my inner thighs around it.

"Fuck. Ash, I need to be inside you." He spoke the words against my lips before waging a full-fledged assault. His tongue swept inside my mouth as his palm cupped my backside, pulling my leg up toward his hip.

"Motherfucking hell."

His tone shot from low and sexy to one of sheer pain.

He'd pulled too high. My leg had brushed right across the deepest welt, scraping the abraded skin and grinding the salty paste I'd just applied down into it.

We sprang apart. His face scrunched up as he looked down at it.

"Shit. I'm sorry," I said, backing away.

His hand reached out for me. "No. No, I'm fine." He sucked air through his teeth.

I laughed. "You're not fine. You're in excruciating pain." I turned and walked back to the first aid drawer, searching for something to help.

He followed me, strong hands gripping my waist from behind. "The only thing that will leave lasting pain is the case of blue balls you're gonna give me if you don't climb on my dick in the next sixty seconds."

His lips met the side of my neck, rubbing the scruff of his jaw against soft skin. I smirked as I found the bottle. Popping it open, I spilled two white capsules into my hand and turned in his embrace.

"Here," I said, holding them out in my palm. "This will help with the swelling."

He stepped back, staring at my offering, as his Adam's apple bobbed up and down. "Nah. I'm good." He held up a hand.

I thrust mine out toward him again. "Don't be a macho jerk. These will help. You're gonna hurt like hell all day if you don't take something."

He plowed a hand through his hair, visibly shaken. "I don't . . ." He shook his head and finally looked me straight in the eyes. "I don't do pills. Of any kind. Ever."

"Oh." I blinked rapidly as my fist curled closed around my guilty suggestion. "I'm sorry. I didn't think—"

"It's okay. You didn't know."

I walked to the wastebasket and let the pills slide from my hand. The room felt too quiet, even with a giant elephant parked between us.

"What did you do after the surgery?" I asked softly.

"Jess came and stayed with me. She manned a bottle of extra-strength Tylenol for three days. Then, I went cold turkey. The doc offered me all the good stuff, but the thought of that just . . . I can't do it."

"How do you recover after games? Your shoulders used to ache . . ."

"Acupuncture. Massage. Good ole grin-and-bear-it."

He stepped toward me, lifting my chin with his finger. "I'm not gonna lie and say that shit is not around me still. There are guys in the clubhouse who hit junk pretty hard. And I won't pretend like I haven't been tempted. There were some shitty nights in the minors when I'd been stuffed on a smelly bus for too many weeks, and I wanted to numb out the loneliness. But, every time I get weak, I think about the look in your eyes when you walked into that hospital room. And I think about not being able to remember almost killing my best friend." His voice shook as his eyes grew glassy and red.

I couldn't help myself. My palms ghosted over the stubble on his cheeks, pulling him down to me. My lips brushed across his, back and forth, sharing the grief of bad memories. His hands encircled my hips again as he tried to take the lead, stealing us back toward where we'd left off.

"I want you to come to New York with me," he whispered the words against my mouth like they were pillow talk instead of an atom bomb.

"Wh . . . what?" I asked, pressing my hands against his biceps to push him back.

Bright blue eyes pierced into mine. I took another step backward, forcing his hands to drop away from my body.

"You got the job. The magazine wants to move forward with the shoot. Micky is getting it lined up. I've been waiting to find the right time to tell you. Come to New York with me. I have to do a stupid appearance at some opening, and we can do the cover shoot and have a little time, just the two of us. I can show you the city."

I walked to the window, gazing out at the sunbirds still day-drinking on the backs of their yachts.

"Ash, maybe what you need isn't space from me. Maybe you need distance from this place. Maybe you need some time away from here to think clearly."

He might as well have been one of those guys in the clubhouse, peddling magic pills and superhuman powders. Everyone had their weakness, their ultimate temptation. His offer was the worst kind of pain.

They'd come that morning.

Two guys with clipboards, wearing Brooks Brothers suits.

Their faces drawn straight from my nightmares.

"Just routine," they'd said.

An assessment of value, a survey of the land. I'd offered them coffee with my head held high, faking like they hadn't hurt my dignity. They'd politely declined. I guess it would've felt weird, taking a morning cup of joe from a woman whose life you were about to steal.

The bank deadline was closing in too fast. My father hadn't sent anything else or responded to my SOS. And, while business had picked up along with better weather, it still wasn't booming by any regard.

I couldn't keep my head up above the tall waves.

If I didn't pay the medical bills, they'd come and take the house. If I didn't pay the balance of the loan, they'd sell the marina. Something had to give.

I was drowning in a sea of red ink.

My options were gone.

The New York money would be good, but it wouldn't be enough. Liquidating assets was next. I could start breaking off chunks myself or wait for the Brooks Brothers twins to come back and sell it out from under me.

Before Brayden and his sister had arrived, I'd listed our two best rental boats for sale. If I could get a good price, I might be able to hold things off long enough to find my father. I just kept praying he'd magically found more work and had a miracle to bring back home.

"I can't."

On a sinking ship, a good captain never abandons the crew.

"The timing is just horrible. I can't leave right now."

"What do you mean, you can't? This shoot is the offer of a lifetime, Ash. It could kick off big things, doing what you love. We can explore the city. Eat our way through SoHo . . . shop at all the used bookstores in the Village. I know you'll love it."

He was the cruelest kind of pusher, hyping his painkillers with wide-eyed enthusiasm.

"I can't, Brayden. Everything is too big of a mess. There are things happening here that I can't explain. And what the hell would I tell my brother? I can't dump this all on him and run off to gallivant with you in New York."

"Ash, you're being ridiculous. I'm talking about a long weekend. Not a month-long sabbatical. This place will be all right without you for a couple of days. You have Logan. Evan and his crew would even come help. Matt could stay with Nathan. He's more than qualified to—"

"I don't know if Nathan is ready to meet Matt yet. I still don't know how he's going to react. He's not done giving me the cold shoulder."

"Jesus, Ash. You're babying your brother too much. What Nathan needs is a great big shove in the right direction. And what you need to do is accept my help to save this place and then come to New York with me." His knuckles cracked at his sides as his voice grew impatient.

"I've been taking care of Nathan just fine," I said forcefully. "And you know I won't ever take your money. You can't buy me, Brayden. I'm not for sale."

"Christ. Are we back to that? Why do you have to be so hardheaded?"

"I have to do this on my own, and this just isn't a good time to leave."

"You have mind-fucked yourself into thinking this place is some kind of penance. You've made it your own jail." An angry hand drove through his hair as he glared at me. "This job in New York is what you've always dreamed about. What happened to the girl who wrote in that composition book? I'm not trying to buy you. I'm trying to give you back a life. I can give you all those dreams we wrote down, Soot. Every single one."

Angry silence spread like wildfire, singeing my skin and filling my eyes. I wondered if this was how he'd felt when he turned down offers to pop a pill or chase a line.

"Dreams don't mean much unless you earn them. Remember the boy who didn't want to ride on his daddy's name?" I asked, biting back. "And the girl who wrote in that book grew up and realized dreams have nothing to do with real life. I don't belong there, Brayden. It's your dream world. Not mine. I'm needed here."

His nostrils flared. He turned his back on me and wove his fingers behind his neck, staring up at the ceiling in frustration. "I have to go up there, Ashley," he said quietly. "I promised Micky."

"I know. Go. It's where you belong, Brayden. We both know that."

He rounded on me again, staring me down with his signature intensity. "I don't want to go without you."

"You have another life. Eventually, you have to return to it. Permanently. We both know that whatever it is we're doing here"—I motioned between us—"can't last in the long run. Ultimately, you have to go back to being a superhero, and I have to go back to being plain old me. Whoever the hell that is."

He wiped his palms across his face in exasperation.

I bounced on my toes a little, trying to feel if the glass slippers were already cracking under my heels.

BRAYDEN

"Thought I might find you here." Jess plopped down next to me, stealing the lukewarm bottle from my hand. She did this cute thing where she wiped the rim before she took a slug from it.

"Better not let Mom catch you doing that."

She puckered her lips as she took another sip of my beer. "How you feelin'?" Her chin tipped toward the remaining welt grazing the ribs on my right side.

"Hurts like a son of a bitch." I closed my eyes and rested my head back against the new futon mattress. I'd replaced half the boards in the loft and had someone come paint and wire new electrical, but I couldn't face the idea of replacing all the furniture.

"You sure you don't wanna take something?" she asked tentatively. She already knew my answer.

She stayed with me all those nights right after my surgery. Including the few where I wanted to bite down on a stick because the thing hurt so bad.

My hand brushed across the scar on my elbow. "Nah. I'll live."

"So, I know you've had a shit day. Mom told me you and Ashley argued. But I have some news that I think you need to know." Her mouth quirked to the side. She did that when she didn't want to tell me something she knew would piss me off.

My sister's sleuthing skills amazed me. My stepfather ran a construction company. She'd worked for him since she was a young teenager. She had a head for business and an eye for detail.

When I hired her as my personal assistant, I thought it would be a way to help support her move to the city. I figured she'd take in my mail and get my dry cleaning in between her classes at school.

But I got drunk one night, her first month in town, and told her my whole sob story. I woke the following morning to a dossier of information she'd stayed up all night collecting. She'd been buried knee deep in this project ever since.

I knew it would be weird for her to finally meet Ashley face-to-face. Other than the unexpected intro, she'd handled it like a champion.

She tugged at her long blond ponytail as she tucked her legs underneath her and scooted a little farther away from me. Whatever she had to say wasn't gonna be pleasant.

"Let's have it."

"She posted these online this morning." She pulled a folded sheet of paper from the back pocket of her shorts. For Sale ads from an online marketplace.

Mrs. F purchased both those boats the summer before Nathan and I started tenth grade. She let us smash bottles of champagne over the hulls. We stole sips from them first, when she wasn't looking.

"Buy them."

Her brow raised.

"Before someone else does."

She nodded and started to fold the paper again, running her fingertips across the crease as she considered her words.

"There's more?"

She bit down on her top lip and nodded. "She had visitors this morning. Assessors. The bank is moving forward. These guys will submit a report that could let the county rezone it for . . ." As her words trailed off, she stared at me in confusion.

Clearly, my expression wasn't what she'd expected from this bit of news.

"You knew?"

I took the bottle back from her and drained the rest of it, washing down the guilt and avoiding her measured gaze.

"Oh God. What did you do?"

I rubbed a hand across my chin. "I'm done playing. I needed to put some pressure on her. This was the only way."

"Fuck, Brayden. She must be freaking out right now."

"Yeah." I nodded and exhaled a shaky breath.

Once again, my actions would cause her more tears. I really fucking hated that part. My hand pressed against the center of my chest.

"Of course, it backfired 'cause it didn't scare her enough to give in to my offer." I sighed and slammed my head back against the mattress a couple of times. "I need you to call Jacobs."

Her eyes grew wide.

"You're serious? You know that will seriously piss her off. And things with Nathan? How do you think he's gonna take—"

"They're gonna know the truth soon enough. I need to make sure everything's in place before that happens." I tried to ignore the pounding in my chest. "And call Vincent. Find out where the hell he is. I need an ETA."

"He checked in yesterday. He had to hole up there longer than expected. He's hoping to leave early next week. Said it might be slow-going though. Doesn't sound like things are going as smoothly as he hoped."

I exhaled against my frustration. The timing had to be right.

"Make sure he knows I want to see him first. We need to get our story straight."

"I hope you know what you're doing." Her tone teetered between skepticism and pity. "I really like her. I don't want her to hate you."

"Her mother said, if I had to, I could fight like hell. It's time to get a little bloody."

CHAPTER 19
BULLETS & BLOOD

BRAYDEN

The door slammed back against the wall. Good damn thing he hadn't locked it. I didn't want to deal with broken glass.

He levered himself up on the bed, obviously startled. "What the hell?"

My hands gripped both sides of the barrel, just like the dudes in the movies. I fought off a smirk as I waved the gun in his direction.

Not gonna lie; the cold metal made me feel like a total badass.

"What the fuck are you doing with that? Have you lost your ever-loving mind? Put that shit down, Brayden."

"You've got exactly two minutes to get your ass up and get yourself in that chair." I used the gun to motion toward the wheelchair, carefully positioned beside Nathan's bed. Straps hung from the ceiling, leverage to help him get up on his own.

"Ashley!" he shouted, trying to look around me toward the door.

"Go ahead and holler like a little girl. No one is gonna hear you. Ashley's not here. I waited at the end of the street till she left for work."

"You had this all planned out, huh? What are you gonna do, big shot? Put a cap in my ass? We both know you could never even hit a squirrel with that thing. Is it even loaded?"

I stared down at my weapon, refusing to let his words tarnish my buzz.

My grandmother never knew about the gun. The summer before

freshman year, we got Bobby's older brother to drive us to the sporting goods store in Easton to buy it. A Smith & Wesson 686 revolver. The mack daddy king of BB guns. I hid it in an old shoebox, tucked on the top shelf of the garage. In the middle of my sleepless night, it dawned on me I'd find the damn thing still hidden there.

"You better get the hell out of my house, or I'm calling the police." He reached for the cell phone beside the bed.

"Don't bother. I already called them."

Dillan took a step through the door. I'd told him to wait out of sight but to listen in, in case I needed backup.

Or in case I accidentally shot the motherfucker.

Nathan was right; my aim sucked. I could put a white ball within millimeters of a target sixty feet away, but I never could shoot down a tower of metal cans with this damn gun.

"You're in on this, too?" Nathan asked, glaring past me toward the good deputy. "You always were at the ready to suck his dick. What the fuck, Dillan? He banging you on the side, too? You know he's got a supermodel girlfriend back in New York; she might not like sharing."

Dillan marched forward, looking twice the badass in his full uniform. He had starched khakis, a big ol' metal badge, and a very real service revolver strapped to his hip. He rounded the other side of the bed, closing in on Nathan.

"I wasn't actually planning on helping him. I just came to make sure you didn't kill one another and force me to do a whole lotta paperwork. But, now, you've pissed me off, so I'm all in." He unclipped the shiny star pinned to his chest and slipped it into his breast pocket. He looked up at me with a short nod. "Grab his other arm."

We both lifted a side, thrusting him up from underneath his armpits.

"What the fuck . . . get off me . . . what the hell?"

Nathan kept protesting as we hefted his dead weight off the bed and into his chair. He awkwardly slumped over when we settled him into it.

We tried to readjust.

"Get the fuck off me. I've got it." He pushed Dillan's arm away and used his forearms to lever himself up to a better position. "Mind telling me what the hell this little ambush is all about? I thought I'd made myself pretty damn clear, Ross. I didn't think I had to spell out that I didn't want to ever see you again."

"I've thought of a million ways to do this. This finally seemed like the best option. You were never going to come willingly."

"Come where? I'm not going anywhere with you."

"Just listen to him, Nathan. This is for your own good."

"Shut the fuck up, Dillan. Don't you have a cat to go save or something?"

While his head was turned away from me, I pressed the gun back under the waistband of my shorts and leaned forward.

Breaking all the rules today.

Might as well go for it.

I punched him. Pretty hard. Right in the upper thigh.

"What the actual hell? Did you just hit me?" Nathan looked down at his leg in astonishment. "Did you really just hit a cripple? Jesus Christ. What's wrong with you? Are you high?"

"You flinched." I couldn't fight back the smile. That shit just broke out all over my face, spreading around like jam on toast.

"What?" He scowled at me. A little pissed off but also a little worried. "Are you on drugs again? Do you have a mental problem?"

"When I hit you, you flinched."

He blinked. Rapidly.

Then, finally, he turned toward Dillan again. "I want to file assault charges. And breaking and entering. And trespassing. And find out if you can charge him with brandishing a firearm or some shit like that. I want the whole book thrown at this bastard. If his daddy hadn't paid off the whole damn town, his ass woulda been in jail years ago."

"How much of it did you feel?" I asked, my voice determined.

I knew I was right. I had to be.

He slowly turned back to me, visibly exhaling. "I don't know what you're yammering on about, half-wit."

"I'm yammering about the feeling you have in that leg. You felt something. How long have you had the tingling?"

His jaw flexed back and forth as he ground his teeth together. His cheeks flamed. "You have lost your fucking mind," he murmured.

"Did it start right after the surgery, or did it take a while? The stem cell grafting is so new, no one knows how long it takes for the nerves to heal after they remove the scar tissue. There have been such varied results with the patients in the study."

"How the fuck do you know about any of that?"

"Because I've been to St. Louis. I've talked to Dr. Hildebrand. He's a brilliant man. You were very lucky to have him as your surgeon."

Nathan's eyes widened. Behind us, Dillan cleared his throat. Neither of us responded. We were far too engaged in a staring contest.

That shit's only fun when you're thirteen.

When you're an adult, it means serious business.

"About six weeks after." His voice stayed small. His Adam's apple bobbed up and down.

I didn't get it. How could a person not be shouting that from the rooftops? I balled my hands up at my sides to prevent myself from doing a full-fledged fist pump.

And from shaking the shit out of him.

If Matt was right—and Matt was always infuriatingly right—this stood a chance of working.

"You need to be in intensive therapy. You need daily massage, hydrotherapy, robotic training. You should have monthly MRIs. There's a doctor in Texas who's seen amazing results with—"

"You don't think I know all that, asshole? You don't think I know how this works? They're my fucking legs! I know all the research. I know all the cutting-edge therapies." He held out his arms. "Look around. Does it *look* like I can afford that right now? Does it look like my family can take one more hit?"

"You don't have to pay for a thing."

"I'm not taking your goddamn blood money. I won't let you buy your way out of what you did to me, motherfucker."

I shook my head and groaned. "You and your sister are singing that broken record like Donny and Marie. It's starting to seriously piss me off. I'm not taking no for an answer anymore. And you don't have to go anywhere for therapy. I brought the best in the business here. Funny, as it turns out, you need daily therapy, and so do I. So, we're gonna be gym buddies again. We're gonna push each other. We just have to get you out of this fucking room first."

His eyes narrowed, but he kept his mouth shut.

"Now, you gonna wheel yourself out, or do you need the town's finest here to give you a good push?"

His nostrils flared. Dillan reached forward to grab ahold of the handles.

"Get the fuck off me, man." Nathan turned to swat at his hands. "I don't need your help."

"You do need our help. And you're gonna smile and take it," I added. "Now, wheel yourself out there and let us help you in the car. Dillan drove. I figured you wouldn't want to get in a car with me."

He snickered, as he pushed his chair past me. "You got that right."

"If you shut up and behave, Dillan said he'd turn the lights on and take the long way around town."

ASHLEY

There were fifteen seconds of eerie quiet before the muffled shouting began, and the car doors slammed shut. My brother offered up a colorful series of curses, and then he and Brayden tumbled through the kitchen door, just like they had a thousand times before.

My breath caught as I saw them silhouetted there, side by side, against the soft gray glow of evening sky. I could almost hear my mother's voice calling them in for dinner and their jeers and good-natured taunting as they tried to settle on the final score to whatever game they'd been sparring at out back.

Those kids were still here.

Buried somewhere beneath new facial hair and old history.

My brother rolled past me, angrily pushing his chair right up to the refrigerator so one wheel hit the cabinet beside it. A permanent groove marred the wood.

"I guess Dillan got ahold of you?" Brayden asked me, still standing in the doorway. He swiveled his ball cap around backward, unveiling eyes labored by a long day's exhaustion.

The fridge door slammed. I turned back toward my brother.

"Oh. So, you were in on this, too? You knew he came over here and kidnapped me at gunpoint?"

"Gunpoint?" I asked, sending Brayden a curious look.

He ran the pad of his thumb across his bottom lip with sheepish guilt. "Kinda a long story," he murmured.

His eyes met mine and then trailed down the length of my body, soaking in my after-work attire of a braless T-shirt and gym shorts.

"Oh, good Lord. I'm still in the room, dipshit. Stop looking at my sister like that, and get the fuck out of our house. You're not the lost little puppy we're gonna take in and feed anymore." Nathan popped the top on a soda and turned to wheel himself out toward the family room. "But, speaking of food, is there any chance we're gonna eat anytime soon, Ashley Jane? I'm fucking starving. This asswipe had a ready-made drill sergeant over there, kicking the shit out of me all day." Nathan's voice trailed off as he exited the room.

The television clicked on to a rerun of *Seinfeld*.

I clutched on to the side of the counter, leaning my lower back against it to brace myself, as I stared at the floor beneath my feet. "How did things . . . I mean . . . does Matt still think . . ."

I'd been a nervous wreck all day, ever since I'd received a message from Dillan about the morning's events. I'd driven straight to the police station and grilled him for details. He'd made me promise not to run over and insert myself. It had taken a few hours to overcome the shock of Brayden's drag-him-out-of-bed methodology. But, once I had, all my thoughts gave way to more fear. Fear that I would give in and secretly let myself believe this could work.

"I know you're probably pissed at me for not waiting and for not including you."

I shook my head, refusing to look at him.

"It had to go down this way, baby girl. I know what I'm doing."

At least he hadn't directly asked me to trust him again.

He stepped closer to me, tipping my chin up with a bent knuckle. His tired eyes softened as they connected with my own.

"Breathe, Ash," he murmured before exaggerating the rise and fall of his own chest.

One side of his mouth turned up when I successfully listened. As I inhaled a long breath. My hands loosened their death grip on the counter and fell back to my sides.

"It went well."

"Really?" My voice rose with skepticism.

I bit my bottom lip, trying to prepare myself for impending hurt. There was always a *but*. It's the word people used right before they dropped the hammer. Only Brayden just stood there and stared at me.

"But?" I finally prompted.

"But nothing. Matt doesn't see any reason to refute his assessment. This can work, Ash. We just have to make your brother want it."

I squeezed my eyes shut. I couldn't stave off the ribbons of emotion uncurling inside me. I'd spent so many years on the receiving end of more bad news, I'd forgotten how to welcome relief.

My eyes startled back open as Brayden's index finger trailed down the side of my arm. He watched it descend before letting his hand fall away.

"Have you thought any more about the trip? About coming with me?"

"Brayden . . ."

Our eyes finally met, inviting combustion.

He moved quickly, placing both hands around my waist as he pulled me against him. His lips brushed softly against my own.

But, just as he started to deepen the kiss, my brother shouted out from the other room, breaking the spell, "Ashley! When the hell are we eating?"

Brayden took a step back, sighing. "Just think about it, Ash. Please." He resettled his hat with the brim facing forward. The move seemed to reset his resolve as well. "I'll be back again tomorrow. And the day after that. I'll keep coming back. Every day until you say yes."

BRAYDEN

"You're doing great. I never thought you'd be able to do this so fast. Let's try three more," Matt said. "Rest longer in between if you need to."

The robotic exoskeleton system, that Nathan lay strapped to, helped work legs that refused to stay useless. Watching him made me want to hum the theme to *Superman* while busting into pansy-assed tears. Yesterday, I'd had to step outside twice, pretending to take phone calls, just to keep my emotions in check. He did two more reps. His small movements surged through my own spine like the national anthem during a gold medal victory.

While I stood there with a case of girlie tingles, his face scrunched up from pain and exertion.

"That's it. You've got this, man." The words of encouragement slipped right out of me. I'd forgotten my new pledge to keep my mouth shut.

He belted out a quick reminder, "Shut the fuck up, asshole. I don't need you talking in my face."

The morning of his kidnapping, Nathan had refused to get out of the car. He'd sat in my driveway with the blue lights still swirling on top of Dillan's cruiser, talking to himself. He went on a nonstop two-hour rant. The passenger seat headrest made friends with his angry fists. He'd called me colorful names I'd never even heard.

Matt made us leave him there. Said he'd seen it all before. A guy couldn't learn to plow ahead to a new life until he left the old one behind.

"Leave him be. He's gotta let the hate drain out."

Since that first day, Nathan hadn't engaged in another meltdown. He still refused to get in a car with me again and claimed he would never even speak to Dillan, but he let Matt pick him up and take him home every day. He listened to Matt's instructions with patience and grace, replying with only quiet nods and gritty determination.

But that original back seat tantrum hadn't finished the job. Nathan's hatred for me needed to ooze out one drop at a time. We'd settled instead into a predictable pattern. His mouth served up short jabs and uppercuts, while I stood there and took it like a man.

"Can you please give this dickhead something to do other than gawk at me like I'm some circus freak?" Nathan called out, pushing himself through one final rep.

Matt smirked as he turned toward me. "He's right. Get back to it, Ross. I'm not running a preschool here."

I tried to refocus on my own workout.

But the reverse rule did not apply.

"Jesus. Is that all you've got? How much weight is on there?" Nathan snickered, judging me from across the room.

I refused to respond.

Responding made it so much worse.

"Moneybags, the Yankees are not gonna pay you twenty-six million next year to look that weak."

I added another weight to the stack on my machine and bit my tongue.

"Seriously, you might want to start working on a new career plan. Can't your daddy score you a gig in the booth? This is the first comeback that's over before it's even begun."

That last one stung a little.

I didn't mind taking his ire. I deserved it. I just would've preferred to stand in front of him while he pummeled me with his fists. Not because I couldn't take the pain, but because the constant belligerence was so unlike the old friend I'd once known.

Every barb he threw my way served up a reminder that the dude I'd loved like a brother might never completely return. Matt kept warning me about that, too. He'd told me stories about guys he'd served with who healed faster on the outside than they did inside their heads.

PTSD could change personalities.

So could bitterness.

Ironically, the daily heckling forced me to work harder. Just like the old days, there was Nathan, pushing me in the gym further than I'd go on my own.

I finished our sessions dripping with sweat but fired up for more. Matt kept cautioning me not to let the insults goad me into pushing too hard, too fast. But I kept using the ugly comments to drive me.

Truthfully, I'd have put up with anything.

As long as Nathan agreed to keep coming back.

After his tantrum subsided that very first day, Matt had walked him through an overview of the program. The strength-building, nerve-healing, mental game that would eventually prepare him to use a special harness system to relearn how to take steps. The process would be slow-going; the whole plan could take a year or more. To buffer that news, Matt had shown Nathan pictures of his buddy Gavin and video of him taking his first steps in the very same contraption we'd have installed here.

Nathan had palmed the bill of his baseball cap while he listened to Matt talk about his friend with unrestrained emotion. He'd thought his response was well hidden, but I'd known better.

My plan had a shot in the dark.

Stuffed down beneath his scruffy face and sullen attitude hid my old friend. And a tiny glimmer of hope. Not that he would ever let any of that touchy-feely crap bubble up to the surface.

"What's it like, fucking Celeste?" he called out to me during our next water break. "That chick has amazing tits. She looked smokin' at that movie premiere you took her to."

I wasn't the only one who'd spent a lot of time doing research the last couple of years. Nathan knew a whole lot about my life in New York.

"Does my sister know about her? I mean, I never figured Ashley would be happy as a token sidepiece. But maybe she's that desperate."

I inhaled, trying to ignore my mashed buttons. I walked to a shoulder machine and dropped down onto the seat, thinking I could grunt my way through what I really wanted to say. It didn't work. Defending Ashley wasn't something I could ever ignore.

I slammed the weight stack down and rounded to look at him.

"Nathan, shut the fuck up. Celeste and I are just friends. And I'm not gonna listen to you talk about your sister like that."

"Whatever, dude. Pretty sure my sister's gone through her fair share of sunbirds, so don't go thinking you have a magic dick or something. Sooner or later, she'll wake up and see the writing on the wall and realize you're an asshole."

He barely paused to reload.

"Weren't you dating the actress from that spy movie and Monica Barnes at the same time? I guess you're used to having a side dish, aren't you?"

"Nathan, try not believing everything you Google."

"What I can't believe is you've had a smoking-hot sister all these years, and we never knew it." Like any true competitor, he aimed right for the jugular. "That chick has legs meant for wrapping around hips."

"Jesus, when did you turn into Bobby? Knock it off. Jess is only nineteen."

"Only? Like that should stop me."

Nathan had crossed paths with my sister three days into our training. She was getting ready to fly home with my mom to spend some time in Oklahoma before the new semester started. Unfortunately, the town car I hired to take them to the airport arrived just as the guys pulled up in Matt's car.

"Nathan, stop talking about her."

"Oh, what? Now, there are boundaries? My sister was up for grabs, but I'm not allowed to look at yours?"

"I will hit you again. You know that, right?"

Matt knocked his clipboard with the palm of his hand, forcing us both to snap to attention. "Look, ladies"—his top lip curled up with sarcasm—"I'm trained to kill with my bare hands, and I'll hit you both if you don't stop jawing at each other."

Peace reigned for a little while after that. By the end of our afternoon session, my brain and body were spent. Luckily, Nathan had also sweat out a good deal of piss and venom.

I brought him a chilled towel and an equally cold beer. "For some reason, I still feel like being nice to you."

"Don't knock yourself out, pretty boy." He took my peace offerings and rolled out onto the back deck in his chair.

I popped the cap off my bottle and followed behind him. "You know you've made incredible progress already. I don't think Matt ever thought you'd build strength up this fast. We're gonna get you walking again, Nathan."

He tipped the top of his bottle toward me. "There's no *we* in this whole shooting match. Let's get that straight right now. You get all the glory for breaking me, but you're not gonna take any of the credit for what's going down now. Don't expect any fluffy thank-yous or for me to wanna suddenly hug it out."

When I didn't respond, he backed down and sat quietly, finishing his beer. I used the short respite to shore up my courage.

"I have a job opportunity for your sister. A chance for her to do a photography shoot."

"You've got her baited right on the end of a hook, don't you?" He jammed a crooked finger into the side of his mouth in a crude demonstration of a caught fish.

"Nathan." I sighed.

"Whatever. So, what's the catch? Why the fuck are you telling me this?"

"The job's in New York. She'd have to travel there with me for a couple of days."

"Great. Well, we both know your rap sheet already includes kidnapping, and word around town is you have a private jet parked on the airfield in Easton. So, what are you waiting for? My permission?" He snickered. "You didn't bother to ask my permission years ago, so why bother now?"

"I already asked her. She doesn't want to leave work. Or leave you."

Drum roll, please.

"So, I've been thinking, maybe you could come with us. It would give you a chance to see Cindi."

"Fuck you. I'm not going anywhere with you."

I blew out a breath. "It was worth a try," I mumbled to myself.

"But I don't give a rat's ass if she goes," he added, much to my surprise. "I don't know why she stays in this damn town anyway."

"She stays 'cause she loves you. And she thinks working hard is the only way to show it."

"Yeah. Whatever."

"And you talk a good game, but you love her, too."

He didn't respond, but he looked away from me.

More hiding.

I know you're still in there somewhere, buddy.

"You know she thinks all this is her fault."

He slowly turned to face me. His eyes told me that fact wasn't news to him.

"She thinks she sent you right into my path that night."

"She did." He paused and swallowed down a swig of beer. "But that doesn't mean I wouldn't have been there anyway."

He bit down on the inside of his cheek. He used to do that right before he stepped up to the plate.

He stared down at the label on his bottle. "She was a mess that night. Couldn't even get into the house. She collapsed in the driveway. I had to carry her inside. She was dry-heaving. Had snot and tears caked all over her face. Wasn't making much sense." He looked back over at me, eyes suddenly deep and intense. "What she doesn't know is, as soon as I got her settled, I would've come anyway. Whether she'd asked me to or not, I would've come to pound your ass for breaking her heart."

I inhaled deeply, sucking his words into my brain.

"Maybe you should try telling her that," I responded quietly.

"Maybe you should just stay the fuck out of our business."

I downed the rest of my beer and stood from where I'd been leaning against the deck rail. I'd beaten my head against the same wall one too many times today.

"I'm sure Matt can give you a lift home whenever you're ready."

"Brayden," he called back to me as I opened the sliding door to retreat, "you were right about one thing. I might not show it a lot, but

I do love her. If you hurt her like before, I will come for you again. And, this time, I'll make sure you're the one left bleeding."

CHAPTER 20
SHOVED

ASHLEY

"We missed you at dinner."

I startled as he rolled into the room. I'd been so caught up in recalculating projections for the month ahead, I hadn't even heard my brother come in the house.

"Hey. Yeah, sorry. I got your text. I just wanted to stay and finish this. Did you guys have a good time?"

"Matt and I just grabbed some crab cakes at Skipper's. It was pretty good. Ran into Dillan. He groveled enough I let him join us."

After a couple weeks of general hostility, my brother was finally showing signs of caving. I assumed the change in spirit came in part from Matt's combat training—his ability to break down enemy resistance. But it was also bolstered by Nathan's own self-recognition. Progress was coming faster than anyone expected.

Even he couldn't deny it.

I didn't want to admit Brayden had been right, but maybe the swift shove was all my brother ever needed.

Subtle differences had started to break through. Nathan hadn't cut his hair, but it was washed and neatly combed back into a tight ponytail. He was wearing a sleeveless athletic jersey that showcased impressive arms. The old, baggy sweatpants had been traded for gym shorts, revealing the legs he used to always keep covered up. They still rested on the metal plates at the bottom of his chair, but his feet no longer twisted awkwardly, like a marionette with too much string.

His jaw still flexed tightly, but he spoke with a little less bitterness as well.

I was afraid to get used to it.

He'd built a camaraderie with Matt. He would leave with him early each morning. And, several times now, they'd spent so many hours working together at the boathouse, they'd ended up foraging for dinner together, too.

"Matt's a good guy, huh?"

"That dude is pretty fucking amazing actually," he answered with a tone of respect I hadn't heard from him in a long time. "Some of his stories are incredible. He did two tours in the Middle East. He's seen some serious shit go down. Did you know he's going through a divorce now, too? Chick fooled around on him while he was on his last deployment."

"Wow. No, I had no idea."

"Yeah, probably good the Yanks hired him to help Brayden. Got him outta dodge while they wait for the ink to dry on the settlement papers. Somehow, she managed to swindle him out of his own freaking house."

I bit my tongue. The truth about Matt's employer wasn't gonna come from me. Nathan was making too much progress, building strength and a new friendship. I wasn't gonna bust that up.

"I can see why you passed up on the offer to join us. Looks like you had far more exciting plans for the night. You working on becoming one of those hunchback old ladies?"

I sighed and straightened up in the dining room chair. "That's about all I'm gonna be successful at."

I'd been sitting here for half the night, poring over the papers now spread in makeshift piles all around me. Yellow Post-it-notes with numbers that no longer made sense were stuck haphazardly to the side of my laptop screen.

"This mess isn't your doing. You know that, right?"

I glanced skeptically around the table at the disaster I'd definitely created on my own.

"I don't mean the papers, half-pint."

My eyes flew up to his. He hadn't called me that name in a very long time. Maybe not since he'd woken up in the hospital and found me crying beside his bed.

"What happened, half-pint? Are you hurt? Where are we?"

He hadn't remembered yet. When he'd first awakened, his brain had been too scattered and scarred to recall everything. The animosity had come later, filling him an ounce at a time as he regained memory and feeling, everywhere but his legs.

I plucked up a sticky note and sadly crumpled it inside my fist. "I just want to be able to keep things going. At least until Dad gets back. Adjusting the slip rates is working, and the new reservations app is great. We've had more steady traffic." I shrugged my shoulders. "It's just not enough. If they rezone the land, I think we might lose it, Nathan. I'm not sure there's anything else I can do."

I knew why my mother had double-mortgaged our whole life. She'd been desperate. Had no choice. She'd wanted him to have all the best care. Mortgaging the family's future to pay for Nathan's doctors and hospital stays in those early years was the only option she'd had. Thankfully, the bulk of my mother's treatments had been covered by insurance. And Nathan's surgery last year had fallen under some special research grant. If we'd had to pay those bills, too, we'd have sunk long ago.

"You've tried your best. No one would ever say different."

I swallowed hard against his unexpected praise. "I just wanted to be able to do this. I wanted to be able to save something." I didn't add, *Since I couldn't save you.* "Losing the marina would feel like losing a whole other part of her. You know?"

"Yeah." He breathed in deeply and rubbed a hand across his mouth. "Sure would be nice if Dad showed himself, huh?"

"I've tried calling every day. No response. I'm getting worried."

"Worrying is all you do. You need to give yourself a break."

I shut the laptop and tried to start stacking some of my chaos into neater piles.

"You should go to New York."

My head shot up as my eyes widened. "How do you even know

about that?" I nodded as soon as the words left my mouth. "Of course. Brayden told you."

"You should go. It's a good opportunity for you."

"Nathan, I can't leave you and the—"

"I'm a big boy, Ash. I'll be fine. I'm considering taking off for the weekend myself. Matt asked me to tag along to DC for a couple of days. There's a friend of his he wants me to meet—a guy he served with who used to have similar wheels." He tapped the sides of his wheelchair.

"Wow. Really? That's great." I tried to hide my utter astonishment.

A few weeks ago, he wouldn't even go out to eat with me. Now, he was talking about weekend trips.

He shrugged his shoulders. "Figured it would be good for me to get out of town, too. Stretch my legs a little."

I blankly stared at him.

"Jesus, Ash." He smiled. A real one. With teeth showing. It almost hurt to look at. "You can laugh. That was a joke."

A joke?

My brow furrowed.

When was the last time you made a joke?

I smiled softly back at him.

"Go. The money can't hurt, right? And it will be good for you. I promise, this mess will still be here when we both get back. Maybe we can sit down together and figure out what the hell to do."

"I feel like I'm having an out-of-body experience. You're telling me to go do something for Brayden?"

"No. Brayden can take a flying leap straight to hell. I'm telling you to go do something for yourself."

"When you come to a fork in the road, take it."
—*Yogi Berra*
Baseball Hall of Fame, Class of 1972

ASHLEY

Counting the number of times I'd flown on a plane didn't require all the fingers on one hand.

Disney World, the year I turned seven. The Grand Canyon, when I was nine. A horrible family reunion in Ohio at fourteen. We hit turbulence on the way home during that last trip. I got so sick in my stomach, my mother dug into the seat pocket to locate the puke bag.

Paper vomit receptacles weren't included on this flight. Neither were real seats or the little packages of peanuts I'd planned to hoard.

"You sure I can't get you anything else, Ms. Foster?"

The flight attendant made me antsy. She kept fluttering around like the butterflies in my belly.

This trip was either a brilliant opportunity or the worst decision I'd ever made. Not that it had truly been my decision. Rocks and hard places didn't provide many comfortable options.

Those Brooks Brothers bank goons were my rocks.

The hard place sat beside me, looking overtly gorgeous and smug.

"No. Really, I'm good. Thank you," I responded politely.

I wanted to throw something at her.

The plane rolled a little to the side. My hands clutched the arm of the couch as a familiar arm wrapped protectively around my shoulders.

She nodded her head back at me, never wavering against the turbulence as she stood in three-inch navy-blue pumps.

"Would you like me to refresh your coffee again, Mr. Ross?"

Would you like me to suck your dick, Mr. Ross?

I mimicked her nasally voice in my head as she smiled wider at him. She had way too many teeth. She'd been ogling him like a starstruck teenager since she greeted us, standing at the top of the stairs as we pulled up beside them.

I couldn't entirely fault her. Brayden looked stupidly delicious in dark jeans, a starched white dress shirt, and a linen sport coat with a silk handkerchief peeking out the front pocket.

I wasn't used to seeing him dolled up.

My Brayden wore gym shorts and faded T-shirts.

He looked older. Sophisticated. More big-city important than quaint-town casual. I wanted to openly gawk at him, too. But, at the same time, I wanted to mess up the perfectly coiffed hair, wrinkle the shirt, and make him look all mine again.

I smoothed a hand over the cuffed hem of my jean shorts. Primping time hadn't been an allotted part of my schedule.

I'd been up before the sun, and had worked a full day, trying to line things up to run smoothly for Logan in my absence. My long afternoon had garnered daydreams of catnapping in the buttery leather seats inside Brayden's car. I'd been fully prepared to live out that fantasy, as he battled through DC traffic to get to the airport. But instead of heading toward the interstate, he'd diverted us to the private airstrip just outside of town.

My sleepiness had long since evaporated.

Replaced by my current state of pins, needles, and annoyance with our overly attentive flight attendant.

"We're fine, Candace. Thank you for everything." Brayden's words were pleasant but firmly dismissive.

Her toothy smile faltered slightly. "Of course. The pilot will let you know when you both should prepare for landing." She disappeared behind the glossy mahogany partition at the front of the cabin.

"Are you sure you're okay?" he asked, his voice filled with laughter as he squeezed my shoulder.

"This plane is"—my head turned to survey the posh space around us—"well above my raising."

He chuckled and leaned over to place a chaste kiss on my forehead. "You get used to it after a while. Beats trudging through National or BWI."

"Nothing about this could ever feel normal."

The private jet wasn't the only thing I had to get used to. An oversize black SUV pulled up beside the plane as soon as we landed. A guy in a tailored black suit, with a neck as big around as my thigh, jumped out. He immediately took Brayden's leather duffel and my small black suitcase.

"Ashley, this is Gino. Gino, meet Ashley."

As the man opened my door, he smiled, revealing a chipped front tooth. "Pleasure meetin' you, Ashley. I hear this is only your second time visiting the city that never sleeps."

"Uh, yeah. I came up once with my mom when I was little. We took the train up to see a show."

"Well, how's about I give you's the five-cent tour on our way to this guy's digs? We've probably spruced up the place since the last time you were here."

Gino was the kind of guy you didn't turn down. He had the body of a linebacker and spoke with a thick Jersey accent that certified he knew all about busting kneecaps. But it was his teddy-bear face that made me want to go along.

Brayden stayed pretty quiet as we took Gino's long way through town—down Fifth Avenue, past the Empire State Building, back up through Rockefeller Center, and across to Times Square. The SUV rolled down the streets like a moving mausoleum, cushioning the blow of potholes and sealing off the noise of the scenes playing around us on all four sides. I cracked my window, desperate to take in the sounds and smells. My face stayed pressed to the glass, reflecting my overwhelmed reaction to the spectacle lying just on the other side.

It looked so totally opposite from the backdrop of my life. Nothing here was green or blue or wide open. I remembered the tall buildings and the feeling of hustle and bustle from my trip as a little kid but seeing it with adult eyes made it feel foreign and new.

The muted palette of colors made my fingers itch for a shutter button.

All the people on the streets were adorned in the same shades of brown and black as the dirt and grime that clung to the sidewalks and buildings. They walked with a slight turn of shoulders, passing one another without eye contact. A screaming baby rolled by, ignored by a mother shouting just as loudly into her phone. Throngs of overly important phone-typers worked while they walked.

Everything about the scene drew me in. I wanted to know the stories of all those passersby. Who were they? Where were they rushing off to?

I wanted to stop them one by one and capture some subtle quality that would humanize and extract them from the blended army marching both ways up and down every street.

My hand stroked the black nylon of the camera bag that sat on the seat next to me.

We got stopped by a throng of tourists, crossing with their faces tilted up toward the famous wall of neon. I followed suit, pressing my forehead against the window to stare up at the massive display.

"Oh my God."

"What's wrong?" Brayden asked, concerned.

"Is that you?"

When he didn't answer, I turned to look at him. He moved back farther in his seat and ran a hand through his hair. His shoulders shrugged. He seemed a little timid, almost embarrassed.

"Sure."

"Holy crap. You're like . . . Godzilla in underpants." I peered back out, watching as two women on the sidewalk giggled their way through taking a selfie.

One held her hand up, pretending to cup the part of Brayden vastly on display. The tight white boxer briefs didn't leave much to the imagination. Neither did the rest of his naked body, plastered up six stories tall.

"I think those women just sexually assaulted you."

Gino chuckled in the front seat.

"This is so surreal."

Unlike all those people I'd studied outside the window, our feet never touched the pavement.

Gino drove us straight down into an underground garage. As soon as the back tires passed by, an industrial-strength metal gate dropped down behind us, carefully shutting off one world from the other. A tall, gray-haired gentleman in another pressed black suit opened my door. His gloved hand helped me out of the SUV. He warmly greeted Brayden before escorting us into a sleek lobby where an elevator waited to whisk us right up to the top floor.

My ears finally popped as Brayden fit his key in the door.

The place was massive. Cavernous ceilings towered two stories above us.

"Holy shit. How many people live here?"

Brayden chuckled in response and carried our bags down a hall that led to more doorways.

A wall made entirely of glass led out onto a terrace that overlooked most of lower Manhattan. A small infinity-edged pool swept across the side. The lights under the water twinkled against the windows, casting prisms of color back into the dark room. Rich, glossy wood and black metal accents highlighted the family room and kitchen.

Brayden returned, flipping a switch to ignite a sleek fireplace that ran nearly the entire length of one wall. I walked toward it, holding out my hands, as if I needed warmth.

Everything else in the room felt cold.

Everything, except the arms that suddenly wrapped around me from behind. The scruff of his chin met my neck.

"I'm gonna order us some bad takeout and fix us a drink. Make yourself at home."

I nodded, while silently questioning how anyone relaxed here.

I didn't even want to touch anything.

His lips gently grazed the skin beneath my ear before he withdrew to the kitchen.

I wandered out onto the terrace. Maybe I'd feel more acclimated after soaking in the Manhattan glow bouncing off the surrounding skyscrapers. Tipping my head back, I searched for the point where the artificial light gave way to the real night sky.

"He was right. There aren't any stars here," I mumbled to myself. I walked all the way to the rail to peek over the side. "Holy shit." I quickly stepped back and sharply inhaled. "How do people live all the way up here?"

I swallowed down vertigo and went back inside to explore.

A framed jersey in the hallway seemed like the only thing in the place linking it to the man who lived here. A little plaque on the bottom had a date and the words *First Game*.

The next door I came to opened soundlessly to a pitch-black room. My hand grappled with the switch until soft light arced through the space. Deep copper walls and sky-high mahogany bookcases surrounded me. Mementos and stacks of well-loved hardbacks filled every inch of them. A large desk dominated the room. Behind it, a spotlight shone down on a spectacular canvas painting.

I stepped closer to it, pulled by the texture and vivid shades of violet and bronze. The dark silhouette of a boy walked across a field at sunset. His outstretched hand tugged on the end of a lasso, plucking a magic boat from a twilit sky.

"It was painted by a friend of mine. Do you like it?"

I turned to look back at him, flustered. He stood, leaning against the doorway with two glasses of wine in his hands.

"It's incredible," I said reverently. I smirked and cocked my head to the side as I turned back to him, uncertain. "Sorry if I'm intruding. The door was shut, and I just got nosy . . ."

"Don't be sorry." He set the glasses down on a table beside a leather sofa and slowly strode toward me with a look in his eye I knew all too well. "This is my favorite room in the whole place. Having you here completes it."

I tried to prepare myself for the onslaught. I'd promised myself I'd maintain some boundaries this weekend.

As he stepped forward, he slipped the sport coat off, slinging it over the back of a chair beside me. He stared down at me as he cuffed the sleeves of his white dress shirt up over the muscles of his forearms. The movement reminded me too much of what lay beneath the starched cotton. And of what sat on full display for the world to see a couple dozen blocks from here.

Brayden evidently had no intention of maintaining any space limitations. He instantly became a part of mine.

One finger traced down the side of my cheek before tipping my chin up, forcing my eyes to meet his. His other hand roughly tangled into the hair at the back of my neck, drawing me closer, like the boat in that painting.

"Having you here is a dream come true. You don't know how many times I've sat here and imagined being with you. Here. Just like . . ." His lips met mine, cutting off his own words and killing any hope I'd had of restraint.

It started out soft and slow. Wet, open-mouthed kisses that quickly drugged my senses. But too much time had passed since we last gave in to what we both needed. We stood there in a puddle of kerosene.

He groaned before his lips pressed down harder. My arms encircled his waist as I pulled his shirt free from his waistband. My nails scratched into the warm skin on his lower back. He groaned again as soon as they made contact. His hands skimmed down over my hips, possessively pulling me against him.

"I can't fucking wait another second, Soot. I can't. Having you here . . . it's messing with my head."

My eyes grew hooded. I whispered his name, granting him the acceptance he craved. My hands cupped his cheeks, drawing him back to me.

I moaned as he sucked hard on my bottom lip. His mouth slanted off my jaw and down across my neck. One hand drew up the side of my body, roughly palming my breast through my shirt and bra. He looked down, watching my flesh plump up in his hand, before he bent his head, replacing his hand with his teeth. I threw my head back and said his name again.

"I'm gonna fuck you in every single room in this place." His words tumbled out against my skin.

I tugged at the hair on the back of his neck, forcing his eyes up to meet mine, as I bit down hard on my swollen bottom lip. His eyes nearly crossed as he stared at it with unguarded need.

His hands traveled the length of my body until he grabbed hold of my ass, dragging me up off the ground, forcing my legs around his waist.

"I wanna lay you out naked on every damn piece of furniture till every single fantasy of mine comes true. Then, I'm gonna take you on the patio until all of New York has heard us scream each other's names."

With my legs still around him, he started to back us out of the room. My eyes stayed shut right until we reached the doorway. I opened them to gaze back into the one space that didn't belong to a stranger.

"Oh my God."

My legs slackened of their own accord, sliding down a little on his hips until he tugged harder, carrying more of my weight. My mouth formed into a perfect O as I surveyed the far wall. I'd missed it on my initial inspection. The change in my mood caused Brayden to look back over his shoulder. My legs slowly slid down to the floor.

I stepped around him, staring at the three large black-and-white canvases hung side by side.

I instinctively moved toward them, my hand now covering my mouth. "How did you? Did you just have these hung up? Where did you . . ." I took another step forward.

"You know that one has always been my favorite," he answered, tilting his head toward the one in the center. "I had it made from my print."

The last time I'd seen that image, it had been lying on the floor of his bedroom, beneath a bed of broken glass.

There, highlighted by a single point of light shining down from the ceiling, were the two of us, tumbling midair off the end of the dock, laughing and clinging to one another.

BRAYDEN

"Good Lord, kid. Why didn't you tell me?" Micky slid his glasses down his nose and ran a hand over the artificially thick hair he'd paid a fortune to have plugged back into his head. "Does she need an agent? I could get her booked."

His brow raised as he nodded his head with a smug confidence that had already calculated how much to demand.

"Damn. I get it now. I'd stay down in Bumfuckville, too, if I had a piece like that. Your father said she was hot, but he didn't elaborate."

He slugged me on the back as Ashley looked up at us from across the room. She was speaking to one of the production editors, pointing to something on a clipboard as she bit her bottom lip. She glanced up again, worry furrowing her brows. I willed my smile to give her some reassurance.

She'd been a nervous wreck from the moment she woke up. When she'd refused to share a bowl of cereal with me, I'd turned her into my breakfast, sliding under the covers so I could force her to relax. I adjusted the seam of my jeans as I replayed the image of her clutching on to fistfuls of black sheets as she came undone beneath my tongue.

Waking up with her in my bed had given me a renewed sense of determination. That was where she fucking belonged, and nothing was gonna stop me from getting her there. Permanently.

She suddenly bent over, picking out another lens from the black bag at her feet. My dick twitched like a crackhead with lines of coke already cut on the table.

"Seriously, are those things real?"

I wasn't the only one enjoying the view.

"Mick," I said with ample annoyance.

He slid his glasses back up his nose and buttoned his Armani suit jacket. "What, kid? I'm old. I'm not dead." He motioned across the room with a bent knuckle. "Your chickadee ever decides to move in front of the camera, you let me know. Not kidding about that. Shit."

He slugged me again. "You two are gonna make fucking beautiful babies."

I choked a little on my own saliva. "Aren't you the one always warning me about carts and horses?"

"With tits like those? I'd shoot the damn horse and steal the cart," he murmured under his breath. "You'd better lock that shit up. Pink diamonds and rose gold. That's what the ladies want these days, buddy. Nothing platinum. That's last year's product."

Mick went through women like most folks dispensed toilet paper. He was the best agent in the business. His bank account proved it. So did his penchant for buxom blondes with a short shelf life. None of them seemed to mind being disposable. He always gave Harry Winston baubles as parting gifts.

"Right now, it's a struggle, getting her to let me buy dinner. You have no idea what it took to get her here."

"Damn. She looks like the cover of *Playboy* and doesn't want your money? I'm tellin' ya, lock that up as soon as possible."

He thrust his fist forward and turned it, a signature move he made whenever he closed a deal. I'd seen it for the first time the day he scored my rookie signing bonus.

His fist opened, and a finger turned to point at me. "You lock her down and then get her the hell out of that shit-ass town. I need you back here twenty-four seven."

"Mick, if I don't manage to fuck this up with her, I might not ever be back here again in the off-season."

"God, don't tell me that, kid. That makes my ulcer bleed." He pulled an ever-present roll of strawberry Tums from his pants pocket and popped two in his mouth at once. "Just make sure she lets you buy her a pretty dress for tonight. The paps are gonna love her on the carpet."

"That's not gonna happen. Ash is nowhere near ready for that. And . . . we're not exactly . . ."

"Not exactly what? You telling me you ain't hitting that? You broke your arm, not your pecker."

I pinched the bridge of my nose and shook my head. "We're not exactly together. Things are . . . complicated. In her eyes, I got high, cheated on her, crippled her brother, and abandoned her in the span of a night. That's kind of a major speed bump in any relationship, Mick."

He pushed his glasses farther up his nose and looked me straight in the eye. The guy had a skeevy fucking way of looking right into your soul. It was how he bought and sold a GM, bluffing he couldn't go higher on a deal.

"Your daddy cheated, fathered and raised a child, and then spent over a dozen years running all over the world, fucking anything with a wet pussy. Now, he's got his Shelly six months pregnant. You still got a lot you could learn from your father." He poked me in the chest. "Anything is possible, kid. Fix it."

"I'm trying." I groaned.

This event tonight wasn't part of my plan. I finally had Ashley here, and instead of doing what I wanted, showing her everything I wanted her to see, I had to work.

"What is this bullshit you have me sentenced to?"

"Aura. Newest scene in town." He clapped his hands together. "A place for the pretty people. Owners are huge fans. Two brothers who took daddy's hedge fund money and don't want real jobs, so they opened a club. They love you. All you gotta do is show up. Smile those pretty white teeth, let some cougars press their tits against your arms, and make sure people think, if they frequent the joint, they might run into you." A pointed finger waved at me in the air again. "And, before you bitch at me, they dropped six large to get you in the door."

"Get you in what door?"

I'd missed Ashley crossing the room toward us. My anxiety weakened as she drew closer to me.

"Ash, I'd like you to meet—" I glared at Micky.

He smirked as he retrained his eyes above her neck. "I'm Michelangelo Moscovitz, madam. My mother gave me a mouthful of a name, so my enemies call me Moscow Micky. My friends call me close to the same. But you, my dear, may call me anything you wish."

She held her hand out in greeting.

Instead of shaking, he took it and brought it to his lips. "It's a pleasure to meet such a lovely creature."

"Okay, Romeo. Don't get your slime all over her." I snickered.

Ashley laughed, obviously amused.

"I was just telling the boy wonder here about the event I have you kids booked at tonight. You're gonna love it." His hands flashed in front of him. "Glitzy new club. Hottest place in town."

Ash looked at me with silent question as I rolled my eyes.

Micky's hands dropped as he tugged smugly on the bottom hem of his suit jacket. "Whatever, ace. The money they're paying you is going to that kids' charity you love so much. Suck it up. I just want your face out there."

I pursed my lips and nodded my head, giving in.

He looked at Ashley and smiled. "Your fella here's a real softy. Anytime I need to get his ass somewhere, I pull out the midget card. Asshole loves the little squeaky snotballs. I roll out a sick eight-year-old, and this guy'll do anything I ask." He snapped his fingers. "I'd love to stay and play, but I've gotta get across town to bleed some more dough outta the Giants for Elksworth. If the bastard could complete a few more passes, I wouldn't have to work so hard."

Ashley beamed at him. It beat the hell out of me, but clearly *all* women found Micky's shtick charming.

"Good luck today, dollface. Tough work, making this ugly mug look good." He pinched my cheek.

She shrugged and grinned. "I'm used to it. I've been suffering through taking pictures of him since before his voice changed, and he decided to grow muscles. He's why I taught myself Photoshop."

Micky snorted. "Jesus H. Christ, I really do like her," he said, grinning at me.

Ashley wasn't the only one charmed.

He turned back to her and pointed. "You ever need an agent, you'd better call me." As he started to walk away, he shouted back at me without bothering to turn around, "Remember what I said, kid. Rose gold. I've never steered you wrong."

"He's pretty much exactly like I always pictured him," Ashley said as we watched him kiss another woman's hand before he made his exit.

"He's a disaster and an institution all at once."

I started to lace my fingers through hers, but she stiffened, reminding me of our deal.

I leaned forward to whisper against her hair, "Sorry. I forgot."

On the ride here, she'd forced me to promise we'd act professional. She didn't want anyone to know we were . . . whatever the fuck category we fit into. Somewhere around 54th Street, I'd promised her, no touching, just as I'd slid my palm up under her shirt and cupped her right breast on top of her lacy bra.

"Brayden."

I hated when she used my name to admonish me. She rolled her eyes at me, too. That shit made me want to spank her. Naked. Bent over my couch, like I'd had her last night.

"I'll try to behave." I reached out and adjusted the strap of the camera around her neck, gently brushing my hand across her nipples as I pulled away.

She rolled her eyes again.

"How are you holding up? Nerves hanging in?"

"I'm seconds away from hurling into the closest trash can. I have no idea what I'm doing, and all these people are watching me," she whispered.

"They're watching because you're beautiful."

"They're watching 'cause they're trying to figure out how the hell I got here, which is funny because I'm pretty much thinking the same." She sighed. "That Henry guy already hates me. I just nixed one of his plans for the second location. His editorial team wanted shots for the inside spread of you throwing. They had some alley blocked off. He had this vision of you in full release with a brick wall and graffiti in the background. It was really fucking dumb."

I sucked in a breath and started counting backward in my head.

"Relax." Her fingers laced through mine, violating her own rules.

My eyes pled silently with hers.

"I told them no. I figured you didn't want to test out your new elbow for the first time in front of an audience."

Squeezing her fingers, I stole Micky's move, bringing the back of her hand to my lips.

"I really do feel like I need to get sick," she murmured.

"Shh. Stop with that. This shoot is no different than Toni's studio back home. Let's just pretend it's you and me, baby girl. You and me and nothing but this lens between us."

I willed her to believe my words.

If I had any hope of seeing this plan through to the end, this had to go well.

CHAPTER 22
JAYWALKING

BRAYDEN

"I have something I want to show you."

"I'm pretty sure I've already seen everything you have to show me."

Ashley's hooded eyes smiled at me from across the back seat. Her legs stretched out across the leather, feet propped up in my lap. I'd plucked her little sneakers off as soon as we climbed into the back of the SUV. The pads of my thumbs dug into her arch until she sighed and let her shoulders finally relax.

"Not that I'd mind seeing it again," she added, laying her head back and closing her eyes.

I reached over her legs to unzip the duffel bag at my feet. "I meant something else, you perv. But I'll be happy to oblige with whatever you were just dreaming about." I smirked as I rifled through the bag for the item I'd tucked in there this morning. "I want you to do something for me. And I promise, it will feel really good." My voice dipped suggestively.

Green eyes fluttered open, intrigued. I held the book out to her in one hand, a black pen in the other. Her eyes widened, suddenly alert. She sat up a little against the seat. Her expression changed to some mix of shock, dashed in with happiness and fear.

Not exactly what I'd been hoping for.

She didn't reach out to take it. She just kept staring at the cover. The word *History* still lay scrawled across the cover. Ironic, since it held our future and our past.

I held the pen between my teeth as I flipped through the pages, bending it open to the right one. She sat forward, moving away from me a little as she tucked her legs beneath herself on the seat.

I held the book and pen out toward her. "You need to cross one off."

Her eyes met mine, brows furrowed, before she glanced back down at the page. "You still have this?" she asked, stunned.

I pursed my lips, fighting off a smile, as I nodded. Ashley took the book from me, tracing the tip of her index finger across her own handwriting and the light-blue lines of the composition paper.

"You could cross all of yours off," she said softly as her finger trailed up the page to my own messier letters.

"Not all of them," I murmured to myself. I held out the pen again. "Today is about you. It's your turn. Cross it off."

"I don't know if I . . ." She didn't finish her thought, but she took the pen.

"You just finished your first photo shoot for a major magazine. You rocked that shit today, Soot. Check the damn box. Mark it off your list, so we can move to the next one."

She glanced up at me with uncertain eyes that frustrated the living hell out of me.

"We're not gonna stop until we've crossed them all off. Today was just the start." My voice grew more forceful, willing her to comply.

Her fingers held the ink down to the page, hovering without making a stroke. "It sort of feels like cheating. I don't know if I earned it." A black dot pressed harshly, bleeding down onto the paper.

"Stop the bullshit in your head right now. Whatever you're telling yourself."

Slowly, she drew the pen all the way across the letters, striking through them.

I took the book and pen from her, stuffing them back in my bag. My finger reached out, tipping her chin up toward me with a little more aggression than I'd intended.

"All I did was get your foot in the door. You did the work. And everyone there thought you were fucking brilliant."

Her face finally softened. Both her hands reached up to frame my cheeks. Relief washed over me on contact. Our lips met with greed pressed between them. I groaned a little too loudly as her tongue flicked across my bottom lip. She pulled back with a timid glance toward Gino in the front seat. I sighed and pulled her in close to me, kissing the top of her head before drawing her to nestle against my chest.

"Dallas," she murmured.

Every time she said that, every time she used that name, knots untied inside of me.

Her fingers toyed with the buttons on my shirt as she continued, "I had fun today. After I stopped acting like a major pussy."

I choked a little on my laughter. But the sound died completely as she pulled back to look up at me with glassy eyes that nearly broke me in half. I cupped her cheek in my palm.

"It was sort of like playing the very best game of make-believe," she added. "I'll never forget it."

I bent my head to brush my lips across hers. "Baby girl, I wasn't kidding. This could be just the start."

The only thing make-believe about the entire day was the indulgent smile she gave me. The kind that doesn't argue but will never agree. The kind that says, *You're fucking nuts, but, hey, that's okay. I'll play along for a while.* I desperately wanted to replace it with the real thing.

Micky's earlier words haunted me.

"Fix it."

Why did that have to be so much easier said than done?

We sat in silence for a while. Gino had moody jazz music playing that made the chaotic traffic jam outside the car unfold in even slower motion. I wanted to get her home. I wanted to strip down everything between us and lay skin-to-skin without any bullshit between us.

When it was just the two of us, nothing felt made up.

My phone vibrated inside my pocket, breaking me from the stupor I'd quickly been sinking toward.

"Ross," I answered without bothering to check the caller ID.

"Brayden, it's Keith."

"What's going on?" I asked, tracing my fingers up the side of Ashley's arm.

"There's been some movement on that one you had me watching."

"What kind of movement?" I scooted up against the back seat more.

"Someone else is sniffing around. I did a little digging. Looks like deep pockets."

"How deep?"

"Riggs Development."

"Shit." My expletive fell out with too much venom.

Ashley stirred in my arms, gazing up at me with a wrinkled brow. I smirked down at her. Rubbing my fingers across her skin to smooth back the worry.

It's okay, I mouthed.

My fake reassurance worked. She settled back against my chest.

"I take it, you've heard of them."

"Unfortunately," I replied.

Fucking cement-box-building motherfuckers.

"What do you want to do?" he asked.

Keith Jacobs had been my financial advisor since the day I inked my first contract. The son of one of Wall Street's most notorious brokers, the guy had grown up watching the *Closing Bell* instead of *Sesame Street*. He believed in buy low, sell high, and invest without emotion.

I could already hear the skepticism in his voice.

He'd been handling this transaction with kid gloves.

I laid my head back against the seat, staring out the window as a man in a gray suit stepped off the curb to cross against the light. He froggered his way between bright yellow cabs in the lanes beside us, obviously late for something so important, it warranted the risk.

"Pull the trigger," I said in a raspy whisper.

Gino tapped the brakes as the gray suit passed right in front of the hood of our SUV. "What the hell are you doin', asshole?" he muttered, shaking his head.

The gray suit leapt up onto the curb. I watched as he disappeared into the throng of people waiting on the opposite corner.

"You sure, man? It needs a lot of work. I know you've got some sentimental thing going with it, but it looks like a money pit."

"I can't lose it," I finally answered. "Do what you have to do."

He sighed. "All right. Might cost you a little more than we thought."

My hand trailed up and down the soft skin of Ashley's shoulder. Her hand slid under the spot where her cheek rested against my chest, right up against my heart. I prayed she couldn't feel how hard it beat inside my chest.

"Doesn't matter. Just close it. Tonight, if possible. Time is of the essence." I stressed my final words.

"Give me twenty. I'll call you back as soon as it's finalized."

After I pocketed my phone, I pulled Ashley tighter against me, wrapping both arms around her so she was trapped between them.

"Everything okay?" she asked.

"It will be," I whispered back, dropping my lips down to kiss the top of her head. "It will be."

ASHLEY

I wanted chocolate. And coffee. And furry slippers.

Not necessarily in that order.

The magazine people had brought lunch in from some swanky deli. I never ate. At the time, the thought of tuna on rye had made nasty things happen in the back of my throat.

Brayden's phone rang again as soon as we got in the door. He took the call to his office, leaving me to pillage the refrigerator by my lonesome. Everything inside it sat perfectly sorted, like the shelves inside a grocery store. No way he'd done it himself.

"Whoever stocked this for him has some serious OCD. And shitty taste in junk food."

I moved a few things around, destroying the feng shui and

making it look like it belonged to the man who lived here.

I'd moved on to digging through the pantry cabinets when the doorbell rang. I padded barefoot across the room to answer it.

"Ms. Foster, good afternoon." Marcus, the white-gloved doorman who'd greeted us yesterday, stood there with arms loaded down. "I'm so sorry to bother you, but Mr. Ross asked me to bring these things up as soon as they arrived. May I?" He gestured toward the room behind me.

"Of course," I said, a bit flustered as I moved to the side to let him in.

He walked to the expansive dining table, too shiny to have ever been used, and unloaded the items onto the glossy black top.

"I usually hold all the mail until Ms. Jessica comes by, but I know she's been out of town a couple of weeks, and I thought I would just bring that up as well. The packages are all addressed to you though." He warmly smiled at me. "A courier just brought them over from Bergdorf."

"Uh, okay. That's just . . . weird," I said, stammering.

There were three huge boxes and two shopping bags with crisp white tissue spilling out the top. He grinned at me. Or rather, at my lack of sophistication.

I'd felt that way all day. Like these New Yorkers had all been schooled in a version of the world three releases ahead of mine. Everything I said to them sounded a little bit backward falling out of my mouth.

"There should be a card for you from Mr. Ross's personal shopper. It'll be in the largest one." He tipped his head toward me and moved back to the door. "Hope you enjoy your evening, Ms. Foster."

He soundlessly slipped out as I continued to stare at the hoard he'd left behind.

I didn't look inside right away. It didn't take rocket science to figure out what the fancy packages held. I went through the stacks of mail instead, carefully sorting out correspondence from junk mail. I put the magazines in one pile, the bills in another. The big manila envelopes got their own stack with all the postage carefully turned the same direction. When I finished, Brayden's mail sat more orderly than the contents of his fridge.

With nothing else to distract me, I finally opened the lid on the largest box, just enough to extract the thick envelope peeking out from the top.

Gretchen. His personal shopper's name was Gretchen VanCleeve. The thick gold stationery held the scent of heavy perfume.

I pretended that's what made my eyes water.

I'd packed my favorite dress. I'd pulled it from my suitcase and hung it in the closet not long after we'd arrived. A plain black sheath that didn't call too much attention. Joey had loaned me a pair of shoes with fancy red bottoms. She'd talked about them for a month after she scored them on eBay last fall.

I smoothed my hand over the top of the box. Gretchen's choices would be beautiful. They would fit me as if hand-sculpted for my every curve. They would make me look sexy and sophisticated.

And would also, no doubt, leave me feeling even more monumentally backward.

I wanted my plain old dress. I wanted to blend in with all the other people. The ones traipsing up and down the pavement my feet had yet to touch.

The dress in that box would turn me into the strange girl on Brayden's arm. The one people would gawk at as they mouthed the words, *Who the hell is she?* The same way all those people at the photo shoot had all day long.

I loved New York and hated it, all at the same time. I'd never felt so alive, yet so utterly out of place.

I abandoned the fancy packages and padded down the hall, ready to ask Brayden where the hell one went in this town to grocery shop for some real food. The door sat slightly ajar. His back faced me as he stared out the window, down toward the street so far below.

"Thanks for taking care of this so quickly." He listened on the other end and then chuckled. "Yeah. You see Chavez tank one the other night?" He laughed again. "The little schmuck talks faster than he throws. At least, the way things are going, I won't be missing any playoff time."

He threaded his free hand into the back of his hair. The jagged red scar on his elbow caught my eye.

One thing marred utter perfection.

"Me, too. Should start soon. Hope like hell it comes back fast. But I can't tell you how much I appreciate all your help. Feels a lot better, knowing I have contingencies in place if things don't work out and everything goes to hell."

He listened again, nodding his head to whatever was being said on the other end.

"I sure as hell understand now why GMs all breathe easier with a stacked bull pen. I'd never really considered the need for backup before this shit went down."

I eased back from the door, feeling foolish for thinking of Twinkies and Doritos while he sat, worrying about his future.

I walked out to the patio. I sprawled out, flat on my back in a lounge chair, so I could stare up at the pink sky fading overtop the sea of tall buildings. I couldn't help but picture what the same sun looked like sliding into a long expanse of familiar blue water.

ASHLEY

They were trying to eat him alive.

Faceless cyborgs with one bright eye.

They climbed over one another, pushing and shoving. They called out with the desperation of drowning men clamoring for the last remaining life ring.

I stood just inside the door where Gino had told me to wait, watching the scene unfold like a bad sci-fi movie.

The man playing the role of the hero couldn't possibly be human. He never squinted against the blinding lights. Totally at ease, he kept one hand in the pocket of his professionally beat-up leather jacket. He used the other to point toward someone in the crowd. Turning his head, he smiled and rotated his shoulders a little, throwing a bone to the guys on his right.

A loud catcall rose above the others. The comment garnered instant reward. The megawatt smile filled me with the oddest déjà vu. A memory of Jack Ross standing near the kitchen sink.

The cyborgs paused, momentarily stunned by the brilliance reflecting back at them. Then, they all lit up again, amped up into an even greater frenzy.

I pressed my hand against the queasiness inside my belly. I'd never eaten anything.

"Ashley?"

I didn't recognize the woman approaching, calling out my name.

She was statuesque. Rich golden-brown hair cascaded around her shoulders. They sat atop a model-perfect figure, highlighted by a deep purple dress. She smiled in my direction before she one-arm-hugged Gino and whispered something in his ear. He turned and nodded at me before walking away, farther into the throbbing darkness of the club.

"Hi, I'm Mia." She held out her hand in greeting. "I'm Brayden's publicist."

I shook her hand and tried to smile back at her. A hand clasped hold of my waist before I could speak.

"Mi-Mi, thanks for doing this." The warmth of Brayden's palm burned through the emerald-green fabric clinging to my skin.

Gretchen VanCleeve had chosen a dress that matched my eyes.

"You okay?" he asked, squeezing me tighter, as his lips brushed against my ear.

"Yeah, I'm good. That was a little intense, huh?" I asked, peeking back over his shoulder.

Heavy velvet curtains swept in place by security guards closed us off from most of the noise and commotion out front.

His shoulders shrugged dismissively. "Another thing you get used to."

He stood right in front of me, his skin against mine, yet I suddenly felt far away from him. About as far as the expanse between his sense of normal and my own. The distance threw me off-kilter.

Not a good thing in four-inch heels.

"I've got a few people I have to talk to. And getting through this crowd might be a little hectic." His hands ran up and down my arms, like he somehow knew this place gave me the chills. His face grew more serious. "Mia is going to take you upstairs. I'll meet you there, okay? Just follow her lead."

I nodded, even more out of sorts. He hadn't warned me we wouldn't be sticking together.

"She doesn't leave your side," he said forcefully, releasing me as he turned to point a commanding finger at his friend.

Mia cocked a hand on her hip. "I told you this afternoon, I've got this." She pointed a manicured finger right back at him. "You just watch your mouth. Don't say anything about Chavez busting ass. This place is crawling with gossip whores. Someone catches you talking trash, it'll be on the front page of the *Daily News* tomorrow. Best revenge on that loudmouthed brat will be you taking back his starting gig. Six months from now, you'll be serving up hundred-mile-per-hour cheddar, and he'll be bussing tables at a minor league park in Scranton."

Brayden nodded and gave a mock salute just as a man in a tan sport coat and dark jeans came through the parted curtain. The guy had the flash of a man who wanted everyone to notice his full money clip.

Mia leaned toward Brayden, speaking in a forced whisper, "Eddie Loweman. You've met once before. Charity golf thing Mark hosted last spring. Wife is Fiona. Two little kids."

Brayden winked at us both. Then, he quirked a brow at Mia and added, "I ever tell you, you're the best in the business?"

"You're going to this Christmas when you give me a bonus check inside a gorgeous Chanel bag." She chuckled and then murmured under her breath, "Incoming."

A boisterous palm clapped Brayden on the back before he could respond.

"Well, they said you'd be here, but I didn't quite believe them."

"Eddie," Brayden replied, dialing up the megawatt smile again as he shook the guy's hand and clasped his upper arm in greeting. "How are Fiona and the kids?"

As flashy Eddie started talking, Brayden made quick, pointed eye contact with Mia. She nodded her head toward him and then smiled brightly at me.

"You look like you could use a drink," she said warmly. "Let me get you through the worst of this crowd, and we'll score ourselves a cocktail. You've had quite the day."

I fell in line a few steps behind her, but I couldn't stop myself from glancing back over my shoulder as three more men joined in on laughing and patting Brayden on the shoulder.

"Those are the guys who own this place. The sooner they get their fifteen minutes, the sooner he's a free man," she said as her eyes followed my gaze.

"Everyone wants a piece of him," I muttered.

"Yeah. Sort of comes with the territory. He's a bright, shiny thing. They all think, if they get close enough, some of it might rub off on them."

I temporarily misplaced my filter. "That's kind of ridiculous."

She stopped walking and giggled, clearly surprised by my assessment. Her head pensively cocked to the side. Her shoulders relaxed, easing her demeanor from all-business to fast friend. "Yeah, you're right. I mean, all he does is throw a white ball for a living."

We smiled at one another, finding common ground.

"Come on." She waved her hand to coax me forward again. "I promise, this place sucks a whole lot less upstairs."

We wove our way through layers of people and loud, pounding bass. We climbed glass stairs that led behind velvet ropes to an area with plush chairs and low couches, all stuffed with bodies.

The whole room pulsed.

Someone brought us frothy pink drinks in tall martini glasses.

We positioned ourselves in a quiet corner near the railing. From up above, we could stalk Brayden as he moved through the crowd down below us. Gino stayed two steps behind him, maintaining a barrier that kept people from closing in on his back. He stopped and shook too many hands, listened to people whisper in his ear, and smiled for camera phones so many times I didn't know how he hadn't gone blind.

"He told me this wouldn't be your scene."

I sipped my drink as I turned to look at her. "Yeah. I'm a little out of my element. In this whole town though, not just this place. I don't think I was cut from the same cloth as any of these people."

"Eh. They're no different than you or me. This town is all about fake it till you make it. Besides, you certainly didn't look out of your element today."

"You were there?"

She smiled. "Yeah. On the fringes. I never got a chance to introduce myself. The kid who took Brayden's spot this season has a big ego and a loud mouth. The media hounds want to pit the two of them against one another. I spent half the day on my phone, saying, 'No comment.'"

My forehead furrowed in response.

"But I saw it all go down. Those shots you got with his fingers trying to cover up part of the scar? That shit was incredible. He never would've given that up for anyone else. He's usually aloof at those things. You have no idea how many times I've told him he has to loosen up, or people will think he's an egomaniacal prick." She chuckled and swirled her drink. "I hope like hell we can talk him into letting them use that shot. He looked . . . I don't know. Vulnerable. And that's not a word people in this town are used to associating with him."

"Brayden has a lot of layers," I said, picking at the crusted sugar on the rim of my glass.

"Yeah? I'm not sure he shows them to anyone else. But he sure as hell let you photograph them all today." She curiously stared at me. "Everyone in that room was buzzing about it. People were dying to know who you are. Truth be told, I'm sort of dying to know who you are. Like I said, Brayden is always pretty closed off about his personal life. All I know is, he cornered me and told me I had to guard you within an inch of my life tonight."

My brows dismissively scrunched together as I looked her in the eye. "I'm nobody. I promise. And I think everyone was buzzing today about why they had an amateur behind the camera."

Her eyes widened. "Are you bullshitting me right now? Girl, they were all whispering behind your back because the sexual tension in the room made everyone sweat. The way he kept looking at you through that lens? Damn. I've never seen a guy make love to a woman from forty feet across the room." She fanned a hand in front of her face. "I spent the other half of my day making sure everyone understood the concept of a closed set. If video of that shoot leaked, my phone wouldn't stop ringing for days."

As she spoke, I turned to watch Brayden. He'd almost made it to the bottom of the staircase. A group of women were clustered around him, clinging and petting. More people trying to borrow his shine. Something he said made them all throw their heads back with robotic laughter. One of them not so stealthily slipped a piece of paper in his back pocket.

"I wish I could lie and say you get used to the jockstrap bunnies, but you don't. You pretty much always want to bash their faces in," she said in disgust. "See the dark-headed guy over there in the blue shirt? The one that skank in the red dress is trying to climb up on?"

I turned to look in the direction she was pointing. Two men stood near the end of the bar, nursing cocktails in tallboys. They were trying to talk to one another and ignore the swell of people crushing toward them. It wasn't tough to peg them. They had that same thing. That polish that made them stand out from the regular folk.

"He doesn't look like he even knows she's there."

"Yeah. He's a good boy," she said, smirking. "That one belongs to me. Tucker Brant. Brayden's catcher. Brayden actually introduced us. You remind me a little of him. He came here, fresh out of water. But he's learning. That's how this town works. It eats you up, spits you back out, and makes you realize you're tougher than you know in the process."

I sighed. "Life's already chewed me up a handful of times. I'm not sure I'd ever survive that again."

BRAYDEN

The dress showed off every inch of her. It clung to the underside of her breasts, pushing them up into a fucking feast for the eyes. It also clung to the backs of her thighs, just enough to accentuate the soft swell of her ass.

I loved it and hated it, all at the same time.

It wasn't Ashley. At all. Neither was the twisted up hair I knew Joey had talked her through step by step on the phone. I wanted to pull out all the pins and jam my hands in her hair, wash off the makeup covering her freckles, and strip her down to nothing but little white panties and a soft lacy bra.

I never particularly liked these events, but this one was driving me straight up a fucking wall. I didn't want any of it touching her—the dark black light, the loud music, or the throngs of nameless attention whores.

I pressed flesh like a puppet, flashing that stupid smile and making small talk, but I kept my eye on her from across the room. I had to be careful. There were a million and one camera phones ready and able. I wasn't gonna give them shit they didn't deserve.

And none of them deserved a piece of her.

Mia had done a great job of keeping her on the fringes, protecting her from the worst of it. She was supposed to explain why I was working the perimeter of the VIP section, circling around them, drawing away the brunt of the crowd.

But I could feel Soot's eyes on me. They kept tugging me closer, pulling me until I finally couldn't fight it anymore. Half a dozen people stopped me as I slowly made my way toward them.

She had a drink in her hand. Her third one by my count. As a rule, I never drank at these things, but I took the glass from her and shared a sip to test its strength. Vodka and sugar coated my tongue.

I needed to find her something to eat.

"How are you holding up?" Mia asked.

"Better now," I replied, never taking my eyes off Ashley as I handed her back the glass. I watched her sip more of the concoction, mesmerized by the way her tongue licked remnants of sugar from her bottom lip.

"Sweet Lord," Mia said beside me. "I have to go find my man. If I wasn't your publicist, I'd tell you guys to go home and make a sex tape. The two of you together are scorching hot." She held her glass out to tap it against the rim of Ashley's in a toast. "Remember what I said. Short and curlies."

They both giggled as Mia walked away.

"Do I even want to know?" I asked, drawing Ashley farther away from the crowd, into a darker corner.

The back of her hand brushed across the front of my jeans, shocking me into attention.

"She thinks I've got a firm hold down here and shouldn't let go."

"Fuck." I slid my hand around her, discreetly grabbing ahold of her ass and pulling her up against me. "I'd like you to have a firm hold down there right now."

"Maybe that can be arranged."

ASHLEY

"This is freaking sinful."

Brayden leaned forward and plucked a gooey glob that had oozed down my chin as I spoke. "This is one of the very best things about living here."

I smiled at him across the candlelight.

For the first time since we'd boarded the plane, I felt fully at ease.

After Gino steered us out of the club, through a secret back door, we'd driven away from the lights and noise and into a quieter neighborhood, lined with darkened storefronts. The buzz of the alcohol had loosened me up enough that I didn't mind the PDA of Brayden kissing me softly in the back seat. I exchanged my heels for a pair of ballet flats, and he plucked all the pins from my hair, massaging his fingers through it as he went.

I was a little surprised when he told Gino we were gonna hop out, explaining he'd called ahead for VIP seats.

We entered the nondescript building through a back alley. The screened door slammed shut behind us—reminding me of home. A short man with a graying beard welcomed us. His age-mangled hands gripped Brayden's shoulders with a happy shake before he escorted us to his most exclusive seats. They'd been fashioned from wooden packing crates that sat beside a large cardboard box— serving as a dining table. Fully adorned, it had a kitschy red-and-white-checkered tablecloth and an empty wine bottle with a candle melting down the sides.

An old woman in a bright blue dress and white apron rushed in to greet us before we took our seats. She sweetly hugged Brayden and brushed kisses across both his cheeks.

"You stay away too long, *ragazzo dolce*," she said with love in her voice. "And this"—she turned and grasped my arms, holding me back for inspection—"*la bellezza*." She glanced back at Brayden. "Just as you said. But you bring her to me even skinnier than her picture." She turned back and pinched my cheek. "No worries. Mama Rosie's cooking will fatten you right up."

She hadn't been kidding.

They'd brought copious amounts of food. Thin pizza with layers of fresh basil and mozzarella. Calzones full of chicken and creamy ricotta. Cannoli as big as my hands.

"I pretty much never want to leave here," I said, now holding my fork full of dough and cheese out for Brayden to nibble.

"I discovered Mama Ro's my third day in town. I'd lost a shit-ton of weight in rehab. Hadn't really eaten in weeks. My father was crawling up my ass about adding pounds as fast as possible. I just wandered in one day, and she started feeding me. Hasn't stopped since. I come after games a lot. Sit back here, shoot the shit with her husband, Mario, and eat my face off. It's not fancy, but—"

"I love it," I said, interrupting as I surveyed the room around us. The little storage room had shelves full of cans and extra linens. For the first time in days, I felt comfortable in a part of Brayden's world.

"I knew you would." He leaned forward and brushed his lips against mine.

Then, he pulled back to look at me with bright eyes I finally recognized. The fake shine had slipped away, replaced with the guy I knew. That boyish grin I used to chase with my camera lens appeared suddenly. I reached out and grasped his face in my hands, silently begging that smile to stay. The air between us grew heavy, weighted by too many hours of building tension.

"Wanna wrap the rest up to go?" he asked, his voice husky as he stared down at my lips.

BRAYDEN

"Brayden. God. That's so fucking good."

She spoke the words against my mouth as my fingers dug harder into wet flesh, and my dick drove into her from behind. Her head was turned back over her shoulder, soaked strands of her hair tangled against her cheeks, as the water cascaded down overtop of us.

I couldn't get close enough. Couldn't squeeze her slippery skin hard enough or bury myself as far as I needed to go. I fought against the nagging feeling that this could all just wash away.

I have today.

I have to make it fucking count.

As soon as we'd made it through the door last night, we made love on the living room rug. The bedroom had been too far away. I'd awoken her sometime in the middle of the night with my fingers already buried deep inside her. Slow, sleepy sex left us tangled in sweaty sheets till early morning, but my need for her still felt insatiable.

Pressing her forward now, I adjusted the nozzle of one wall jet, forcing bursts of water straight against her clit. Her mouth opened wide, shocked by the sensation it created. Her eyes met mine, glassy and drugged by the burning need to fall over the edge.

I slowed my thrusts, holding her right on the cusp of oblivion. The sound of our wet skin smacking together synchronized with my own panting gasps.

I was barely holding myself together.

Her head fell back. Tormented by the delicious rhythm, she started pressing against me, forcing her ass to meet my hips. I stared down at it, roughly palming her round flesh, fighting the need to give in and plow deeper. Her arms lifted up behind my neck, pulling my lips back down to hers. She smiled against the onslaught of my mouth.

My hands slid up her body, gripping her breasts so I could pull her back harder against me. Her hands came down to press overtop my own, gaining more traction as she moved even faster, taking what she pleased. Her muscles clenched, running up and down the length of my cock with white-hot strength.

"Holy fuck, baby girl."

I gave in. I could never deny Ashley anything, and the animal inside me couldn't hold off anymore. I grabbed ahold of her hips and increased my pace as her palms splayed flat against the wall in front of her.

"Please, please, please." The words strung together in one long plea as she wound tighter around me. Her mouth fell open again as her legs started to shake.

Wet skin smacked harder. She screamed as her cunt started fisting around me like a vise.

I slowed down as the tension left her body, like a taut piece of string that had finally snapped. She laughed and turned her head again. Fluttering eyes opened to meet mine.

"Sorry. You turn me into such a screamer. I always thought those chicks in the porn videos were faking."

"I'm not sorry at all." I thrust into her slow and lazy, letting her come down from the high.

I kept fighting back the regret that I'd left her long enough for other men to have her. Blocking out the mental images was hard enough. Wondering if she'd screamed for them made me nearly insane.

I kissed the side of her neck and mumbled in her ear, "But let's talk about the porn you're apparently watching 'cause I could be down with that."

I chuckled as she reached back to swat me on the chest.

We smiled at one another, goofy, holy-shit grins that made too many nerve endings burn again. I pulled out and pumped my dick in my hand before spinning her around to face me.

"I'm not done with you," I murmured against her mouth.

I pressed the creamy flesh of her breasts together in my hands. My dick bobbed up and down against her belly, overeager to reconnect. Leaning down, I sucked one of the puckered nipples into my mouth, softly biting her before laving at it with a flat tongue. Water bounced off the back of my neck, splashing down onto her skin, as her fingers tugged at my hair, holding me down to her.

My hands squeezed their way down her body, following the rivulets of water that pooled in lines down her soft skin. Pressing her back against the wet tiles, I knelt down, curling two fingers inside her as my tongue darted back and forth across her sensitive clit.

"Brayden. God. So, so good. I don't think I can . . ." Her body started quivering again. Her nails dug into my scalp. "I can't . . . I can't . . . oh, Jesus."

She came on my tongue again, laughing and gasping for air at the same time. As I slowed my ministrations, she pushed against my shoulders, forcing me down against the tiled floor.

"You know I hate that word, *can't*," I said, leaning back onto my forearms as she straddled my hips.

"I know." She smiled and brushed the wet hair back off her face. "But I might keep saying it 'cause I really like the way you fuck it right out of me."

I hissed out a breath from her dirty words and from watching her slide down to her knees, positioning herself to sink down onto me. She took me in so slowly, one fucking delicious inch at a time. Making me want to mutter that same damn word because I didn't know if my dick could take the torture. My mouth fell open against another panting exhale.

She grinned like the devil in a skirt and crown. "I'm not done with you either," she whispered wickedly against my mouth.

Her arms tangled around my shoulders as I let my arms slide out from under me, lying all the way back against the wet tiles. She sat up, lacing her fingers through mine as she began to swivel her hips in mind-fuckingly shallow circles. Then, in one swift motion, she sank all the way down onto me.

I cried out her name as she made that sound.

The one I freaking dreamt about.

It vibrated in the back of her throat as she tilted her head back and let the water soak down over her hair. Her breath came out in short gasps. I could already feel her start to bear down. Her hips rolled forward and back, working me just the way she wanted. I braced my elbows back and drove up to meet her.

"God, you're beautiful when you're about to come all over my dick."

That throaty sound exploded again as I felt her fall over the edge.

I sat up, twisting our legs together as I fiercely hugged her body to mine, feeling her nipples slide against my chest. I couldn't hold off much longer. Couldn't fight the need to get off.

Or to say the things exploding in my head.

I kissed her temple, her cheeks, and her lips. She giggled lightly, a short, happy sound that filled up my damned soul. She buried her face in my neck, biting lightly across my collarbone.

My body begged for release.

So did my heart.

I mouthed the words I needed to say.

Silently.

Over and over again against her wet hair.

She pulled back, so her hands could cup my face. Hooded eyes stared down at my lips before her mouth captured my own. We stayed like that. Connected. With no space, or worry, or hesitation between us.

One day.

I only had one day left to build on that feeling.

We don't always recognize the moments in life where we hit a fork in the road. Paths merge right in front of us. Blind curves materialize, twisting our actions before we can see a final destination. We make crucial decisions and don't even realize they'll alter our course.

But I knew. Without a doubt.

We were finally standing in the spot where two roads diverged. Today, I had to convince her to keep walking toward me. Brick by brick, I had to lay the groundwork.

I would never get this shot again.

She leaned back on her forearms. The extra space should have stretched our connection, but it only made it more intense. We stared at one another and then watched as our bodies joined in the most elemental of ways.

"Brayden, come with me. Please."

I couldn't fight it anymore. I had to give in.

I would give her anything. All of me. Whatever she wanted. I had to make her see that. Tears I didn't want her to see burned the whites of my eyes.

I quickly pulled out of her, spinning her body and gripping her breasts to spoon myself around her. She whimpered as she turned her head to look back over her shoulder. I drove my tongue into her mouth as I reached between her legs to stroke circles across her clit. She started to ride my wrist without shame.

She whispered my name against my lips. "I need you inside me."

"Hold on to my neck, baby."

She reached her arms back, doing as she'd been told for once. I watched my dick slide in between her folds, disappearing, as she gasped. I held her tight, trying to work her without sliding across the wet floor. Both of our chests were heaving like we'd just run a race.

"Fuck. Fuck. Fuck," I chanted and groaned, fighting against the impossible tightness in my balls. "It's you, Ashley. Swear to fucking God, it's always been you, baby girl." Those words were as close as I could get to the three I wanted to say.

She knew I was on the edge. My dick hardened like steel, driving inside her. Her head turned again. She stared into my eyes with wordless intensity.

Believe me, baby.

Believe in me.

We stayed locked like that until the burning forced both our mouths open wide.

"Fill me up, Brayden," she begged in a low, husky tone. "Give me everything."

Her words threw me over.

Everything. Everything.

You're my everything.

Both arms circled around her, holding her back against my chest, sheltering her from the hard tiles, as I pistoned ferociously. I spilled into her in hot spurts that forced her to throw her head back against my neck as she came one more time.

Her body slackened against mine, as spent physically, as I suddenly felt emotionally.

I drew her back to me again, kissing her shoulder, her neck, and the skin beneath her ear. I wanted to whisper the words again. They smoldered like jet fuel spilled inside my brain. I mouthed them against her cheek.

"I think we've sufficiently christened your shower." She giggled.

I grinned. "You don't know how many times I've already christened this shower while chanting your name."

She turned, looking up at me with such happiness I just about gave in and said everything I wanted to out loud. The smile on her face filled dark spaces I'd kept covered up for way too long.

The last time I'd seen it, we'd been standing in her mother's kitchen. She was busy packing a picnic while I tried to cop a feel.

Now, she was back in my arms, finally letting the weight on her shoulders temporarily slide away. She was my Ashley again. Young and carefree.

One day.

God help me. It has to be enough.

Stay. Stay. Stay.

I had to convince her to walk alongside me.

To choose a shared path.

I'd never be able to let her go.

ASHLEY

"I didn't mean it as an offense. I just think it's kinda weird," I said, laughing, as Brayden leaned over the bowl to take another spoonful. "You have milk on your chin," I added, dropping the spoon back into the bowl, so I could wipe the dribble away from dark stubble.

To my gleeful surprise, he'd produced a box of Cocoa Puffs he kept hidden in the back of a pantry cabinet.

"I knew you had a stash somewhere." I'd jumpy-clapped, before hopping up to sit on the counter as he poured a big bowl.

He stood in front of me, positioned between my legs so we could share. Hyped up on sex and sugar, I felt a hundred eighty degrees different than the previous morning.

"I mean, haven't you ever noticed that your feet never touch the sidewalk? You can't tell me you haven't thought about it."

"I really haven't, to be honest," he replied, feeding me again.

"It's like there are two different New Yorks. The one enjoyed by the royal class"—I tucked my free hand against my waist, pretending to bow to him—"and the one the commoners get to deal with. You guys get ushered right to every door. You spend all your time at the top of every building, where the sun still shines. All the dirt is so far down, you never see it. Everyone else is out there, trudging from place to place, sweating their asses off, and trying to ignore the body odor of the dude one seat over on the subway."

He blankly stared at me, dropping the spoon down into the bowl as he smirked and shook his head. "Today, I'm gonna change your mind. I'm gonna show you all my favorite places. And, by the end of the day, I promise, we'll both smell like BO."

I loved it all. Every ounce of grime and grit.

The honking horns, pushy people, and wad of gum on the bottom of my shoe. The used bookshop where we sat on the floor and read to one another from page-ruffled paperbacks. The gallery where I met the talented friend who'd painted the massive canvas in his office. The park where we watched men play chess. All of it spoke to me, in a melody I'd never heard, but instantly knew by heart.

My feet hurt. And they were filthy. I quickly realized why no one else walking by us sported open-toed shoes.

"How do you feel about a little breaking and entering?" Brayden asked as we descended stairs to the subway.

We'd only walked half of the city. The other half, we'd tunneled beneath while stuffed into smelly train cars with an intriguing cross section of humanity.

Gino had laughed through the phone when Brayden called at seven a.m. to give him the day off. *"She wants to ride the subway? Well, good luck with that."*

Good luck indeed.

The people-watching was unparalleled. The guy going down the stairs in front of us now had a three-piece suit and a Coach briefcase; the girl behind us had a neon-pink beehive hairdo and tattoos that wrapped around her neck.

"Damn. I suggest you get a little down and dirty with the commoners, and suddenly, you're resorting to a life of crime?" I bumped his hip with my own.

"Smart-ass," he muttered as he grabbed on to one of my hands and led me toward the right turnstile.

As we waited on the platform, I swung our arms back and forth like I had as a young girl, smiling up at him with bright eyes.

"Are we talking two or twenty years if we get caught? 'Cause, if it's on the lower end, I'm in."

He leaned down and kissed the tip of my nose. "Two, I think. I have an in with the owner. I don't think he'll mind if we bust a window."

"How far do we have to go?"

"It's not far. Switch from this to the five train, and we're there."

I loved having no sense of direction. All day, each new corner brought me something undiscovered. I'd spent most of my life feeling like my world dropped off at the heels of the Chesapeake and the far east edge of town. Wandering around, to all of Brayden's favorite haunts, gave me a new appreciation for the breadth of the city. What had overwhelmed me the day before, now felt like the very best adventure. Letting myself get swallowed inside the sights and sounds and smells helped me finally fit in.

Of course, I was the only one who did.

Brayden didn't look like the shiny superstar today; he looked like my very own prince. He hadn't bothered to shave again, and he had his old red hat and a plain gray T-shirt that hung a little looser, camouflaging the fact that his body would never be ordinary.

But, even dressed down and walking the streets like a commoner, Brayden had no chance of totally blending.

People occasionally whispered and bumped each other. A couple of people gave him head bobs of appreciation. The owner of the little diner where we'd eaten lunch refused to let us pay. On the way out, Brayden had left a wad of cash with the guy at the end of the counter, instructing him to pay for everyone else's meals.

To those who saw beyond his disguise, my prince was a king.

I couldn't stop touching him. I tugged on his belt loops. I intertwined my arm with his. I stood on my tiptoes to kiss his cheek or neck. Being next to him felt like a fairy tale.

When we popped up out of the subway, I started to believe in elves and fairy godmothers.

Gone were all the tall skyscrapers and bright lights. The army of bodies gave way to mostly empty sidewalks. Trees poked up out of the cement, filling the muted shades of the city with bright pops of unexpected green. Townhouses dotted both sides of the streets.

Wrought iron railings lined steps that led up to shiny black doors. Picturesque balconies jutted out of second stories. An old woman stood out on one, watering pots filled with ferns and bright red impatiens. I half-expected her to spontaneously burst into song.

My fingers itched for a shutter button.

"Is this a movie set?" I asked, turning a full circle with my arms out wide.

He laughed and stopped my twirling by tugging me into his chest. Blue eyes sparkled in amusement. "No. This is the Upper East Side."

"It's amazing. I don't ever want to leave." I tipped my head back, laughing.

The megawatt smile almost blinded me.

"Come on, our life of crime awaits us." He threaded his fingers through mine as he guided me toward the end of the block.

We turned down a side street that had an opening to an alley, flanked by tall brick walls straight out of a British storybook. Halfway down, he stopped near a green wooden door. He used the side of one shoulder to force it open and then stuck his head inside.

He turned back to me and smiled. "Watch your step. It's pretty overgrown."

Without caution, I stepped through the doorway and straight into a page torn from a child's tale.

Lush greenery hung from white painted trellises. An old marble fountain sat motionless, coated with a patina of neglect. Beside a rusted table, two chairs sat slightly askew, as if someone had gotten up from afternoon tea and never came back.

Brayden lifted some vines out of our path and nervously smiled back at me again. We passed through an archway in the trees and emptied out onto a massive stone patio. I tilted my head back at the same time my mouth dropped open.

It was gorgeous. Four stories of a massive white stone house. Towering windows surrounded by detailed marble carvings. Some of the glass was broken, and ivy crawled, unfettered, up over one side of the first floor, but none of that could tame the magnificence.

"This can't be real," I muttered in amazement.

Brayden grinned as he bent and picked up a small rock. Without any forethought or ceremony, he wound up and threw it at the thin window beside the back door. The glass shattered into jagged shards.

"Hold on a sec." As he stepped forward, he took off his hat and pulled his T-shirt over his head.

I tried not to get distracted as he balled the shirt around his hand and reached in, punching his way through and twisting the doorknob open from the inside. He turned and held an arm out, inviting me toward felony. As I stepped toward him, the irony finally dawned on me.

"Brayden, you just threw that rock."

His brows furrowed with question.

"Full windup." I curved my fingers around an imaginary fastball, demonstrating.

"Well, hell." He cocked his head to the side and readjusted his cap. "Had to try it out sometime, right?" His lips morphed from a tiny smirk to a full grin.

My own personal megawatt appeared again.

He was turning me into an addict.

BRAYDEN

"My real estate agent thinks I'm nuts. He brought me here with the idea that it was a teardown. Had plans to gut it and build a whole new house." I sighed and apprehensively looked at Ashley. "You think I'm crazy?"

"For breaking into your own house?" She turned and grinned at me. "Yes. Definitely. For buying this place and wanting to save it?" She held her arms out and turned in a full circle, soaking in the massive great room. "I can't imagine anyone wanting to tear this down."

I followed after her, pointing out the work I knew had to be done first. At some point, the old plumbing had mostly given way, and water damage had rotted floors and torn through plaster. The electrical looked like one big fire hazard, and every single window would have to be restored or replaced.

But the bones were still strong.

They were just lying there, hidden, waiting for someone to love.

"It's a massive undertaking; that's for sure."

"My father thinks I'll be dead by the time it's all done."

She paused at the bottom of the curved staircase that led up to my best surprise. Her hand gripped the mahogany newel post. "Well, we both know your father isn't always right about everything," she mumbled before starting up the stairs. "What's up here? Is this a whole 'nother floor?"

I couldn't answer. Too much emotion and nerves clogged in my throat. I'd let her see it for herself first. I kept hanging back as she reached the top of the stairs and turned. Her profile exposed enough of her face. Her mouth hung open in awe.

The same expression I'd held the first time I saw it.

"Brayden . . . what is . . ." She stepped farther into the room.

I followed her close behind, watching as she walked the perimeter. Her fingertips danced across the sheets that covered everything over. The whole room lay draped in ghostly white. The ceilings towered fourteen feet above us, flanked by windows that stretched just as high. The back wall, opposite all that glass, remained the only source of color. The entire expanse was plastered in layers and heavy splotches. Every shade. Every color. Dots of ink and stain, painted and splattered over what must have been an entire lifetime.

"The man who used to own this place is close to dying. He's in hospice care now, but before that, he'd been in assisted living for years. That's how the house fell into such disrepair. I went to visit him last year after I saw it for the first time. I wanted to know the stories this place could tell.

"He moved into the house in the late forties after he got back from serving in the war. It was a wedding gift from his parents. He picked the place solely based on the light in this room. His young bride was an artist, an oil painter. She used this as her studio. He said she worked here every single day until she passed, twelve years ago.

He got tears in his eyes when he talked about this wall."

Ashley smiled in response and stepped toward it, holding her hand out to barely graze the texture.

"It started as a joke. His wife accidentally flung some paint onto it while trying to chase him from the room. Guess, in his younger days, he tried to distract her a lot." My voice dipped suggestively.

Her bright eyes acknowledged my meaning. "It's incredible. It must've taken her years."

"He caught her one night a decade or so later. She'd dragged a massive house ladder up here, and was perched all the way up, throwing paint toward the ceiling."

We both craned our necks, staring upward.

"There are so many layers. The way the colors all overlap. It tells their story, doesn't it? You can see all their years together. It's messy and crazy, but beautiful all at once," she murmured.

Warmth built inside me, relief that she was experiencing it in the same way I had.

"This has to be saved. This whole wall," she said, her voice growing determined as she used both arms to motion toward it. "It can't come down. You can feel her . . ." Her shoulders shrugged. "I don't know . . . it's her soul or something. She's still alive in this room. This whole space is special. All these old windows . . . the light in here on a sunny day . . . it must've been an incredible place to work."

"I know." I closed the space between us, wrapping my arms around Ashley from behind, resting my cheek against her hair as we gazed outward. "As soon as I saw this room, I knew. Knew I had to have it. And knew there was no chance in hell I could let it be torn down."

I pulled back to turn her in my arms. I could already picture her here. Dressed in little jean shorts and a tank top with her hair pinned up in a messy bun and a camera lens stuck to her face. Soft lights splashing against this huge backdrop.

Now or never.

"I knew you'd feel the same way about it. This is why I wanted you to come. To the city. To this place. I wanted you to see this. You're right. This house is a massive undertaking."

My lips brushed across hers, hungry but restrained all at once. Tightness stretched across my chest, blooming inside me.

"I don't want to do it alone."

A sound made me stir. Something out of place. My hand stretched across the sheets, uncomfortable that she'd rolled too far away.

"Soot," I mumbled.

One eye opened. The comforter was pulled back on her empty side of the bed. How had she found the energy to climb out from under the covers?

We'd enjoyed a quiet night. We'd strolled around the streets down near the park till we'd found a little hole-in-the-wall with outdoor seating. We'd lingered over a bottle of red wine. Ashley had wanted every detail about my meeting with the old man who owned the house. I'd told her about the gallery where some of his wife's work still hung. Ever so gently, I'd slid in the notion that I'd take her there.

The next time we come back.

She hadn't given any real reaction. She was shit at lying to me, so I'd figured she hadn't let all the stuff I'd dumped on her add up in her head just yet.

I'd talked her into a cab ride back to my place. Mainly because the buzz of the wine and the frayed nerves of the day had left me with a burning need to have my hands all over her. My fingertips had traced circles on her upper thigh the whole way home.

We'd watched a movie, lying on the couch with our arms and legs tangled and my mouth permanently affixed to her neck. By the time the credits rolled, I'd had her shirt unbuttoned, so my palm could cup a lace-covered breast.

We'd brushed our teeth side by side, sharing a tube of Colgate. I'd watched as she slipped a satin nightgown over her head and crawled under the covers beside me. We'd made love like grown-ups. Under the sheets. Slow and easy. Lights still on.

The way she'd stared into my eyes twisted new knots inside me. It'd felt like she could see all the way down. Past every good intention.

And past every half-truth and lie.

I could taste it. All the things I'd wished for.

The happy ending I'd been working toward for so fucking long.

I'd made her come half a dozen times and shot off twice myself. I couldn't help it. I'd wanted to fill her up so full of me, she couldn't ever walk away. I'd wanted to pour myself into her until we couldn't tell anymore where one of us stopped and the other began.

I needed her to stay.

Stay.

That motherfucking word.

For once in my life, I just wanted it to stick.

We'd fallen asleep, intertwined, our bodies naked and raw. I wanted to keep Ashley here forever, locked away with me, where nothing outside of us could change her mind.

I'd slept more soundly with her in my arms. I must've been half-comatose to miss her climbing from our fortress.

I needed to go and bring her back.

Throwing back the covers, I padded naked down the hall toward the soft light in the great room. The door to the terrace sat open. She stood out by the rail, her satin gown billowing around her legs in the summer breeze.

Modesty didn't hold me back. Her head turned slightly to glance over one shoulder, signaling she knew of my presence.

"Nice pajamas," she muttered sarcastically.

"Not my fault you're overdressed." My lips met the soft skin of her shoulder. My fingertips slid the thin strap down her arm. "What are you doing out here in the middle of the night? Come back to bed with me. I'll help you fall back to sleep."

I sucked on the spot just above her collarbone, scratching her skin with my chin because I knew it drove her insane. When her body stayed rigid, I lifted my head and turned her in my arms. Tears lined the bottom rims of my favorite green eyes.

"What's the matter, baby girl?" I pressed my forehead down to hers, wanting to fill her sadness with feelings of something familiar.

"I loved every single second of today." Her eyes squeezed shut.

Tears spilled over, sliding down over perfect cheeks and freckles.

The backs of my knuckles gently grazed across them. "Then, why are you out here, crying?" I asked gently.

"Today was a taste of the life we could've had." Her eyes opened, staring back into mine.

A vise gripped ahold of my chest. Something prickled up the bottom edge of my spine.

"Soot"—my hand cupped her cheek—"this is the life I'm waiting to give you. That was the whole point of today."

"But I have another life that needs me. And you already have everything figured out. You have this whole city by a string. You can't just pluck me up and smash me into your dream world." She held both arms out. "Where do I fit in here?"

"You fit beside me. You always have. That's who you are. Who we are."

"I don't know who I really am. I've never had a chance to find out."

"I want to be the one to give you that chance. That's all I want. You just have to let me."

I didn't want to understand why that made her little smile so sad.

BRAYDEN

Ashley came into the kitchen, wearing a sunny cotton dress and little white sneakers. Her long, dark hair was still damp, pulled into a low ponytail at the back of her neck. Her lashes were dark, and her lips were shiny, but nothing else covered her freckles.

I instantly wanted to take her back to bed.

"What time is our flight?" she asked.

I set my coffee down and checked my watch. "We have about six hours. Is there anything you want to do? I just need to get through some of my exercises real quick, or Matt will have my ass tomorrow for skipping too many days in a row."

She bounced a little on her toes, turning her ankle over on the side, like she used to when she got nervous as a kid.

"But I can get it done fast, and we can do something if you want," I added hurriedly.

"No, I don't want you to rush. I actually was thinking about going for a short walk. I want to pick up something to take back to Joey. There are tons of those shops with the poop emoji pillows or a Statue of Liberty Pez dispenser. I have to take her something to assuage the fact I'm not bringing her back a pair of Jimmy Choos or a Louis Vuitton. I could do it while you're working out and then meet you back here. I'll be fast, and I promise not to get lost."

"Are you sure? Why don't I come with you and save my workout for tonight? I don't like the idea of you going off alone."

Okay, I *really* fucking hated the idea, but I was trying to seem gallant instead of creepy.

"I'll be fine. Really. It will be an adventure to go on my own. Prove to myself I can do it."

Fuck. There's no way I can stop her now.

I threaded my hands behind my head. "At least let Gino drive you. I can get him to . . ."

Her arms wrapped around my waist. She rose up on her toes, pressing her lips against mine. I quickly deepened the kiss. When she lightly bit down on my bottom lip, my hands grabbed ahold of her ass and started to lift her back toward the counter.

"Uh-uh. No, buddy. We've got stuff to do. If you behave now, maybe we can find a way to break in that fancy airplane of yours later on."

"Don't tease me," I said against her lips.

She pulled back and adjusted her ponytail. "I've got this. Really. I'll be back before you're done working out."

She was already halfway out of the room.

"Be careful. Make sure you have your phone."

"I'll be fine. Stop being so overprotective," she called back. "You know, I took care of myself the last couple of years and managed to stay alive without you lording over me."

Her words drove the knife deeper.

"I can't help it where you're concerned," I murmured too softly for her to hear.

The door swung shut behind her.

I'd already dialed by the time I reached the terrace.

"S'up, boss?"

"Ashley is about to exit the front door. Can you swing around and follow her? Not too close. She said she wanted to go for a walk. I just want to make sure she's—"

"Yeah, yeah. I got her. Just walked out." He paused and whistled. "But doesn't look like she's going for a walk, boss. She's getting in a cab."

"What?"

"I assume you want me to follow after them."

"Fuck," I replied, running an angry hand through my hair. "I knew she was up to something. Yes. Stay with her. Let me know where she goes."

I hung up on him and immediately hit speed dial. I needed to figure out where the hell the rest of the Fosters had run off to. All three of them would add a few more years to my life if they learned to fucking follow directions.

ASHLEY

My mother was the only one who knew about this place. My secret died with her.

So did my dream of ever stepping foot here.

The people all looked friendly. They dressed differently than the folks I'd seen all over the city. More colorful. Almost bold. They were the type that naturally rebelled against fitting in.

As I got close to one of the buildings, a guy with a dark purple hoodie and a head full of long dreads stopped to look back and hold the door for me. He had a beautiful smile.

"Oh, no. Thanks. I'm waiting here for someone," I said. The white lie slid off my tongue.

There was a little courtyard between two buildings, filled with abstract metal sculptures. I sat on a nearby bench, pretending to study them.

Last night, I'd told Brayden I felt like I'd glimpsed the life I could have had.

Coming to see this completed the circle.

I could picture myself here. Backpack slung over my shoulder, camera affixed to my neck, laughing as I hurried by with a few friends. I sat on that bench and dreamed about what that would feel like.

If things had just broken a little differently.

Brayden's mother had talked about dominoes that tumbled. And my mother had always believed we'd end up where we belonged. I needed to make peace with the idea that maybe this place *wasn't* where I was supposed to be. But the pull I felt, sitting on that bench, made me feel like those dominoes had all fallen on top of my head and crushed me, rather than pushing me toward the place I needed to end up.

I started to rise, ready to say my goodbyes and make my way home, when my phone vibrated in my pocket.

I fumbled for it, muttering to myself, "Jeez, of course, he has to check up on me. He's so mental sometimes."

My brother's name surprised me.

We'd exchanged a handful of texts all weekend. He'd been having a good time with Matt and his buddy. They'd talked him into going to a Nationals game. He'd sent me a snapshot of them standing next to the mascots of a bunch of overstuffed presidents.

He should've been home by now.

"Hey. How's it going? You guys make it back safe?"

He didn't respond.

I could hear him breathing into the phone.

"Nathan?" Alarm laced my tone. I imagined him fallen somewhere, struggling on his own without me there to help. "What's wrong? Are you okay?"

"I'm fine, sis. It's not me. I'm . . . I'm good."

"What is it? Oh God, is it Dad? Did you hear from him? You're scaring me, Nathan. Speak."

"That dude from the bank was just here."

"Oh, shit. Mr. Garrett? What did he want?"

I glanced around, feeling foolish for coming here. I couldn't afford to let myself get caught up in such selfish thoughts. My real life was not a fairy tale. The last twenty-four hours made me temporarily forget.

I caught the last part of his response.

It jolted me upright.

"What? What did you just say?"

BRAYDEN

"What's the status?"

"Something weird is going on," Gino answered.

My stomach sank.

"I tracked her down into NoHo."

"What the hell is she doing there?"

"I don't know. We're at a school. That artsy-fartsy place. My neighbors had a kid who went here a couple years back. Kid was like a sculptor or something. Like that could ever fucking pay the bills." He snickered.

A glimmer of something that felt suspiciously like hope bloomed inside my chest. She'd gone to the art institute? Maybe I'd gotten through to her last night.

Why lie about going there?

"Did she go inside? Did she talk to anyone?"

"Nah. That's what's weird. She wandered around the outside of a couple buildings, just kinda studying the people walking in and out. Then, she sat on a bench for a while, staring into empty space. She didn't seem bothered or anything, so I just let her be. But then she got a phone call. And there was some kind of argument. I crossed the street to get closer, and by that time, she was crying like a school kid with skinned up knees. Tears all running down her face and everything. If you don't mind me saying, chick is still a knockout, even with mascara running all over the place. My Pamela cries like that when the Hallmark Channel plays those damn Christmas movies. She looks like a hot freaking mess though."

"G, where is she now?" I asked, impatient.

"She got back in a cab. I'm trailing behind them now. She's on her way back to you, boss. But she's definitely not happy."

"Fuck," I groaned, defeated as reality broke over me. "She already knows."

"Brayden, we have to go. We have to leave right now. I have to get home. As soon as possible. Can we get the plane to leave faster?

Can I just get on a regular flight or something?"

As soon as Ashley tumbled through the door, those words started spilling out. The tracks of mascara that Gino described before, now wore a path down both her cheeks.

I followed her all the way to the bedroom. She flung her little black suitcase on the bed and started piling her things back into it.

"Coming here was a huge mistake. I should never have left. Maybe I could've stopped them. I can't believe they'd just take it. Just fucking take it without any warning. Years of people's lives, and they don't even care. Don't even have the decency to give any warning. Pulled the fucking rug right out from under us. My father. My God. What am I going to tell my father?"

She stopped moving. Her hand flew up to cover her mouth. Fresh sobs broke from deep inside her chest. My whole body shook as I stepped tentatively toward her, waiting to see if she'd punch me in the face.

She didn't resist.

Quite the opposite.

She let me wrap my arms all the way around her, let her body sag against mine. Her wet cheek pressed against my chest as her arms clung to me.

"Can we please get home fast? We need to go, Brayden. Take me home."

The way she'd said that churned my insides even more.

We.

Home.

There's a feeling you get right before you slide into home plate. It's this gut-wrenching need to just get there. To reach that target and know you're safe. It's what propels you to do whatever's necessary. To thrust your legs out from under you and literally throw your body into the dirt.

Ninety feet stretched between the bases.

I only had an inch left to slide.

I could taste it.

Please, God.

"Shh." I smoothed my hand down her back. "I'll get you there, baby. I just need you to calm down and let me help you."

She pulled back, looking at me with sad eyes. "I wish there were a simple fix. Maybe if I'd listened . . . maybe if I hadn't been so hardheaded. But, now, I'm too late. Now, it's done. And there's nothing I can do. Nothing anyone can do to get it back from the Brooks Brothers twins."

I leaned down to rest my forehead against hers. Breathing her in like old times.

"Ashley, talk to me," I whispered.

She lightly kissed me on the cheek and then pulled away to sit down on the corner of the bed. Her chest visibly rose and fell. I watched the movement, counting my breaths along with hers.

My whole world tilted on a precipice.

"Nathan called me while I was out. Mr. Garrett, from the bank, came by the house first thing this morning. He was upset and wanted to see me. Nathan forced him to talk." She licked her lips, gathering the courage to find her next words. "They sold the marina. My mother had leveraged everything before she died. The loan payments were just . . ." She heaved out another breath and trailed off. "We defaulted on the second mortgage late last year. Technically, the bank took ownership a few months ago. I appealed. I wrote letters. Old customers helped. The freaking town council wrote to the bank on our behalf. I came to an agreement with the bank. If my family could redeem the loan balance, we could get it back. There was no one crazy enough to buy it, so the corporate suits agreed."

I squeezed my eyes shut, unable to witness the devastation on her face.

"I know. I know," she said, mistaking my pain. "Mr. Garrett told Nathan some company just came in and made an offer the bigwigs couldn't turn down. They've talked the county into rezoning it, so they can build. I've lost it, Brayden. Everything my parents worked for.

"I have to find my father. God. Can you help me do that? I've got to find him as soon as possible. I can't tell him this over the phone.

His heart is already broken. I don't know what this is going to do to him."

"I can find him. I have people who can—"

A phone ringing interrupted me.

"Oh, shit. That's mine. Where did I leave it? Nathan was gonna call me back."

She wandered back toward the living room. I could hear her talking softly. I walked to the end of the hall, hovering in the doorway, as piece by piece, my whole world began sliding over the cliff. The hope I'd felt, hearing about her sitting outside that art school, became a cruel memory. One last bitter pill jammed down my throat.

"What did you say the name was? Why is that so familiar? Wait." Her voice took on a sudden edge. "Say it again."

I couldn't feel the dirt beneath my feet, but I could see the catcher standing in front of home plate with a shit-eating grin and the ball already tucked in his mitt. I'd never slide under his glove. All that work, all the hours, all the years . . . I'd never beat the tag.

"It's a, what?" she added, harshly now. "You're sure?" She paused again. "Nathan, I have to call you back."

She dropped her phone down onto the kitchen counter. For the first time since she'd walked back into the apartment, she stood absolutely still. Her hands twisted in front of her. Black and white tiles slid into place, aligning just before they began toppling over, one by one.

She started moving all at once, rushing past me as I tried to grab for her arm. I called out her name.

She threw open the door to the office. Her hand hit the wall, flipping switches, drowning the room in light. I stood in the doorway as she walked to stand right in front of the painting.

"I missed this before. When we were talking about it." Her voice grew eerily calm. "You had this painted, didn't you? By your friend? This wasn't something you picked out from his finished work. We saw his other stuff. It was a lot different than this." She turned and briefly faced me before returning to stare at the image. "He painted this specifically for you."

She stepped closer, zeroing in on the boy standing at the bottom, lasso in hand as he pulled the cluster of stars down toward the earth.

"He has a ball cap on. Backward. He's you. You're the boy." Her whole body remained motionless, but the color drained from her face. "What's this called?"

I didn't respond.

"It's the constellation, isn't it? Like Hercules. You love them. I forgot. The telescope in the boathouse. Those night sails with my dad. Those books you used to read. We went to the planetarium one summer. You were fascinated by it all." She turned her body toward me but didn't look up. "What's the name of this painting, Brayden?"

She pressed her lips together.

I couldn't feel my feet anymore.

"Tell me!" she shouted.

A breath, I could not feel, whooshed out of my lungs with the same hiss as helium draining from a popped balloon. The tightness gripped ahold of me. My inhaler lay hidden in my bottom bathroom drawer. There was no way I'd count myself back out of this one. My fingertips already tingled, and my breathing was growing too short, too fast. I held on to the doorframe.

She burst past me, almost running. I thought it was to get away from me. But I could hear her screaming. I turned in time to see her standing over the dining room table. Her arm swept out, shoving the neatly stacked piles over in one fell swoop. Magazines and envelopes scattered every which way.

She cried out again—a terrible sound, like a wounded animal in pain.

I could feel it in my bones.

I started counting again. Not the backward math to calm myself down. An estimate of the number of steps to the bathroom drawer.

I had to get there.

She bent and picked up a large manila envelope, thrusting it toward me like a knife. It might as well have been. I held on to my ribs, feeling like it'd struck me from across the room. The numbness claimed all feeling, but I could hear myself panting.

"Argo Navis. That's what it's called, isn't it? The boat constellation. You have a painting of it on your wall. And this envelope came addressed to A. Navis, Inc. With your address." She stared down at the words on the label.

So fucking careless. I just hadn't even thought about it.

Jess usually got my mail.

"It's you. You stole it, didn't you? Why? Tell me, why the fuck would you buy the marina out from under us?"

"It was time, Ashley. I had no choice."

"Did you trick me into coming here, so you could steal it? Why would you do that? Is this some kind of sick need for control? You can't manipulate us this way and expect us to trust you again."

"I'm not stealing anything. I'm trying to save it. We're all on the same team here, Ash. There were others. It was me or a group of developers who would've come and leveled the place. I wasn't gonna stand by and watch that happen. I made a promise to your mother."

"Oh Jesus. Don't hide behind my dead mother." She turned away from me, staring out toward the wall of glass windows.

"It means something to me, too, you know. I need to know it's still there. That it will *always* be there to come back to."

Her shoulders sagged as her hand flew up to cover her mouth again. "He was right, wasn't he? My brother warned me. Just like before. And, just like before, I didn't listen to him." She rounded back to face me, even angrier. "You're terrified of not getting your fancy life back, so you're trying to buy your way back into your old one. That's what this all is. Me, St. Michaels, the marina. I heard you on the phone the other day. Telling someone you'd learned to always have a contingency. It's all connected. We're your backup. I'm your plan B."

I strode toward her, forcing the anxiety down deep, channeling a last surge of adrenaline to keep myself lucid.

"I asked you to let me help a million times. You wouldn't give in. Your pride was gonna cost—"

"My pride is all I have left."

"It doesn't have to be, goddamn it. I can give you all of this." I tried to hold my arms out wide. They only made it a quarter of the way. "This is the life we could be living. Together."

"I don't want to be your puppet on a string. You can't force this on me. I'm not a little girl who you make choices for. I deserve to be more than someone's safety net."

"Is that what you think?" I gripped her chin, fighting against the pins and needles beneath my skin, as I forced her to face me. "You can really look me in the eye and say you believe that's all this is? I did this because I love you. I've always loved you. From the second we met. From before I even knew what that word meant. I've always taken care of you. And I will until the day I die."

Empty green eyes stared through me.

I couldn't tell if she'd even heard a word I said.

"You're going to be fine, Dallas. You're always fine." Her voice grew hauntingly calm. An eerie resolve spread across her face, wiping away her anger as it added to my fear.

Chills shot up the base of my spine.

In my mind, I saw my feet come out from under me, sliding for the plate as the catcher's mitt thrust out toward me. The leather scraped across my skin while the umpire's fist prepared to call the out, sending me back to the dugout, back to the purgatory of a man who had nothing to show for his effort.

Stealing home is the biggest risk in baseball. Those who succeed are called winners; those who fail live in hell.

The hell of getting close enough to taste it.

I was so close. So close.

"You're going to be the shining star all those people out there love." She pointed to the window. "You'll be the prince of Gotham again, walking on air, living in a castle. You don't need a backup plan. You don't need me. I wish you believed that. I wish you could've found that out on your own without coming back. Without finding me and making me fall back in love with you again."

Shell-shocked, I shook myself to make sure I'd heard her words. I quietly uttered her name and stepped closer. She shook her head back and forth. Her hand held out, repelling me back. I tried to grab on to the sides of her arms, but without my full strength, she easily brushed her way past and walked out of the room.

She reappeared with a suitcase beside her.

"Ashley, stay, and let's talk this out."

She didn't respond.

She opened the door and crushed my heart. She walked out on me without looking back. For the second time in my life, I had to let her go without putting up a fight.

I half-crawled to make it there. As I pulled open the bottom drawer, a familiar burn built inside my skull. That deep yearning for numbness hadn't crept up on me in a very long time. It had been lying there, dormant, waiting. An addict's need for easy oblivion never totally subsides.

I sucked two breaths from the inhaler and then gripped on to the side of the bathroom counter until the pressure began to ease.

I pulled my phone from my back pocket.

"She's on her way down. Don't let her get in a fucking cab. Take her to the airport. The jet is on standby. And, Gino, Vincent is in St. Michaels with the delivery. Make sure he's there to greet her on the other end."

"I'm on it, boss. Anything else I can do for you?" he asked carefully.

Gino had seen plenty in his days. He knew my girl leaving by herself spelled out a sad twist of fate.

"Tell the flight crew to circle back for me. I'll be waiting."

Waiting it out.

I'd spent too many years doing that already.

I took another puff from the inhaler and then sucked down a full, cleansing breath.

The time for waiting was over.

I had to lay down my hand. Had to spread out all my secrets and lies. Problem was, before that could happen, I had to get her father to come clean.

In more ways than one.

"Yours is the light by which my spirit's born:
you are my sun, my moon, and all my stars."
—E.E. Cummings

BRAYDEN

I drove straight to the marina, knowing I wouldn't find her there. Vincent had dropped her off hours ago, and still sat parked at the end of her street, watching over the house.

By the time I arrived, the pink fingers of evening were stroking down through the water. They laid to rest the bluster and noise of late day sunshine. Docklines clanged solemnly against moorings. Loose halyards slapped against their masts. The vacant maritime symphony kept time with each step I now took toward my fate.

I found my delivery.

Standing at the rail on the aft deck of *Toward Happiness*, staring out across the water.

Robert Foster was the first man I'd ever admired. The first man I'd ever wanted to emulate. He laughed easily, spoke in a quiet voice, and always maintained a steady demeanor—even back in the days when he'd been coaching us on a ball field and we'd been majorly fucking up. When he would come to conference with me on the mound, he wouldn't yell or fuss like every other coach I'd ever had—before or since. And he'd never taken the ball from my hand.

I'd tried to give it to him once, in a district final game, after I'd walked two chumps and let a third get a cheap hit that two-hopped the fence. He'd immediately thrust it right back into my palm.

"No, kid. I don't want the ball. It's right where it belongs. I believe in you, Brayden. Bases loaded doesn't mean you give up. Means you make 'em look that much more foolish when you strike their next three out. Now, get out of your head and throw that sucker right through your catcher's mitt."

He didn't hear me as I first approached.

That gave me time to stand back and study him.

Mrs. F always used to joke that he looked like Robert Redford, with lighter hair and a better ass. I could still see the resemblance. He'd aged though. Not in the way years soften skin or whiten hair, in the way a man looks after he's carried around too much pain.

I never saw him after that night.

That was the weirdest part. We'd never exchanged angry words or tearstained goodbyes. I saw him for the last time two weeks before the accident. I was picking Ashley up for school. Running late for work, he gave me a short wave as he jumped in his truck.

Our relationship didn't peter out or explode in a ball of fire. It just broke off, silently consumed by the void my mistakes created.

I'd come here full of impatience and frustration.

Ready to do battle.

I'd planned to tell him how this had to play out and to insist he help me. But standing there now, feet from him, I realized just how fucking stupid that plan really was.

This man was the father I'd always wanted to have. Regardless of my age or stature, I would always face him as that same little kid, still desperate for his acceptance.

Too many feelings tangled up in my throat. Remorse. Pain. Gratitude. They heaved up to the forefront as I swallowed back childish tears and finally cleared my throat.

He glanced briefly to the side without fully turning, exposing a beard I'd never seen him wear.

"You didn't have to send your goon down to get me. I was ready to come home," he called out.

"She needs you," I responded defensively.

He slowly turned to face me, leaning back against the rail. His eyes swept the length of me. I took a deep breath, waiting for the wrath I felt was sure to come—the hatred I'd feared during four long years of exile.

"Jesus. Look at you." A soft smirk combined with sad eyes. "My memory still stores the lanky kid, but there's a man standing before me."

I ran a hand across the stubble on my chin, feeling the anxiety uncoil inside me as I soaked in the acceptance hidden beneath his words. Relief propelled me forward. I stepped toward the rail, positioning myself beside him so I could stare out at the water and try to catch my breath.

"I know Ashley needs me," he added quietly. "Part of me stayed away because I didn't know how to face her. I left her with a huge mess. I just . . . I had to fix myself before I could fix anything else."

"Yeah." I nodded. "I know something about that, too."

He turned beside me, gripping on to the rail and staring out in the same direction. "Nice little boat you've got yourself here. Takes up some prime real estate. Probably good you've got a connection with the new owner."

I licked my lips, trying to stop the words from spilling out of my mouth too fast. "I didn't buy the marina 'cause I wanted to pull it out from under you. Your kids are probably both gonna tell you that. But that's a lie. I bought it because it's the only part we have left of her, and I couldn't stand by and watch you all lose it. I already have lawyers working on transferring the deed back into your name. You'll own it free and clear by the end of the week."

I had intended to have it all transferred before anyone found out. Instead, I'd put them back in a place where they had to trust me. Where they had to believe I was telling the truth. Trust and forgiveness. They grow up the vine together, dependent and intertwined. Now, instead of earning just one, I had to beg for them both at once.

He stayed silent for so long; I grew uncomfortable. Pressure built behind my eyes. His open palm drummed against the rail as I waited, anxious for his reaction.

He took a deep breath before he began, "The night before I cashed the first check, I tried to kill myself."

"What?" I turned to stare at him, wide-eyed.

"I kept finding little notes she'd left. All over the damn place. As soon as she got sick, she must've started writing them. The first couple weeks, I pulled the house apart, searching for them all. Some were practical. Instructions on how to wash laundry. Recipes. Reminders about everyday life. Some of them were love notes. Deep thoughts she had about our life together. Things she wished we'd made time for. Things she was thankful we'd accomplished. As you can probably guess, reading them pretty much tore me up." His voice clouded over.

He wiped a hand across his mouth, collecting himself for a moment.

"I was working late that night, trying to figure out how the hell to get out of the hole we'd put ourselves in. I found another one, stuck inside the top desk drawer. I thought I'd already found them all, but I pulled out a pen, and there it was. It only had two words on it." He turned his head to look me in the eye. "Move on."

"Easier said than done," I muttered.

He nodded his head and snickered. "I sat at the desk with my grandfather's shotgun between my knees. Just staring down the barrel. I couldn't come up with a way to save this place on my own. And the only way I could imagine moving on was to join her."

"Shit." I wiped both hands down my face, trying to mask the image his words left behind.

"But I couldn't go through with it. I kept looking up and seeing the faces on all those photos on the wall. The next day, I went to the bank and cashed the first check. Then, I went home and got stinking drunk for the first time. I knew I was opening Pandora's box. Knew what it would do to them if they ever found out the extent of their father's weakness. And I knew what it would do to you to suddenly have me make an about-face and take your money."

His hand gripped my shoulder. "Son, I didn't send back all the other checks before it to throw charity back in your face. I didn't cash them because I wanted more for *you*. I prayed you'd stop sending them. If they stopped coming, I'd know you'd moved on with *your* life."

"I couldn't. I can't."

"I know, kiddo. I know. Moving on, easier said than done."

A bond formed around our shared words. He paused as we both watched a sleek thirty-six-foot cutter cruise by, blowing pretty hard toward the mouth of the bay.

"You still love her, don't you?"

His words surprised me. I hadn't recovered yet from hearing them being passed back and forth that morning.

"I love all of you." My voice cracked.

His hand squeezed my shoulder again.

"I had to buy the marina. I promised your wife . . . I promised her I'd take care of it. Of you guys. I owed you all that much." My words rushed out as fast as my thoughts.

"Son, you don't owe me a thing."

"I do. I owe you everything." I dragged a hand through my hair as I prayed I could talk about this and hold it together. "I know what you did. I always thought it was her. But she told me. The last night, before she died, she told me it was you."

He pursed his lips and nodded, obviously surprised.

"Why did you do it? If those lab tests hadn't gotten screwed up, I could've been formally charged. I was high as a kite when I hit him. I took that crazy shit and destroyed your daughter and then half-killed your son. But you saved me. Why? Why did you do it?"

He turned, facing me head on.

"Because I could've saved you all. I should have. Brayden, long before you failed Ashley and Nathan, I failed you. My mistake enabled yours. I knew you were struggling. Nathan knew it, too. He thought he was covering for you, but I knew why you both were fighting so much. I tried talking to your father. But that wasn't enough. I should've done more. I helped raise you. In so many ways, I thought of you as a son. I shouldn't have turned a blind eye. The whole town had turned you into a goddamn shooting star, but I should've seen you were falling apart. I should've forced you to come stay with us."

"You couldn't have stopped me." I held my arms out. "All of this. This whole mess. It's all my fault. And it kills me that you and your daughter spend one second blaming yourselves. Why does everyone take partial credit for something that should solely lay at my feet?"

"Because blame seldom lands in one place, son. We all played a part. And, now, we all have to play a role in putting things back together."

"How do we do that? Your daughter feels betrayed again. Your son is never gonna forgive me. And we can't get your wife back." The last part spilled out before I could think of how harsh it would sound to suffering ears.

"You're right. We can't get her back." His voice faltered. He took a deep breath, finding fresh resolve. "I've spent thirteen months hiding at the bottom of a bottle, reminding myself of that. But we can save this place together. We can all be a part of it."

I hung my head. His words sounded like my plan.

The one I'd built up under my life like a house of cards on stilts.

I didn't know anymore. My faith was gone. The certainty that Mrs. F gifted me before she died, was swept away by the tears on Ashley's face that morning. I didn't know how to find it again on my own.

"I don't want you to transfer that deed solely into my name. I want you to split it among the family. Even. Four ways."

I looked back up at him, surprised. "Four?"

"Nathan. Ashley. Me. And you."

I stood there, shell-shocked. His hand gripped my shoulder again, steadying me with a father's strength. I brushed the back of my hand across the corner of one eye, knowing I had no chance of holding that shit back now.

I shook my head, wanting to respond, but knowing I couldn't speak. None of this was how I'd imagined this conversation going down.

"Guess we best be getting me over to the house. There's a little girl over there who's probably dreaming up ways to skin us both alive."

I swallowed.

"You want to tell her the whole story together?" he asked.

That had been my plan. To come clean. To make her see. Force her to understand. Now, I didn't know right from wrong anymore.

White lies, lying end to end, eventually form a string long enough to bind you.

"I don't know what to do. I don't know where to go from here. I'd convinced myself for so fucking long that I knew what was best for her. That I was best for her. I thought I could ride in here and save everything and make her look at me again like she used to—before that night. I've spent all this time going to get the stars. That's what I had to do. Go get them, shove them in my pocket, and bring them back to her. But what if she doesn't want them? What if I'm not *it* for her? I just don't know anymore."

He chuckled.

I turned to look at him, confused.

"Sir, with all due respect, I'm not even sure the way I feel about your daughter is normal. I've always thought this was love, but I don't know if—"

His chest rumbled with deeper laughter, cutting me off.

"You feel like you can't live without her? Like every other thought has her wrapped around it somehow? The big stuff, like what you want to do with the rest of your life, and the little stuff, like the way a fistful of strawberries smells like her hair?"

I exhaled loudly. "Yeah. Pretty much."

He slapped me on the back. "That's love, kid. And, trust me, I don't know if you can find that twice in one life."

I muttered a curse.

"Brayden, we can play this however you want. But I gotta tell you, there's nothing in this world I wouldn't do to spend five more minutes with my wife. Nothing. I'd sell my soul to feel Lizzie in my arms one more time. After I went through about half a bottle of Patrón one night, I said that very thing to a bartender. Guy had a gold cross hanging from his left ear and a dream catcher hanging from his right. He reminded me that I'd get those five minutes again someday. When the time was right." He pointed upward. "Told me the universe had its own plan for me. I just had to sit tight and wait it out."

He looked up, staring at the sky, before he added, "Hardest damn thing in the world is to look up and realize we aren't always steering the ship."

He slapped me on the back again. "I've gotta wait for another lifetime to get my girl back. If I were you, I wouldn't wait that long for yours."

ASHLEY

I turned on the porch light when I heard a car pulling up the driveway. I knew he would come. He could never leave well enough alone.

I'd spent the whole night shouting at him in my head. Finally saying some of that shit out loud was gonna feel mighty good. I marched out to the top step, ready to let him have it.

He opened the door and stood there, one hand pressed on top of the roof of his pretentious car. He didn't move further. Didn't pound his way up the steps and manhandle me, as I'd predicted. He just stood there, patiently staring at me with those stupid blue eyes.

Something about them looked different. More at ease than I'd expected. Almost peaceful.

I'd never seen Brayden Ross do peaceful.

It had to be another trap.

"If you came here to bully me more and force me to—"

The other door opened. I watched in shocked disbelief as his passenger climbed out.

My hand clutched the doorjamb. "Daddy?"

ASHLEY

The hot water felt like heaven. I sighed as I laid my head back against the chair, letting the jets pummel the ache of a double shift.

I hadn't stepped foot back at the marina. They were over there, Brayden and my father, acting all chummy and smug. Sketching out big ideas based on my mother's dream. Poring over permit applications. Resurrecting plans for the Labor Day party.

I'd doubled up my hours at Foxy's to avoid them.

"So, you sat there, across the table from him, and just didn't speak?"

"Pretty much," I replied.

As I had driven home, I'd noticed the shop light was still on. Soaking my feet in Joey's pedicure chair was worth putting up with her third degree.

"I can't believe your dad invited him to dinner. Just like that,"—she snapped her fingers—"all's forgiven? Do you even know yet where your dad's been all this time? How Brayden found him so quickly?" Joey asked. "That's fishy as hell."

"Yep. Stinks to high heaven, doesn't it? And they both just sat there and acted like everything was hunky-dory. Brayden showed up with a pile of paperwork for us to all sign and a bottle of champagne. Nathan and I just sat there, pretending to eat, while we tried to figure out what the hell was going on."

"It's so mysterious. Your life is so exciting. Nothing like this ever happens to me," Riley said sadly, plopping down on the technician's stool beside my chair.

"Yeah. That's how this feels. Exciting," I replied sarcastically. "It would just be nice if one of the bastards came clean with the full story."

"Have you ever told him about the note from Coral Lynn?" Joey asked quietly.

I sat up straighter. One of her brows arched at me from across the room.

"It wouldn't matter."

"My point is, maybe he'd like to have the full story, too," she replied.

"It wouldn't change anything."

She shrugged self-righteously.

Riley sat forward on the stool, eyes wide. "Tell me. Please. I hate the Taylors. Coral Lynn's little brother was the first person at school to torture me when my belly started showing."

I sighed and glanced back at Joey.

"Oh Lord," she said. "Throw the kid a bone."

"Coral Lynn sent me a letter about a year ago. She'd been having an affair with one of her professors." I rolled my eyes.

"Of course she was," Joey added dryly.

"She thought the guy was perfect. Thought they were soul mates."

"Hard to have a soul mate when you don't have a soul," Riley muttered.

Joey chuckled in agreement.

"Yeah, well, he'd promised he'd leave his wife for her. He wanted to marry her once she was done with school. They had this whole white-picket-fence thing going. Then, she walked in on him banging his teaching assistant in the middle of office hours."

"Karma," Joey called out behind her balled up fist and a fake cough.

"So, why'd she write this all to you?" Riley asked. "So you'd know she got what she deserved?"

"Her letter said she'd realized then and there what it felt like to walk in on a broken heart. She felt guilty. She wanted me to know the way things looked that night weren't exactly what they seemed."

"He didn't sleep with her?" Riley's eyes grew wider.

"No. They slept together. But not in the way she forced me to picture. She'd found him half-passed out. The room was dark. She took her clothes off and climbed into bed." I took a deep breath, reliving the image I'd never completely purge. "He thought it was me. He called her by my name the entire time."

"He thought he was fucking you?"

I pursed my lips and nodded.

"That is messed up." She punctuated each word. "So, if that chick hadn't tricked him and let you walk in on it, none of the shit you've gone through would have happened. This whole mess is *her* fault. God, I really hate the Taylors."

I listened to her words and let them rattle through my head. A year ago, my reaction had been pretty much the same. I'd raged to Joey. Eventually, I'd allowed myself to cry about it. We'd lit the letter on fire over the vanilla-spice candle she kept burning to cover chemical smells in the shop.

"She was just another domino," I replied softly.

"I still think you should give him a chance. I mean, hell, if a guy got a tattoo that pointed straight to me, I'd be his backup plan. All night long," Riley added, laughing.

"Pointed straight to me?" My brows furrowed. "What are you talking about?"

"His tattoo. The compass. Another customer asked him about it the last time he was here. The little numbers shaded above the words. He said they're the latitude and longitude to the old boathouse on his property. You didn't know? Isn't that where . . ." She turned to Joey for confirmation. "That's where you told me they used to get it on, right? Like some kind of love shack?"

My mouth fell open. I'd been so interested in the meaning of the scrolling words, I'd never paid close attention to the rest of the details. I closed my eyes and envisioned the dark ink. My mind turned over our conversation about it.

He'd had it for years.

I pictured tracing it with my fingertips as we lay in his bed our last morning in New York.

That memory flipped a switch.

Another mental picture.

"Oh God."

I stepped out of the tub, tracking wet footprints across Joey's clean floor.

"What's wrong?" she asked, alarmed.

I fumbled my way to the front desk, spinning the mouse to light up the computer screen, trying to peck my way through her password. I hit the keyboard in frustration.

She leaned over me to type. "What are you searching for?"

"Google that constellation."

She looked at me with confused hesitation.

"Argo Navis. The one I told you about. From the painting. Google it."

She typed slowly, bringing up a list of images.

"That one. There. Zoom in."

I stared at the screen. Mute and confused as familiar names danced in front of me.

"That tattoo. The compass. It's part of it. The painting left that part out. My God, Joey. They're all him."

"Ash, you're scaring me. What does this all mean?"

"I've gotta go."

I grabbed my purse and headed for the door, still barefoot.

"Ashley! Wait. Where are you going?" I heard my best friend call after me.

I didn't have time to stop. I couldn't explain.

Not until I went and demanded the answers for myself.

"It was all you, wasn't it?" My voice broke into their jovial conversation.

All four of them looked up. They were seated around the patio table, take-out containers from Lucky's in front of them. My brother and Brayden were both still sweaty from an evening workout that I knew my father had gone over to watch. Matt sat at the end of the table, the innocent, about to get caught in the fallout.

"Ash, honey, you're just in time for some food. Did you eat already?" My father pushed his chair back and started to stand.

"Answer me." My eyes never wavered from Brayden's.

"The life insurance company. The grant for Nathan's surgery. My mother's medical bills. The company you used to buy the marina. Vella Indemnity. Pyxis International Trust. Carina, LLC. A Navis, Inc." The names spilled off my tongue in one long string. "They come back to the same place, don't they? A boy pulling stars from the sky. A man with a compass tattoo. It was all you. They're all parts of the same constellation."

He wiped his mouth with a napkin and then balled it up and threw it on his plate. I didn't miss the slight gesture that accompanied it.

He glanced up at my father.

They had a brief, silent exchange.

"You knew." It was a statement, not a question, but it still came accompanied by my surprise.

My father ran a hand across the short beard covering his chin.

"You knew he was doing it? That's why you weren't upset about the marina. You already knew."

My father cleared his throat. "I knew about the insurance money. I wish like hell your mother and I'd had the forethought to pay for life insurance. But we would never have had the money for the premiums. Those checks were from Brayden. Yes, I knew." He looked up at Brayden and nodded. Then, he turned to look at my brother. "I didn't know about Nathan's surgery though. Or your mother's care."

My father looked back at Brayden again as his face filled with emotion akin to gratitude and praise.

Nathan sat completely still, staring down at his forgotten food.

Brayden pursed his lips and nodded to my father in another silent exchange of thieves who had a plan. He quickly pushed his chair back and stood with a heaving breath of resolve.

He walked slowly around the table, prowling toward me, like he would if we occupied the room alone. Blue eyes tried unwrapping me. I crossed my arms over my chest, shielding my heart and warding off the intensity of his gaze.

"I was going to tell you. Once you calmed down." The words fell out with that assertive, commanding tone he used to hold me in place.

It reminded me a whole lot of his father.

"How am I supposed to trust you when everything between us is based on lies?"

"The only lie between us is you thinking, for one single second, that I came back here for myself. I came back here for you. That's been my plan since *day one*. And the sooner you settle down and realize that, the sooner we can get back to where we belong."

His hand rubbed across the skin on his biceps, across the coordinates that brought him home to me.

I thought he'd just washed in with the tide.

Turned out, he had a map.

CHAPTER 29
STORM CHASERS

BRAYDEN

"I love the way this place smells. You know what I mean?"

"Nothing else like it on the planet," I agreed, gazing across the field.

Nathan sucked in a deep breath as he squinted in the same direction. "How are we gonna tell him?" he asked, lightly tossing a ball in one hand before looking down to study the red laces.

"I'm not sure we can. It might break him. Dillan's always been the most fragile-hearted among us."

"Go figure, for the guy who carries a gun." He snickered and tossed the ball again.

We watched as the ragtag bunch of kids finished running between the foul poles and then piled back into the dugout in a pubescent heap of sweat and dirt and loud.

None of them looked in a hurry to follow their coach's directions and clean up their shit. They were too busy pouring water over one another. They did that far more successfully than anything we'd watched them do on the field.

Dillan barked commands at a couple of them before he jogged over toward our spot near the bleachers.

"So, what do you think? A little rough around the edges, but they'll come along. Remind you of us once upon a time, huh? Did you see Petersen? He's making progress, right? I think he's my starter." He nodded his head, affirming his own musing without any input.

He turned as one of the kids dumped the entire Gatorade cooler. "Shit. Hernandez, stop making a mess." He stalked back toward his team.

Nathan turned and stared at me with a blank expression of shock. "He's kidding, right? Isn't Petersen the redheaded kid with the unfortunate acne? He can't hit the broadside of a barn. He's never even met a strike zone. Probably thinks it's an app he can buy on his phone."

I ran a hand across my mouth, unsuccessfully trying to contain my chuckle.

"Don't laugh, man. I'm serious." Nathan's own laughter bubbled up. "This team is gonna kill our legacy."

"That Dawson kid has a pretty decent arm," I said, trying to grab some optimism. "Great velocity at least. He knows how to come over the top. Shitty aim, but we could work on that. Maybe we should come again tomorrow and give him some tips."

"Swear to God, Dillan is too much of a choirboy for this job. This team needs someone to yell bloody murder at them. They have no respect for the double play. They use their shins to field the ball more than their gloves. And they have no idea how to get a decent lead off the bag. That's just for starters."

"Why don't you take over as head coach?"

He cocked his head back and put his hand on his chest. "Me? Are you nuts?"

"Yeah, you. You always were a slave driver at practice. Made me work twice as hard as I ever wanted to."

"You were always a pussy. Still are."

A couple of weeks ago, that comment would've been hurled my way with the backing of hatred and anger. But, as soon as the remark spilled out, he shrugged his shoulders and smirked.

While uncovering the truth behind my lies had unveiled more of Ashley's wounded pride and wrath, it had finally softened her brother a bit. Beneath the cracked veneer of the man who sat beside me, I could finally see some of my old friend peeking out. Every day, a little more of him emerged. I kept holding on to hope, with both my hands knotted into fists.

We watched as the kids started tumbling out of the dugout, whooping and howling their way toward the parking lot.

I blew out a breath, mentally preparing for vulnerable crap Doc Wolfe would love. "I feel like a fucking pussy right now. I threw for the first time yesterday."

"Yeah? How'd it go? You as bad as Petersen?"

"Just about. Threw thirty reps from forty-five feet out. Felt like a girl."

"That what you were thinking the whole time?"

I shrugged.

"Where's the cocky A-hole who used to think he could do no wrong? That dude who used to go up to bat, pointing fingers at the fence or waltzing up to the mound while eating a candy bar, like he was going to a summer picnic?"

I snickered.

I'd forgotten about the day I did that.

"I think they carved all that out on the operating room table," I replied.

Nathan pursed his lips and nodded to himself.

He smacked both hands onto the arms of his wheelchair before suddenly bursting forward, pushing himself toward the heap of gear left on the infield grass. He leaned over to rifle through an equipment bag, chucking stuff everywhere.

"What the fuck are you doing?" I called out.

"I got an idea."

"The kids just picked all that shit up."

"Stand up, and act like you still have two balls intact," he called back. "My first rule is, there are no pussies allowed on this field."

As I stood up and ambled toward him, he started pulling out chest pads. He'd already strapped catcher's guards to both shins.

"Hand me that mask," he said as I stepped closer.

I tossed one to him, shaking my head at the same time. "You look ridiculous. What the hell are you doing?"

"I'm your new head coach. Second rule"—he waved two fingers—

"don't question me. Get that bucket and count off forty-five paces."

I stood, motionless.

He loudly clapped his hands together. "Let's go. Stop thinking, meathead. Just throw the damn ball at me."

"Nathan, don't take this the wrong way, man, but this is a really bad idea." I looked down at the wheels on his chair.

"What? You so worried you can't throw strikes, you think you'll hit me?"

"Something like that. I could kill you."

"Well, you already tried that once. You weren't that good at it."

I squeezed my eyes shut.

"Fuck. Did they cut off your balls *and* cut out your sense of humor?" He laughed down deep in his gut.

My eyes opened wide as hope bubbled up in my hands. I knew the smile that lit up his face. My old friend wore it all the time.

You don't know how much you miss something you've lost until you find it.

"Stop thinking." He slammed a ball down into my palm. "Throw. Preferably strikes 'cause, yeah, I don't really wanna get hit."

I blankly stared at him. While he was verbally poking at me, he'd strapped another chest pad across his lap. His chair looked like some kind of storm-chaser-intercept vehicle. The ones those shitheads on cable used to run down tornados.

He already had his extra hand tucked safely behind his back.

The dude meant business.

"You said you thought I could coach. Well, here we go. You're my first student. God knows, if I can fix you, I might have a chance with Petersen."

"Fuck," I muttered to myself, repeating his expletive.

If this idea didn't lead to serious bodily injury, it had the potential to give us *both* some confidence for the future. How could I take that from either one of us? I sure as hell wasn't ready to rob him of anything else.

I picked up the bucket of balls and started counting off paces.

Dillan stopped dragging the infield to stand and watch. "What the hell are you idiots doing?"

"Don't ask," I said to myself, turning to stare down at my former best friend turned lunatic.

My chest tightened. I breathed through it, willing the nerves to stay down in my belly.

He smirked behind the mask he'd pulled down over his head. "Come on, ace. Dazzle me."

I chuckled at the familiar line from his favorite movie. He used to say that shit in the front yard. Taunting me till I'd throw harder. Teasing me till I'd gun one into his mitt so hard, his palm would sting.

The noise around us died away, muted by the blood rushing through my ears. I could hear my own heartbeat, but all I could see was his glove. He pressed the leather together, opening and closing like he always did. Helping me zero in on my target.

The unease fell away. That foreign feeling, that had plagued me my first time out, totally disappeared. I turned the ball over in my hand, feeling the laces against my fingertips. I stared down at it for a minute, seeing my skin pressed against the white leather.

"God, that feels good," I muttered aloud. My smile bloomed as I heard a muted call over the static in my head.

"Come on, you pussy. I ain't got all night."

I got set, slightly bending my knees, feeling my weight ground me as both my hands rose up to my chest, preparing for duty.

I started to turn, lightly lifting my leg.

"Nice and easy, man," he called, his voice no longer taunting. "You've got this shit."

It happened before I could think about it. An easy toss. Form and function instead of power. Muscle memory that could never forget. I curled and uncurled, twisting at the hips, before I hurled the ball forward. I followed through till I tapped my left shin.

The *thwack* of it hitting Nathan's glove combined with Dillan's voice calling out, "And he's back, ladies and gentlemen."

Nathan's smile blossomed behind his mask. The sight of it seared into my brain.

"Again," he sharply called out.

I found a rhythm. For the first time ever, slow and steady felt amazing.

Thirty reps came way too fast.

Nathan and I sat on the bottom row of the bleachers, drinking beers I'd brought over in a cooler.

"Good thing Dillan had to go to work. Pretty sure this is breaking a half-dozen laws," I said, popping a cap off another one for him.

He chuckled. "Dillan needs to break a few laws and go get himself laid. Guy is wound too damn tight. Is your sister coming back for the Labor Day party? Why don't you let him have a shot at that?"

"Jesus," I muttered.

"What? At least, that way, she's protected from Bobby. You know what's gonna happen once he waltzes into town and gets a look at her."

"Surely law school has turned him into a gentleman by now."

He snorted. "Are you kidding? Nothing could put lipstick on that pig."

I smirked and sipped my beer. For the first time, being with Nathan felt almost like old times. Comfortable. Like déjà vu I didn't want to slip away.

We sat near the bleachers, nursing our lukewarm beers and enjoying the smell of grass and dirt mixing with crisp summer night air. I'd missed all of this. The ball. The cheap beer.

And the company of my best friend.

He finally broke the truce by poking at the elephant. "For what it's worth . . . I thought you went off and forgot all about us. I thought . . . hell, I don't know what I thought."

I picked at the hem of my shorts, unable to face him. "How can I ever make this right?"

He stopped his bottle halfway to his mouth. "You're earning it." He smirked before glass touched his lips.

I brushed my hand against my arm, realizing he could read the words inscribed there on my skin. "I forgot you took French."

"That's a wussy tat, man. I can't believe your teammates don't give you shit about it. Good thing your jersey hides that thing. It makes you even uglier than you already are." His words didn't match his broad smile.

I grinned back at him and shrugged my shoulders.

We settled into silence again, content to sit beside one another and watch the automatic sprinklers kick water across the outfield. We sat like that till the six-pack drained, and the sinking sun hollered out last call.

He sniffed loudly, breaking into the tranquility. "Ash will come around," he said simply.

I bent my head and picked at my thumbnail. "I don't know. It's been two weeks. She won't return my texts or calls. Doing everything she can to avoid me."

"She's scared of needing anyone. She needed you before and lost you. She needed my mother and lost her. She thought she was managing on her own. Keeping our heads above water. Now, she's realized she had someone beneath her, holding her up the whole time."

I nodded in agreement. "Ash has always been scared to lean."

"She'd rather have everyone lean on her." He paused and then added, "Give my sister some time to get her legs back underneath her. Then, she'll come around."

I looked up at the sky. Newly woken moths fluttered around the field lights, frenzied with need. I felt the same way, as I wondered if my legs were far enough beneath me now to finally say the words I needed him to hear.

"Nathan, I came back here to fix my arm, to help your family, and to somehow, someway, tell you how fucking sorry I . . ." My voice cracked. Pansy-assed tears, there was no use fighting against, clouded my eyes.

"Shit. Are we about to have a moment?"

I turned to look at him.

He grinned when he saw my watery eyes. His fist jabbed my shoulder. "Damn. We are, aren't we?"

He looked down and shook his head. He exhaled through his nose and stared out at the field as he started to speak in a more serious tone, "I don't remember the accident. Not a single thing about it. My memory cuts out somewhere near the end of our street. Cindi was humming to something on the radio, trying to calm me down. I was ranting. Planning out how I was gonna break you. Chinese water torture. Burn your house down. Leave you in a bloody pulp. That kind of thing."

I nodded my head. "I wish like hell that's how it all went down."

He palmed the bill of his cap. "Well, guess now's my chance to finally say what I wanted to that night." He turned to look me in the eye. "After I beat the shit out of you, I was gonna drive your ass to my house. I was gonna make you grovel and swear and beg. And I was gonna enjoy watching. But then I was gonna tell you this. My sister is the best damn thing that ever happened to you. I was gonna tell you you'd better fight like hell to get her back. I wasn't gonna let you give up on her."

"I never did."

"I see that now. And, sooner or later, she will, too."

I sighed and pinched my fingers against the bridge of my nose.

"Besides, you've got another job to do now," he added, smacking a closed fist into his opposite hand, simulating a ball and mitt the way only true ballplayers do.

"What's that?"

"I assume, sooner or later, those guys who pay you the big bucks are gonna expect you to get your ass back to the city. You need to take Ash with you when you go back to New York."

"She's not even talking to me, man. How the hell do you think . . ."

He finally turned to look at me again. "She has a scholarship waiting there for her."

I blinked. My eyes widened.

How had I missed that?

"She doesn't think I know anything about it. I heard her arguing with my mother about it once. She deferred enrollment. Said she had to care for a family member." He paused and then added, "I don't need her holding my hand anymore."

"Holy shit."

"I called them last week, explained the uniqueness of our situation. They said someone would meet with her, talk out options for financial aid. Maybe even reevaluate the scholarship for next fall. I figure she can show them some of her new stuff. Maybe someone up there will like those shots she took of your ugly mug."

"I'll get her there. I'll do whatever I have to do."

"I know." He tapped me on the knee with the closed side of his fist. "I know you will. You've always taken care of her."

I sat there, dumbfounded, searching for a plan that made sense.

"Come with us." The words just popped out of my mouth. "She wants to see you. I think it would be good for you to see her." I intentionally didn't use her name, shielding him from that pain.

"I can't."

"Nathan—"

"No, I don't mean it like that." He exhaled a breath. "I'm just not ready yet. I will be. Someday. It's just . . ." His voice broke. The whites of his eyes quickly grew glassy and red. "When I go to see Cindi, I'm damn well gonna walk my ass off that plane."

His smile slowly broke out, blossoming across his face again, the same way it had after I threw that first ball. It looked the same as the one I had grown up with. A perfect match to the one in that photo of us with heads covered in whipped cream.

My Nathan. My best friend.

"And you'd damn well better have a front row seat at Yankee Stadium waiting for me when I get there," he added lightly.

I swiped at my eyes. I couldn't hold it in. That same feeling I'd had while standing in that grass, getting ready to throw. Everything foreign and strange fell away. The old familiar snapped back into place.

"God, I've missed you," I said without thinking.

I hadn't even planned for it.

Vulnerable spilled out without even trying.

I'd have to send Doc Wolfe a check in the morning.

He swiped at his own eyes and bumped me in the shoulder. "Jesus, bro, let's go buy another six-pack or something. We look like a couple of girls."

ASHLEY

"I brought you some dinner."

I looked up at my father with tired eyes.

"It's my tuna casserole, so don't get too excited." He set one of my mother's old Tupperware containers down on the desk.

"Thanks," I said, leaning back from the computer. "I just got to thinking that I never sent all these invoices."

"You need to teach me how to do that. Your mom never wanted to show me the program, said I would do it backward and make twice the work for her." He smiled softly as he spoke of her.

It broke my heart a little and made me happy for him at the same time. Before, he couldn't even mention her name without breaking down and leaving the room.

"I don't mind doing it. It's probably easier for me to just keep—"

"Ashley, honey, you've done enough."

"I just have a few more left. They'll be late if they don't go out tomorrow."

"I wasn't talking about these invoices."

My brows furrowed as he held out a hand.

"I mean, you've done enough around here." His head tilted toward the door. "Come and take a walk with me."

I saved my work before I pushed back the chair. I tugged at the end of my braid and followed my father outside, feeling apprehensive about what he possibly had to share. I didn't have the strength to dive beneath any more white lies.

We walked to the end of the longest pier, all the way down to an empty slip bench that had a spectacular view of the evening's pink-painted sky.

"It's a beautiful night, isn't it?" he asked. "I missed cool evenings like this while I was down in the Caribbean."

I nodded my head as I sat down beside him.

"Did your mother ever tell you how we picked St. Michaels?"

"I thought you found a sale ad for the marina in the paper?"

"That might have been one more partial truth. Or it was just your mother's way of being kind."

He fell silent again, scratching at his beard, as he stared out at the water. I sat patiently, giving him time to mull over what he needed to say.

"I was going through a tough time. I'd leave for work every day, feeling even wearier than the last. Your mother claimed my job was sucking my soul out an ounce at a time. But I don't even know if that was it. I'd checked all the boxes. Great wife. Great kids. Nice house. Steady job." His index finger made check marks in the air. "I kept asking myself, *What's left?* I felt lost. Guilty for my life not feeling like enough. Sad that I just felt caught inside a big, blank space. I'd come to a weird intermission—a place in life where I'd run out of dreams.

"I couldn't acknowledge how bad it had gotten until I came home one day to find her with the car idling in the driveway. There were grocery bags on the back seat, stuffed with a few changes of clothes, and she'd hung an ugly dream catcher Christmas ornament from the rearview mirror. She said you kids were packed off to stay with some friends while we went on a soul-seeking mission."

I smirked as I leaned my head down to rest on his shoulder. The love filling his voice helped me picture the scene he described so clearly.

"The whole thing seemed crazy. We weren't the spontaneous road-trip types back then. At first, I didn't want to go."

"How did she talk you into it?"

"How do you think?" He chuckled.

"She gunned the engine and told you to get your ass in the car?"

"Close. Your mother told me she wasn't going to wait for me to come home with a girlfriend or a motorcycle, like all the other guys on our block in the throes of a midlife crisis.

"'We're going wandering,' she said. And we weren't coming back home until I found what I was looking for." He smiled and then continued. "We started out in Baltimore. Ate piles of crabs and drank beer till we remembered we were too old for hangovers. We left there the next day and headed east by the flip of a coin. Crossed the Bay Bridge around lunchtime and finally had to stop here for gas."

I tilted my head up to look at him.

"I know." He laughed. "We started our journey 'cause I was running on empty; We ended up in this town 'cause we ran out of gas."

I couldn't squelch my own smile.

"Your mother fell in love with all the shop windows. She wanted to roam around, so we decided to spend the night. We were sitting on the end of the dock over by the old Inn, watching all these fancy boats come and go and making up stories about the people on board.

"Your mother said, 'Wouldn't it be fun to get the chance to talk to them? To know their real stories?'

"We walked into town that night, and she plucked up a magazine from in front of the real estate office. And there it was. An ad for a cute little house and a For Sale sign overtop a picture of this beat-up, old marina."

He swallowed a few times, fighting with images the story had recreated. I laced my fingers through his to remind him that he wasn't alone.

He squeezed my hand before he continued, "She had some bills in her purse. She pulled them out to use the backs of the envelopes as scratch paper. We sat there and drank cheap red wine as we came up with a new plan. We just knew. We knew that night, this town was where we fit. We made new dreams."

"I've never heard any of that. I never knew you'd planned it all that fast," I said quietly. I paused before adding, "Mom told me once that I was stuck and needed to wander. She really believed in that, didn't she?"

"It's how she lived her life. It's one of the last things she said to me. *'When you feel lost, don't be afraid to wander.'*"

All the months he'd been gone suddenly added up. He'd been following her direction. Keeping one last promise.

There was a lot of that going around.

"Did you find what you needed?" I asked softly.

"As selfish as I was for leaving, I did. I wasn't sure I could stay here. Not without her. I wasn't sure what dreams I could have left now. Even when my dreams changed, they'd always included her." As his voice warbled, he pulled me tighter against him. "But missing you guys, helped me remember that I have something to live for."

His cheek rested atop my head. I took a full breath for the first time in months. There could never be a safer place than in my father's arms.

"This is still where I belong. And it's the closest I can be to her right now." His hand smoothed over my hair. "I'm sorry it took me so long to realize that. I left you here, holding on to this whole mess, all alone. You did a beautiful job, Ash."

"Daddy, I let the whole thing fall apart." My words rubbed against the soft cotton of his shirt.

His lips pressed into my hair. "Hush, my girl. You did not. You held everything and everyone together. And that's why I wanted you to hear this story." He pulled away from me, so I'd turn to look at him. "It's your turn. It's your time to wander now. You need to go out and find what sets your heart on fire. Find where you belong." He paused and then added, "And who you belong with."

"I don't know what I want. I'm not used to having choices."

"That's the beauty of your mother's idea. You don't have to know where you're headed. You just can't get stuck."

We sat quietly. I leaned my head against his shoulder again, letting myself breathe in the familiar scent of his aftershave, watching his fingertips drum against my knee.

A calmness settled over me. A stillness I hadn't felt in . . . maybe years. I'd grown so used to living with constant worries, my mind didn't quite know what to do with the empty spaces left behind. They allowed for feelings to flow too easily.

"I still love him." My admission came out so softly, I wasn't sure he'd even heard me, until he snorted in response.

"Well, God knows, that boy is certifiably nuts about you." He shook his head. "Like truly nuts."

We both smiled sheepishly.

"I just don't know where I belong. I don't know my own dreams anymore. And I'm not sure where I fit in, in Brayden's new world."

"You don't have to be sure of anything right now. All you have to do is keep moving forward, one step at a time, until you get your sign. When you see it, I promise, you'll know." He leaned forward and pulled something from his back pocket. "I almost forgot. These are for you. In case you need somewhere to start sketching out your own plans."

He handed me a small stack of blank white envelopes, tied together with sailor's twine. Tucked beneath the string lay a tourist-shop blue pen with *St. Michaels* running up the side."

Down an unknown road to embrace my fate.
Though that road may wander, it will lead me to you."
—*"Go the Distance"*
Hercules

CHAPTER 31
BUTTERFLY

ASHLEY

I spent a week thinking about the things my father had said. I stood in the background, watching as everyone else started picking up with life.

My father taped my mother's *Master Plan* drawing to the refrigerator. He and Brayden began interviewing architects. My brother went, all on his own, to let Joey cut his hair. Evan and his buddies helped hang posters around town, advertising the reinstituted Labor Day bash.

Brayden kept showing up at the dinner table, usually still hot and sweaty from pulling two-a-days and helping Nathan with some harebrained scheme to retrain the JV baseball team at the high school.

I avoided being alone with him, but I could always feel his eyes on my skin. I wasn't ready to talk. I needed to figure myself out before I could focus on him.

Or us.

Everyone around me suddenly had a purpose. A place to be. I tried my normal pattern. Like a robot, I sat behind the desk in the marina office and schlepped drinks at Foxy's. But none of it felt the same. Wearing my former life gave me vertigo. Just as my father had described, I ended each day wearier than the last.

When Joey scored concert tickets on Friday night, I gladly offered to take her shift. But Preston and his buddies ruined any chance of the quiet night I'd hoped for. They showed up at four o'clock, already rotting from hard day-drinking. Bad went to worse an hour later when Brayden and Matt came in, ready to plow their faces into burgers. Quietly dodging both their tables turned me into a human pinball.

I was in the back hallway, reaching down on a cart for a pallet of clean glasses, when a warm hand splayed against the back of my thigh, just under the hem of my skirt.

"You shouldn't have this on at work. It's too damn short."

As I straightened, his chest pressed in against my back, hiding his hand as it slid farther up to squeeze my ass.

"Leaves nothing to all these bastards' imaginations." His breath fanned against my ear. "Mine's already picturing it up around your waist." His fingers slid beneath the thin strap, popping the elastic lace of my thong against my skin. "Fuck, baby girl, I'm trying to be patient. But how long's it gonna be this time? How long are we gonna go on pretending like we can keep our hands to ourselves?"

I turned slightly, looking down at his chest in my peripheral. "I'm working," I said haughtily as I kept steady concentration on not pushing back against him. I didn't want to give him what he desired most. I still wanted to exact some form of punishment.

"So am I. Working on getting you out of this skirt and back underneath me."

"Brayden."

His hand slid ever so slowly down the crack of my ass before withdrawing. His other hand threaded up into my hair. I waited for the kiss I knew was coming.

"I want to see you. Alone." His lips hovered inches from mine.

"Why? So, you can manhandle me and try to get your way?"

"So, I can fuck some sense into you. And see how pretty this skirt looks lying at your feet," he said, his lips pressing onto mine.

I tried to maintain my composure, to not topple headfirst into his weird gravitational pull. But his tongue traced my lips back and forth, soft and sweet, until I had no choice but to cave. My fingertips dug into his biceps as I stood on my tiptoes for better reach.

He groaned. "Please, Ash. You and I both know you wore this thong tonight for a reason."

"Preston's out there. How do you know I didn't wear it for him?"

He pulled back, looking down at me with bright eyes. As he started to completely pull away, I grabbed his hand. He glanced at my fingers and smiled teasingly.

"What are you doing?" I asked, alarmed.

He backed up two steps, still grinning at me. "Just gonna run and commit a quick homicide. I'll be right back."

"Brayden."

He reached out and gripped my waist between his hands, pulling me back against him. "I was kidding."

"So was I." I cocked my head to the side and added cheekily, "I wore it 'cause I was running low on laundry."

His expression sobered as his thumb traced my bottom lip. "We have to talk, Soot. You can't hide from me forever."

"I know," I replied softly. "I'm just not ready yet."

He gave me a brief, hard kiss and a short nod. "You know where to find me."

He licked his bottom lip before he turned and walked away, forcing me to watch his tight jeans and strong shoulders move back out into the bar.

It took me an hour to compose myself. A damp thong chafed in unfortunate places. I could feel his eyes all over me, fucking me senseless from thirty feet away. When I took them a second round, his eyes swept over me, settling on my lips with a gaze so sultry, Matt had to cough uncomfortably into his fist.

As I turned to walk away, I heard Matt murmur, "Dude. Is there a pay-per-view fee included with this meal? Or is soft porn on the menu?"

I was ringing up another order, at the register next to the bar, when someone grabbed me from behind. Surprised Brayden would make another public display, I turned on him with wide eyes and a smacking hand.

I immediately stepped back in surprise. "Preston."

I pushed him until he staggered back some more. Unfortunately, not far enough to cover the stale stench of man sweat and beer.

"Are you trying to lose a hand?" I asked harshly.

"Come on, sweetheart. No hard feelings here. You are looking way too hot tonight, and I've gotta go back to school soon. What time do you get off work? Let's go have some fun."

I watched over Preston's shoulder as Brayden got up from his table and threw down his napkin. From the set line of his jaw, homicide no longer looked like a joking matter.

Preston was too drunk to even notice his imminent demise.

I tossed my hair over my shoulder and pressed my hand against the Ivy League idiot's chest, pretending to play with the buttons on his shirt. "You know, that would be great and all, but you're just still such a mystery to me."

"I am?" he said, drawing his neck back in surprise. He teetered a little from side to side.

"You are. I always thought that thing people said about men who had big hands was true, but you just seem to be an exception to the rule 'cause your dick is just way too small," I said it with a sweet smile, in as loud a voice as possible.

An old guy seated in front of a tall schooner at the end of the bar choked on a mouthful of beer.

The guy's friend slapped him on the back and called out, "Hey, buddy, catch a clue. She ain't goin' home with ya."

A younger guy sitting two stools down joined in, hollering out, "I think they make a pill for that."

"You're such a bitch." Preston's words slurred as he scowled down at me.

I cocked my hip to the side and scratched my chin, feigning deep thought. "You're right. But I'd rather be labeled a huge bitch than be known as a tiny prick."

The two guys at the bar chuckled again.

Preston glared at them before he tucked tail and stumbled back to his friends seated out on the deck. He never saw Brayden standing in the background a few feet away.

I closed the distance between us. "I told you, I can take care of myself."

He tweaked the tip of my nose. "I'm starting to see that now, baby girl."

———————

BRAYDEN

When she slapped the napkin down on the table and said, "Last call, boys," I almost didn't look down. I figured the best view was walking away from me.

But then I noticed the black ink magnified under the bottom of my glass.

Our place in an hour.

Instinct forced me to flip it over to the other side.

We're gonna talk first.

I smirked at her from across the room and stuffed the note down into my front jeans pocket.

I knew we couldn't climb out of this hole by fucking first and thinking later. I wanted this to be right. All of it. That meant, I had to come totally clean. No more lies.

Black or blue or white.

I got there early, so I could turn everything on and light the candles Jess had told me to buy. She'd helped me add all the girlie stuff. The white lace and fuzzy pillows were all her doing too.

Ashley hadn't seen the place since all the work was completed. That played to my advantage now. I needed to talk. If this place left her a little bit breathless, I would have a fighting chance at getting her to actually listen.

Thirty minutes later, the door slid back.

"Weird," she muttered. "It doesn't creak anymore?" She pulled herself up the ladder and stopped at the top.

Her look of shock filled hopeful places inside me.

"Holy shit. What did you do?"

"You like it?"

She climbed the rest of the way up and turned a one-eighty. She looked like a princess inside one of those fussy snow globes.

I'd left the futon. I'd changed the mattress and bedding and added real tables beside it, but the base was still the original. All new electrical had allowed me to replace the sad, old Christmas lights with hundreds more; tiny little pinpoints were clustered in long strands draped from the ceiling. A canopy of gauzy mosquito netting hung below them, softening their glow. The candles were everywhere. In rustic lanterns and a little chandelier that hung near the window.

"This is insane. When did you do all this? It's . . . magical." She sat down beside me, looking up at the lights, awestruck. Her hand ran across the back of the futon's whitewashed wood frame. "I'm glad you didn't get rid of this."

"This is where I first made love to you. You'd have to burn the place down with me in it to get this thing out of here."

She smirked and shook her head. "My dad's right. You really are nuts," she muttered.

I took a deep breath and wiped my hand across the scruff on my jaw. "Well, since you've started with the topic of my sanity, there's something I have to come clean about."

Her brow raised.

"It's the last thing. I promise." My index finger drew an *X* across my heart.

Leaning forward, I pulled the folder from where I'd set it on the coffee table and placed it in her lap. Her fingertips traced over the outside edge, giving away her anxiety. Slowly, she pulled it open.

I'd put them in chronological order.

Not by date.

By stalker threshold.

She was in every single one. Helping Nathan down out of the truck. Sitting outside the café with her mother. Tying up a boat at the marina. Laughing with Joey, walking out of her shop.

All of those felt pretty benign.

She kept turning. Page after page, until she hit the first of the ones I had seared deeper in my skull.

Walking out of Foxy's, smiling up at Tim Loeman. Holding hands with Preston, coming out of the movies. Kissing Preston in his car outside her house. The next one zoomed in on him unbuttoning her shirt.

She rested her hand on top of the photograph, covering the image of her skin with her own flesh and blood.

"I told you, I'd never stopped watching you, that I couldn't believe you didn't feel my eyes." I blew out a breath. "This is what I meant."

"How . . . ? When . . . ?"

"I hired someone. A private investigator."

"You had me followed?" Her brow scrunched up. She still wouldn't look at me. "For how long?"

I leaned forward with my elbows on my knees, lacing my fingers behind my neck to ease the tension. "A few years," I finally mumbled.

She paged through the remaining shots until she came to the end. She softly closed the folder and placed her hand back on top like a weight.

"Guess, now, you understand how much restraint I've been exercising by not rearranging that sunbird's face."

She tossed the file back onto the table. The corners of several photos slid out the top.

"You were never my plan B, Ash. Getting you back has always been my objective. From day one." I sat back up, turning to look her in the eye again. I couldn't read her expression. "Say something. What are you thinking?"

Her eyes searched my face. "I think you're a fucking lunatic. A controlling fucking lunatic. You have been since . . . Lord, maybe since you used to yell at me for riding my bike with my shoelaces untied."

As her words trailed off, her hand reached up to rest against my cheek. Her thumb scraped back and forth across my skin. Her words held bite, but her actions eased the ache in my chest.

I slid my hands around her waist. Her free hand gently framed my opposite cheek.

"So, I guess that makes you my lunatic."

My mouth got ahead of my brain. My lips crushed down onto hers, celebrating my own relief.

I kissed her until we were both feeling edgy and breathless. I finally pulled back to rest my forehead against hers, the taste of her still wet on my lips. The back of my throat burned with the words I needed to finally say out loud.

"I've loved you my whole life. Since before I knew what I felt had a name."

Her hands stroked my cheeks. "I know," she whispered, smiling with double meaning as her mouth descended onto mine.

She took tiny, soft pecks at my lips before stopping to stare down at them. I pressed my hands overtop hers. Worry suddenly furrowed her brows. I wanted to lift my hands and wipe it away. To say all the worry lay behind us now. As long as we were together, everything from here on out would be all right.

"What is it?" I asked.

"We have more to talk about, Brayden. There are things I have to come clean about, too. I know my brother told you about the interview." Her thumb rubbed across my mouth when her words drew forth a smile. "I'm going to New York."

My smile grew wider.

"Alone."

I blinked.

Once. Twice.

A third time for good fucking measure.

"What?" I finally asked, lips moving against her fingers.

"I'm taking the bus up next week. By myself. No fancy private jets. No drivers. No security detail."

I nodded slowly, feeling the scrape of my Adam's apple and the knot in my chest. This was some kind of test. One of those damn chick curveballs that hit you square in the nuts.

I had to tread carefully.

"At least stay at my place."

She shook her head. "I'm gonna stay overnight with Cindi. She called last week. I finally picked up the phone. We talked for a long time about . . . everything. She offered to let me stay with her."

I swallowed again. Her fingertips smoothed over my forehead, trying to wipe away the confusion and worry I wasn't hiding very well.

"Brayden, after the accident, I lost more than just you. I lost me, too. I lost the chance to figure out who I am. I have to stand on my own two feet for a while. I have to do something for myself. Without you looking over my shoulder all the time."

With a quirked brow, she glanced at the folder lying strewn across the table like a junkie's dirty paraphernalia.

"I have to piece together who I am and what I want to do. I can't do that if I go from being my family's caregiver to a superstar's girlfriend. I need to just be me for a little while. Figure out who the hell that is."

I squeezed my eyes shut, trying to block out the bottomless fear that gutted my insides. It came hand in hand with guilt and shame and double-edged need—the same feeling I'd had the first time I woke up in rehab and reached for the nightstand drawer.

Watching over Ashley fixed me. Since I was a little kid, looking out for her had centered me. It gave me a fucking reason to exist. Even after I'd left, I never stopped. There wasn't a twelve-step program in the world that would break me of that habit or teach me to curb that need.

"You can't ask me not to take care of you. I've been doing it since the day you tumbled into the library. I don't know how to stop. I can't." That word. It ground out of my chest, the garbled speech of a drowning man.

"We don't do *can't*. Remember?"

"Where your safety and well-being are concerned . . . I can't, Ashley. I won't."

"Brayden, I'm not asking you to step out of my life. I just need you to step back and give me room to explore. I need to stumble every now and then. I need to make my own mistakes and build my own dreams. That's the only way I'll ever feel like I've earned them. I have to do that alone. Without the help of your shoulders, or your money, or your last name."

I pulled out of her embrace and stood, fighting back emotion I didn't want to show. I turned my back to her, but I could still see her reflection in the window, walking toward me like an angel I didn't want to let go.

Her arms tightly circled my waist. The side of her cheek pressed against my back.

"There's so much I could do to help you. We can get you set up in that school. We can rent out my place and get something closer to the campus while we work on the townhouse . . ." My words trailed off as my voice warbled.

Her hands smoothed over my chest, rubbing straight into the familiar pain. "I sat here so many times and listened to a boy who didn't want to ride his father's coattails. Dallas, you have to understand where I'm coming from. You're the shiny star with the big shadow now. I have to try this on my own."

I turned in her arms, threading my hands into her hair. Tears burned behind my eyes. "Don't send me away again."

The words sounded tiny in my ears. Just like the voice inside all my nightmares as a kid. All the times I dreamt of calling them out to my faceless mother.

My chest tightened more.

"I won't. I can't. Not ever again," she replied, her voice raspy with her own emotion.

"Stay," I said, demanding. The voice of a desperate man replacing that of the child.

"I promise to always stay, if you promise to give me some room to fly."

She brushed her lips across mine. It eased some of the pain in my gut.

"I love you," I whispered.

How many more times could I say it? How many times would it take for her to believe the truth?

She smiled softly in response as her fingers started fumbling with the button casings at the front of her shirt. Watching her skin, exposed inch by inch, bit into my already raw nerve endings.

She kept going, until thin black lace appeared. It swirled and dipped, molding to her breasts and running down the length of her torso. Slowly, she slid her shirt down off her shoulders, uncovering the entire corset that laced around her. She unzipped the back of her skirt, letting it fulfill my mental image of it falling to the floor.

She looked incredible, like every single fantasy I'd ever had. But I was afraid to touch her. Afraid I suddenly didn't have a plan. Didn't have a clue of how this would play out.

I had to follow her lead.

Her hands pulled on my own, drawing them up to cup her breasts. Her fingertips danced down the sides of my biceps and under the hem of my shirtsleeves, tracing over the edges of my tattoo.

"Make love to me," she said quietly. "Right here where we began."

"Why do you say that like this is the end?"

"Because it is. It has to be," she replied.

I stiffened, but her fingers dug into my skin, holding my reaction at bay. "Brayden, I've lived my whole life, chasing after the dominoes someone else set up for me. I've stood by and watched as the blocks fell into place around me. Wondering where the trail of them would lead. Wondering how many more had to fall."

She stared up into my eyes. She had that look. The one her mother had borne the last time I saw her.

Certainty.

"Have you ever watched one of those videos of a whole room filled with thousands of dominoes?" she asked wistfully. "Long strings of black-and-white tiles that'll go on forever if you let them. All it takes is one person, pulling out one little tile. If just one is out of place, the chain reaction ends. You and I have both lived with regret and pain. We've lived both sides of forgiveness. I'm ready to put down my own tiles. I'm ready to start again. Without all the pain of our regrets."

"That's what I want, too," I murmured.

"To do that, we have to be whole people. On our own. We have to learn to forgive ourselves, Brayden. It's the only way. This is an end. It has to be if we have any chance at starting over."

EPILOGUE 1
ALL SIGNS POINT HOME

ASHLEY

Once a week, he sent me flowers with a handwritten note.

Never on Monday or Friday. Not at the beginning or the end. He sent them in the middle. A random Tuesday morning or Wednesday afternoon.

The artist in me wanted to believe he did it on purpose, symbolically marking the middle place of our years together. We weren't standing at the starting line, those young kids fueled by hormones and teenage lust. And we weren't the settled-down couple who had it all figured out, like the ones I watched rushing through the streets to get home to one another at the end of each day.

We were somewhere in between.

And that was okay.

Our relationship stayed under wraps. Heavily guarded. Brayden knew I wasn't ready for the spotlight or prepared for the big, shiny label that came attached to being his girl. He sheltered me from his public world, protected me from his crew of friends and foes whose feet never touched the pavement.

I guess it gave him something to do.

He worked hard at giving me space. The first time I got lost on the subway, trying to meet him, he didn't even yell.

Or come to save me.

My white knight waited patiently, inside the lobby of the movie theater, until I found my way to him. Once I got settled, he half-sucked my face off in the back row of the balcony, to make sure all my faculties were still in working order.

I didn't tell anyone about him. He often joked about turned tables, but he willingly became my dirty little secret.

My roommate, Krissy, fell in love with my mystery man. She sang his praises every time I described some of the vague details of the past or romantic snippets of what he promised for the future.

When the deliveries arrived each week, she would steal the cards and read them aloud in a dramatic voice. She fanned herself after the sweet, sappy ones and pretended to stuff the naughty horndog ones inside her bra.

He left the cards unsigned. Instead, at the bottom of each one, he penned a simple line, *I hope you know.*

I almost slipped a couple times and used his real name, but I caught myself before ruining it.

The secrecy was better anyhow.

Krissy had grown up a diehard Mets fan.

Brayden and I spent lots of quiet evenings at his apartment, but I never stayed over more than one night. I brought my things back and forth in a beat-up old backpack, refusing the empty drawers he kept cleared for me.

We ate in more VIP seats, at discreet little spots like Mama Rosie's. I helped him work on restoring the old townhouse by pretending to be his decorator.

It was sort of fun, hiding out again, reliving the old days of stolen kisses. It helped me stay focused.

On me.

On working.

On making my own name complete.

By late winter, *his* name was everywhere. On the side of the buildings in Times Square. On the little placards atop every cab in town. On the posters strewn about on the subway. Micky and Mia were both hard at work, putting the prince back on his throne.

They interviewed him on every news station. They talked about him in the papers. If the city's hope and expectations could fuel strikeouts and home runs, this would undoubtedly be the team's big year.

I worried about the pressure becoming too much. I watched for signs of implosion, scared we'd been in this place before. Only, now, instead of a couple thousand, the town population reached the millions.

He had to go back out there and prove he had it.

To himself first.

Then, to the rest of the city.

He worked tirelessly. Muscles hardened. Bones grew weary. I saw him less and less as spring training loomed.

I started to sneak into his apartment in the early hours of the morning before I had class and he had to work out. Each day I would crawl under the covers and into his arms, softly questioning if he was still okay.

Every time, he'd roll me on top of him, thrust deep inside me, and sigh sleepily, "I am now."

I had to miss his first preseason game. It killed me not to catch the broadcast. I had a presentation to give. A portfolio review to apply for a summer internship. I had the chance to go to Paris and work for a magazine as a Fashion Week correspondent.

Joey was still shitting herself.

I sent Brayden a text beforehand and watched all the highlight footage on my phone. His smile, when his teammates piled on top of him, made me wish I'd been there to see it firsthand.

But, instead of celebrating his continued success in the warm Florida sunshine, I was left plowing through my last assignments before mid-semester break.

Krissy and I had both suffered through a tough week. She had a Historical Styles test from hell, and I had a paper due in Elements of Visual Thinking—my least favorite class.

She texted me as soon as she turned in her exam.

Meeting up with the crew at Digby's for drinks. Margaritas on me. We sure as hell

deserve them.

Digby's was our favorite hole-in-the-wall, within walking distance from campus. By the time I arrived there, our friends were already huddled around the corner of the bar, staking their claim on prime happy-hour real estate.

Jonesy flashed a dimple at me and got up to offer me his seat. He nodded to the bartender to pour another drink. "Did you get your grade back from DeLuise on the Narrative Strategies project yet? That guy totally busted my balls."

"You know Dr. DeLu-Loser didn't bust Ashley's balls, Jonesy. For one, she doesn't have any, and two, she's the teacher's pet. She's gonna spend all summer with him in Europe," Victor said, from the seat beside me.

I smirked at him and rolled my eyes. "Try turning the next assignment in on time, Victor. It might help."

"Roasted," Jonesy said, laughing as he stuck a finger to his tongue as if putting out a match.

An image on the TV above the bar distracted me from their ensuing antics. I let their banter fall into the background as I stared up at his picture on the screen. A new headshot appeared next to old statistics. The commentators spoke without sound. I tried to catch up with the rolling captions at the bottom of the screen.

"Ross has been looking pretty good, huh? You a Yankees fan?" the bartender asked, setting down my drink and breaking into my awkward reverie.

"Seriously? How could he ever look bad? He is one fantastic pile of man," Victor said, piping up beside me. Since breaking up with his latest boyfriend, Victor had been suffering from a serious case of on-the-prowl.

"He's the only reason to ever watch the Yankees," Krissy added in agreement as she glanced up at the screen. "They should just show him from behind every time he pitches."

"Amen to that sister," Victor said, drawing out each word. "Just look at that fine ass. I'd take an eyeful"—he made a squeezing motion with both hands—"or a handful of that any day."

I quietly sipped my drink as their conversation slid further down the hill of inappropriate. The coverage cut to an on-field reporter, a sweet young thing who'd clearly scored her job based on the assets below her neck. She stood on the edge of the on-deck circle, talking as practice played out in the emerald grass stretched out behind her.

I loved watching the cadence of the players tossing the ball around the infield. The crisp colors of their practice uniforms popped in the late day sun. Their footwork, the twist of their shoulders and hips, and the easy strength behind each throw, felt as beautifully synchronized as the chorus lines playing down on Broadway.

The scene made me oddly homesick.

The wide shot cut back to the reporter, who was now thrusting her microphone toward a familiar face. The megawatt smile blinded her, too.

He needed a haircut. Edges of scruffy-sex hair peeked out from under his hat, just below his ears. He'd gotten a lot of sun; the golden tan on his neck and cheeks made his bright blue eyes stand out even more.

I longed to feel them on my skin.

I tried to look away from the screen. To add intermittent commentary to a conversation that had moved on to actors with the best rear view. But seeing Brayden's face eased that homesickness still lingering in my belly.

I pressed my hand against it, willing it away.

The interview wrapped. The broadcast moved on to reel footage from Brayden's first game. Him warming up in the bull pen. His cap held over his heart while school kids sang the anthem. Taking his first walk out to the mound.

Mentally, I narrated the choreography of the routine I knew would come next. He would slap his glove against his left leg twice. He'd scuff the rubber six times while he tipped his hat forward and back. He'd take three practice pitches before a short nod to his catcher. A creature of habit, he'd done the same thing at the start of every game since the summer before he turned fifteen.

It all played out just as I'd expected, except for one small addition that instantly struck me dumb.

I watched in slow motion as the bartender mimicked the same gesture. Another guy at the end of the bar followed suit. My head shot back to the screen as he started to take his trio of pitches. The sports talk guys reappeared on the screen.

"Hey. What was that?" I loudly called out to the bartender.

The conversations around me quieted with the shocked alarm in my voice.

The bartender looked at me, surprised by my outburst.

"What was that thing with the lips and . . ."

"This thing?" the guy asked, repeating the signal.

"Yeah. What . . . what is that?"

"That's Ross's thing. Apparently, he's one superstitious motherfucker. He does that before every game. Always has. Since he started down in the minors, I think. He taps his lips twice, puts his hand on his heart, and says something no one understands to the sky. It's his trademark. Supposed to bring him good luck. Now, all the fans do it, too. Kinda a prayer to the baseball gods, know what I mean?"

I barely heard his last words.

Liquid pooled in my eyes.

"He probably made it up, so he seems like a real guy. Some PR rep probably thinks it makes him more likable," the faceless guy at the end of the bar chirped up.

I stared down at the stem of my glass as I swiped at my wet cheeks.

"Honey, are you okay?" Victor asked, suddenly alarmed. He placed a hand on my shoulder.

"Ash? Ash, what is it?" Krissy asked, coming to stand beside me.

"That's our sign," I said softly.

I pointed up at the screen to where I'd seen him do it with my own eyes. "It means . . . that's the sign we'd give for . . . we used it . . . to tell each other . . ." Tears slid faster down my cheeks.

Her hands gripped my shoulders, trying to calm me. "What does this mean? You're not making sense. You're freaking me out."

"This whole time, I've been hiding, and he's been secretly telling the whole world. It means . . . I've always been part of his plan." I looked up at her and smiled. "He loves me. He always has." I squeezed my eyes shut and imagined words on a torn sheet of paper.

Find a way to show Ashley I'll always love her.

"He's been telling me since day one. I just never saw it."

Her mouth hung open. She looked up at the screen and then back down at me. "Holy shit. Are you telling me Brayden fucking Ross is your mystery man?"

"He's the love of my life." I pointed back to the TV and giggled. "That's my sign. That's where I belong."

"Well, Jesus fucking Christ, Ashley. I thought maybe it was a married man. Or maybe some dude twice your age. Maybe some hotshot CEO who couldn't be seen with a coed. But Brayden freaking Ross? No. This just . . . I can't believe this," Krissy said, rambling.

I hopped down off the barstool and grabbed on to her arms. "I have to call his sister. She'll know how to find him. Krissy, focus. How do I get on the next flight to Florida? I need to get to a memorabilia shop. I need a number eighteen jersey. Do I have time for that? Shit. There's a lot to do."

Krissy was already typing furiously on her phone. "I can get you there tonight out of JFK. It's gonna be tight though. Jonesy, we need to borrow your car. Victor, close your mouth; you're drooling. Go to the shop down the street and get her a Ross jersey. You"—she pointed at me—"we have fifteen minutes to get you packed. I hope you're ready to run."

The air around me filled up with summer come early. Suntan lotion and popcorn. Hot dogs and children's laughter. They combined into a heady combination of happiness, baseball, and life.

I didn't grow up sitting in a wooden pew at church on Sunday mornings. I sat on hot metal bleachers, watching my brother and Brayden play out doubleheaders. My preacher wore a dark blue collared shirt and a face mask. Instead of hymns, he sang out balls and strikes, forcing us to believe he knew better than we did.

Now, I stood down the fence line, feeling like I wanted to drop to my knees at that same altar, a born-again sinner who'd found her way back.

I soaked it all in, the homespun majesty. The pops of pure white balls against leather, the pristine uniforms, and the greenest grass I'd ever seen. It rolled out like a thick blanket, the only thing still spread between him and me.

I'd missed so much. So many of his firsts.

I didn't want to miss any more.

When I'd called Jess on my way to the airport and learned his next start was the following afternoon, my own plan had quickly formed. I'd checked into a little roadside motel near the field and spent a sleepless night trying to be patient.

I knew exactly how I wanted this to go down.

Now, I just had to find him.

"Excuse me, sir?" I called out to the burly older gentleman standing down the line from first base.

His bright yellow jacket read *Security* across the back.

He kept his back turned, trying to ignore me. I called out again and gave him pleading puppy-dog eyes when he finally looked my way.

"Can you help me?"

"Whaddaya need, missy?"

"Uh, I'm trying to find Brayden Ross. I'm a friend of his." I held up the plastic badge hanging around my neck.

Jess had instructed them to hold it for me at Will Call.

"Nice try, sugar. You know how many times I hear that a day?"

"Oh no, I'm not a psycho, I promise."

"Yeah, that's what they all say. Ross has a girlfriend. Don't waste your time."

A ball rolled over near the fence as he served me his parting shot. The first baseman jogged over to retrieve it. He slid his sunglasses down to suggestively look at me.

"Ross might have a girlfriend, but I don't, honey." He turned and asked the dude for a pen, signed something on the ball, and then trotted back over to hand it to me.

I glanced down at his digits scrawled between the laces. "Uh, thanks, but I'm sort of spoken for." I pressed it back toward him.

He tilted his head and looked at me funny. The guy wasn't used to being turned down.

"Oh, shit. Are you really her? Are you the mystery girl?" He looked over his shoulder and called out, "Hey, Larry! Go tell Ross he's got a visitor."

I watched the old man grumble as he walked across to the other side of the dugout.

I smiled as soon as I saw him. Standing near the fence behind home plate, Brayden was signing a ball for a little boy whose bright smile was missing two front teeth. He spoke to him before ruffling his hair and smiling for a picture. I watched as he moved down the line, taking time, forming a connection with each fan. After two more kids got a turn, the old man tapped him on the shoulder and whispered in his ear. Brayden gave a kid back his ball and finally looked up in my direction.

His eyes brushed past me and then snapped right back. His mouth gaped open a little, his expression not too unlike the awe on the faces surrounding him. A smile blossomed on his lips. My smile. The one he'd reserved for me since our first days in the library.

I grinned in response. He quickly said something to the group around him and held up a finger before he started toward me, slowly at first and then gaining speed.

I'd temporarily forgotten Brayden's teammate was still standing beside me, watching everything unfold.

He flipped his hat around backward and gave me a cocky grin. "If things don't work out with Ross, you be sure to come back and see me."

When Brayden was a few yards away, he called out my name. The sound came with a question mark attached, like he needed to make sure it was really me in the flesh. I smiled softly as I placed two fingers over my lips and then down over my heart.

He broke out into a jog. On the way, he called out, "Sampson, get away from my girl."

The first baseman chuckled as he started back to his post.

Brayden's arms engulfed me over the fence, tugging me against his chest, so my feet momentarily left the ground. He kissed the top of my head and then gripped my shoulders, pulling back to see my face. He flipped his hat around, blinding me with bright, happy eyes.

"This is the best damn surprise I've ever gotten. You're here. You came."

My palms reached up to ghost over his cheeks. "Kiss me."

"What . . ." His question died as his eyes searched mine. He hesitated and then glanced over his shoulder. "There are cameras everywhere. Reporters and fans and—"

"I know. It's okay. I don't care." I raised up on my tiptoes and wound my arms around his neck. "Kiss me, Brayden. It's time."

His megawatt smile eclipsed the sun.

As his lips met mine, he softly murmured, "Welcome home."

ASHLEY

There were a million things to love about Paris. Quaint cafés. Centuries-old buildings. World-renowned art. But the way the city lit up at night was what I would always love most. My little-girl dreams looked just like the Champs-Élysées bathed in twinkling light. No matter how many times I'd been here the last couple years, the sight never got old.

Sadly, I'd spent most of this latest trip walking that street alone.

My schedule had been packed all summer. An entire athletic wear campaign, three magazine covers, and this catalog shoot for an up-and-coming designer the fashion world had dubbed the next Ralph Lauren. Being in high demand was great; it was also tiring.

Of course, this job just happened to coincide with the late July stretch. After the all-star break, the Yankees followed up a home stand against the Sox with a long trip out west.

Two time zones farther away.

But, this weekend, we were going to make up for it. Brayden had flown for twelve hours, leapfrogging across the country and an entire ocean, so he could hold my hand, walking beneath those glittering lights.

And, so he could help me find my way back home.

I'd already found my way there. In his arms. An hour after he got off the plane yesterday.

"Did you get a good one?" he asked, smiling.

I flipped through the pictures on my phone. We'd gone up to the top of the Eiffel Tower like a couple of silly tourists, laughing and snapping ridiculous selfies.

"This one is hysterical," I said, holding it out for him to see. "Even when you're being a goofball, you're still way too pretty. I'm putting this one on Instagram. Your fangirls will spend all night Photoshopping their faces over mine."

Usually, that would've garnered a witty retort, but he just smiled sheepishly and ducked his head to look out the window.

I put my hand on his knee where it bobbed up and down. "You okay?"

The car slowed to a stop. Vincent got out in the front.

"What's this? Where are we?" I asked, trying to look around him.

He cracked open the door.

Vincent nodded to him and then added, "Everything's in place, boss."

The door swung open farther. We were parked in front of a white stone building. Red velvet ropes and a thick carpet spread between us and the door.

"What's going on?" I asked again.

Brayden hoisted himself out of the car and reached a hand back to me. "Another surprise. We're gonna knock two more dreams off the list tonight. Half mine, half yours." He shook his hand, coaxing me to take hold of it and follow his lead.

Vincent had walked ahead of us to hold the door.

I stepped over the threshold, straight into another fairy tale. One dotted by familiar smiles. Deep purple walls lay beneath black-and-white prints. Huge canvases were highlighted by pinpoint lights that brought them alive. I strode forward, my mouth hanging open as I realized the significance.

Every single one was mine.

At the center of the back wall, huge, scrolling letters spelled out my name.

"How did you do this? What is this?"

"Our story," he said. "As told by your lens."

"How did you get all these here?"

"Nathan helped me."

"He did?"

We walked slowly, studying our own faces. Watching them age and grow wiser. The backgrounds changed. There were people we'd loved and lost. People we'd lost touch with. And some people we'd never let go.

Seeing them all together, stacked side by side, in a time line of years, completely overwhelmed me. My work had appeared in magazines. On the sides of buildings. On TV. But I'd never seen so much of it all in one place. I'd never connected all the dots at once. Never laid them out in one long row where I could finally see the greater pattern unveiled.

As we neared the back wall, I started to begin putting my feelings into words of thanks. But, as I turned, I suddenly realized the space was larger than it had first appeared.

Leading into a second room were a series of shots I had taken my first year in art school, for a class on motion and perspective. They looked larger than life. Dominoes tumbling into one another. The blur of the little white dimples as the blocks connected, toppled, and leaned.

"There's more?" I asked, already moving forward.

The second room was different. Bright white walls glowed under candlelight. Hundreds of lit votives were lined up, pressed together, like the prayer vestibules in Notre Dame. It cast a mood, a feeling of stepping onto hallowed ground.

At the end of the space sat one pure black wall. A spotlight shone down on it, highlighting the empty spot where something lay missing.

"What's going there?" I asked, pointing.

"That's where we'll hang the picture you take of us. On our wedding day."

I suddenly turned around, my mouth open wide.

He was kneeling down on one knee.

"Oh my God."

The brightest light in the room shone from the box in his hand.

"This is where my half of the dream comes in. The part where I ask you to change the name on the wall to Mrs. Ashley Ross."

My hand covered my mouth until he reached out to take it.

He slid the ring onto my finger. "Say yes, Soot."

I slowly sank down to my knees, mirroring his position. I stared down at my hand again before grasping his face in my palms and pressing my lips to his. "Yes."

I could feel his mouth smile against my own.

"Yes. Yes. Yes," I repeated against his lips before pulling back to look into his eyes.

"I love you."

For the first time in our lives, he didn't object to me saying those words aloud.

"I love you, too," he replied with the biggest, goofiest grin of all.

As my mouth found his again, I softly whispered, "I know."

"It ain't over till it's over."
—**Yogi Berra**

ABOUT THE AUTHOR

Harlow Cole is a former journalism student, turned techie, turned mother, who finally decided at age forty-plus what she wants to be if she ever she grows up. Her writing journey first began in sixth grade, when she and her best friend penned boy band fanfiction in an old spiral notebook. Harlow is a connoisseur of peanut M&Ms, brand-new school supplies and angst-filled love stories that always end happy. At fifteen, she met her first love. They've now been married for twenty years. They reside in suburban Washington, DC, where Harlow moonlights as a taxi driver for their farting beagle and teenage twins.

You can help feed Harlow's social media addiction on any of the following channels:
Facebook: @harlowcolebooks
Instagram: @harlowcole
Pinterest: @harlowcole
Twitter: @harlowcolebooks

For more information on upcoming releases,
visit *www.harlowcole.com*

Made in the USA
Columbia, SC
17 April 2021